Starcrossed
COLORADO

Copyright © 2025 by Hannah Shield

STARCROSSED COLORADO (Hart County Series Book 1)

All rights reserved.

No part of this book may be reproduced in any form or by any electronic or mechanical means, including information storage and retrieval systems, without written permission from the author, except for the use of brief quotations in a book review.

This is a work of fiction, and any resemblance to real events or people, living or dead, is a coincidence.

Ebook Cover Photography: Wander Aguiar

Cover Design (Ebook and Print): Angela Haddon

Produced by Diana Road Books

HART COUNTY BOOK 1

Starcrossed
COLORADO

HANNAH SHIELD

Prologue

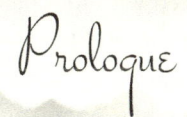

ASHFORD, THREE YEARS AGO

LORI HAD A SECRET. Correction: a secret from *me*.

"What time will you be home tonight?" I asked her over breakfast. Maisie squirmed in her seat beside me, studying her pancake bites with the infinite fascination of a three-year-old.

Lori shrugged, averting her eyes. "It's book club at Silver Linings. You know how the girls and I close the place down. You shouldn't wait up."

Wrong, I thought.

Book club had been two nights ago, and Lori hadn't been there. One of the moms had stopped me yesterday and asked, *Is Lori doing okay? We haven't seen her around much lately.*

Lori checked the clock and stood, already dressed in the scrubs she wore as a dental assistant. "I'd better get going. Can't be late. We have a tooth extraction scheduled first thing."

"Of course. Can't upset the great and powerful Dr. Carmichael."

Lori sighed. "Ashford, please don't start."

"I'm just not your boss's biggest fan."

"You're hardly anybody's fan. Except Maisie's." She stroked our daughter's hair.

I grunted. Yeah, it was true.

Unlike me, Lori hadn't grown up in Silver Ridge. She'd had no support system here at first, apart from mine. But when I'd left active duty, Lori had agreed with me that Hart County, Colorado, was the best place to raise our child.

Maisie had been a beautiful accident. The result of a single night between me and my best friend. As far as Lori's father had been concerned, marriage was the only option, and I'd readily agreed. After the shitty way my siblings and I had grown up, I'd wanted to give Maisie a safe, stable home. And of course provide for the mother of my child, a woman I cared deeply for even if we weren't in love.

We had agreed, from the get-go, that we could see other people as long as it didn't affect Maisie.

I mean, *I* didn't see other women. But that was my issue, not Lori's.

She stooped over Maisie, giving her kisses and smelling her hair. "Bye bye, buttercup. I love you."

"Love you, Mommy," Maisie said with a mouth full of pancake.

"I'll pick you up from Auntie Grace's, and we'll have a fun afternoon. Okay?"

Maisie nodded.

Before she left, Lori held out her fist to me. I bumped it. "I'll see you later," she said. "Try to have a good day."

"I'll try. Be safe, okay?"

"Always."

We were a team. No matter what, I had to remember that.

I went about my day. Taking Maisie to my sister's house for the morning while I met my training clients. Then teaching my afternoon martial arts classes while Maisie was with Lori.

But the whole time, I was stewing.

We had to talk. And it couldn't wait any longer. It had to be tonight.

If she was seeing some other man, she didn't have to lie. If she wanted more with this mystery guy—if she wanted to end our marriage—then I guessed we could talk about that too. Maybe it had been inevitable.

The problem was this. Lori and I already had a secret that we'd kept from everyone here in Silver Ridge, including my closest friends and family. It had seemed necessary. Even innocent. Little more than an omission.

But secrets had a way of multiplying.

Maybe the more secrets you had, the easier it was to live with them. Even if the lies were eating away at your insides. You got numb to the pain.

After putting Maisie down to bed, I sat on the couch and waited for Lori to come home. But when a knock came in the middle of the night, it wasn't her.

Two grave-faced deputies from the Hart County Sheriff's Department stood at my door.

"I'm sorry, Mr. O'Neal. There's been an accident."

ONE
Ashford

"Hold on, you did *what*?"

Dixie arched a white eyebrow. "You might want to adjust that sassy tone, hon."

I crossed my arms, fully aware of the way it made my pecs and biceps bulge, but Dixie was not impressed. She was five-foot-nothing and had celebrated her seventy-ninth birthday, again and again, each of the last several years. I was about three times her size and had black belts in three different fighting styles.

Yet my landlady's iron stare put me in my place like I was a little kid instead of a thirty-four-year-old man. Every damn time. Probably because she'd known me since I was in diapers.

"I'm just surprised," I grumbled. "This is coming out of the blue."

"Hardly. I gave you notice of the new commercial lease terms a couple months back."

"And I said I'd find a way to pay you the higher rent. I've been working on it."

"Sure, dear, but wishes and hopes aren't going to pay for my condo on Miami Beach. Not trying to be harsh here. It's just true."

Noisy voices and laughter filtered over from the lobby. Parents arriving with their kids for my afternoon Brazilian Jiu-Jitsu class. For the last several years, O'Neal Martial Arts had been operating from this storefront a block off Main Street. We got enough business to keep the lights on. Personal training on the side paid well per hour, and I'd slowly been adding to my roster of clients. Very slowly.

But growing a business in our small mountain town was a challenge. Add in health care and taxes, keeping our apartment habitable and my kiddo happy and occupied now that it was summer break...

I was struggling. Yet it was a sucker punch to the chest to have Dixie come in here today and make it so painfully obvious.

I couldn't cover the increase in rent, so she was going to lease out the commercial space to someone else during the mornings. *My* space. What the hell?

Dixie patted my forearm. "You'll only have to turn over the classroom for a few hours a day. The new renter is a music teacher. Needs a place to hold parent-and-tot music classes for the summer, and this building is a perfect fit."

"What about my personal training clients?"

That eyebrow of hers made another trek upward. "Like I don't see you with your clipboard over at the gym when I'm taking my Zumba classes."

Okay, that was fair. I didn't have a gym setup here, so I usually met my private training clients elsewhere. But I'd been thinking of hiring another teacher and expanding our class offerings. There was no way I could do any of that if I lost my training room for half of each day.

"Who is this so-called music teacher? I don't know any music teachers in Silver Ridge." Except for Mrs. Stuckey, who'd been giving piano lessons out of her basement for the last hundred years or so. I couldn't imagine Mrs. Stuckey leading a roomful of screaming toddlers through nursery rhymes.

"Her name is Emma Jennings. She's arriving soon from California."

"*California?*" I sputtered.

The vein at my temple twitched. My blood pressure was probably reaching unhealthy levels. This was my turf, and now I'd have to make room for some carpetbagger who wasn't even from our town.

My daughter and I lived in the apartment upstairs. It was a separate rental, effectively giving us the whole building. I didn't want some stranger hanging around and nosing into my private business.

Also, I didn't like the name *Emma Jennings*. Couldn't say why. She sounded unpleasant. And trust me, I knew a thing or two about unpleasant.

"What if Maisie doesn't like this woman?" An even worse idea occurred to me. "What if this Jennings woman doesn't like Maisie?"

"Who wouldn't like Maisie? She's a doll."

"Exactly. We don't know."

Dixie tutted. "Emma has family over in Hartley and comes well-recommended. But you're missing my point. She already signed her lease, and it starts the first of the month. The deal is done. So stop being an overgrown baby and accept it, Ashford O'Neal."

Groaning, I tipped my head back and glared at the low ceiling of my tiny office. This sucked. Because deep down, I knew Dixie was doing me a favor. She'd been charging me below-market rates for years. Now she'd found another way to cover the rent increase until I could make it work myself. *If* I could ever make it work.

I rubbed a hand over my beard. "Okay. I'll give it a try. But I'll have the higher rent for you soon. I'll figure it out somehow. Just in case this summer person is unreliable and falls through."

"Works for me."

"I appreciate you giving me a deal on the rent for so long."

"Oh, don't even mention that." Dixie glanced at the huge rose-gold watch on her tiny wrist. "Is it about time for those tykes to do their kickboxing? I want to stay and watch. It's so stinking cute."

"It's a grappling art, not kickboxing, but...yeah. Sure."

Still reeling from Dixie's news, I left the office and went down the hall to where the kids had gathered in the lobby. My gaze went straight to Maisie, as if drawn by a magnet.

My little girl. I loved my family and friends, and I'd do anything for them. No matter how much they might get on my last nerve. But always, *always*, Maisie was my number one.

She had my chestnut-brown hair. My straight brows, which usually looked more worried than a six-year-old's should. And she had Lori's delicate nose, heart-shaped face, and emerald-green eyes.

The memory of my best friend twanged a hollow place in my chest.

Maisie made a beeline in my direction. "The big hand on the clock is close to the top, Daddy. You were almost late."

"*Almost* doesn't count. I was just chatting with Miss Dixie." I leaned down to smooth Maisie's hair and kiss the top of it, sneaking a quick whiff of her strawberry-soap scent. Same thing Lori used to do. It calmed me like nothing else.

Standing, I raised my voice and said, "Let's go, class! Who's ready to rock?" I opened the door to the training room, and the kids flooded inside. "Ollie, hands to yourself. Quiet down, everyone. Who remembers what we talked about last week? What's the best kind of fight?"

"One with a flying spin kick!" somebody shouted.

"No. Especially not in jiu-jitsu. Who knows the real answer? What's the best kind of fight?"

"One we can stop before it starts," Maisie recited.

"Exactly." *That's my girl*, I thought. "We only fight if we have no other alternative."

Except life had a tendency to knock your feet out from

beneath you with a flying spin kick just when you thought things were okay. I wasn't talking about rent increases, either.

Bad shit happened, and good guys didn't always win.

I wanted to keep that harsh reality away from my daughter for as long as I possibly could.

TWO
Emma

"Come on, baby. Don't do me like this. Haven't I always been good to you?"

I caressed the steering wheel of my 2001 Nissan Altima. She'd been making weird noises for the last several miles. Clanking. Then some kind of grinding. None of it good.

"You can do it," I cooed. "We're almost there. Baby, please."

Stella whimpered from the passenger seat. Then leaned over to lick my cheek. I appreciated the moral support.

The drive had been going so well until now. I'd left West Oaks, California, yesterday morning. Stopped in a secluded area on the Nevada/Utah border to get a few hours of sleep overnight. Stella had cuddled up with me to keep us both warm. Maybe sleeping in my car in the desert wasn't the safest idea, but it had worked out fine. What my overprotective father didn't know wouldn't hurt him.

From there, the morning had gone without a single hitch. But what was a new adventure without the unexpected, right?

Perhaps not *completely* unexpected. Maybe I should've paid for a trip check on my Nissan before leaving. Or gotten those repairs that I'd kind of, sort of known were inevitable. And possibly more expensive than this poor old chariot was worth. But

I had paid for this car with my own money, and that meant something to me.

We just had to make it a little teeny bit farther.

I had only five miles to go when the concerning noises turned dire. My gas pedal started to go. Then I saw smoke leaking from inside the hood.

Oh, come on.

I managed to get over to the shoulder and sputter to a stop right in front of a billboard that read, *Welcome to the Hart of Colorado. You're Going To Love Hart County!*

Hmmm. I sensed irony.

Checking my phone, I confirmed what I'd already suspected. No service. "Shit," I muttered.

Stella licked my cheek again.

I looked over and smiled, stroking my fingers into the golden fur at her neck. "We're gonna be fine. A little walk on a summer evening never hurt anybody, right?"

Right.

Heaving a deep breath, I got out and patted the hood of the car. "Thanks for a good run." She'd gotten me almost the entire distance to Silver Ridge, and for that I was grateful.

Maybe it was fitting that my old car had expired. When I wiped my slate clean, I was thorough about it, wasn't I? Like the way I'd blown up my entire life during the last semester.

Nobody could accuse me of doing things half-assed.

My downfall had begun last October, not long after I'd started my grad program in music education at a prominent school in Southern California. I'd been so proud and more than a little starstruck.

To earn some extra income, and also because it sounded fun, I took a gig as a violinist for a local theater company. That director. Wow, he had been charming. Floppy hair, a million-dollar smile. Somehow confident and self-deprecating at once. Always staring at his messy stack of papers, pushing his black-framed glasses up his nose, while most of the women and half the men in the play couldn't take their eyes off him.

It started out innocently. For the longest time, I insisted there was no way he could be flirting with me. But one day, I ran into him at a popular lunch spot, and we got to talking. He invited me back to his office. *Definitely* flirting. I knew what he wanted, and I wanted it too.

Freeze frame, right there. If only I could tell myself to turn him down. That the thrill wasn't worth it.

We kept our relationship a secret, since he was my boss. The sex had been hot, too. In his office, my apartment, backstage after hours...

Stella had never liked him. That should've been a clue.

Looking back, I felt so stupid. He'd used every trick in the book on me. How had I not seen it? But when you wanted to believe in something bad enough, I guess you could convince yourself of anything.

I could, anyway.

Then, a few months ago, his wife returned from a stint teaching in London. Yes, that's right. He'd hidden the entire fact that he was *married*. And it turned out she was a professor at my school. In the *music department*, where I was a master's student.

The whole thing exploded, and soon, everybody knew. The faculty, the students. When I told the administrators I wouldn't be back next year, they didn't fight me on it. If anything, they were relieved.

I was in desperate need of a new beginning.

So here I was in Hart County, Colorado, taking some time off in a different state to figure myself out. With hard work and some luck, I would have things settled by the end of the summer. Ideally, I would be able to move to a different grad program to finish my master's. I'd missed the usual deadlines, but I had an advisor pulling for me. I was already waitlisted at one school, and I had several other prospects. I believed it would work out because it had to.

My family would never need to know the real reason I'd transferred. And all of that bullshit would be so far behind me that it couldn't touch me.

I shook myself off, like I could already imagine it gone.

Stella jumped out and sniffed at the wildflowers growing along the shoulder. I went around to the backseat to grab the essentials. My hair fell forward as I checked the contents of my messenger bag. It held Stella's treats, my wallet and phone, and my journal and pen. Things I couldn't live without.

From the trunk, I grabbed my violin case. I debated for a moment over the guitar, finally deciding to take it too. My case had a padded strap. I could carry it a few miles, no problem. My keyboard in the backseat was another story. Unless I could somehow rig a harness on Stella's back...

My retriever mix perked up and looked at me, furry brows knitting like she knew what I was thinking.

"No, you're right. That would be ridiculous. The keyboard will wait." So would my music books and my suitcase full of clothes. I was wearing cutoff jean shorts, an old Nirvana hoodie, and sneakers. Good enough to get me where I was going.

I closed and locked up the car. Snapped Stella's leash onto her collar. "And we're off. Our new adventure awaits."

THREE
Ashford

I HAD BEEN in some intense situations in my life. Like deployments to war zones. Teaching martial arts to a room of five-to-ten-year-olds didn't rank at the top. But it wasn't for the faint of heart either.

And yet, aside from any moment I got to spend with Maisie, this was the brightest part of my day. Teaching these wild hooligans to focus their intention. To be strong, but also peaceful. Ready for anything.

Lessons I still needed to practice myself.

I took the kids through today's lesson. An older boy from the teenage class assisted me. It was all going fine until little Ollie Carmichael said, "Mr. Ashford, watch this!" And proceeded to jump in the air, kicking wildly. His foot caught me in the crotch.

Thankfully I was wearing a cup. Because *safety first*.

But still. Ow.

"You okay, sir?" my teenage assistant mumbled. Most of the kids had gone quiet. And the parents were probably watching in the lobby through the one-way glass.

"Sorry, Mr. Ashford." Ollie looked terrified, but it had been an accident. Mayhem seemed to follow that kid.

I cleared my throat. "I'm good. Ollie, we need to go over the safety agreement. We can discuss it later with your mom. Let's wrap things up, kids. Closing circle."

The world had it out for me today. And it was so far from over.

When I dismissed the class, my brother was the first smirking face I saw in the lobby. He edged past the stream of children to reach me. "You all right?" Callum asked. "Looked like Ollie's ready for his black-belt test. He almost took you down."

"Almost doesn't count, Uncle Cal," Maisie chimed in as she dashed by.

I scratched my forehead with my middle finger. "I'm just peachy. Thanks."

Callum snickered like the annoying little brother he would always be, even though he was only two years younger than myself. "And I *almost* feel sorry for you."

"You're still taking Maisie after this, right?" I asked. "I have to check out that equipment I found on clearance."

"'Course. I wouldn't miss getting ice cream with my favorite niece. And *all* the toppings. We're walking straight over after this."

I decided not to complain about ice cream being a poor dinner choice. "I just can't handle any more changes of plan today. I've reached my limit."

"Ah." Callum nodded sagely, hands in the pockets of his ripped jeans. "This about the music teacher?"

"How do you know about that?"

"Heard Dixie telling some of the moms."

Wonderful. The news had hit the Silver Ridge mom network. By tomorrow, everyone in town would know I couldn't afford my rent.

I spent a few minutes chatting with parents of my students. But soon, the space had cleared out, leaving only Callum, our sister Grace, and our friend Piper Carmichael, who was Ollie's mom. Maisie and Ollie played with their little action figures by the window. Well, Maisie played, while Ollie was dancing like fire ants were crawling up his legs.

Secretly, I wondered why Maisie couldn't have picked a sweet, quiet kid for a best friend instead. *Kidding.* Except not really.

Piper, who was almost as tall as me if you counted the blond bun atop her head, leaned in with a smile. "Sorry about my child today. Glad to see you're walking upright."

"I'm fine," I grumbled.

Callum snorted. "It wasn't as bad as that day Ashford was babysitting us at the library. Remember the skateboard trick he tried to do on the front railing?"

Piper laughed. "Oh yeah. That was epic."

"I hate you both," I deadpanned.

Grace nudged me with her arm. "Whatever, big brother. You love us."

"I love *you*, Gracie. Because you're nice. Most of the time."

"And you, Ashford, are an incurable asshole to everyone except Maisie and Grace," Callum said, still grinning. "Most of the time." Luckily, the kids weren't listening.

"But he's *our* asshole," Piper quipped. "He always took care of us."

"Tried, at least." A smile creased the corners of my mouth.

Grace was the baby of the O'Neal family. Then Callum was next youngest, then me. Eldest was our brother Grayden. Yes, I could admit I had a soft spot for my youngest sister, but Piper was like a sister to me too. She and her older brother Teller had lived across the street when we were kids, and they'd been there for us through everything my family had gone through—my mom's death, my dad taking off.

Then Grayden's issues. Hadn't seen or heard from *him* in over a decade.

My point was this: I had reasons for my asshole tendencies.

Once we'd reached adulthood, we'd scattered for a while. But except for Grayden, we'd all made our way back home.

One night, wasted on tequila and sharing our tragic heartbreaks, Piper had dubbed our friend group the "Lonely Harts" club as a joke. H-a-r-t because we lived in Hart County. And the unfortunate name had stuck. Probably because it was accurate. We all had terrible luck with romantic relationships. Happily-ever-afters belonged in movies, not reality.

But we had each other. I could trust each of them with Maisie. If I hadn't had their support through the last several years? I had no idea what I would've done.

Yeah, I loved this family. Even crotch-kicking Ollie.

It was my job to protect them.

Before I said goodbye, I gave each of them a hug. And then an extra-long hug and kisses for Maisie, who jumped into my arms like a tiny koala bear.

"I love you bunches, Daddy."

"I love you bunches too, monkey. Even more than yesterday. I hope I don't run out of room in here."

That made her giggle, like it always did. I cherished every one of those moments. Because you never knew if this goodbye would be the last one you got.

✧

The rest of my afternoon was a bust.

I trekked forty minutes out to another town to check on some used equipment and supplies. A martial arts school was going out of business, which was depressing as all hell. Like a nightmare vision of my possible future. The owner refused to negotiate on price, so I left with only a few training mats that I could've gotten elsewhere. Waste of my time.

Then I stopped at a mega-chain grocery looking for Maisie's favorite granola bars, and the place didn't even have them. I grabbed a tub of the protein powder Callum liked instead.

Now, I was driving back toward Silver Ridge as the sun was setting. Mountains zig-zagged across the horizon. Twilight shadows spread across the valley on either side of the two-lane highway. Aside from a dark abandoned car by the side of the road, my truck was the only vehicle in sight. I just wanted to get home.

Dammit, I was tired.

My phone rang, and I glanced at the number on the screen. Discomfort tingled up and down my limbs.

I knew that area code.

Didn't matter if I blocked this number, because another would inevitably call again. Always the same person who I didn't intend to speak to. I never answered.

The ringing finally stopped.

Then, because the universe had a sick sense of humor, I realized where I was. Almost to the mile marker where Lori had died on that awful night three years ago.

Figured, didn't it?

I still didn't know what she'd been doing out here that night. Or what secret she'd been keeping. I probably never would. But the sympathetic faces of those deputies reappeared in my mind. Their words echoed.

There's been an accident.

I rubbed my forehead. A headache throbbed between my eyes.

Then I saw a figure up ahead by the side of the road. Long legs, long hair. Like a ghost appearing out of the past, if I'd believed in things like that. But this person was real.

Real *stupid* for walking along the shoulder where she'd easily get hit.

Carrying something bulky, too. She'd have trouble getting out of the way if a car came toward her. It pissed me off so much my vision feathered.

What did this girl think she was doing, being so careless?

Then she turned and stuck her arm out, thumb pointed up. Hitchhiking, of all the idiotic things. Did she have a death wish?

Nope, I wouldn't let that happen. Not on my watch. Not tonight.

FOUR
Emma

It was a beautiful evening. Deep blue sky, orange clouds, songbirds soaring. An old wooden cabin sat in the distance. The air smelled fresh and sweet. Purple, yellow, and pink wildflowers crowded the surrounding valley, and the setting sun lit up the red rocks of the cliffs.

We passed a small white cross, a marker for someone who'd died here, which added a touch of bittersweet melancholy.

Stella smiled, tongue lolling. She was loving this too. If we weren't beside the highway, I would've let her run off-leash through those wildflowers.

Yet I would've driven past all of this, only barely noticing it, if not for my car breaking down. "See? This summer is going to be just what we needed. I can feel it."

After a mile of walking, though, I was slightly less enthusiastic. Had my guitar always been this heavy?

I sighed with relief when I heard a rumbling engine. Thank goodness. Somebody heading into Silver Ridge. Surely they wouldn't mind giving little old me a ride into town. If the driver turned out to be a creep, I had my pepper spray in my satchel. And Stella.

I turned, smiled, and stuck out my thumb.

A black Dodge Ram roared along the asphalt. It had sped up, and I thought for a moment the guy was going to blow past me. But he didn't. Instead, he slammed on his brakes, window buzzing down as he reached me.

The man inside was in his thirties. Muscular and broad-shouldered in his T-shirt. A baseball cap covered his hair. And he was *not* smiling back.

In fact, he was scowling like I'd personally offended him.

"What do you think you're doing?"

I sputtered a laugh. "Um, what?"

"You shouldn't be walking out here. Much less hitchhiking. Do you have any idea how dangerous this highway is?"

I glanced right at the deserted asphalt, with its wide shoulders and nearby fields of swaying wildflowers. Glanced left. It was getting dark out, but hardly the mean streets of LA. "Did you stop just to tell me that?"

"No," he snapped. "I assume you're heading into Silver Ridge. I'll take you."

What was this guy's problem? "You know, I think I'll walk. Or wait for the next person to stop."

"The next person could be a serial killer."

"How do I know you're not?"

"You don't. And that's the issue."

I laughed. "But how does that reassure me?"

He shifted into Park, threw open his door, and got out. The truck was still running. The guy rounded the front bumper, hands on his hips. Black-ink tattoos stretched over his forearms, and his T-shirt said *O'Neal Martial Arts*.

Stella backed up, getting closer to me. I patted her head. But my other hand was ready to grab my pepper spray. "I'm armed. Just to let you know."

"Glad to hear it. I wouldn't recommend getting into the cars of strangers. Even my daughter knows that, and she's six. But I also wouldn't leave anyone in my family out here alone, and I assume you have a parent or friend who'd say the same."

My eyes really wanted to roll at his scolding tone. But he was correct.

I glanced through his backseat window and saw a child's booster. Plus a variety of toys and food wrappers littering the upholstery. So he couldn't be that bad. Some serial killers had daughters, but they'd probably be luring me with kind promises and candy. Wouldn't they?

He held out his hand, beckoning impatiently. "Up to you. Just make up your mind. If you're coming with me, I'll put your stuff in the cab. Is it yes or no? I don't have all night."

"Okay, Mr. Grumpy. Geez. But if you mess with me, my dog will tear your face off." That was wishful thinking. But Stella would, at the very least, give him a stern growl.

"If I mess with you, then I hope he does."

"She. My dog's a she."

"Even better."

I almost laughed again. This guy was something else. *What exactly*, I couldn't tell.

But at least he'd get me to Silver Ridge. That had to be progress.

I took off my guitar case and handed it to him. He studied it for a moment before placing it in the backseat. After I gave her a nudge, Stella jumped in next. Immediately, she started rooting around the floor mats for dropped Cheerios or whatever else was down there.

I climbed into the front. "It's not like I was out here on purpose. My car broke down."

He slid into the driver's seat. "The sedan on the shoulder about a mile back?"

"Yep, that's me."

He squinted at the violin in my lap like it might be filled with drugs or weapons. "Are you new in town?"

"I'm new, yeah. Here for the summer. I'm Emma."

The guy grunted, face pinching like he was in pain. No clue what *that* was about. Stomach issues?

"I'm Ashford." He put the truck in gear and took off down the road. But to my surprise, he made a U-turn and started heading the opposite direction from Silver Ridge.

"Hey, where are you taking me?" I wasn't panicking yet, though I tightened my hand around the pepper spray.

"Back to your car." He said it like it was obvious. "You must have a suitcase or something. You'll need it tonight."

I relaxed against the seat. "Oh. That's true, yeah." I had no idea when I'd get my car towed into town. That would cost money, and most of mine was spoken for.

When we reached my Nissan, he made another U-turn and pulled in behind it. We both got out, and he waited for me to unlock the trunk. He squinted suspiciously at the keyboard case.

"You want all this?"

"Yes. That's why I brought it with me close to a thousand miles."

We transferred the rest of my stuff to his truck. Which *was* probably what a serial killer would do if he planned to erase evidence of my existence later. But Stella was sitting happily in his backseat, so I decided to roll with it.

"Where are you staying in town?" he asked.

I gave him the address, and he said he knew it. We pulled back onto the road.

I did not know what to make of Ashford. One minute, he was a bossy, abrasive jerk. And the next, he was almost close to decent. He was odd.

But a serial killer? Nah. Probably not.

"So you're some kind of musician?"

I could've made a snarky comment about his powers of observation, but I assumed he was just trying to make conversation.

"I guess I'm a musician." Though I hadn't played or composed anything outside teaching assignments in months. "I'm getting my master's in music education."

"That's why you're here for the summer? To teach?"

"Yep."

He frowned at the windshield. His gaze slid to me. Then away again. "Do you have experience teaching?"

"I do, actually. I've been giving lessons to kids for years." Including all through my years in college.

"You seem young."

"I'm twenty-three. Not that it's really your business."

"Doesn't seem right to show up for the summer knowing you'll leave soon. Kids get attached."

My face scrunched. "Teachers come and go all the time. Kids are adaptable. Especially little ones."

"But most small businesses fail. How do you even know people in Silver Ridge want music lessons?"

"Because everyone likes music. What is your problem, exactly?"

The small muscle at the side of his square jaw pulsed. "Just pointing out things you might not have considered."

This time, I didn't hold back my eye roll. "Okay."

Houses and buildings started to appear. We were coming into Silver Ridge. I was eager to get a sense of it, and also for a distraction from the giant grump beside me.

The architecture was eclectic. A mix of western, Victorian, and newer construction, accentuated with lush flowerbeds and historic streetlights. Fairy lights draped above the patios of restaurants along Main Street, where diners laughed over dinner. Teenagers played frisbee at a park across from a red brick town hall complete with a clock tower.

Stella and I were going to adore this place.

"You're renting a commercial space from Dixie Haines, right?" Ashford asked.

My head turned sharply toward him. "How'd you know that?"

He pressed his lips together. "Dixie mentioned your name earlier. She said we'd be sharing the same building. I run the martial arts school there."

O'Neal Martial Arts. That explained the T-shirt. Dixie had

told me I was renting a shared space, but she hadn't mentioned the exact business I'd be dealing with. "So you knew who I was."

"Look, this is really bad timing for me. That building has been mine for years. I live in the second-floor apartment. I've been meaning to add more classes during the day so I can afford Dixie's rent increase, but how can I do that if you're using the space? It's a Catch-22."

"Were you hoping I'd give up and leave if you raised enough doubts about my summer plans?"

"Pretty much."

"That's a dick move."

He cringed. "I'm not proud of it."

At least he could admit that. "I understand your concerns, but I have a signed lease. We'll have to deal with each other. I'm sure we can work it out."

"I'm not trying to be rude here. But I have a kid to provide for. Running a business is hard enough without upending my daily routine. Much less cleaning dirty diapers and spit-up left all over from toddler music time."

My spine straightened and my jaw clenched. Yet I still managed to smile. "I assure you, I will clean up after my classes."

"That remains to be seen." Ashford stopped the truck. "We're here."

We'd parked in front of a sprawling, multi-story Victorian house that had seen better days. A harsh streetlight lit up the brown lawn. A couple of shutters hung askew, and trash littered the yard.

I opened my phone to check the address again, but this was definitely the location of the room I'd rented. Not the commercial building I'd be sharing with Ashford, obviously, but where I'd sleep. The Ponderosa Apartments.

Those online pictures had been extremely misleading. But they took pets, offered month-to-month leases, and the apartment came furnished. So I wasn't eager to complain.

"This boarding house is a dump, by the way." Ashford

propped his elbow against his door. "Hasn't been updated since the last century."

I smirked. "I wasn't asking for your opinion. I think it looks great."

"Really."

"Yep. Historic charm."

"That's real estate code for *old dump*."

"You really are a jerk."

"So I've been told."

I jumped out of the truck, slamming the door closed. My skin was hot all over, my heart racing. Setting my violin case carefully on the grass, I opened the backdoor of the cab.

"Stella. Come. Let's go."

She sat in the backseat, smiling. Then she put her paws on the center console, pushed her muzzle into the front seat area, and licked Ashford's bearded face.

That traitor.

He leaned away from her tongue but rubbed her neck. She ate up the attention. "Go on," he said. "Your mom's waiting."

Stella bounded out of the truck. I glared at her accusingly, and she had the grace to look guilty.

We were going to have words later about loyalty. No matter how hunky the man in question might be.

Ashford got out to help unload my stuff. "Just leave everything here on the grass," I said. "I'll take it up myself."

"You sure?"

"Wouldn't want to inconvenience you any more than I have." And yes, I was being sarcastic.

He frowned at the building, then at me. Then shrugged. "If you're sure."

"I am. Just like I'm sure I'll love it here, and that the people of Silver Ridge will adore my music classes. I'm going to have a fantastic summer. No matter what you might think."

"Suit yourself."

"I plan to." Which maybe didn't make sense. What did that

saying really mean, anyway? But I didn't care. Ashford could keep his opinions—and his big tattooed muscles and his doggy neck scratches—to himself.

Welcome to the Hart of Colorado?

So far, not so much.

FIVE
Emma

THE NEXT MORNING, I tied Stella's leash to a railing outside Silver Linings Coffee on Main Street. "I'll be back in a few. You be good now. No more cozying up to strange men."

Stella tried her sad doggy eyes on me. And of course, they worked.

"All right, I'll buy you a treat if they have one. We could both use a pick-me-up." There was a dog bowl here on the sidewalk, half full, so Stella had her drink already. Now, it was my turn.

The bell on the door jingled cheerfully as I pushed inside. I was supposed to meet Dixie Haines here later, but I'd shown up bright and early to scope things out myself. I hadn't slept well and needed copious amounts of caffeine, stat.

Also, I planned to make use of the coffee shop's wi-fi, since the wi-fi at my apartment was apparently broken. Among other things.

When I reached the counter, a tall woman with blond hair and a warm smile greeted me. "Morning, what can I get you?"

"One of those doggy treats." I pointed at the bakery case. "And your biggest vanilla latte. With as many espresso shots as you can legally serve in one cup."

Her eyes narrowed. "Oh, this sounds like a challenge. I love it." She tapped on her order screen. "Rough night?"

"It certainly wasn't the best." I wasn't ready to call the Ponderosa a dump, like Ashford had. But the paper-thin walls, clanking pipes, and drafty windows weren't ideal. Who knew it would get so cold at night here in the summer? Well, the internet probably knew. But not me.

The lumpy, thin mattress hadn't helped with my restfulness either. Or the ominous-looking stains on the apartment ceiling. I hadn't dealt with my car yet, either, but all that would wait until after coffee.

"I'll throw in an iced mocha donut, on the house. Always perks me right up." She winked.

"That sounds amazing. Thank you so much. Maybe my night wasn't great, but you're turning my morning around fast." I handed her some cash. "Keep the change. I'm Emma, by the way. I'm new."

"Piper. Wonderful to meet you. Is that your retriever out front? She's gorgeous."

"She is. And thank you."

"Welcome to Silver Ridge."

"I appreciate that." At least some people around here knew how to make a newcomer feel welcome. While I still had her attention, I dug a leaflet for my music lessons from my messenger bag. I'd printed them before leaving California with the info Dixie had given me. "Any chance you have a community bulletin board and wouldn't mind me posting this?"

Piper read the text on the paper, eyes widening. Then she looked over at me with a whole new level of understanding in her expression. "You're the music teacher! I've heard about you."

"All good, I hope."

Her head tilted back and forth. "Well, I'm friends with Ashford O'Neal."

My heart sank. Had he already been bad-mouthing me around town? What the heck was that man's vendetta against me?

Thankfully, Piper laughed. "From the look on your face, I would guess you've met Ashford already. Don't worry. His bark can be bad, but his bite is no worse than your golden retriever's." She nodded at the window, and I turned around to find Stella, tongue out, gleefully accepting tummy rubs from passersby.

"Maybe. But Stella likes just about everyone. Ashford definitely doesn't like me."

"Just ignore him when he's being surly. That's what I usually do." She plucked the leaflet from my hand. "I'd be happy to hang this up for you. And I'll spread the word. I love the idea of parent-and-tot music classes. Are you going to offer lessons for older kids? My son is seven."

I nodded eagerly. "I plan to. I wanted to assess interest first. I play violin, piano, guitar, and I have experience with one-on-one lessons. That's the kind of teaching I prefer. What do you think he'd be interested in?"

Slow down, I told myself. The woman was at work, and a couple of customers were in line behind me. But could you blame me for being excited? She was my first potential client.

"Not sure about which instrument. Ollie might be the drums type. He's a fan of loud noises. But not so much sitting still."

I laughed. "I'm sure we can figure out a good fit for him. And an affordable price. Private lessons don't have to break the bank."

"I would love that. I'm so glad you came in today, Emma. I'll have your order right out."

I turned away, fizzing with optimism. *See?* I thought. *This is going to be great.*

While I waited for my latte, I walked over to the far side of the café, where bookshelves stretched along the wall offering used books for sale. I saw sections for both romance and thrillers, two of my favorite genres. At the other end of the shop, there was a fireplace and a collection of comfy, overstuffed chairs. No fire going, since it was June and sun shone through the front windows.

The most striking feature of the cafe, aside from the butcher-block coffee counter, was a huge handmade quilt with designs of mountains and trees hanging in a prominent spot.

I could already tell I would be spending a lot of time here. When I wasn't teaching my classes and private lessons, of course. *Take that, Ashford.*

Piper called my name. I went up to grab my order, then sank into a chair by the fireplace. The first sip of my latte zipped through my veins. Dang, the woman had made good on her promise. I glanced over at the counter, catching Piper's eye, and lifted my cup in thanks.

Once I'd connected to the coffee shop's wi-fi, I checked my messages. I'd managed to text my mom, dad, and stepmom last night that I'd arrived. Cell service had been enough for that. But not much else. I sent my stepmom, Madison, a longer check-in, followed by a message to my uncle Aiden and his wife over in Hartley. I'd have to get over there to visit them one of these days. Once things had settled down for me in Silver Ridge.

Against my better judgment, I logged on to my socials. My friends from music school hadn't written. Seemed like they wanted to pretend I didn't exist anymore.

That hurt more than anything else. The fact that none of them had given me the benefit of the doubt in that awful scandal.

But I did have posts and messages waiting from my high school and college besties. Thankfully, none of them knew about what had happened last semester, and they never would.

I sank my teeth into the mocha donut, moaning at the perfect play of coffee, chocolate, and carbs across my tongue. Piper was officially my favorite person in Silver Ridge.

I still had a few minutes until Dixie was supposed to arrive, so I poked around online. And then, without giving myself much chance to think about it, I googled *Ashford O'Neal* and *Silver Ridge, Colorado.*

I took another bite of donut while my eyes scanned the results. There was a website and some social pages for O'Neal Martial Arts. Somehow, the man had managed a smile for the cover photo of his business page. It annoyed me how handsome he was. Also, the way his biceps and pecs popped beneath his tight T-shirt.

Moving on.

I perused the next few results, mostly killing time. But then my eye stopped on a news article. *Highway Fatality Under Investigation.*

I clicked on the article and gasped as I read it.

It was from three years ago, and recounted how a young mother named Lori O'Neal had been hit and killed by a car on the highway outside of town.

Her husband's name? Ashford O'Neal.

I remembered that small white cross I had seen yesterday. It hadn't looked that old. Could that have been for Lori? My heart went out to Ashford and his family. Especially to his daughter, who I assumed was the one Ashford had mentioned yesterday. That poor girl. To lose her mom like that, in such a tragic way...

In fact, the entire incident yesterday hit differently. Ashford's reaction to seeing me out there. The way he had seemed so angry. Had he been thinking of his wife's death?

I finished reading the article, followed by another I found from about a week afterward, which cleared the driver of the car of any wrongdoing. Lori had run out onto the highway at night. The driver of the car hadn't been able to stop in time. They'd called the paramedics right away, but it had been too late. A tragic accident.

She'd run onto the highway. Why? What had she been running from?

"Emma? Is that you?"

I looked up and found an older woman standing beside my chair. Chin-length white hair, reading glasses on a long chain.

"Dixie?"

"Guilty as charged."

I stood up and gave her a hug. "It's so good to finally meet you in person."

We'd been communicating by email so far. But I'd sent her a scan of my driver's license for the credit and background checks, which was probably how she'd known what I looked like. Now that I was standing, it was obvious how petite she was. Way shorter than me, and I was no giant. Dixie wore a pair of shiny gold platform sneakers, which added an inch or two to her frame. Besides making a dramatic fashion statement, naturally.

"I love the shoes," I said.

"Why, thank you." Dixie held me by the shoulders to look me over. "Aren't you a stunner. The young men of Silver Ridge are in for a shake-up. We've got plenty of eligible bachelors eager to show a girl a good time, if the walks of shame I see every morning are anything to judge by."

I snorted a laugh, my face heating. Dixie did not have a quiet voice, and I was pretty sure half the coffee shop was listening to us.

"Any man waiting for you back home in California?" she asked pointedly. "Or women, for that matter?"

"No men for me at the moment. But I'm not interested in romance anytime soon. I plan to stay out of trouble." I'd had more than enough man-related trouble already.

She hummed. "Doesn't sound like fun to me, honey, but you do you. Shall we walk over to the building? Show you the space you're renting for your music classes?"

"That would be great." I grabbed the rest of my latte, waving goodbye to Piper.

On the way out, I stopped to untie Stella's leash. Dixie rubbed Stella's flanks and accepted a flurry of face-kisses. "What a sweetheart. Maisie is going to love this one."

"Maisie?" I asked.

"You'll see." Was I wrong, or had Dixie's tone taken a turn toward mischievous? "I have two Lhasa Apsos, but they live in Florida now with my boyfriend Pedro. He's Cuban. Such a gentleman. Barely speaks any English, and I only know three words in Spanish. It's heaven. Would you like to know what the three words are?"

"I will pass." I struggled to breathe as I suppressed another laugh. "Do you think you'll move there permanently?"

"Oh, no. I'm a snow bird. I love the mountains in the summer. Plus my son and his hubby live in Golden. Have to get those grandkid visits in."

As we walked down Main Street, Dixie pointed out the sights to me. The clock tower, the florist, the best boutiques. "Stay away from the Seafood Hut. They ship their trout in frozen. And there's the vet. You'll want their number. I'll text it to you."

"Okay," I said, just trying to keep up. Those gold sneakers moved fast. Stella trotted along, taking it all in and stopping occasionally to give a light pole a sniff.

We turned onto a side street, this one dotted with colorful gingerbread houses converted into businesses.

"Before we get there, I'm afraid there's a problem we need to discuss," Dixie said.

"Oh? What's that?"

"His name's Ashford."

Ugh. My mood soured. "Actually, I'm well aware of that problem. I met him last night. He's not happy about sharing the building with me."

Dixie side-eyed me. "It's not personal. Ashford can be a bit...territorial. He's a single father. Been through more downs than ups. He'd do anything for that little girl. She lost her momma a few years ago."

Once again, sympathy rose in my chest. How could I stay annoyed at him when he'd been through something like that?

"I stumbled onto an article about his wife's death." Maybe not stumbled. More like I'd been online-stalking the man. "Terrible thing to happen."

"It was. Lori was a wonderful mother. But truth is, the loss hit Ashford the hardest."

"I'm sorry to hear that."

As we walked, I had the strangest feeling. The hairs rose on my neck, and unpleasant tingles broke out across my back. I looked behind us, wondering if somebody else was there, but the street was quiet.

It was probably just the subject matter we'd been discussing. Lori's death.

"Something the matter?" Dixie asked.

"No, sorry. Just looking around."

A block later, we came up to a huge two-story brick building. It was painted blue, with white trim and a sign reading *O'Neal Martial Arts*. "We'll order a sign for your music school and put it in the front window there," Dixie said, pointing.

"I don't know if I'd call it a school. And it's just for the summer."

"Shouldn't sell yourself short, hon. I say, wherever you are, make sure people know it." She unlocked the door and ushered me inside. "I'll give you the two-cent tour."

"Can I bring Stella in with us? She's very well-behaved."

"Fine by me. Wouldn't want her to get lonely."

Just inside, there was a small lobby space with a rectangle of one-way glass looking into a teaching area. Floor mats were stacked along one side of the classroom, along with other neatly arranged equipment.

I braced myself to see Ashford again, but it seemed no one else was here.

Dixie showed me a bathroom, a small kitchen, and the storage closet, which held more supplies. Overall, I was impressed. It was tidy, but far from sterile. I pictured where I might store my instruments and the items I needed for the tot classes. My keyboard would be the most difficult, since it was a full-size digital piano. I'd need to get creative there. It was doable though.

"What do you think?" Dixie asked. "No regrets, I hope?"

"This will work great. Might need a bit of rearranging. But I like it."

Most importantly, the vibe was right. I could imagine kids

here, learning and having fun. Parents connecting. A community. Ashford had already done that work. No wonder he was protective of what he'd built.

"It's lovely," I added.

She opened another door. "This is Ashford's office." It was a tiny room, filled to the brim with boxes and a paper-strewn desk. A purple stuffed dragon sat in his desk chair. "Looks like Maisie's been in here."

"The dragon is appropriate." I would stay out of the office, lest he breathe fire at me.

Dixie smiled as she shut the door. "I've known Ashford since he was a boy. He's wary of change because he's dealt with too much of it. But when it comes to what's *good* for him, he's not so great at seeing it."

I wasn't sure what she meant by that. Knowing what I did now, I could look past his icy reception. So long as he stopped trying to scare me away from running my classes.

There had to be plenty of room here for the two of us. I was willing to share if he was.

✦

I asked Dixie if I could stick around for a while after she left, even though my lease hadn't technically started yet. I had planning to do.

Stella lay in a sunny spot beneath the front window, while I set down my messenger bag and took out my journal and gel pens. I made a circuit of the first floor again, this time jotting down ideas and sketching out how I envisioned arranging things. I would have to check with Ashford and get his input, of course. But I wanted to have a proposal that he couldn't refuse.

This man didn't want to make room for me. So I'd have to make it as painless as possible, while also letting him know he couldn't scare me off.

But I could still make it fun.

As I made notes in my journal, I found myself humming a melody. I couldn't place it at first. It took me a moment to realize it was something new. For the first time in months, I'd actually found a glimmer of inspiration.

I sat down crosslegged in the middle of the classroom and tried to capture the notes on paper before they flew away.

But I wasn't fast enough. The melody evaporated from my head as soon as I tried to write it down.

"Why does this keep happening?" I asked. I heard Stella's collar jingling, though she stayed where I'd asked her to. Because she was a very good girl.

Why couldn't my brain be a good girl too? Just cooperate with me on remembering a simple melody?

Sighing, I pulled up some music on my phone instead. I found my favorite playlist of the moment from the artist Ayla Maxwell. She was an absolute beast on the piano, and she added in poppy vocals and inventive lyrics, which had made her a legend even though she'd only been recording a few years. I was in awe of her. Not like I wanted to be an international pop star, but the woman was a powerhouse of creativity.

If just a little of that fairy dust could rub off on me, I would take it. Didn't matter if I was performing up on a stage or taking a class full of moms and toddlers through a lineup of silly songs. I wanted to give it my very best.

I stood up and tucked my journal under my arm, head bopping as I went into the lobby.

And then I nearly screamed as a tiny person jumped out in front of me.

"Hi. Who are you?"

My hand went to my chest, rubbing it like I needed to get my heart going again.

A girl stood there, around five or six years old, with bright green eyes and a white ribbon tied in her dark hair. This had to be

Ashford's daughter. Which meant her dad probably wasn't far behind. I paused the music on my phone.

"I'm Emma. I'm going to be teaching music classes here."

"Wow, really?" Her little nose wrinkled up. "But what about my dad? He does classes here too. He's the best teacher ever. I take Brazilian Jiu-Jitsu." She said the words slowly, pronouncing them carefully. Like she had been practicing on it a lot.

"I know, I've met your dad. We're going to share."

She shrugged. "Oh, okay. What was that music you were just listening to? Was that you? Are you a singer? Can you teach me to sing?"

Before I could answer any of her questions, Stella got up from the ground and came over to say hello. As soon as Maisie saw her, she gasped. "Are you kidding me? You have a puppy?"

I smiled as I went to hold Stella back. I could tell she was getting excited at the prospect of meeting a new person, and Stella adored kids.

"She's not really a puppy anymore, but she loves to play, and she's very friendly. This is Stella."

The girl waved. "Hi Stella, I'm Maisie. I always wanted a dog."

"You can pet her if you like."

Maisie's eyes went comically round. She only hesitated a half second before going to her knees and hugging Stella around the neck.

Tears sprang into my eyes, because I was a total softie like that.

Stella sat calmly, smiling and panting as Maisie petted her. It wasn't my business, but I couldn't help thinking of how this little girl had lost her mom. Dogs were the best at providing unconditional love and comfort.

"She's really nice," Maisie said.

"She is. Stella's my social director."

"What does that mean?"

"It means that Stella makes friends for me wherever I go."

"Can I be friends with you?"

"If your dad says it's okay."

She studied me, then nodded. "I like your smile. It's a friendly smile. You must have lots of friends."

"Thank you, Maisie. But here's a secret about me." I leaned in. "I'm a little bit shy."

Her eyes widened again. "Me too! It's not a secret, though. I'm not supposed to have secrets."

"Oh, hmm. That's fair." I'd stepped into one of those kid-safety things. "I didn't really mean secret. It's just something most people don't realize about me. I'm an introvert. I like having time to myself to think, which means I don't always feel like peopling. But Stella helps remind me to be social."

"What's that fancy book?"

"This?" I held up my journal. It was bound in blue leatherette with embossed flowers. "It's the place I write down what I'm thinking. Like a diary."

"I can read a lot of books. Even ones with chapters. And I can write really good, too."

"I bet you can. I bet you're top of the class."

Maisie laughed, a sweet and musical sound.

I decided to turn Ayla Maxwell back on, and I let Maisie flip through the pages of my journal while she petted Stella with her other hand. I doubted a six-year-old could read my messy cursive. I could barely read it myself.

"Mais?" a deep voice called out, just before Ashford appeared in the hallway.

The man did cut an excellent figure. Ashford didn't have a ball cap on today. His brown hair was rumpled, and he wore snug athletic pants and a black T-shirt with the silhouette of a fighter on it. A martial artist? Was that a term?

Unfortunately, his handsome face turned stormy in an instant. "What's going on here?"

I stood up. "Dixie let me in."

"It's not the first of the month yet."

"True, but I needed to do some planning."

He flinched. "Can you turn that noise off? It's like nails on a chalkboard."

Okay, so not a fan of Ayla Maxwell. I pressed pause on my phone screen.

"Maisie, you shouldn't be down here," Ashford said, though he'd softened his tone. "I asked you to head upstairs while I was making my phone calls. You didn't listen."

"But the dog, Daddy. I was petting her."

"There shouldn't be a dog here either. Go upstairs and pick up your toys, monkey. Aunt Grace will be here soon. I need to talk to Miss Emma."

"But Daddy—"

"No buts, please. Go."

"Fine." Maisie gave Stella another hug, showing a streak of defiance, then scowled at her dad as she marched past him. The two of them looked so much alike it almost made me laugh.

"Six going on sixteen," Ashford muttered.

"Maisie seems great."

His glare refocused on me. "You can't just come and go. My apartment is upstairs. This is my home. I need to know who's here when I send my kid inside."

So much for all those sympathetic feelings I was having. For the daughter, yes. The dad? Not so much.

"Can we not do this, please? Let's fast forward." I made a grumpy face and dropped my voice. "*I'm Ashford, I'm super territorial and unreasonable.*" Then I smiled. "Oh, hey, I'm Emma. I'm a nice, innocent music teacher. Dixie did a full background check on me. I lock doors, and I would never allow an unvetted stranger around your kid. *Thanks Emma, I feel much better.* The end."

I held out my hands like I was saying, *Ta-da*.

His frown softened. Just a tad.

I picked up my journal from the floor where Maisie had left it. "If you've got a few minutes, I had some ideas to make room for my stuff. I don't have that much. I promise."

He shook his head, glancing away. "This isn't a good time. I need to meet a client for a personal training session in ten, and my sister's on her way. I was just on the phone with the mechanic. He's a friend of my brother. I arranged for your car to be towed, and it arrived at the shop, but I didn't have your number."

"Seriously? Oh my gosh, thank you. That was on my list for today, but I was worried about the cost. I'm a little short on funds at the moment."

He sighed like I was the biggest inconvenience he'd ever encountered. "I can make sure you get the friends and family discount."

"That's...surprisingly nice of you."

"It happens on rare occasions."

"Do I detect a hint of sarcasm? Do you actually have a sense of humor in there somewhere?"

"Maybe. It's rusty. Might not be salvageable."

A smile tugged at my lips. Stella sensed her opportunity and approached, nudging Ashford's hand with her nose. He ruffled her ears.

"How are the Ponderosa Apartments?" he asked.

I tensed up, smiling again but with my lips closed. "Just fine."

"You sure? You might want to talk to Dixie. She could try to help you find another apartment. Assuming there's anything available at this point, since the summer tourists have already arrived." His tone was full of judgment. As if he was really saying, *A smarter person would've figured this out ages ago.*

"I can handle my own living arrangements."

He shrugged like he didn't believe that.

My frustration broke through.

"What's your issue with me, really?" I asked. "Is it that I'm young, and you think that makes me irresponsible? Is it that I'm not from here? Or you're judging me because my car broke down? What?"

"I don't have an issue with you. Not a personal one."

"Bullshit." I sighed and grabbed my bag. I'd had enough of

him for today. Maybe Ashford wasn't a terrible guy, but he didn't seem to think much of me. "I'll be back later."

"On the first of the month."

"Nope. Before. So we can plan where my stuff will go."

He made a grumbly sound. Too bad. I didn't need his permission to be here.

When the summer ended, he could rejoice that I was gone if he wanted. For now, I was sticking around Silver Ridge. He had to get used to it. I wasn't going anywhere.

SIX
Ashford

"Daddy, is it time to wake up yet?"

Inside, I wanted to shout *no* and hide my head under my pillow. But I was a grown man and a father. So instead, I pretended to be asleep.

Maisie stood beside my bed. I could feel her staring at me. "Daddeeeee." She poked my forehead. "It's light outside. I want to go down and see if Emma and Stella are here yet. Can I?"

Groaning, I sat up and rubbed my face. "No, you may not. Emma won't be here for a couple hours at least. It's too early."

"But I'm dressed already. And I made breakfast."

I blinked, eyes adjusting to the familiar sight of my daughter. She'd put on the fancy dress Grace had bought her last Christmas, and she'd styled her unbrushed hair with a unicorn headband, complete with plastic horn. I hoped the kitchen wasn't too awful of a mess right now.

"Breakfast, huh? Enough for me?"

"Of course. I made lots."

Oh, boy. "But I'm too hungry to wait." I lunged forward to grab her. "And you're so sweet."

"I'm not!" Maisie shrieked and laughed as I carried her out of my room, pretending to chew on her midsection. *Now*, I was awake.

A little while later, we were eating soggy cereal at the kitchen table. Maisie had only left a small puddle of milk on the counter. A few flakes on the floor. Could've been worse. She hadn't quite filled the cereal bowls to the brim, but it was close.

It had only been a week since Emma had arrived in Silver Ridge, and my kid was already obsessed with the new music teacher. Every day, it was *Emma this* and *Emma that*.

In fact, it seemed like the whole town had caught the same bug.

Yesterday had been Emma's first parent-and-tot class. The room had hit capacity, which meant babies and toddlers were crawling everywhere when I'd spied on her through the one-way window.

Because I had no shame. Or, apparently, better things to do.

The people of Silver Ridge just *loved* Emma Jennings. Meanwhile, I'd been working my ass off for years to build my customer base. When I'd complained about the situation, Grace had told me to try *smiling more*. Then she'd cackled maniacally.

Real funny.

It wasn't that I disliked Emma Jennings on a personal level. I didn't have an "issue" with her like she'd claimed. Couldn't a guy just be a curmudgeon in peace?

Maisie perked up. "I think I heard something. Is it Emma?"

"Not yet, monkey. Be patient."

"But time is moving too slow."

"Really? To me, it's always moving too fast."

She huffed, the perfect picture of a mini teenager. "Can I have music lessons with Emma?"

"That's too expensive for us right now."

"But Ollie is going to learn piano. He'll get to see Emma more than me."

"Somehow, I doubt that."

I wasn't completely unaware of Emma's charms. Like her

lustrous dark hair and her seemingly flawless skin. The way her mouth quirked when she was being sarcastic. And she had curves in the exact places most likely to draw my eye.

She was just *everywhere*. My daughter's favorite new subject of conversation. An invisible presence in my workspace with her instruments and rhythm toys and flowers-mixed-with-vanilla scent.

I could smell her in my own damn apartment now. I couldn't get her out of my mind.

Maybe Maisie had the right idea. Time slowed around Emma. It felt like a looooong time until the end of summer.

When it was finally a reasonable hour, we heard keys in the lock downstairs. Maisie popped up from her seat. "Can I?"

"Rinse your dishes first." I watched her dash around, standing on her tiptoes by the sink, then added, "And put on shoes!"

She rushed down the stairs to meet Emma in the lobby.

I followed at a slower pace, sipping a second cup of coffee and double-checking my phone calendar for today's schedule. The sounds of Maisie fussing over the dog rose up the stairs. Another battle I'd lost. Emma seemed to think this was a pet-friendly zone, and I guessed Dixie had confirmed it. Nobody cared what *I* thought about it.

"Morning, Ashford." Emma stood at the mouth of the hallway I'd just entered, looking casual in faded shorts and an over-sized button-down, her hair tied up in a knot.

A warm feeling simmered low in my belly as a wave of floral vanilla hit me.

"Hmmm," I responded, taking another sip of coffee.

"Friendly as usual, I see." She brushed past me on her way to the storage closet, while I headed for my office. When I reached the door, I found a note waiting there for me.

Don't move my keyboard again. It was fine where it was.

-Emma

The hell? I grabbed the note from the door, crumpling it in my fingers. She couldn't have just said it to me in person?

Okay, I had left her a note last night asking her to do a better job picking up the baby toys. I'd found a tiny noisemaker under a training mat. Or rather, Ollie had found it yesterday afternoon. It had caused a distraction in my five-to-ten-year-old class.

I glanced over my shoulder at the direction she'd gone. I assumed she was in the kitchenette. Brewing some of the weird, froo-froo tea that now occupied half the shelf in there.

I didn't have time to deal with her right now. Or preferably, ever.

I got Maisie to her morning day-camp activity. They were meeting at the park, which was conveniently right down the street from the gym. I had two training appointments today. Clients I'd been working with for a while. It all went smoothly, and I was able to get in a workout of my own.

At least *some* things went like they were supposed to.

When I got back home, I heard Emma's class underway. I had no idea where the dog was. Seemed like Emma had arranged another place for her pet during her class times, which was good, because I certainly didn't want to take care of her animal. Not my responsibility. I had enough of those already.

I squinted at the floor of the lobby, looking for dog hair, but didn't spot any.

Taking a sip from my water bottle, I stopped in front of the one-way mirror. Emma was in there with a guitar on her lap, singing and swaying. Several moms and a dad sat in front of her, holding their squirming children in their laps. She did have a nice voice. High and clear.

I'd never done any classes like that with Maisie when she'd been that age. Had Lori? I would guess not. There hadn't been anything like this in Silver Ridge then. Unless Lori had driven to a nearby town, like Hartley.

It pained me when I thought about how much I didn't know about my best friend, even though we'd been trying to make a life together.

I shook my head, shaking off thoughts of Lori as I always did whenever they rose in my mind.

Then I went to sit in my office and tapped at my computer, answering emails and paying bills. Exciting stuff. The guitar music and singing coming through the wall set my teeth on edge.

I knew I was being slightly unreasonable. It wasn't Emma's fault that O'Neal Martial Arts had been slower to grow than I would've liked. I had helped her move her things in. Listened to her ideas for how to rearrange all my stuff that had been here for years. I'd made room for her here.

But inside, I was constantly bracing myself against her presence. Probably because she had to be so stinking positive about everything. Who was that cheerful all the time?

Except for when she was dealing with me, of course. I brought out Emma's sardonic side. A distinction I surely deserved.

Did I have to be so uptight with her? Maybe not. But I had the feeling that, if I didn't draw some kind of line in the sand, she would end up taking over. And most of the town wouldn't have a single problem with that.

I grabbed my pad of Post-it notes and jotted out another message.

Trash pickup is tomorrow. Don't forget to empty the diaper pail and re-latch the bear lock on the trash cart. VERY IMPORTANT.

Ashford

Then I marched over to the kitchenette and stuck the note to her box of tea. There. If she preferred to communicate with me in writing, fine by me.

A nagging voice, which sounded distinctly like my sister Grace, told me I should be the better man and find a way to get along with her. Otherwise, it was going to be a long three months.

I told that voice where it could shove its advice. Right in the diaper pail.

✧

Once upon a time, whenever I'd been home on leave in my Army days, my favorite spot to meet up with my friends had been Hearthstone Brewing Company.

They'd done renovations since then, updating the wood-paneled interior with modern light fixtures and sleek new chairs and tables. But thankfully, the low-key energy was still the same. The concrete floor was just a bit sticky from spilled beer beneath my boots.

It had been a long-ass day, and I needed to unwind.

I didn't hang out here every night like I used to back in the day. I was a home-for-dinner kind of dad, unlike my own had been. But tonight, Maisie was at a Parents' Night Out event at the community center. Free babysitting, mostly by teenagers from the local high school. Grace was there to help supervise. Whenever there was a community-building event around Silver Ridge, Grace inevitably had a hand in it. By day, she was an accountant for several local businesses.

As I wove between tables to reach the bar counter, I spotted my brother Callum working the taps. He was the brewery's assistant manager. My buddies Judson Lawrence and Elias Camden were already here, perched on two barstools with a free one next to them. Perfect.

I sat down and nodded hello. "How's it going with you two?"

"Can't complain," Judson said softly. His cowboy hat shadowed his features.

"I can," Elias quipped. "Did you see the score on the Rockies game last night? Brutal."

Callum made his way over. "What can I get you, big brother?"

"Amber ale. And some nachos."

Callum nodded, grabbing a pint glass. "It'll be awhile on the food. Kitchen is backed up."

Damn summer season. "There should be a tourism tax," I said. "Places are getting too crowded. Barely any room for us locals." We had been inundated with tourists, especially in the last year since a small ski resort had opened on a nearby mountain. Now that it was summer, they were offering lift access to mountain bikers.

Elias laughed, clapping me on the shoulder. "Please don't run for mayor or town council anytime soon, man. I've been appreciating the uptick in business. If only we could find a better way to get them here during the shoulder seasons."

Callum handed me my beer. "I've been enjoying all the pretty new faces."

I snorted. "I bet you have."

My brother's favorite pastime was finding tourists to hook up with. He was a volunteer firefighter in addition to working at the brewery, and the firehouse had a prominent spot on Main Street. He never had any trouble charming the out-of-towners.

Tonight, his olive-green T-shirt said ARMY across the front, and his cap read Silver Ridge FD. Because he liked everyone to know his business at all times.

"And speaking of new faces," Callum muttered, lifting his chin and gesturing to something behind us.

Somehow, I already guessed what I would see.

Piper sat with a few of her girlfriends at a table. And there was Emma. She had on the same casual clothes as this morning, but her hair was down and curled. Her profile was visible, a smile brightening her blue eyes.

I couldn't see the blue from here, of course. But I knew they were blue. Just like I could smell her sweet floral scent from across this crowded brewery.

The woman was inescapable.

"The new music teacher." My little brother's voice was laced with innuendo. "Ashford's been pissy about her the last week, but I really don't see the problem."

I bristled, swiveling back to frown at him. "What's that supposed to mean?"

Judson sipped his porter. "I think Callum's referring to her many pleasing physical attributes."

Elias snorted into his rum and coke. "Watch out, Ashford. If your little brother doesn't snag her, this cowboy wordsmith over here will." He nudged his elbow at Judson.

"Nobody's going to *snag* Emma." I crossed my arms, elbows thunking on the bar top. "And if they did, it's nothing to do with me."

The three of them exchanged amused glances.

Why had I come here again?

Judson was in fact our resident poet, though he tried to deny it. You'd never know it looking at him. He was six-foot-six, a former defensive tackle on our high school team. They used to call him The Wall because nobody could go through him.

That talent had extended to a college football scholarship and a blink-and-you-missed-it stint in the NFL. These days he was a rancher, having taken over his family's cattle business. Their property was out in the valley about a thirty-minute drive from town.

Elias was slightly smaller than Judson but a lot mouthier. He had shaggy dark-blond hair and a trimmed beard that didn't quite hide his dimples when he smiled. Elias and I had both been on the high school wrestling team. Much cooler than football, in my opinion. Elias didn't have the black belts I did, but he could almost rival me at grappling when we sparred.

He also owned Flamethrower Burgers & Brews right up the road. Most nights, you could find him behind the counter.

Tonight was a rare time we were all out together. But Elias didn't mind us coming to Hearthstone, even though technically they were his competition. No such thing as too much beer in Colorado.

Callum grabbed some empty glasses and stacked them in the dishwasher. "Uh huh. So you really have zero interest in the gorgeous woman sharing your space every day."

"She's way too young. I've got eleven years on her. She's only twenty-three."

"So? She's running a small business, just like you. People like her classes a lot. I hear she's great with Maisie, too. Pretty *and* sweet. What more do you want?"

"How do you know so damn much about her?" I grumbled.

"Because Callum is popular with the local moms," Elias muttered, drink in front of his mouth. Judson snickered.

Callum flipped them off, his smile not breaking, then turned back to me. "Then I take it you're one-hundred percent not going to make any moves on Ms. Jennings."

"A hundred and ten percent. It's not happening."

"Good." My brother glanced at his watch, the G-Shock I'd given him for his birthday five years ago. "My break is in ten minutes. I'm going to introduce myself to her, since I haven't had that pleasure yet."

A hot flash of anger pounded my temples. "You're not screwing around with the woman who stole half my lease."

"She didn't steal anything. *You* missed your opportunity." Callum pulled a dish towel from his jeans pocket. "Just like you're about to do now." He walked to the other end of the bar to serve another customer, leaving me fuming.

Judson and Elias were quiet. But I could still hear all the shit they weren't saying.

"Why is tonight all about judging *me*?" I asked. "Can't somebody else serve as the whipping boy?"

Elias finished his drink and pushed the glass away. "We all know Judson likes to keep his love life to himself. As for me, I'm still the pathetic guy who's trying to get over his divorce. If I start spilling my guts about my problems, it'll just depress the hell out of the rest of you. I don't want to be responsible for that."

Judson clapped him on the shoulder sympathetically.

Elias's wife Holly had left Silver Ridge a couple of years ago to move to Denver. It had come as a shock to everyone, including Elias, because they'd been the golden couple of our high school. Nobody expected them to break up. Just went to show, didn't it? No happy endings.

"Piper didn't name us the Lonely Harts for nothing," Elias said.

My back muscles tensed. "Well, she can rescind my membership. I'm not lonely."

My friends' silence said they didn't buy it.

My nachos finally arrived. As my friends and I ate, Callum left his dish towel with the other bartender and went to take his break. My gaze followed him across the room from the corner of my eye.

He said something to the occupants of Piper and Emma's table. Female laughter drifted over.

"You're really not gonna go over there?" Elias asked.

"Nope." I gulped the rest of my amber ale, lifting a finger for another. "I'm enjoying my night off."

But I glanced over again. And I saw Emma look up at Callum. She smiled at him, head tilting. My brother leaned down to say something in her ear.

Before I'd even realized I was moving, I was out of my seat. I swiped my fresh pint of ale from the bar. Then I was striding across the room, with Judson and Elias's low laughter trailing after me.

SEVEN
Ashford

BY THE TIME I got there, Callum had pulled up a seat right next to Emma's.

I grabbed a free chair from another table, scooting in beside Piper. She grinned at me and lifted her beer. "Parents' Night Out, amiright?"

I clinked glasses with Piper. "That's where Ollie is?"

"Where else? Not like he'd be at Danny's." Her ex rarely took their son overnight, always having some excuse. Piper's older brother, Teller, was happy to spend time with Ollie, but Teller was also chief of the Silver Ridge Police Department, so he often had his hands full. I didn't see him here tonight.

In fact, I had trouble paying attention to anything except Emma and my brother on the other side of the table.

Emma pointed at his shirt. "Army? You served?"

"I did." Callum hooked his thumb in my direction. "Ashford did too."

Emma's blue eyes lingered on me. "I have a couple of uncles who were Army. My dad was a Navy SEAL."

"Was he stationed at Coronado?" Callum asked.

"Yeah, when he wasn't deployed overseas. But we ended up in

West Oaks. It's a small beach town not far from Los Angeles. My dad and stepmom are both law enforcement. West Oaks PD."

I drummed my fingers on the table. "Close to LA. That tracks," I muttered.

At my words, Emma's head turned, and her eyes locked on mine. "How does it track, exactly?"

I shrugged. "You just seem like a Californian. Like everything is breezy and simple."

She barked a laugh. "I don't think everything is simple. Far from it. You've never been to California, have you?"

"Why do I need to? We see plenty of it in movies and on TV. Can't get away from it. People are obsessed with celebrities. It's ridiculous."

"Sure, but you're making an awful lot of assumptions about a big place. And a lot of assumptions about me."

Callum cleared his throat. On my other side, Piper poked my arm. "Can you tone it down a few notches?" she murmured. "Chill."

Hey, not my fault if the music teacher got easily offended when a guy expressed his opinion.

Callum took out his phone, tapping the screen with his thumbs. "Just googled West Oaks. Location looks sweet."

I noticed how he was leaning closer to Emma. Close enough to brush against her. I took a gulp of beer and thudded my glass onto the table.

"Emma, what brought you to Silver Ridge?" Piper asked, changing the subject.

"She's on summer break from college," I supplied. Then both Piper and my brother glared at me again, and I said, "What?"

Emma smirked. "It's *grad school*, not college. I have my bachelor's degree. I'm on summer break, but my plans changed pretty suddenly. I'm looking to transfer. My last program…" She sat back in her seat, blowing out a long breath. "It wasn't a great fit. Mostly because my ex-boyfriend is there. So it's better for me not to be."

Callum winced. "Sounds like there's a story behind that statement."

"I would need to be a lot drunker to tell it."

An ex. Made me wonder about this guy. What had happened? What had the guy done to her that she'd run to another state to get away from him?

Not that I needed to know. It was just curiosity.

"No confessions necessary," Piper said. "It doesn't have to be *that* kind of night. Unless you want it to be."

Emma laughed. "Maybe another time. I have a class to lead in the morning. It won't be good for my reputation if I show up hungover." She bit her lip. "The gist of it is, I ran from a disastrous breakup. I'm here to find my way again."

Callum put a hand on Emma's arm. "Well, whatever happened, I think you're brave for coming out here alone."

I snorted. My brother was laying it on thick. I shifted my weight in my chair.

"I do have family over in Hartley," Emma said. "Not like this is a foreign country."

"But still, they're not in Silver Ridge," Callum went on. "That takes some guts. Even when I enlisted in the Army, I did it knowing my two older brothers were already there. Piper's brother too, though Teller decided to be all impressive by joining Special Forces."

Emma's gaze shot back to me.

Piper stood up, putting her hands down on the table. "I propose a round of shots. We need to welcome Emma into the Lonely Harts club."

"The what?"

"Piper's pet project," Callum explained. "We commiserate over being single. Or something like that. *I* happen to like being single."

"I never said I have a problem being single," Piper protested. "We're commiserating over the bullshit we've all gone through in the name of love."

I grunted in annoyance, and Emma's eyes cut toward me once again. "I don't think Ashford wants me as a member of any club he's in. Assuming he's a member?"

Callum snorted. "Oh, he's a member all right. Practically the mascot."

I would never wish bodily harm on anyone in my family. Not even Grayden. But the glare I was giving my younger brother might indicate otherwise.

"You can join anything you want," I said to Emma. "I'm sure I couldn't stop you."

Her smirk broke into a full-on smile. "Now that is the truth."

Callum went to the bar to get a tray of whiskey shots for us. On his way back, he brought Elias and Judson along with him. Neither of them were likely to turn down a free drink. Cal passed the tray around, and we each took one. Even me, though I thought this was stupid.

"Let's officially welcome Emma to the Lonely Harts club." Piper winked. "You're one of us now."

The whiskey went down smooth. Callum had gotten the good stuff. As I swallowed, licking my lips, my gaze found Emma's again. I couldn't explain why. I just knew that, out of anything or anyone else in this room, my eyes were determined to settle on her.

✧

After another hour or so, our group started to scatter. Piper wanted to play a round of pool before Parents' Night ended. I wound up back at the bar with Judson beside me, drinking another round of beers.

Callum wandered over, draping his towel over his shoulder. "You didn't walk Emma home?"

I shook my head. "Elias offered to drive her. It's on his way, and he didn't drink much."

"And you let him?"

"Why the hell wouldn't I?"

"No reason." Callum looked amused.

"Just FYI, I'd rather you didn't make a move on her. I have to see the woman every day. It'll make things awkward if you hurt her feelings." My brother was a one-night-and-done kind of guy. Some women didn't want to accept that.

"That's your only objection to me going after Emma? The awkwardness?"

I tightened my grip on my glass. "Pretty much."

Also, the thought of Callum with her made me itchy all over. It didn't sit right.

I would've offered to walk her myself if nobody else had stepped up. Just to make sure she was safe, because I'd do the same for anyone. But Elias was okay too. He wouldn't try to hook up with her. Probably.

As for why I cared so much who Emma hooked up with...I wasn't going to examine that too closely.

Callum picked up some empty glasses, swiping the bar top clean. "I doubt Emma's interested in me, anyway. She couldn't take her eyes off you."

I almost choked on my mouthful of beer. "Only because she can't stand me. And I don't care for her. The dislike is mutual."

"Nah, I'm not buying it," my brother said. "I know chemistry. You and Emma? There's chemistry."

"You don't know what you're talking about."

"Hey, Judson. You know what I mean. Right?"

Beside me, Judson chuckled softly. Then nodded.

I shifted on my bar stool. "Both of you can keep your opinions to yourselves."

Callum sighed. "Ashford, how long has it been since you got laid? Or at least got off with anyone besides your own hand."

I glanced around. "Would you lower your voice? I teach these people's kids."

"Nobody's listening." Still, Callum lowered his volume and

leaned across the counter. "Women are interested in you. I've heard the complaints that you're unattainable, and it's not for lack of offers, man. Has there been anyone since Lori? Even with her, I'm sure it was a while since...*you know*."

Judson looked on sympathetically.

Callum and Judson both knew the nature of my marriage to Lori. After I'd returned stateside from my last deployment, she and I had tried briefly to start something. It had seemed right. Falling for my best friend. We'd both wanted stability. Love. To find a safe place to land when so much in the world was ugly and uncertain.

Only, neither of us had fallen very far. The spark just wasn't there. We'd realized we were better off as friends than lovers. By then, she'd missed her period. And then came those two pink lines.

I would never call Maisie a mistake. She was everything. But by mutual agreement, our marriage had been platonic. We'd even slept in separate rooms.

And no, there hadn't been anyone else. Not then. Aside from a few very occasional encounters, not since.

"I don't have the time for that," I said. "I have a kid at home. People are counting on me. Unlike you, I can't be irresponsible."

Callum laughed, not taking my insult personally. "You're the one who pointed out you see Emma every day. Why not take advantage?"

"Because of a million different reasons. Like the fact that she can't stand me. She's too young. She's leaving at the end of the summer."

"Isn't that a pro versus a con? They call it a summer fling for a reason."

I glanced over at Judson. "Can you talk some sense into him?"

"I'm staying out of this."

My brother was out of his mind. "I am not interested in Emma that way. Period. The end."

Callum grabbed my empty glass and set it aside. "You want to know your real problem?"

"Not really."

"It's that you want to keep your world small because you're scared."

I glared at the mirrored wall above his head. "Fuck off, Cal."

"You think that if you allow someone new into your life, you'll be responsible for her too. But Emma's a grown adult. She's young, but she gives every indication of being able to take care of herself. That doesn't have to be your job."

I shook my head, continuing to glare at the wall.

"After what happened to Lori, you're scared of letting anyone else down. But you deserve more in your life. Your daughter does too."

Anger surged into my throat. Pounded at my temples. I loved my brother, but I was also so tempted to hit him right now. "Not another word. Unless you'd like to have it outside."

Callum threw his towel down and walked to the other end of the bar.

"You all right?" Judson asked. "If you ever need to talk…"

"No." I pushed back, getting up from my seat. "I need to go pick up Maisie. It's getting late."

Callum had stepped way out of line. What I needed was to stay focused on running my business and taking care of my family. I didn't need anything else. Couldn't afford to need anything else.

Because when you stopped being careful, that was when everything fell apart.

✦

Maisie was a wild bundle of energy when I picked her up from the community center. The kind of overtired and hyperactive that Lori and I used to call "toddler drunk." Once I had her in the truck, she was sound asleep within five minutes.

I carried her into our building with her soft, heavy head resting on my shoulder. She barely stirred as I tucked her into bed. I patted her quilt around her and smoothed her hair from her peaceful face.

My heart was full at moments like these. As long as my girl was safe and happy, things were okay. I didn't need anything else, except for people to leave me alone.

Callum didn't know a damn thing.

Quietly closing the door to Maisie's room, I made my way down the hall. I passed the extra bedroom along the way. What had once been Lori's room. We used it for storage or for guests, like when Grace stayed over to help with Maisie.

I didn't look inside.

In my own room, I set my phone and wallet on the dresser and stripped to my boxer briefs.

Summer was my favorite season in Silver Ridge. Our apartment never got too hot or too cold at this time of year. Juggling Maisie with my work schedule was more complicated in summer, but we also got to enjoy lazy walks outside, with breezes blowing through the groves of aspens that bordered Main Street and days that seemed to last forever in the best way.

When Emma had appeared, I'd thought she would throw a wrench in my summer. But maybe it wouldn't be so bad having her around. I would have to ignore my brother's idiotic innuendos, but that wasn't Emma's fault.

She was sweet to Maisie. Hard for me to hold a grudge against someone who was nice to my kid.

My phone buzzed with a text, and I grabbed it, possessed by a sudden instinct that it was Emma. We'd exchanged numbers. What if she hadn't gotten back to her apartment okay? What if something was wrong?

I cursed when I saw an anonymous number. That fucking area code.

UNKNOWN
You can't ignore me forever, Ashford.

"You're wrong about that," I said to my empty bedroom, blocking the number. I was nothing if not stubborn. Switching my phone to Do Not Disturb, I tossed it angrily onto my dresser.

Was I just pissed off about an unwanted text?

Or was I actually disappointed that Emma hadn't written?

I blamed Callum. He'd put ridiculous ideas into my head, no matter how much I'd tried to push them away.

Fine, I was attracted to the woman. But there was zero chance of me hooking up with her. There would be no summer fling. All those reasons I'd listed earlier still applied.

Unfortunately, I was all worked up and restless as I slid under the covers. My brain wouldn't be quiet. And that wasn't the only part of me demanding attention.

I was hard.

How long had it been since I'd jerked off? Three days? Four?

Groaning, I rolled over and faced the ceiling. Orgasms were a basic physical need. Usually I took care of it in the shower. I'd been preoccupied lately. Stressed.

But right now, the apartment was quiet. I didn't have to be anywhere. Nobody needed me.

I slid my hand into my boxer briefs. My fist closed around my shaft. A moan rumbled from my chest, surprisingly loud in the silence. Whoops.

Quickly, I kicked off my covers and jumped up to lock my bedroom door. If Maisie woke up and needed something, she would knock.

On my way back to the bed, I stripped off my briefs altogether and lay on my back in the middle of the mattress. I'd managed to keep one hand on my aching cock the entire time. I slowly slid my fist up to the thick tip.

Mmm, yes. This was exactly what I needed.

I bent my knees. Shivers spread across my body as my breaths came fast and shallow. My fist worked down to the base of my cock, squeezing, then sliding up again. Nice and tight. Just how I liked it.

I tipped my head back, eyes drifting closed.

Against the backdrop of my mind, I saw lustrous, dark hair. Plush lips on a shot glass. Long fingers plucking the strings of a guitar. Then those same long, delicate fingers pushing my hand away from my cock to take over.

She would stroke my shaft. A little hesitant. Nowhere near enough.

Fumbling for my nightstand, I found the lube I kept at the back of the drawer and poured the glistening liquid over my cock.

"Nngh," I moaned, speeding up the pace. My fantasy kept unfolding. That same gorgeous woman bending over me to take my cock into the velvety warmth of her mouth. I snapped my hips, imagining I was pushing into her mouth instead of my fist.

"*Emma*," I gasped.

My release splashed onto my stomach in hot pulses. Waves of pleasure wiped my mind clean for a few perfect seconds. I lay there panting as I came down from the high.

So...yeah. That had just happened.

But it didn't mean anything. I didn't need any new complications in my life.

There would be no summer fling between me and Emma Jennings.

EIGHT
Emma

I WOKE to a loud rumbling sound. And then a heavy weight crashing down on top of me. I was terrified for a split second until I realized what was going on.

A thunderstorm. And Stella had leaped up into bed with me.

"Come here, you big scaredy-cat." I yawned. "There's barely room for me in this twin, much less you. We'll have to cuddle." Luckily, Stella had never refused a cuddle in her life.

Thunder rumbled outside again. It sounded like we were in for a rainy day.

But if you asked me, music classes were the ideal indoor activity.

After the success of my parent-and-tot class, I now had three older students booked for private lessons. Two piano and one guitar. Summer was the perfect time to get started, and the kids were all sweet. Including Piper's son, Ollie. He was a ball of energy for sure. But I had taught plenty of kids before, and I also had two much-younger siblings. I knew all the tricks.

After a slightly rocky start in Silver Ridge, everything had been looking up lately. Even Ashford had been slightly less annoying the past several days, ever since the night I'd seen him at the brewery. As my journal reflected. I'd spent less time complaining about him in there.

My apartment was the only part of my summer plan that was still on unsteady footing. This place was drafty, and it had a persistent smell of mildew. Especially in the bathroom. But it was fine. I was getting used to it.

When the first few drops of moisture hit my arm, I thought Stella was slobbering on me. But no, she was already slobbering on my shoulder.

I sat up quickly, looking around. My eyes slowly traced upward to the ceiling.

Drip, drip, drip.

"No!" I scrambled out of bed, grabbing for the small trashcan to catch the raindrops currently falling inside of my apartment through that ugly water stain on the ceiling. Which apparently wasn't an old leak, but a *very active* one.

I threw on some clothes, grabbed my phone, and called Sheldon, the on-site property manager. He didn't answer, so I marched down to his apartment on the first floor.

I knocked for a solid two minutes before Sheldon cracked the door open. "Dude. Do you know what time it is?" The smell of stale marijuana wafted from behind him.

"Yes, actually, I do. It's much earlier than I wanted to be awake. Because it's raining *inside* my apartment."

"Have you tried closing the window?"

"Is that supposed to be cute?" I was sure another tenant would've reported this leak before. But I decided to give him the benefit of the doubt, taking the time to describe it in detail. "Look, the roof has to be fixed today. It's right over my bed. I can't live like this."

His bloodshot eyes drifted downward, suddenly taking interest in me. Except he seemed to be interested in my body instead of my words. "I guess I can call our handyman, but—"

"No butts. Make the call. Somebody needs to be out here to fix it. *Today.*" I spun on my heel and went back to my apartment.

When I got upstairs, I realized I'd been wearing my pajamas with no bra that whole time. No wonder the guy's eyeballs had gone to my chest. Gross.

Stella jumped up from the corner where she'd been hiding from the thunder.

"It's going to be all right. I told Sheldon what's what, and I'm sure he'll get this fixed."

Now, we just had to move on with our day.

Once I was cleaned up and dressed, and I'd moved as much of my stuff away from the leak as possible, we headed out the door. First stop was Dixie's. She'd been watching Stella off and on while I held my classes. She lived in a cute cottage a few streets away from Main.

Dixie answered the door with towels for Stella. I'd warned her we would be walking as usual, since my car was still out of commission. "Want to come in and dry off too, hon?"

"It's not so bad." I pointed at my umbrella.

"Except umbrellas don't help much when the rain's going sideways. We rarely get it this bad. How's the roof at the Ponderosa? Has it sprung a leak again? I swear, some landlords have no standards."

I felt my smile slip, but I put it right back in place. Dixie had not been thrilled when she'd heard where I was living. There weren't many other rentals available, though, and none in my price range. "There was a small leak. But—"

"You know my couch is available. Oh, and my dear friend Shirley had her spare room open up. Her forty-year-old grandson still lives in the basement, so you'd have to share a bathroom..."

"Nope. The Ponderosa is working out great for me."

The skepticism was clear on her face, but she nodded. "All right. But if you change your mind, you just let me know. It's bingo at the community center later this afternoon, if you'd like to join. Dogs welcome. They aren't allowed to serve liquor, but I bring my own pitcher of margaritas. I can save you one."

My smile returned in full force. "I'll think about it. Thanks,

Dixie. Better go. I was up early, yet somehow I'm running late." I handed her the bag with Stella's food, toys, and treats for the day.

Dixie's offer of her couch had been tempting. Her house was cozy and inviting. Smelled good, too. Not a single whiff of mildew.

But I was a grown woman with a college degree. I could handle my own shit. And it wasn't that bad, really. This was adulting. Who had ever said it was supposed to be nothing but sunshine and rainbows?

I glanced up at the clouds just as a few rays of sunlight broke through. And there actually *was* a rainbow.

I took a deep breath, feeling steadier already. I refused to let this day get me down.

✦

I'd started calling Ashford's building the Big Blue Monster because of its blue painted brick and imposing facade. Also because of the grumpy man who lived inside. It now had a small sign proclaiming *Music Lessons* in the window. Not the fancy sign Dixie had offered, since I had no idea what to call my "music school," but this was all I needed for now.

I left my wet umbrella by the door and my waterlogged shoes on the mat, then went straight for the kitchenette, where I filled the electric kettle with water to make some tea. Just what I needed. It would warm me right up. I brushed damp strands of my hair away from my cheek. Dixie hadn't been exaggerating about the sideways rain.

Then heavy footsteps thudded in the hall, coming my way.

Ugh. Really?

Ashford's bulky form appeared in the doorway, hands on his hips and a deep scowl on his expression. "Emma, I told you last week about the bear latch on the trash can."

"I know. I got all your stupid notes." I set the box of tea on the counter, determined to stay calm. "I always make sure the trash is secure."

"Except clearly you didn't, because this morning I found trash strewn all over behind the building. An animal got in there overnight."

"*What*?" The back of my neck heated. *Calm.* I would not lose my temper with this man. "That's not possible. I checked the latch yesterday before I left. It was secure."

He waved an arm toward the back of the building. "Are you claiming that somebody else with opposable thumbs was skulking around here during the night messing with my trash can?"

Anger bubbled inside me despite my efforts to keep it down. "*Our* trash can, Ashford. It's *ours*."

"Same difference."

"No, it's not." *Deep. Breaths.* "Let's just get it cleaned up." I took a step toward the door.

"I already cleaned it up."

I spun back around to face him. "You should have waited for me to help you."

"I don't need help picking up trash."

"You know what? I don't care what *you* need." My finger poked into the broad wall of muscle that was his chest as I advanced on him. "That signed lease means I have every right to be here. That makes this place my responsibility as much as it is yours."

His nostrils flared. "You're mad that I didn't make you pick up trash?"

"Yes, actually. I am."

"Fine. Next time there's a mess, I'll save it for you."

"Perfect. I can't *wait*."

We were suddenly standing very close. His eyes narrowed, studying my face. "Why are you all wet?"

"Because I walked here. It's storming outside. As I'm sure you noticed."

"I did, but I wore a raincoat when I went out there. That's what sensible people do."

My throat felt hot and thick. Tears burned behind my eyes. I was so dang sick of Ashford and his attitude. His assumption that I couldn't do a single thing right.

"I didn't remember to pack a raincoat when I left California." The last word caught in my throat, so I turned and walked away. No way would I cry in front of him.

In the storage closet, I took some more deep breaths. *Lots* of deep breaths. Then changed into a spare set of dry clothes. Thank goodness I'd left a few things here just in case. I'd been preparing for incidents involving baby spit-up, but my spare outfit worked for a rainy day too.

Then, as I dug through my messenger bag, I realized I'd left my journal at my apartment in the chaos of this morning. To someone like Ashford, it would probably seem silly that I was so attached to my diary. It was a comfort thing, knowing I could open it up and write down whatever I was thinking. Such as, a rant about the impossible man I had to share a space with. Now it was too late to go back to my apartment for it.

It'll be fine, I told myself.

I grabbed a basket of toys and carried them to the big room to get ready for my first music class. I was spreading out the mats when Ashford walked in and stopped a few feet away from me. I didn't look up.

"Want to yell at me some more?" I asked testily.

"Actually, I thought you might need this."

I lifted my head. Ashford held out a steaming mug with the string of a teabag sticking out of it.

"You made me tea?"

"The water was boiling. Since I chased you away from the kitchen, I figured the least I could do was bring this to you."

"You didn't chase me away," I mumbled, accepting the mug. The warmth of it glowed against my palms.

"No, I did." He scratched his forehead. "Look. I'm sorry I was an asshole earlier. If you say you secured the latch, I believe you. And even if you forget sometime, it's not the end of the world. I... shouldn't have been a dick about it."

Huh. This was a first.

I shrugged, taking a small sip of tea. "Apology accepted."

"I brought this as well." He held up a jacket in his other hand. "Spare raincoat. I can hang it on a hook by the door."

"Thanks."

I chewed my lip and considered what else to say. But Ashford took off, leaving me wondering if any of that had really happened.

After both of my parent-and-tot classes and a private lesson were over, I sat to wipe down the mats. Running footsteps descended the stairs and came into the lobby. I knew exactly who it was before she appeared.

"Hi Emma! Did you see the rainbow?"

I smiled. "I sure did. Wasn't it pretty?"

Maisie was a little rainbow in her own right. She never failed to cheer me up when she was around. Funny that such a difficult man would have such a sweet daughter.

Except Ashford *had* made me feel better earlier.

I was still frustrated with him. He'd been a pain in the butt since I'd arrived in Silver Ridge. But the summer would be far more pleasant if we found a way to get along. Was that possible?

I was ready and willing to find out.

"Can I help?" Maisie sat down next to me, picking up the spray bottle and holding it with both hands. When I nodded, she sprayed, and I wiped. We were a good team.

"What were you up to this rainy morning?" I asked her. "I was running late, so I missed seeing you."

"I had summer camp. Instead of the park, we had to stay inside today and watch a movie. I liked it, though. It had a talking dog and cat. Then Daddy picked me up and we took Aunt Grace some soup for lunch." Her little nose wrinkled. "The movie was fun, but I like the park better. Watching the chipmunks is my favorite."

"Chipmunks are pretty cute."

"I don't like thunder and lightning. It's too loud."

"Stella would agree. Thunder scares her, and she jumps up in my bed to cuddle with me."

"I would love if Stella jumped in my bed! Why were you late? Was it because Stella was scared?"

"Well, no. We had a small mishap at my apartment. But it was fine."

"What's a mishap?"

"That's when something goes wrong."

Her little mouth made an O shape, and she nodded with understanding. "Daddy had one of those today too."

Right on cue, Ashford's deep voice rumbled through the wall. He was in his office. I couldn't make out the words, but the man was not happy.

"Was it about the trash can?"

"No!" Maisie laughed like I'd said something hilarious. "It's 'cause Aunt Grace is sick. She was supposed to watch me later, but she can't now."

Ah, the picture was starting to come together. "That's why you took soup to her for lunch? Because she's sick?"

"Yeah, of course." Except when Maisie said that, it sounded like *a course*. "But now, Daddy can't find a sitter for me."

"When exactly does he need a sitter?"

"For this afternoon." Maisie squirted the mats with cleaning solution again. Then she blinked a few times, glancing up at me through her long eyelashes. Puppy-dog eyes if I had ever seen them. And I was something of an expert.

"What are *you* doing later, Emma?"

"Mais, you don't need to be in here," Ashford said, surprising me and Maisie both.

He had one hand braced against the door frame. From my seat on the floor, he looked ridiculously tall. But even from down here, I could see the worry in his eyes.

"It's okay. Maisie was helping me clean up."

His daughter held up the squirt bottle of cleaner. "See?"

"Perfect. You can help me clean the kitchen when we get upstairs." He hooked his thumb, gesturing for her to follow him.

Before either of them could go, I blurted, "I hear you need a sitter."

I told myself this was just about Maisie. I did love spending time with her. But I was also thinking of that cup of tea Ashford had brought me earlier. His apology.

He rubbed a hand over his beard. "I'm teaching a law enforcement workshop at the Hart County Sheriff's Office. It's in Hartley. Grace has a cold, and a couple other sitters I called can't do it. But I'm going to ask Dixie."

"She's got bingo at the community center," I said.

"Fuck," he muttered.

"*Daddy!*"

"What? I said *truck*."

"No you didn't!"

He frowned and looked to the side. "If Dixie's busy, I can try Callum."

"But you're mad at Uncle Callum." Maisie crossed her arms, a mirror image of her dad. "You said you don't want to talk to him because he's a D-word."

I lifted my eyebrows, wondering which D-word.

Ashford scratched his nose. "Thanks, Mais. Can we go before you share any more of my private business?"

"But Daddy, Emma could watch me. Pleeeease?"

I got up from the ground, brushing off my hands. "I could do it. I'm free the rest of the day."

A bunch of different thoughts seemed to pass through his mind, like he was torn between yes and no. "You don't have to bail me out."

"I know I don't *have* to. I would be happy to do it. I like hanging out with Maisie."

She clasped her hands together and aimed her puppy-dog eyes at him. "Please, Daddy?"

I saw the exact moment his resistance fell.

"Okay. That would be great. Thanks."

"Yay!" Maisie threw her hands in the air.

Ashford walked closer to me. "I can pay you."

"No need to pay me."

"Then I'll owe you." He said that like it wasn't a position he enjoyed being in.

"Just keep being nice to me. We'll be even."

"I guess I can be nice."

There was something in the tone of his voice that sent a rush of tingles all the way to my toes.

"Meet us back here in an hour?" Ashford asked.

"Sounds good. I'm going to swing by Silver Linings to see Piper. Want a coffee?"

"Nah. I'd better not go any deeper into debt with you. I'll be stuck paying it off the rest of the summer." That time, he'd managed a half-smile. A minor miracle.

That crooked grin also increased his attractiveness by a hundredfold.

Yikes.

Warning bells were already pinging in my head. *Nope. Don't even think about it.*

NINE
Emma

OVER THE LAST couple of weeks, I'd made a habit of visiting Silver Linings Coffee most afternoons. Their wi-fi was much faster than my apartment's, even when it was actually working. The coffee was great, and the vibes were the perfect level of cozy.

And most importantly, I got to visit with Piper whenever she was around.

"Quite the storm this morning," she said as she made my vanilla latte.

"Stella was not happy."

"Oh no. Poor puppy. But at least the sky has cleared up." She nodded at the front window, which showed pure blue and sunshine. "Welcome to Colorado weather. I've seen snow in July."

"Seriously? I'm not ready for that. I didn't even bring a raincoat with me." I made a face. "Which is my fault completely, but I just didn't think of it when I was packing for a summer trip."

I'd gotten over that embarrassment. Ashford's change in mood, combined with the prospect of spending time with Maisie later, made me able to laugh at myself.

"I don't blame you. I'm happy to loan you anything you might need."

"I'm set. Ashford loaned me his extra rain jacket."

Piper almost dropped her jug of milk. "*Ashford* did?"

I shrugged. "He saw how wet I got walking to work and took pity on me, I guess."

She just stared another moment before going to the espresso machine. "Wow. How gentlemanly. I've known the guy most of my life, and he's never given *me* any of his clothing to wear. He must really like you."

I barked a laugh. It was loud enough that a few heads turned. "He's barely starting to tolerate me."

"Still. For Ashford, that's quick progress."

Piper passed my latte over, and I stepped aside while she helped another customer. Taking a sip, I glanced at a display, which held an assortment of gifts for book lovers. There were bookmarks, mugs, stickers. But the notebooks with beautiful covers caught my eye. Made me miss my journal. Maybe I'd have time to run back home and get it before babysitting.

Then I saw a notebook with iridescent unicorns all over the cover, and that gave me an idea.

When the register was free, I grabbed the unicorn notebook and set it on the counter. "I'll take one of these, too."

"Excellent choice." Piper rang me up. "I have a break in a bit. Want a sandwich? I make amazing paninis, and they're huge. I'll share one with you. On the house."

"You have a bad habit of giving free food to paying customers."

"What can I say? Food is my love language."

I weighed my options. I'd meant to run by my apartment. But sharing a sandwich with my friend sounded so inviting. "I'd love that." I already knew she'd refuse any more money from me, so I added several bills to the tip jar. "I just have to be back at Ashford's in an hour. I'm babysitting Maisie."

"Hold on, Ashford is trusting you to babysit Maisie?"

"Ouch. And I thought you liked me."

She shook her head. "It's not you. You're totally trustworthy. Ashford's the problem. If he accepts you, you're *in*. But he does everything he can to keep people *out*. He usually needs to know someone for, like, a year before he'll leave his daughter with them."

I shrugged. "He seemed pretty desperate."

Piper hummed thoughtfully.

Fifteen minutes later, we were tucked into a corner table with gooey cheese oozing onto our fingers. "You're a wizard with a sandwich," I said with my mouth full. "If I dated women, I'd be asking you to marry me right now."

"Sadly, even if I dated women, I would say no. Because I will *never* get married again. But since you brought up the topic of dating..."

"Uh oh."

"Can we talk about Ashford again for a sec?"

"Why?"

"Because you don't seem to realize how remarkable it is that he gave you his own clothing to keep you warm. *And* he's letting you take care of his little girl."

"He also made me a cup of tea. It doesn't mean anything."

She set her sandwich down on the butcher paper it had been wrapped in. "A *cup of tea*?"

"Don't make it something it's not. You were there at the brewery last week. You know I'm not his favorite person."

"Mmhmm. But things change fast, it seems." Piper took another dainty bite of her sandwich. "If he were interested, would you?"

"Would I what?"

"You know." She pumped her eyebrows. "Take a ride on that stallion."

I coughed as a glob of cheese nearly went down the wrong way.

"I would be tempted," I said once I could finally speak again. "He's a good-looking guy. Don't get me wrong. But the last time I fell into bed with an older man, it didn't end well."

"The ex you mentioned before?"

"Yep."

My ex had convinced me to believe everything he said because I trusted his experience and his judgment. He'd made me feel unsophisticated in comparison to him. What a mistake that had been.

"I think you'd be good for Ashford, though. It would help him relax if he had a little fun instead of being so serious all the time."

"What about you?" I asked.

"*Me* date Ashford?" She looked horrified.

"Not Ashford." I was surprised at how vehement I sounded. "I mean, someone else. Do you have your eye on anyone?"

"Remember how I said I'd never get married again? That includes falling in love. Not for me." She sighed, wiping her mouth and hands on a napkin. "My divorce was awful. I can't imagine going through anything like that again."

I squeezed her hand. "I'm sorry. That's rough."

"Things got really bad about three years ago. Danny, that's my ex, fought with me constantly. Often in public. Danny is a dentist. Dr. Carmichael."

"I've seen his office up the street."

"I walk by it every day. Joys of breaking up in a small town. But anyway, we would end up yelling at each other in front of his staff." Her eyes got a faraway look. "Lori O'Neal was Danny's dental assistant."

"Ashford's wife?"

She nodded. "Lori and I had always been friends, but with my marriage collapsing in front of everyone, I felt awkward around her. And that was right before she died. I wish I'd spent more time focused on Lori and not reacting every time Danny picked a fight. One day I came into the dental office, and Lori was crying. I asked her what was wrong, and she wouldn't tell me. I didn't press the issue. But I had this feeling it was about a man."

"A man who wasn't Ashford?"

Piper leaned in closer. "Well, she and Ashford weren't

together that way. They were allowed to see other people as long as they kept it separate from Maisie."

"Oh."

Piper cringed. "Maybe I shouldn't have told you. I feel like the worst gossip right now. You're way too easy to talk to."

"I'll take the blame if you want. But you were sharing your own experiences. No crime in that."

"I know. After her death, I told Ashford about how Lori was upset. It felt wrong not to. He didn't know what it meant either."

"Maybe she was afraid to tell anyone. Or didn't want to disappoint him."

"Whatever it was, she took it to the grave."

A cold shiver traced down my back. "And it was definitely an accident? Not...intentional, somehow?"

Now I felt like the gossip. But I came from a law enforcement family. Questioning these kinds of scenarios was second nature.

"There was an investigation, and that's what the police ruled. A tragic accident. Ugh, I'm sorry. This conversation took a really depressing turn. Divorce and death."

I squeezed her hand again. "Seems like you needed to talk about it."

She blew out a breath. "And now, I need to get back to work. Let me know if you want to hang out later. Ollie and Maisie love to play together. I'm taking Ollie to his baseball summer league this afternoon, but we'll be free after."

"Thanks."

I gave Piper a big hug. Truth was, we *both* needed it.

✧

Before I left Silver Linings, I stopped by the bathroom to fluff up my hair. I tried not to think too hard about *why* I was doing it. The rain earlier had left me with messy waves, and it didn't look half bad.

When I reached the Big Blue Monster, I went inside and climbed the stairs. There was an external door that led directly to these stairs as well, but that one required a key I didn't have.

I paused on the upstairs landing. I'd never been up here before. Ashford had emphasized that it was *his home* only about a million times, making clear that this area of the building was off limits.

Shifting the strap of my bag on my shoulder, I knocked firmly a few times. Voices and running footsteps came from inside.

The door burst open, revealing Maisie with a big grin, and Ashford right behind her. "Mais, you can't just open the door like that. You have to check who it is."

"But it's Emma." She grabbed my hand and started pulling me into the apartment. Zero hesitation there.

Ashford had to step out of the way, and I almost brushed up against him. Different T-shirt than this morning, this one even more snug around his muscles. If that was possible. His slim-cut pair of athletic pants hugged him in exactly the right places.

"Hey," he said.

"Hi." Why did I sound so breathy?

"You made it on time."

Ah, there it was. His personality. "Of course I did."

"Emma, this is the kitchen," Maisie said. "Over there is our living room. That's where we watch TV."

I snickered. "Oh, really?" There were framed family photos on the wall, different combinations of Ashford, Maisie, Callum, and Grace. Several showed Maisie with a pretty, golden-haired woman who had to be Lori.

"This way to my room."

"Hold on. Your dad probably wants to give me some instructions before he needs to go."

Ashford walked into the kitchen. "Emergency numbers are on the fridge. She can have *one* bag of chips or *one* pack of cookies. Otherwise, there's cut-up veggies and fruit for snacks."

Maisie rolled her eyes and heaved a sigh. Six going on sixteen.

"There's Netflix for kids on the TV. Don't put on anything else."

"Oh darn. I had my heart set on HBO."

He stared at me. "I assume that was a joke."

I smiled and shrugged.

"Keep the door locked, and I'll text when I'm on my way home. Should be three and a half hours or so."

"I thought I'd take Maisie over to get Stella. She's at Dixie's house. And then we can head to the park for a while."

"Is that another joke?"

Maisie jumped up and down. "Daddy, that sounds so fun. I want to see Stella and play at the park."

"Mais, I don't know..."

"I didn't get to go this morning at camp 'cause it was raining. Pleeeease?"

I bit my lip, unsure if I'd stepped out of bounds by suggesting the park excursion. Ashford studied me. "You won't let her out of your sight?"

"Not for a second. But if you prefer, we can stay here instead. There's plenty we can do indoors, and I can get Stella from Dixie later." Hopefully that wouldn't cause any problems for Dixie's bingo plans. She'd said dogs were welcome at the community center.

"Daddy, *no*," Maisie whined.

"You can go to the park," he said, though it looked like the words pained him. "Just be careful."

"We will," I promised.

He had to give Maisie several hugs before they separated, and he held my gaze intensely as if he was repeating the words. *Just be careful.*

"We're going to have a great time," I assured him. "I'll text you with plenty of updates." Often his distrust of me got on my nerves, but not this time. I understood. Maisie was his whole world, and I would never do anything to jeopardize her.

We left together, Ashford heading to his car while Maisie and

I set out on foot. I'd taken the spare key to their apartment, snacks and water bottles, plus a small first-aid kit he'd foisted on me. We made quick time to Dixie's place, Maisie tugging on my hand the whole time because she was so excited to see Stella.

"Ashford's letting you babysit?" Dixie asked when we appeared at her door.

I just nodded, since I'd been through all of that with Piper already. I didn't need someone else getting the wrong idea about me and Ashford.

I had high hopes that we'd find a way to get along, maybe even be friends after this, but that was it.

I would not be riding *any* stallions this summer, thank you very much.

On our way, we passed by Silver Ridge Dental. The sign in the window showed the smiling face of Dr. Daniel Carmichael, who I now knew was Piper's ex-husband.

No wonder I hadn't trusted that perfect smile the first time I'd passed this sign. In my experience, men who were too charming were trouble.

Once Maisie and I reached the park, I took Stella off her leash so she could run around the open green space. Maisie took off after her, and I kept a close eye on them both.

Stella was so sweet and patient with the little girl. Always circling back around to let Maisie catch up.

Maisie got tired after a while, so we found a spot on a bench to eat our snacks. Stella drank water from a collapsible bowl I'd brought. My dog also eyed some leftover puddles from the morning's rainstorm, but I gave her a stern word to warn her away. If I returned Maisie with her cute outfit all muddy, Ashford wouldn't be impressed.

Maisie popped a chip into her mouth. "My mom used to take me to the park."

My entire body went still. "Yeah? That must've been wonderful."

"She pushed me a lot on the swings. She was really pretty and nice. Like you."

Oh, God. That hit me straight in the heart.

Maisie had been three when her mom died. Some people didn't have any memories from that age. I was glad that Maisie did.

"Thank you," I said. "You must take after your mom then, because you are very smart and an absolute sweetheart."

"Can we listen to that music again?"

It took me a moment to recall which music she meant. "Ayla Maxwell? The singer on my phone the other day?" I pulled up the playlist. Maisie nodded, crowding beside me to look at the album cover on my screen. It showed Ayla with her hair in a dramatic up-do and sparkly green shadow around her eyes.

"Wow. She's beautiful."

"She is." Ayla was also the most famous pop star in the world right now, though I didn't expect a six-year-old to know that. "She looks a little like you," I said. "Bright green eyes like yours."

Maisie fluttered her lashes and lifted her chin proudly, then went back to her snacks. "Do you have a mom?"

I smiled. Maisie kept me on my toes with her rapid changes of topics. "Sure. I have a mom, and a stepmom who's married to my dad."

"Really? Are your moms alive?"

Ugh, another pang. "They are, yes. I'm close to both of them. They're awesome. So is my dad."

"My daddy is the best. Except when he won't let me do stuff."

"My dad's the same. He can't tell me what to do anymore since I'm grown up. Well, he tries, but I don't have to listen. He does it because he loves me though. He wants me to be safe and happy."

"Yes. That's what dads do." Maisie nodded sagely. "Can we play fetch with Stella now?"

"Absolutely."

"Do you think Stella likes me? Even as much as she likes other dogs?"

"Look how much fun she's having with you." I pretended to think. "If you were a dog, what kind would you be? A Maisie-doodle?"

She laughed like that was the funniest thing she'd ever heard. A sound full of joy.

After fetch, we went to the playground. I helped Maisie on the swings. Then she pumped her legs to keep going. Stella sat by my side and watched. A few other kids appeared, and I said hello to their parents or sitters or whoever was with them.

Meanwhile, I took pictures with my phone and sent them to Ashford.

ME

> Look who's having a great time at the park.

About ten minutes later, the response came.

ASHFORD

> Wish I was there.

And to my surprise, I kind of wished he were there, too.

My day had started out awful. But now, it was the best day I'd spent so far in Silver Ridge.

Until I kept noticing the stranger in a dark blue rain slicker.

He, or maybe she, was standing between some trees in a wooded area of the park. The person had their hood up, their face shadowed. They were average height, medium build. But something about the build seemed male. The raincoat was odd, since the skies were clear now.

At first, I ignored him. But after a while, I couldn't shake the creeping feeling that his eyes were on us.

"Hey, kiddo," I called out. Maisie had run over to a kid-sized climbing wall. I didn't want to shout her name, just in case that creep was listening. "We're going to head home now."

Was I overreacting? Maybe. But I didn't want to take any

chances. Strange men hanging out alone near children's parks were a definite *no*.

"Not yet! Please, Emma? I have to reach the top."

"It's time to go," I said, more firmly this time. "I'm counting to five, and when I get there, your feet need to be on the ground, missy."

"Nooo."

"One, two, three..." When I reached five, Maisie jumped down to the ground and fell to the grass. I cringed, worried she'd hurt herself, but she jumped up. The knees of her pants had grass stains.

"Where's Stella?" she asked.

I looked around. A wave of worry hit me.

There was no sign of Stella anywhere.

TEN

Ashford

My session at the sheriff's headquarters in Hartley went well. It was a joint training with other area departments, including the folks from Silver Ridge PD who'd driven in for the workshop. I taught the officers a variety of defensive moves based on Krav Maga to use against aggressive suspects without causing undue harm.

Teaching courses like this didn't pay a ton, but I never turned down the opportunity.

"Thanks, Ashford. Great class," Sheriff Douglas said afterward, shaking my hand. He was around my age with a reputation for being diligent and fair. Unlike a lot of elected sheriffs, who might skip a training session in favor of sitting at a desk, Douglas had been out on the mat with his deputies. He'd served as a Marine, and he had some skills.

"There's a rumor that some of my deputies are grabbing dinner at Last Refuge Tavern after this," the sheriff said. "You should join. Same with you and your officers, Chief Landry." He nodded at Teller, the chief of our tiny Silver Ridge department.

But Teller shook his head. "I've got some work to do back at the station."

He was Piper's older brother. Teller and my brother Grayden had been best friends when they were younger, but then Teller went and served honorably as a Green Beret for almost twenty years until he was wounded, while my brother took pretty much the opposite path.

Teller was polite to me and my family, but we hadn't talked much since he'd come back to Silver Ridge. He had a good reputation as chief though, and was around for Piper and Ollie. Hard to ask more of a man than that.

"I'll have to skip this one as well," I said. "I'm anxious to get back to my daughter."

And actually, back to Emma.

From the pictures she'd sent, it had looked like she and Maisie were having a blast. I wanted in on that. I was ready to admit that I'd been wrong about the park outing.

Wrong about several things.

Dammit, Emma was proving to be much more than I'd expected. Great with my kid. Talented. No pushover, which I respected. And she was really, *really* fucking pretty. So pretty it was a personal attack on my willpower every time she smiled. Looking didn't do any harm though.

Emma didn't need to know that she'd starred in several of my fantasies the last week. Maybe I should've felt guilty about picturing her in various not-safe-for-work scenarios with me.

But I didn't.

I *did* feel guilty for almost making her cry. I'd gotten worked up about the stupid trash can, and like an asshole, I'd blamed her. I'd made her sad.

Angry was one thing. But seeing her *sad*? No, that was just wrong.

Some people in Silver Ridge might accuse me of having no heart for anyone outside my family, but it existed. Way down deep.

I got on the road and decided to head straight to the park,

hoping they were still there. Locking my truck by the curb, I walked across the grass and spotted Maisie on a low climbing wall. Emma stood a few feet away, hands on her hips. I felt a smile tug at my mouth.

A flash of golden fur barreled toward me on my left. Stella ran circles around me in excitement, as if I was her long-lost best friend and not a guy she barely knew.

"What're you doing over here?" I grabbed her by the collar and knelt to rub her belly, just to keep her from jumping up and getting dirt on my black T-shirt. That was the only reason.

I looked up in time to see Maisie leap down from the climbing wall. That made me grit my teeth, but she appeared to be fine.

Then Emma started turning this way and that, hand pressing to her chest. She seemed upset.

Stella and I started toward them. When Emma saw me, she clapped her hands to her mouth. She grabbed Maisie's hand, and together, they ran to meet us.

"Daddy!" Maisie let go of Emma and jumped into my arms. Stella barked excitedly.

"Hey, monkey. Missed you."

"We had so much fun. We got Stella from Dixie's and did the swings and ate snacks." I set her down. "Daddy, watch! I can play fetch with Stella."

Maisie picked up a stick and threw it. The stick only went a few feet, but Stella obligingly ran over to grab it. Maisie wrestled it from her mouth and tried again, the two of them playing more of a running game than a throwing one.

Then I realized Emma had her arms wrapped around her middle, shoulders tight, a frown marring her features.

I rested my hand on her back. "Hey, what's wrong?"

"I couldn't find Stella. And before that, there was somebody watching us. And I thought..."

"Wait a minute, slow down. Somebody was watching you? *Who?*"

"I don't know. Wearing a shiny blue rain slicker, so I couldn't see his face. It just didn't feel right. I decided we should leave, and I went to get Maisie. But then Stella was gone. It freaked me out."

I stood up straighter, scanning the park for somebody in a blue raincoat.

The person was gone. Had they taken off when I arrived? What would have happened if I hadn't come? Would this person have followed them home?

Silver Ridge was a pretty safe place. Most of the time. But that didn't stop awful things from happening.

"Glad I got here when I did." I still had my hand on Emma's back. She leaned into me as we both watched Maisie and Stella play. Meanwhile, I kept glancing around us, all of my senses on high alert. More than anything, I wanted Emma and Maisie to feel safe.

I was here now, and one thing was certain. I wouldn't let anyone touch them.

Eventually, Emma relaxed beside me. "Whoever that person was, he left. Maybe I was wrong, and he wasn't watching us at all."

"Maybe. I appreciate you being cautious and looking out for Maisie."

"Always. I might not be great with cars, or possibly trash cans, but I wouldn't let anything happen to Maisie."

Her tone was light, but I tried to convey my sincerity when I replied. "I believe you."

She looked up at me, blue eyes blinking.

I was suddenly aware of how close we were. How good it felt, how *right*, to be touching her like this. I wanted to put my arm around her shoulders and tug her against my side.

Reluctantly, my hand slid away from her back. Because those were not thoughts I should be having.

Maisie ran over with Stella on her heels. "Did you see me, Daddy?"

"Sure did. You're the dog whisperer."

She cracked up. "I wasn't whispering. You're so silly."

"That's me. Your silly dad," I deadpanned.

Emma bit her lower lip and grinned. Damn, I wished she wouldn't do that.

"I guess I should leave you to the rest of your evening," she said.

Maisie's eyes turned to saucers. "Not yet! You should have dinner with us. Daddy, can we take her out to dinner to say thank you? Please? That would be nice, wouldn't it?"

"I swear, I didn't prompt this," Emma murmured. "You don't have to."

But I shrugged. "I did say I'd be nice."

"Can we go to Flamethrower and get cheeseburgers and extra tots and shakes too? 'Cause it's a special occasion? They even have a patio for Stella. Please?"

"Special occasion, huh? Then I'd better say yes. If Emma wants to go." I turned to her. "Would you join us?"

"I'd love to."

"Yay!" Maisie shouted. "Shakes!"

"You just got played, big time," Emma said under her breath.

"Probably." Luckily, I didn't care. Dinner was the least I could do as a thank you for watching my kid.

Not *just* so I could spend more time with Emma, though that was a side benefit.

"Want to walk there?" Emma asked. "It's so beautiful out. Plus I doubt you want more dog hair in your truck."

I grunted. "We'd better walk."

"You were just fearing for your upholstery, weren't you?"

"I was thinking of what an enjoyable stroll it would be." I gestured at the trees and sky and…whatever.

"Right."

Her teasing smile went straight to the least appropriate parts of me. *Nrgh.*

I reminded myself that my kid was close by. That sobered me up.

Emma put a leash on Stella. Maisie insisted on holding the leash, which I thought was a bad idea because that dog had forty pounds on her. But Emma assured me Stella would stay calm.

Since it was summer, the sun was still high though it was dinnertime. I noticed details of my town that I must've missed in the last few weeks. When had all these flowers bloomed? Everything was so green.

"Oh, I wanted to ask you something." Emma dug into her messenger bag. I kept one eye on my daughter ahead of us and one on what Emma was doing. She produced a book-like object with unicorns on the cover, but no title written on the outside.

"What is that?" I asked.

"Shhh," Emma scolded me, hiding the book in her bag. "It's a surprise. Don't be so loud."

"I'm not loud."

Maisie looked at us over her shoulder. "You're very loud, Daddy."

"Ganging up on me, huh?"

Emma smiled so big that a small dimple appeared in her cheek. "I bought it earlier," she said, far quieter than me. "It's a blank notebook. I thought Maisie could start a diary, or just draw in it. Whatever she likes. But I wanted to check with you first and see if it's okay."

"Sure. That's...I think she'll like it." I cleared my throat.

"Good. I'll give it to her later." She closed her bag. "Tell me about the workshop you were teaching."

Yeah. That was much safer ground than how sweet she was being to my kid. Time to talk about my badass martial arts moves. I stuck out my chest, flexing a bit for good measure.

Me, getting misty-eyed because this gorgeous woman had bought a unicorn notebook for my daughter? Nah. Never happened.

I'd deny it until the end of time. Or at least until the end of the summer.

✧

"You're kidding me," I muttered.

We had just turned the corner, and Flamethrower was up ahead. But the line stretched out the door and partway down the block. It was a Thursday night in summer, so maybe I should've expected this. Damn tourists taking over my town.

"That's okay," Emma said. "We can entertain ourselves while we wait."

I kept grumbling, but after a while, I gave up. Honestly, it took more effort to stay in a bad mood when she and Maisie were around. Between the dog and my kid, we made new friends and said hello to a bunch of people I knew. So maybe it wasn't *all* tourists.

Just before we went inside, Emma tied Stella's leash to a railing by the patio and made sure she had water available. Maisie tugged at my arm. "Daddy, can't Stella come in with us?"

"Nope. No dogs allowed. We'll come out here and find a table after we order."

"Not fair." Maisie pouted and stomped her little foot. But people on the patio were already fawning over the retriever. She was going to be fine.

Still, I noticed that Emma kept casting nervous glances through the windows as we headed inside. She'd really gotten a scare in the park.

"I'll keep an eye on Stella," I said. "I have a clear line of sight."

Emma exhaled. "Thanks. I'm being ridiculous."

"Nah, I get it." Unable to resist, I let my fingertips brush the inside of her wrist. She exhaled again and didn't move her arm. The contact lingered.

We reached the counter, where Elias was taking orders. I knew how that was. Running a small business meant you filled in anywhere and everywhere.

I gave him an up-nod. He grinned when he saw us. "Well look

at you, O'Neal. Out and about. Emma, right? I remember you from Hearthstone."

"Yep. Nice to see you, Elias." Now she was grinning at him, and I didn't like that as much.

"All right, we're holding up the line. Let's order."

"He's just a ray of sunshine isn't he?" Elias joked, still focused on Emma.

"He has his moments."

"Ashford, I've got a Peaches and Cream Ale on tap. My latest brew made with Palisade Peaches. Do you want an 18-ounce? Or just a pint?"

I glared. Elias knew I hated fruit in my beer. He thought he was funny.

We ordered burgers, a kid's meal for Maisie, plus a sampler platter of tater tots and three chocolate shakes. I was going to need an extra-long session at the gym tomorrow. Did Emma work out? She had to. I leaned back, gaze sneaking down toward her ass in those shorts. When I looked up, Elias was giving me a smug, closed-mouth smile.

"Don't say it," I muttered as I swiped my debit card.

"Not saying anything. Callum told me how you jumped down his throat. I'd rather stay on your good side." He handed me a number for our table, and we went out to the patio to find an open spot. Maisie went straight to Stella, showering her with hugs and pets since they'd been away from each other for ten minutes.

"What happened with Callum?" Emma asked as we sat down. "I seem to remember Maisie saying you called him a D-word."

I bit back a smile. "Dumbass. As in, my brother couldn't keep his dumbass opinions to himself." I wasn't even mad at him anymore. He'd made some decent points, now that I had distance from that conversation. Even though he was still wrong overall. I found Emma attractive, but that was the end of it. "Callum doesn't know when to shut his mouth. But we'll probably make up by tomorrow."

"You have another brother, right? Callum mentioned him the other night."

Which was a topic I liked even less. But at the same time, I didn't mind telling her. "Grayden is the oldest. He's not in our lives anymore. Not since he was courtmartialed by the Army, got handed a dishonorable discharge, and went to prison."

There wasn't any sugar-coating my brother's fall.

"Oh. Wow. I don't blame you."

"I prefer not to discuss him in front of Maisie."

"No problem. I won't mention him."

My daughter ran back over to us, wiping her now-messy hair from her face. "Daddy, can I play with those kids?" She pointed at a small group that had gathered around the dog.

"After we eat, okay?"

"Hey, I've got something for you," Emma said, pre-empting Maisie's protests. She pulled the unicorn notebook from her bag and set it on the table.

I nodded when Maisie looked to me for permission. She picked up the notebook, marveling at the shiny designs on the cover. "What is it?"

"Your very own notebook, but not just any notebook. This one is special. It's a journal. A place for you to write things down, or draw, or anything you like. A place to hold all the treasures inside you that want to come out."

Maisie's mouth dropped open in awe. "I have treasures inside me?"

"You do. Everybody does, if they know where to look."

"Even Daddy?" Maisie giggled. "He gets really mad when he can't find things."

"Even him." Emma's blue eyes slid to me, her head tilting. "Do you need a journal, Ashford? I can get another unicorn one."

"I'm good, thanks."

Maisie wanted to start on her journal right away, so Emma gave her a pen. The food arrived soon after, and I had to confiscate the notebook for a little while to make my kid eat, even though Flamethrower burgers and tots were the pinnacle of cuisine in her opinion.

"I want my journal to be just like yours, Emma," Maisie announced, cheeks full of tots. "You must have lots of treasures in you because you're so shiny."

Emma set down her burger. "That is the sweetest thing anyone's said to me. Thank you."

We kept eating, but my eyes were doing that *thing* again. The one where I kept going back to Emma. Drawn by an irresistible force. My daughter had the right idea.

Emma was shiny. Way too shiny for me.

✧

We were almost done eating when Piper showed up with Ollie. They pulled up a table to join ours. "Are you still pissed at Callum?" Piper asked.

I rolled my eyes. "Give me a break. Did somebody write an article in the local paper? Take out an ad? It's not that big a deal."

"I dropped by Grace's a few minutes ago. I was bringing her a get-well-soon package." Piper sipped her drink. "Callum was there too."

"I'll call him tomorrow," I grumbled. "Just so he'll stop whining to everyone."

Piper snickered. She knew she was stirring up shit.

"Is Grace doing okay?" Emma asked.

Piper swiped a tot from our basket. "She has a bad cold. It was so sweet of you to step in and watch Maisie, Em. How did it go?" Piper eyed me as she said that. Probably watching my reaction.

She liked to claim she didn't gossip, but everyone around here gossiped. It was a small-town rule. It sucked. Especially because my private business seemed to be the topic way too often.

I drank my shake while Piper and Emma chatted, and Maisie and Ollie petted Stella. Finally, the sun was going down, and I couldn't fit another bite into my full stomach. "We should head out soon."

"Okay. I'll be right back." Emma got up to use the restroom.

"I have an idea," Piper announced, once we were alone. "Maisie should come play with Ollie for a bit. He wanted to show her his new Lego set. And you can walk Emma back to her place. Feel free to take your time."

I knew what was going on. This was a conspiracy.

She had *definitely* been talking to Callum.

"Stop meddling."

"Who, me? I don't meddle. Just trying to be a good friend. To *both* of you."

I stood up, collecting our baskets and napkins. "For someone who claims she's through with love, you seem pretty interested in other people's love lives."

Piper shrugged. "It's a hobby of mine."

"Set up Grace with someone instead."

"Believe me, I'm working on it."

I didn't even want to know.

But I decided to take her up on her offer. Just so I could make sure Emma got home safe. I threw away our trash, returned the baskets, and met Emma when she emerged from the ladies' room.

"If you're heading home after this, I can walk you. Piper's going to keep the kids for an hour or two."

"Okay." Emma smiled, adjusting the strap of her bag. "Thanks."

I kept my hands in my pockets as we walked toward the Ponderosa Apartments. I didn't need the temptation to touch her again. Even though I wanted to, and that urge kept getting stronger.

Damn my friends and family for meddling with my business. For being so obnoxious as to want me to be happy.

A summer fling wasn't going to make me happy. It would be nothing more than a distraction. I couldn't afford distractions. And Emma Jennings had already turned into a big one.

Besides, why would a beautiful woman in her twenties, with a sunshiny personality and her entire future laid out for her like a buffet, want to deal with me? I came pre-loaded with a shit-ton of baggage.

"Thank you for dinner," Emma said, holding Stella's leash as we made our way down the sidewalk. "I had fun tonight."

"Me too. We shouldn't make a habit of it though."

"And why is that?"

"Because a couple of months from now, you'll be getting ready to leave. Maisie will be sad when you go. I don't want her to get too attached."

"Sorry to break it to you, but I think Maisie is already attached. To Stella, for sure. Maybe even to me. You can't stop her from caring about people."

I glanced down the street, pressing my lips together. "It's not that simple."

She sighed. "It's your call if I spend time with your daughter or not. But I thought you and I got along really well today too. Just admit it, Ashford. We're friends. You like me."

"Are you sure you want to be friends with me? It's not that great."

"I beg to differ. I think you're a pretty nice guy. When you choose to be."

I wanted to smile at her the way she was smiling at me. Wanted to reach out.

But I couldn't let myself. Because if I reached for her, what if I didn't want to let go?

"I'll see you at work tomorrow."

"Sure. See you at the Big Blue Monster."

"The *what*?"

"That's what I call it. Blue bricks. And those two windows on the second floor look like eyes."

My smile broke through my defenses. "I never thought about it. But they do."

"Admit we're friends," she said in a sing-song voice.

"I'll consider it."

"And I'll consider that a win."

She and Stella went inside the building. I wasn't happy to see that there was no lock on the outer door. Would the owner of the Ponderosa get angry if I came over here and installed one?

Hmm. It would be a pain in the ass. But I was seriously considering it.

I crossed the street, but I didn't leave yet. A light switched on in a third-floor apartment. Was that hers?

She was home safe. It was getting dark. I should probably go.

Instead, I stood there with my thoughts going around and around in the same circles. Wanting something that I shouldn't, *couldn't*, have.

When I turned to go, I caught sight of a figure standing beneath a tall cottonwood tree. The person wore a long blue jacket in a fabric that caught the fading light when he shifted. A hood shadowed his face.

A navy blue rain slicker. Just like Emma had described seeing at the park. The person who'd been watching her and Maisie.

What the fuck?

"Hey, you," I called out, starting toward him. "Excuse me."

The guy bolted, dodging out of sight.

"Hey!"

I cursed, my muscles tensing to follow. But he hadn't done anything illegal. And while I'd been hanging out with cops today, I wasn't one myself.

If the guy came back, though, he could waltz right into Emma's apartment building. For all I knew, there was a back door and the creep was heading there now.

I took out my phone and tried calling Emma. She didn't answer.

I crossed to the entrance door, went inside her building, and started up the stairs. Except I didn't actually know which apartment was hers. It could be anywhere.

Nice job thinking ahead.

But I had to warn her that the same creep from earlier might be hanging around. I would offer to call Teller. The Silver Ridge PD station was less than a mile away. If Emma wanted to, we could file a report.

Then I heard a woman shout. It had come from the floor above.

I barreled up the steps.

ELEVEN
Emma

I went into my apartment, switched on the light, and dropped my bag to the carpet. Stella sat on her haunches, blinking up at me.

"He's a tough nut to crack, that one."

I'd never met someone so frustrating as Ashford O'Neal. So determined to be a hard-hearted grouch when I *knew* he was a good guy underneath.

"I'm wearing him down," I said to Stella. "It's hard work though." I walked toward the tiny kitchen to pour some food in Stella's bowl. She dove right in. "Why is he so resistant to us being friends? Is it me? Piper said he's like that with everyone, but I don't know."

He thought Maisie would get attached. That she'd be sad when the summer ended. But *I* was already attached. Not just to that sweet little girl, but to the glimpses of her dad's softer side that I'd seen so far. It wasn't enough to qualify as a crush, but it was getting close. Which was all kinds of foolish. The last thing I needed was more guy-related drama.

"And yet, he keeps being so handsome. What's a girl to do?"

Stella tilted her head, chewing.

Then I remembered the leak.

I'd been so up in my head, I'd forgotten all about it. It felt like ages since the rainstorm this morning. Sheldon hadn't texted me about the status of the repairs, either.

I just hoped the leak was fixed, even if they'd had to make a stop-gap repair. I assumed there would be bigger repairs needed, like replacing the ruined drywall on the ceiling, but that was an issue to figure out tomorrow.

Stella followed at my heels. I turned on the light in my bedroom. The whole place smelled damp and musty.

It had not been fixed.

There was a red mop bucket placed on the bed frame to catch the drips instead of my tiny trash can. Someone had been in here. But that wet spot on the ceiling bulged downward more than ever, like any minute it would collapse.

Where was I supposed to sleep?

I looked around for the belongings I'd stacked this morning to keep them away from the leak. My bedding, my pajamas from last night, some books. I'd been in too much of a hurry to carry it all into the living area. But they weren't where I'd left them.

Someone had moved my things to beneath the window. And now, there was dampness showing around the frame.

The window had been leaking too. Unbelievable.

When I knelt down, I found my stuff soaked with dirty rainwater. I groaned. My pillow, my blankets. Everything was wet. This *sucked*. I sorted through, figuring out what else was ruined.

Beneath a blanket, I found my journal.

"No," I whispered.

Stella barked, shuffling her feet against the carpet. She pushed her nose against my cheek. But I couldn't stop staring at my journal. The pages were totally waterlogged. The ink had run. One tore as I tried to turn it.

I felt sick.

Maybe it shouldn't have mattered so much to lose this small object, but I'd put my heart and soul on those pages. I'd written down my pain over what had happened with my ex. The shame I still felt over the entire scandal. And so many other things too. I'd tried to turn that heartache into something beautiful and meaningful, even if only to me.

And now it was just...ruined.

I yelled a sound of frustration. I'd had it with this apartment. Stella barked just before I heard someone call out, "Emma?"

Was that Ashford? It sounded like he was in the hall. I stumbled over to my front door and opened it. Ashford was in the hallway, his back to me. He whirled around. The tightness in his expression turned to intense worry as he strode toward me.

"What are you doing here?" I asked, voice thick.

"What's wrong? What happened?"

"It's..." The words got stuck in my throat.

Ashford put a hand on my shoulder and steered me back into my apartment. Stella's tail wagged, and she kept looking from Ashford to me, both excited and confused. I heard him flip the lock. He stalked around my apartment like he was searching for something.

"What happened in here?"

He'd seen my bedroom.

Ashford stormed back out, fists clenched. But his frown relaxed as he reached me. "How long has that been leaking? It looks bad."

He eased me down onto the tiny loveseat, squeezing in beside me. He was so warm and solid. His arm went around my shoulders. I leaned against him, letting my weight fall into his side. Stella sat at my feet, her head on my knee.

"It was the storm this morning. That leak opened up. I'd seen the stain before, but I didn't realize it was a current problem."

"Did you report it to the landlord?"

I bristled, inching back. "Of *course* I did. I told the property manager who lives downstairs. Sheldon. I'm not an idiot."

"No, you're not. I wasn't suggesting it. Looks like Sheldon didn't do his job."

I shook my head. "I was busy all day. I didn't have a chance to check up on him. Just got here and found...this *mess*." I waved a hand at my bedroom, but I realized I was still holding my sodden journal.

Ashford took it gently from my grip. "What's this?"

And that's when I lost it.

Hot, humiliating tears cascaded down my face. I turned my head, wiping the teardrops away as fast as I could.

Why did I have to do this in front of him?

The moment couldn't have been any more awkward. I had no idea why Ashford had come inside my building, but I had no doubt he was about to find an excuse to take off. He didn't want to see my embarrassing display of emotion. He barely even liked me.

"Emma. Hey. It's going to be okay." His voice was as deep and rumbly as usual, yet also softer than I'd ever thought possible. He set my journal on the coffee table. "C'mere."

The arm around my shoulders pulled me in tighter, and I went right where he guided me. My face pressed into his chest. His other arm closed around me so I was surrounded by warmth and his masculine scent.

I sobbed into his T-shirt. There was no stopping me now.

But he just sat there and held me, murmuring gentle words. "It's going to be okay." Stella got in on the act too, trying her best to crawl into our laps.

Eventually, my tear ducts ran dry. Ashford's hand went to the back of my head, smoothing down my hair.

Stella cocked her head, looking up at us forlornly. He reached over and petted her head too.

I'd melted into him like a sad blob of drippy candle wax. There was probably snot on his shirt. I hiccuped, knowing I should move but really, really not wanting to.

"What are you doing here?" I asked. "I thought you left."

"I saw someone hanging around near your building. He was wearing a blue rain slicker. I tried to confront him, and he ran off."

This night kept getting worse. "The creep from the park? Did you see what the person looked like?"

"The hood of his jacket was up. I tried calling your phone. You didn't answer. That's why I came inside. I wanted to check on you."

"I didn't hear it. The cell reception's not great in here, and the wi-fi is iffy. But thank you." The thought of that creep following me home was scary. But the feeling didn't fully register. My emotions were already pretty busy at the moment.

I managed to peek up at Ashford. He looked down at me with a crease between his brows, tenderness in his intense, dark eyes.

My palm was pressed to one muscular pec just above his rapidly beating heart. My own heart lurched, a nervous thrill moving lower into my belly.

It had been a while since a man had held me this close. Especially one who was comforting me like he actually cared.

And my body chose this moment to register just how incredibly, irresistibly sexy Ashford O'Neal was.

I had to look like a disaster right now. Skin blotchy from crying, eyes bloodshot. Also sweaty. Couldn't forget that. Probably smelled bad. I wiped at my face.

"Have you checked on Maisie?" I asked.

"I was just thinking about it. I'm sure Piper's got her, and they're fine. But I'll text."

I extricated myself, already feeling colder after leaving that comfy position. "I need to go talk to Sheldon about the leak." I should've already done that, instead of breaking down and crying. But I was grateful that Ashford didn't point it out.

He jotted a text on his phone. "Hold on a sec. I'll come with you."

"You don't have to do that."

"I know. But I think I should."

I didn't have it in me to argue. Once again, Ashford was stepping in because he thought I couldn't handle myself. Was he wrong, though? I hadn't even been able to find myself a decent apartment. Or remember to pack a raincoat.

He finished his text and got up, stowing his phone in the pocket of his athletic pants. "Come on." Ashford reached for my hand and pulled me toward the door.

"Stay," I told Stella. "We'll be right back."

Ashford held my hand all the way downstairs. When we reached Sheldon's door, the one with a plaque labeled *Property Manager*, Ashford rapped on the wood with his knuckles. The sounds of a TV came from inside.

"I'm familiar with Sheldon," Ashford said. "He was in Callum's year at school. He's a weaselly little jerk."

"Trust me, I know. When I was here this morning to complain about the leak, he stared at my chest like my boobs were doing the talking."

Ashford's eyes flashed dangerously just as Sheldon's door opened.

"Yeah?"

Ashford crowded the other man in the doorway. "Is it true that Emma told you this morning about the leak in her ceiling?"

"Uh, yeah. But—"

"Sounds like you didn't listen to her."

"I—"

Ashford cut him off again. "No." He hadn't touched Sheldon, but the pure menace in his expression made it seem like he might. "You're going to shut your mouth so Emma can speak. And this time, you're going to listen. With respect. Or we're going to have a problem. Got it?"

Sheldon swallowed, nodding.

They both looked at me.

I crossed my arms. "It's obvious that leak isn't new. It should've been addressed before. I expect a reduction in my rent for every day it's not fixed."

"The roofers couldn't make it out today. And it'll probably be a while before the damage gets ripped out and redone. This stuff takes time."

Ashford's scowl intensified, one corner of his mouth lifting.

Sheldon closed his mouth.

"*Reduction in rent*," I repeated. "Also, there's a leak coming from the window too. Someone was in my apartment and moved my things. I'm guessing it was you. But you put my stuff right under the window. I expect you or the landlord to replace any of my belongings that got ruined."

The things that were replaceable, anyway.

"Did you get all that?" Ashford asked. "Need to write anything down?"

"No," Sheldon mumbled. "I got it."

"Good."

I nodded sharply. "I expect to hear from you first thing in the morning with details on when the contractors are coming."

I spun on my heel and headed back upstairs. Ashford came up behind me. Once we were inside my apartment, he asked, "Are you okay?"

I took a deep breath. "Thanks for coming with me."

"Sheldon shouldn't need me standing there to treat you respectfully. That's bullshit. But I'm glad I could help. You didn't really answer my question, though."

I knelt to rub Stella's flank. I could tell she needed reassurance. "Am I okay? Not really." My head hurt and my nose was stuffy from that crying jag. My stomach ached. "Not feeling so great at the moment."

"This is a setback," he said. "But you can't let it get you down. You're the most optimistic person I've ever met."

"And where did that get me?" I gestured at my barely habitable apartment. My ruined journal on the coffee table.

Ashford was quiet. When I looked over, he was staring off to the side and scowling.

"You probably need to go," I said. "Maisie's waiting."

"Yeah. But you're coming with me."

"What?"

"I'll help you pack up. You're coming to stay with me and Maisie."

"Ashford..."

"I'm not leaving you here. There's probably mold growing in the ceiling. And there was that guy who was watching your building and might have followed you. And Sheldon downstairs. I'm not thrilled that he has a key to your place."

"I can figure it out. You don't want me to be your problem."

"You are *not* a problem. I am sincerely sorry if I ever made you feel like one." He sat down beside me on the floor. Stella leaned in to give him a nice, sloppy lick, and he grunted. "Come stay with us, even if it's just a night or two. Otherwise I won't be able to sleep because I'll be anxious about you."

"We can't have that."

"Is that a yes?"

My lips curved with a small smile. "Stella will have to come with me."

"Is she going to leave my apartment intact?" He eyed the dog, and she gave him an innocent *who, me?* look in return. Ashford sighed. "I guess we'll need her food and all that."

"And her bed and toys."

"Show me where all this stuff is. I'd better call my brother. We'll need a vehicle to carry it all. Callum can get my truck from the park and drive it over here."

"You're speaking to him again?"

"I guess I am now." He got up, then reached out his hand to pull me up too. "Come on. Pack your suitcase."

"Are you sure? Really?" I wanted to give him one last chance to change his mind.

"Yeah. Easiest decision I've made in a while."

✦

When Callum showed up at my door, he gave his brother a hug and asked me how he could help.

Callum bent to pet Stella, who was happy to have a new face to lick. Unlike his older brother, he laughed and seemed to love it. "So you're staying at Ashford's?"

"Just for tonight." I doubted the repairs would be finished to my apartment, but I could see about that room Dixie had offered. The one at her friend Shirley's, where I'd have to share a bathroom with her grandson in the basement. *Ugh.*

"Or you could stay at Ashford's longer." Callum grinned at his brother. "I have the feeling Emma's going to fit right in at your place."

Ashford rolled his eyes and went to grab Stella's doggy bed. Which I took as confirmation that he didn't want me moving in for the rest of the summer. Not that I had any intention.

He was doing me a favor. He'd been amazing tonight. Like Piper had said, once you were in with Ashford, you were *in*. But I didn't want to wear out my welcome.

Luckily—for better or worse—I didn't have much to move. No furniture, and my bedding was done for.

Callum drove us to Ashford's. While we carried my things inside, Callum took off for Piper's to pick up Maisie. It had to be close to her bedtime. I was exhausted myself. Crying always wore me out.

This had been such a long day, full of ups and downs. I needed sleep so I could start over again tomorrow.

I kept Stella on-leash as we went upstairs to his place. Ashford unlocked the door and held it open. "Come on in."

Just a few hours ago, I'd been here as Maisie's babysitter. Now, I would be staying overnight. It wasn't so different really. This was temporary, and I was a guest.

But it *felt* different as I followed him past the living room. "That's Maisie's room," he said, pointing. "Bathroom's opposite."

I smiled. "I remember."

He scratched his forehead. "Right." He suddenly seemed sheepish. It was cute. "This is our spare room." Ashford pushed the door open and hit the light switch. There were some boxes stacked up against one wall. A futon against the other. "We use this space for storage, but I can move the extra stuff out of here."

"Don't worry about it. This is great." Now *I* sounded awkward. Maybe because this hot dad who also happened to be sweet had brought me up to his apartment, and the bed was *right there*. "There's room for Stella's things in the corner."

She perked up, hearing her name.

Ashford helped me get things arranged. By the time Stella was comfy in her new spot, the door to the apartment burst open again.

"Emma!" Maisie shouted. "You're really here?"

Stella went running. There was lots of excitement, both Maisie and Stella dashing around the living room until Ashford sternly told them both to calm down.

I explained about the leak in my roof. Maisie wasn't too interested in those details. She was thrilled to be having a sleepover.

"Daddy, can't Emma and Stella sleep in my room? Pretty please?"

"No, monkey. They need their own space, and so do you. In fact, it was your bedtime five minutes ago."

"But I have to show Emma." She went and got her new unicorn journal from Callum. He'd carried it in for her. She opened the journal to the first page. "See?"

I studied the pictures and words she'd drawn. There was a yellow dog-like creature with STELA scrawled beside it. "Wow. This is beautiful. Stella will love it too. But don't let her get too close. She might love it so much she'll try to chew on it."

Maisie giggled. "Okay."

I said thanks to Callum, and he took off. Then I decided to make myself and Stella scarce during Maisie's bedtime routine. Just to help her calm down enough to sleep.

There were a lot of big feelings happening inside the Big Blue

Monster this evening. Stella curled up beside me on the futon while I tried to work through mine. Would've been easier if I'd had my own journal. But snuggling was a close second.

Eventually, there was a soft knock at the door.

"Come in," I said. The door wasn't closed all the way, so Ashford pushed it open. He stood in the doorway, shoulder leaning against the frame.

"Finally got her into bed. Bedtime stories have been read, and the white noise machine is on." Ashford spoke softly so we wouldn't disturb Maisie next door.

"Sorry. It's my fault she was up late."

"Don't be sorry. She was excited."

I got up and walked over to him. But I stood just inside the room, like there was an invisible barrier between us. A line that neither of us could cross.

"She's attached to you, just like you said. I kept trying to convince myself that was a bad thing. But she's happy around you. That can't be bad."

I meant to agree, but I got a little lost in his dark brown irises. They had flecks of gold and amber. The moment stretched out. But it wasn't uncomfortable. There was a different kind of tension. A feeling like warm honey poured through my veins.

His gaze shifted down to my mouth.

I forced myself to look away.

Ashford stuck his hands in his pockets, shifting his weight. "I'll see you in the morning then."

"Okay. Thank you again."

"Night." He smiled before walking toward his bedroom.

TWELVE
Ashford

"Daddy, something's wrong."

"Hmm?" I sat up fast, though I was still half asleep. My heart rate instantly revved into overdrive. "What? What is it?"

"It's Emma."

I blinked, remembering what had happened last night. Finding Emma near tears in that dilapidated apartment. Seeing her cry. I had been physically incapable of leaving her there. Only a monster would've done that.

And then, once she was in my home, I'd almost kissed her.

What kind of an asshole was I, tempted to make a move on a vulnerable young woman who needed my help? Exactly that kind of asshole, apparently. *Hi, everyone. It's me.*

I got up, put on a T-shirt and sweatpants over my shorts, then followed Maisie to the guest room. The door was closed, and canine whimpers came from inside.

"See?" Maisie said. "Stella's upset."

I knocked gently. The whimpers increased, and there was a muffled groan that sounded far more human. "Emma? You okay?" I opened the door a crack. The room was dark.

Before I could stop her, Maisie squeezed past me and inside.

She went to the pile of blankets on the futon where I assumed Emma was bundled up. Stella followed at her heels.

"Emma? Are you in there?" Maisie lifted the top of the quilt.

"*Mais*," I warned, taking a careful step forward. Then I heard Emma answer in a strained voice.

"Not feeling so hot, Maisie-doodle. I have a migraine."

Shit. "I'll be right back," I said. "Hold on."

I went to the bathroom to wet a washcloth with cold water. When I returned, Maisie was sitting on the futon beside Emma. After hesitating a moment longer, I crossed the small room. Emma blinked up at me, hair spread over her pillow and her blankets pulled up to her chin. She looked too pale in the daylight bleeding through the blinds of her window.

"Thought you could use this." I held out the cold washcloth. With a grateful sigh, she took it and draped it over her forehead.

"Thanks."

"Are you nauseous?" I asked.

"Yeah. Trying to lie still."

"We have saltines."

"I can get them." Maisie jumped up and ran for the kitchen. I hovered there, contemplating what else I could do.

"How'd you know about the cold compress?" Emma asked. "Do you get migraines?"

"Lori used to. When she was stressed."

"That's a trigger for me too. Also crying. Did plenty of that yesterday."

"Need to cancel your music classes this morning?"

She grimaced. "Ugh, yeah."

"Don't worry about it. I can handle it. You use that sign-up app, right?"

Emma unlocked her phone, and I navigated to the app to send a cancelation message to everyone who'd registered. By then, Maisie had returned with a small plate of saltine crackers, and also a glass of orange juice that was precariously full.

"Thank you both. I just need a little quiet and dark and rest. I'll probably be doing better this afternoon."

"Don't worry about going anywhere until you're well."

Maisie tugged at my shirt. "Daddy, shouldn't we stay with Emma today?"

I was feeling the same thing. But there wasn't much we could do for Emma except let her rest. I'd been through this same thing with Lori.

Maisie had day camp this morning. I had a training session with Elias.

Emma bit the corner of a saltine. "I promise I'm fine. *Please* don't cancel your plans because of me. That'll make me feel even worse."

That settled it. "Come on, Mais. Let's get ready. Stella will be here with her. We'll be back this afternoon." I steered her out of the room. Maisie pouted as she got dressed and sat down for breakfast.

Just before we left, I brought Emma a cup of hot tea. She was asleep, so I left the mug on the table by the bed.

"We shouldn't have left her," Maisie said with a dramatic frown, little arms crossed in the backseat on our way to camp drop-off. Yep, she was mad at me.

"Sometimes grown-ups have to take care of themselves."

"But you helped Emma when you brought her to live with us. 'Cause her partment was leaking. That was taking care of her, wasn't it?"

"I was trying to. Yeah."

"Then why won't you take care of her now?"

Geez. My kid was only six, but she had an advanced degree in guilt-tripping. "It's just different. Okay?"

She stuck out her lower lip and glared at the window.

After drop-off, I headed to the gym to meet Elias for training. He was already warming up on the treadmill when I walked up. "What's with you?" he asked. "Would've thought you'd be smiling."

"Why?"

Elias grinned smugly. "Callum told me about your pretty new roommate. How's that going?"

Seriously, the small-town gossip network was bad enough. But my siblings took it to another level. "Emma's not feeling well today. Maisie's upset that we left her at the apartment."

"Oh. Damn." Elias hit stop on the machine and stepped off. "Do you need to take off? We're doing the same routine as last time, right? I can run through it myself."

"No, you paid for me to whip your ass into shape. Let's hit the weights. Squat rack first."

Since the moment Emma had shown up in Silver Ridge, I had been trying to keep her at arm's length. But there was another part of me that wanted to pull her closer. A very stupid part of me.

I had to draw the line somewhere before I did something I couldn't undo.

Yet an hour and a half later, after returning my truck to its usual parking space, I found myself a few blocks away on Main Street picking up supplies. Laden with bags, I trudged back to the Big Blue Monster. That name had already stuck. Those windows really did look like eyes. How had I never noticed it?

I tried to be quiet as I went upstairs and unpacked my purchases in the kitchen. No sounds came from the guest room. But when I tiptoed over to check, her door was open.

Emma leaned against the pillows with her eyes closed. Her hair was damp like she'd taken a shower. She smelled like lavender and vanilla. I hadn't been able to name the flower before, but now her shampoo and body wash were in my bathroom.

Stella snoozed beside her. I didn't want to disturb them. I was about to sneak away when Emma opened her eyes.

"Hi. You're back."

"Finished my morning session." I leaned into the door frame. "Dixie is going to pick up Maisie from camp and entertain her for a few hours. I told her you're not feeling well. Dixie said she hopes you feel better soon." Actually, Dixie had asked me to give Emma a get-well hug for her. I figured that was a bad idea. "I grabbed some things from the market. For whenever you're hungry."

"You didn't have to do all that."

But I did, I thought. Couldn't help myself. "No big deal. How's your pain?"

"Not great. But not the worst. The nausea has mostly passed."

"Do you feel like having soup? I have chicken noodle or tomato."

"Tomato sounds good. Thank you."

A few minutes later, I carried a tray with two bowls of soup and more saltines into the guest room. "Mind if I eat in here with you? I'd sit at the kitchen table, but seems weird for us to eat in two separate rooms."

"I don't mind at all. Stella, down please. Good girl."

I clenched my teeth. Hearing her say those last two words just made me imagine myself saying them. In a very different kind of situation.

The only place for me to sit was on the bed. Which didn't help. I placed the tray over Emma's lap, then carefully sat on top of the blankets next to her so I wouldn't jostle the soup.

"Didn't know you could have such a delicate touch," she said.

"Me? I'm like a panther when I want to be. Pure stealth."

Emma snickered and dipped her spoon into the soup.

The lights were low, and we ate in companionable silence. Once Stella figured out there was food, she tried joining us, but Emma snapped her fingers and told the dog to stay down. "It's not your turn, Stella. You just have to wait."

I smiled at their interaction. Usually, the pets-as-children thing annoyed me. But not when Emma did it. "How long do your migraines usually last?"

"The worst of the pain and nausea might be a day. Then I'm really exhausted after. I hate missing things because I'm sick."

"How often do they come?"

"Depends. Once every month or two."

"That sucks."

For some reason, my statement made her smile. "It does. But it's really nice to have roommates to bring me soup and crackers. And hot tea."

My phone rang at full volume. I cringed, grabbing it out of my pocket and switching it to silent. Thankfully it wasn't Dixie. It wasn't a number I had any intention of answering.

"That's a Los Angeles area code," Emma said.

Damn. So she'd seen my screen.

"Oh, is it? I wouldn't know," I lied. "Must be a wrong number. Hey, I bought ice cream. I'll go get it."

Shameless change of subject. But I wanted to head off any more questions.

In the kitchen, I scrolled to my recent calls and blocked that number. *When the heck is she finally going to give up?* I wondered.

Then I pushed the subject out of my mind. Because it seemed like the answer was *never*. And that scared me more than I would ever admit.

◆

"Which flavor?" I brandished the two options, one bowl of each.

I'd bought two kinds of ice cream at the market. Mint chocolate chip, which Lori had always liked when she had a migraine. And chocolate. Since Emma had a chocolate shake yesterday, I'd figured that was a safe bet.

Emma bit her lip, looking from one to the other. "Can we share? Unless you don't want my germs. Migraines aren't contagious," she joked.

"I think I can take the risk." I scooted back into my spot beside her. I'd also brought a paper bag with me, tucked beneath my arm, but that was for later. I set the bag on the floor and handed Emma the bowl of chocolate. "Here you go."

We traded bowls halfway through. My gaze followed as she licked ice cream from her spoon while I did the same to mine.

The lower half of my body responded, cock firming up against my inner thigh.

Calm down, I told myself. The poor woman was sick. But apparently I had a weakness when it came to Emma Jennings. In all kinds of ways.

Stella jumped up on the bed, and this time, Emma didn't bother scolding her. The dog watched us forlornly until I gave up and said, "Here," holding my bowl out.

Stella made short work of licking the bowl clean.

"She'll love you forever now," Emma said. "Won't be able to get rid of her."

"Yeah, yeah. I got tired of the puppy eyes." Hopeless. I was hopeless. "I picked up something else while I was out."

Setting the dish on the nightstand, I leaned down to grab the brown paper bag I'd left beside the bed. Stella pushed in between us, so I had to reach over to hand Emma the bag.

"What is it?"

"It's nothing really. Just saw it in the window at Silver Linings when I was walking by."

She opened the bag. "Oh my gosh. Ashford. This is... I don't believe it."

"If you don't like it, I can exchange it. Or return it."

Emma pulled out the new journal. It had a white leather cover with stars and shiny gold on the edges of the pages.

I hadn't exactly seen it in the window. I'd had to hunt around, and Piper had suggested this one.

"You like it?"

"I can't believe it," she said again. Her fingertips traced the soft cover, and I couldn't help imagining those fingers on my skin instead.

Nope. So not appropriate.

I shrugged. "It's not exactly like your other one. But I figured this could fill in. Seemed like the journaling thing was important to you."

"I love it so much. Thank you." She hugged it to her chest.

"You're a very sweet man, Ashford, even if you spend a lot of energy pretending you're not."

Cue the discomfort. "Eh. I don't know. Just don't get used to it."

Emma settled against the pillows. "Do you need to go?"

"Not yet." I hadn't looked at the clock for a while. Checking now, I was glad to see we had another hour.

"Would you tell me more about you and Maisie? It will distract me from the pain." She batted her eyelashes.

I laughed. "And you say my daughter knows how to play me. You're much more dangerous."

"I *am* a musician. Playing things is my speciality."

When she put it like that, how could I deny her? Even if the story was pretty depressing.

I stretched out my legs and started talking.

I told her about my mom having a stroke when I was thirteen. How my siblings and I had taken care of each other, since our dad hadn't been interested. I didn't talk about myself like this. Pretty much ever. But something about Emma made it easy.

Stella lazed half on my lap, half on Emma's. I let myself sink into the pillows, and while I was talking, our arms ended up touching. Emma's head found its way to my shoulder.

I told her how I'd met Lori on base. Her father had been a colonel. An overbearing tyrant of a man, especially to his wife and daughters. He'd never gotten violent with them. That would've risked losing face and being disciplined by his superiors. But he'd berated his family every chance he got until his wife and then Lori's sister left. Lori was the only one who stayed.

"We were close friends for a long time. Kept in touch through every relocation. Then after I came back from my last deployment, Lori showed up on my doorstep. I guess we both needed something good. Maisie showed up nine months later."

"Sounds like it was meant to be."

I smiled, my gaze tracing patterns on the ceiling. "I've never described it that way. But it does feel like Maisie was meant to come into our lives. She's what we both needed."

Emma shifted against my side. "I should tell you. I already heard a little about Lori from Dixie and Piper. They said she was a great mom."

"She was. I miss her like crazy." But I felt like I should make things clear to Emma. I just didn't want her to misunderstand. "Lori and I weren't together, though. Our marriage wasn't romantic. This was her room, actually."

She paused, glancing around at the darkened space. "You don't mind me being here?"

"Not at all. It's been three years."

"But emotions don't keep time that way."

I sighed, my eyes drifting closed. "I guess not. Most people expect me to be over her death. Especially because we weren't in love."

"It's okay if you're not over it."

Callum, Elias, and Judson kept urging me to date. Same with Piper. They all meant well. I knew that. But for me, it wasn't about *my* needs. Or even my heartbreak. I didn't have a broken heart, not in the traditional sense. I was *angry*. Furious that I'd lost my best friend. That my daughter didn't have her mom. That Maisie had to count on me for everything, and what if I wasn't good enough?

"I just wish I knew *why*," I admitted. "Why Lori died."

"I read a news article about the investigation. I googled you, and it came up."

I chuckled. "You cyber-stalked me, Jennings?"

"I feel guilty. That's why I'm confessing."

"I forgive you." I opened my eyes and turned my head. Emma was looking at me. Blue, blue eyes. So fucking pretty.

There was a lot I would forgive her.

"What did this article say?" I asked.

"That she was hit by a car on the highway. She ran into the road. But Piper said it was definitely an accident."

I hesitated.

"It was, right?" Emma asked.

"The elderly woman who hit her couldn't stop in time. Lori had parked at a nearby trailhead, and she walked the trail through the meadow there. It was summer then, so it was probably full of wildflowers. Like it is now."

I pictured how those fields of flowers had looked a couple of weeks ago. The day I had met Emma.

"She stopped at an old abandoned cabin," I said.

"I think I saw it from the road."

"It's on the trail. She dropped her phone nearby. After that, why she was there after dark and ran onto the road, nobody can say. But the elderly woman who was driving the car claimed she saw *two* people by the highway. Someone else was with Lori. And the driver said... She said this other person pushed Lori into the road."

"Oh my God. Did the police find any evidence to support that?"

"No. Nothing. The driver's glasses prescription was out of date, and it was dark out. The police thought she was either confused or saw a double image. But I don't know. I still have Lori's phone, and I've gone over what's on it a hundred times with no luck. If there were incriminating messages, she must've deleted them. I knew she was keeping secrets from me."

"What do you mean?"

"A feeling I had. I was going to ask her about it. Didn't get the chance. I wish I could force it all to make sense, but I can't."

"I'm sorry," Emma said again.

"Me too."

I looked down at her big blue eyes. And suddenly, I was leaning in. My nose brushed the side of hers. I wanted desperately to kiss her. Press her down to the bed. Take comfort in her, and let her take comfort from me. Take anything she wanted.

The hell is wrong with me?

She was sick, and I was thinking about stripping her naked.

"Close your eyes," I whispered. "Get some rest. I'll be here."

Emma took a deep breath, exhaled, and put her head back on my shoulder.

✧

The alarm on my phone blared. I rubbed my face, and Emma stirred beside me. We'd fallen asleep.

"You need to go?" Emma asked.

"I do." Didn't want to, though. I'd been comfortable. Couldn't remember the last time I'd taken a nap. "Dixie's going to bring Maisie over before the kids' jiu-jitsu class. I need to get things ready. You need anything?"

"Could you take Stella out for me?"

"Of course. Anything else?"

"Not right now. The ice cream helped. And the sleep." But when she sat up, her mouth twisted like she was still hurting. "Maybe Dixie could come up while she's here. I need to ask her about her friend's spare room. See if it's still free."

"You're settled in here. Why not stick around?"

"You agreed to give me a place to stay for a night. Maybe two. I know you'd rather have your space."

I ran my fingers through my hair. "This could work out for the both of us. You'll have an easy commute to work. And you could help me out by watching Maisie sometimes."

"You really wouldn't mind? Are you sure?"

"Absolutely." Did I know what I was doing? Not a clue. All I knew was that I wanted Emma close. I would know she was safe, and it would make Maisie happy.

"At least let me pay rent."

"We'll work it out. Later. When you're feeling better."

"Okay." She seemed lighter already. More like herself. "Thank you, Ashford. Really. I don't think I've expressed how grateful I am for everything you've done for me. I didn't even think you liked me."

"Hard to dislike someone who's good to my kid."

But it was more than that. Despite my denials and excuses, it wasn't just Maisie who was getting attached.

Basically, I was screwed.

I'd already almost kissed her twice. How much longer could I resist?

THIRTEEN

Emma

By the time I woke up on Saturday, I felt like myself again. If a little more worn out than usual.

Tilting my head to the side, I listened for the sounds of Ashford and Maisie talking, laughing, moving around. But the apartment was quiet. I couldn't remember if Ashford taught on the weekends or not. Maybe he had another personal training client?

I picked up my new journal from the nightstand and ran a hand across the smooth cover, thinking of Ashford. He kept surprising me. We had spent over an hour straight-up snuggling in my bed yesterday when he was trying to make me feel better. We'd taken a nap together. An intimate kind of moment to share. Now, we would be living together through the rest of the summer.

And I was pretty sure he'd almost kissed me yesterday. *Again.* I hadn't felt my best, but I would've kissed him back. Maybe kisses from Ashford could be my new headache cure.

If I had wanted to avoid the temptation of falling for another older man, this was *not* the best way to go about it.

After journaling for a bit, my stomach started rumbling, and I went to find some food. After eating little more than soup and ice cream yesterday, I was ravenous. Also I needed to focus on something other than the ridiculously sexy man I was living with.

Unfortunately, the kitchen didn't help. Everything about the space reminded me of Ashford and his daughter. Poking around in the cabinets revealed juice boxes and snack packs. One of the few items that could only be for him was a box of protein bars.

My curiosity got the better of me once I had some food in my stomach. Instead of going straight back to my room, I ventured further down the hall to Ashford's.

His door just so happened to be open, and I just so happened to look inside. His bed was unmade, which only made me think of Ashford lying there. Tangling up those sheets with his long legs. The room smelled like him, hints of cinnamon and clove and anise.

Heat prickled all over my skin.

Ashford was gruff and difficult, sure. But when it counted, he had shown me more kindness and generosity than my ex ever had in the entire time I had been with him.

It made me want to do something more for Ashford. Cleaning up the kitchen and living room seemed like a small gesture, but one he would appreciate. I grabbed my AirPods, queued up some music from one of my favorite contemporary composers, and got to work.

What kind of music does Ashford like? I wondered.

I lost track of time. Until someone tapped me on the shoulder, and I whirled around, yanking the AirPods from my ears.

A woman in her late twenties stood there. She jumped back, hands going up. "Sorry! Didn't mean to scare you. You didn't hear me when I came in. I'm Grace. Ashford's sister."

"Of course. Hi, I'm Emma." I set aside the cleaning supplies and wiped off my hands.

"Believe me, I've heard *all* about you. Yet somehow, I keep missing the chance to meet you." She held up a takeout bag from Flamethrower Burgers & Brews. "Thought I'd swing by with lunch and say hello. I heard you've been out of commission with a migraine. How are you feeling?"

"Much better. You had a cold, right?"

She made a face. "I did, and it was the worst. I hate being sick."

"Same. It's really sweet of you to drop by. Ashford and Maisie are out though."

"I know. Ashford takes her to the farmer's market in the square every Saturday. I will admit I came here with an agenda. I was hoping to chat with you alone."

"Uh oh."

She laughed. "I promise I'm not that scary. Just...curious." Grace glanced around the kitchen. "This place looks amazing, by the way. So clean."

"Trying to help out, since Ashford's done a lot for me lately. He's a great guy."

"He is." Grace smiled again, but I felt the way she was assessing me.

We unpacked the food she'd brought. To my surprise, not burgers. "Elias makes really good turkey-avocado club sandwiches. I asked for blue cheese dressing on the side. Might sound weird, but it's my favorite."

"I'm up for it. Bring me all the cheese."

She held up her hand for a high five. "Yes. I can already tell we're going to get along."

Grace looked like her brothers, with her straight nose and the prominence of her jaw. But all of her features were the feminine version. Her bright brown eyes matched theirs, hers with even more flecks of amber, though partially hidden by her oversized glasses.

She'd tied her hair up with a pencil. Unlike Callum and Ashford, hers was lighter, a mix of brown and gold with auburn tones. Grace was stunning, but she had the kind of beauty that could go unnoticed because she was so unassuming.

"So you moved in here." She dipped a corner of her sandwich

in the dressing. "I was surprised when I heard that from Elias. Especially because Ashford hadn't told me."

There it was. The awkward part of the visit. "It happened a couple days ago. When you were sick with the cold. I babysat Maisie, and Ashford walked me home afterward. I was staying at the Ponderosa Apartments."

She grimaced. "That place? No offense, but it's kind of…"

"A dump? Trust me, I'm well aware. We got all that rain, and my ceiling was about to fall in. Ashford offered me his guest room. It was incredibly kind, and I'm so grateful."

Last night, I had given notice to Sheldon at the Ponderosa that I wouldn't fulfill my lease. Dixie had assured me that she and her friends would pressure the landlord to return my security deposit. Which meant I could use that money elsewhere. Maybe toward getting a new car, once I'd saved up more, since my old Nissan was never going to recover.

Grace frowned at her sandwich. "Like you said, my brother is a great guy. But he hasn't known you very long. It's one thing to help out a friend. But inviting you to live with him and Maisie? It was sudden. Really sudden."

"Are you asking if I'm sleeping with him?"

"Since you mentioned it…"

"I'm not." I almost told her that it wasn't her business, but that was a tough call to make. Ashford and Maisie were her family. Of course she was protective of them. "I realize it might seem like I'm trying to take advantage. But I already told Ashford I'm going to pay rent. Plus helping out around the apartment and taking care of Maisie."

"He trusts you with her. That's impressive. And it's obvious how much she likes you. The past few weeks, she's hardly talked about anything except Emma the music teacher." Grace folded up her trash into a neat square. "Here's the thing I'm worried about. Ashford hasn't dated anyone since Lori. I know he seems tough on the outside, but my brother feels things intensely. He always has. He's the kind to make sacrifices for the people he cares about."

"I gathered that. But I told you I'm not dating him."

"I'm just asking you to be careful. Don't start anything with him unless you're sure about what you want. Ashford has been through too much in the last few years. I just want to look out for my big brother, since that's what he always does for me."

"No, I get it." My first reaction was to defend myself. She didn't know me. If Ashford was interested in me, his sister wasn't his keeper. "But it's not necessary."

"Good." She blew out a breath. "I brought cookies for dessert. Silver Linings has these amazing chocolate-dipped shortbread ones. You in?"

"Absolutely. Bring it on."

What would Grace say if she knew my past? I had slept with a married man. Not on purpose, of course. But I still blamed myself for not seeing the truth. If Grace had known that, then there was no way she'd *ever* want me involved with her brother.

That wasn't the real issue though. Grace had reminded me of all the legitimate reasons Ashford and I shouldn't cross the line. But when I got close to him, I seemed to forget everything except how much I liked him.

✧

My bedroom door was open, but Ashford still knocked. "Hey, there you are. What's been keeping you so busy?"

"I have a bunch of new students for private lessons. Just doing some lesson planning." I closed my journal and set aside my pen on the nightstand.

Ashford stuck his hands in the pockets of his athletic pants. Those sexy, formfitting ones. Which I should not be noticing.

"I thought maybe you were avoiding me."

My gaze shifted away from him. "Why would I do that?"

Since Grace's visit, I'd been making an effort to keep my distance. At least as far as Ashford was concerned. I had been filling in as a babysitter for Maisie whenever he asked, and in the evenings, the three of us had cooked dinner together a few times. Those were some of my favorite parts of each day.

But after Maisie's bedtime, I always made sure I was busy in my room. No alone time between me and Ashford.

Because that was the way of temptation, and I was determined to be good.

"Aren't you supposed to be teaching your jiu-jitsu class?" I asked.

"Not on Fridays. What are you up to?"

"Just about to take Stella on a walk." At that magic word, she looked up from her doggy bed, where she'd been lazing.

"I'll go with you. We should hit up the park."

"Maybe another time. I need to run some errands. It'll be boring."

I got up from the futon and went to squeeze past him through the doorway. But then Ashford said, *"Emma,"* all low and growly, making me freeze right there an inch away from him. Like that bossy tone had connected with some instinctual part of me and forced me to be still.

He rested his elbow on the door frame above my head. I blinked up at him, endorphins flooding my body at having him so close, his scent in my nostrils, his heat like my own personal sunbeam.

"I think you *are* avoiding me. What I want to know is why. What did I do?"

I swallowed, bracing my hands behind me against the other side of the door frame. "Nothing. I promise."

He studied me for another long moment. "Okay. Then how about I help you with your errands, and then you and Stella come with me to the park. Maisie is playing baseball with Callum. Piper and my sister are going to be there too. Same with Elias and Judson."

"A meeting of the Lonely Harts club?"

He groaned. "I hate that name. But yeah, I guess. Club meeting. There's a cart that sells bad hot dogs and half-melted popsicles. Dogs and kids running wild. A Silver Ridge summer tradition. Stella will love it."

"She will?"

"Yep. It's doggy paradise. You don't want to deprive her, do you? Look at that face."

We both looked at Stella, whose eyes ping-ponged between us. Her tail wagged.

I didn't want to say no. Besides, I wouldn't be alone with Ashford. We'd be surrounded by his family and friends, including his sister.

I assumed Grace would be keeping a watchful eye on us.

"I guess I could save my errands for another day."

One side of his mouth curved, a sexy half-smile that made my breath catch. "Good answer."

On our way to the park, I could hear the laughter and shouts of dozens of people from a couple of blocks away. The park was a happening place in Silver Ridge on a summer Friday night.

The Lonely Harts crew had a red gingham picnic blanket laid out beneath a huge shade tree. Over in the grassy area, Callum gently pitched the ball to Ollie. They had a tee set aside, I assumed for the younger kids. Maisie stood with her glove in the air in the outfield.

"I'd better head over there and help," Ashford said. "Callum is dangerously outnumbered." He reached out and squeezed my arm before jogging away, such a small, simple gesture. Yet it made me feel like I belonged here. And set off a flurry of tingly sensations in my stomach.

I let Stella explore a bit, and then we went to cheer on the ball game with the others, especially when Maisie got a base hit off the tee.

Piper nudged me. "Ashford is great with the kids, isn't he?"

I nodded, aware of Grace a few feet away. "You're like the devil on my shoulder," I murmured.

Piper laughed evilly. "I'm very innocent, I'll have you know."

"I don't believe that for a second."

She was right, though. Ashford's grins came easier when he was surrounded by kids, and it seemed like the usual stress he carried had disappeared. I loved seeing him like that.

And every time he looked in my direction, it was hard not to think that smile was for me, too.

This wasn't just a fleeting attraction or a silly crush. I was starting to develop actual feelings for the man.

I just had to keep remembering all the reasons nothing could happen between me and him. No matter how much I wanted it.

FOURTEEN

Ashford

I SWUNG the plastic bat a few times. It made a singing sound in the air.

"Showing off for Emma?" Callum asked under his breath as he passed me, heading out to pitch.

"Fuck off."

"So inappropriate. There are children present."

"Fuck off, *please*."

The kids weren't close enough to hear us. They were over getting popsicles and crowding around Stella. Several of us guys had taken the equipment to play a quick game.

Also, I was very much showing off for Emma. As much as one could with a plastic bat and wiffle ball.

Callum pitched. I hit a line drive and jogged to first base, glancing in Emma's direction when I got there. Her eyes were on me, which filled my lower belly with anticipation.

Not like I had anything specific to anticipate. But my body had ideas lately, and it wouldn't listen to the rational voice of my brain.

Over the past week since Emma had moved in, I'd needed a lot of solo sessions in my bed and the shower. It was like my libido had suddenly woken from a long sleep, and it was *ravenous*. Yet the woman had been spending as little time around me as possible, and that lack of her attention just made me crave it more. It was embarrassing. I wasn't usually that guy. I was steady, dependable, responsible.

And here I was, stealing a base during a pickup wiffle ball game in hopes of impressing a woman who wasn't interested in me.

At least all the kids cheered.

I ran past the stump we were calling home base. The game didn't last much longer, and after checking on Maisie, I found a spot on the picnic blanket near Emma. She was wearing cutoff denim shorts and a tank top, and she leaned back in a relaxed posture with her hands braced behind her.

"Having fun?" I asked, tipping my water bottle to drink.

She nodded. "You were right about the hot dogs. They're pretty bad, and yet somehow they taste so good going down."

I sputtered and wiped spilled water from my face. Emma had a devious little smile, though she had her eyes on Stella romping around. Maisie had let her off leash.

"It's that summertime effect," I said. "Everything tastes better when the grass is green and the sun is shining."

"That must be it."

I bent my legs and rested my arms on my knees. "I'm teaching a women's self-defense course tomorrow afternoon. There's an open spot. You should come."

What are you doing, O'Neal? I asked myself.

The answer: something I shouldn't. But these days, ever since Emma had appeared in my life, what else was new?

Her gaze flew to mine. "What about Maisie?"

"Grace or Callum will watch her. That's usually what I do when I teach on the weekends."

"But isn't that my job now?"

"Not when you have other plans. Like joining my class. Useful, too. This is stuff everyone should know."

"I know basic self-defense. Dad and stepmom are cops, remember?"

"Then I'll teach you some advanced moves." I kept my gaze steady on her face instead of drifting down her body like I wanted to. "Come on. It'll be fun."

She chewed her lip, hesitating. "Okay. Sure."

I smiled and looked out over the park. The sun was going down, yet as I watched my kid laughing and playing with Emma beside me, everything seemed brighter. Even if my latest bright idea wasn't such a good one.

Maybe I didn't care any more.

✧

After introducing myself and my high school-aged assistant, Timothy, I started off the class with a few easy moves to warm everyone up.

"The first thing you always want to do is to listen to your instincts. If you feel uncomfortable, say something. Make noise. Don't be afraid to be loud and obnoxious. It's how I go through life every day, and I'm doing just fine."

There was polite laughter, as usual when I made that joke, lame as it was. I always tried to keep things light in these classes.

Of course, this afternoon I had a very attractive distraction warring for my attention.

Emma's hair was swept into a high ponytail, and she wore a tight pair of athletic leggings and a crop top.

She was mouthwatering.

Every time I looked in her direction, I forgot what I was doing. Not the kind of impression I wanted to make on any of my students, but her especially.

"Now, sometimes it's impossible to avoid a physical confrontation. So we're going to practice some moves to create distance between you and a potential attacker. It's all about moving fast and being aggressive." I demonstrated the first techniques on Timothy.

"Everyone pair off to practice. Groups of two or three. Be sure to stay on the mats."

I made my rounds, giving instructions and suggestions, and correcting form. Yet I noticed from the corner of my eye that Timothy had drifted to Emma's side of the room and stayed there.

He had just graduated from Silver Ridge High a couple of months ago. Thought he was hot stuff. There was also an odd number of ladies in the class, so he had appointed himself Emma's partner.

Nice try, Tim. If anyone was going to be giving Emma extra attention, it would be me.

I chose not to think about the fact that he was nineteen, far closer to Emma in age than I was.

Slowly, I made my way over.

"Tim, I think Mrs. Stuckey over there needs some help. Go give her a hand?"

Mrs. Stuckey had taken my self-defense classes before. She did look like she needed supervising. She kept waving her arms like she planned to karate chop the young mom next to her.

Tim tried to hide his grimace, but he wasn't quite fast enough. "Yes, sir."

I watched him cross the room. Then I turned to Emma. "Show me what you've got so far."

"Sure you can handle me?"

Her flirty tone sent a thrill of arousal through me. "Let's find out."

When I approached, she barred her arm to shove me back. She had more strength than I'd expected. "Nice."

"Told you I've got moves."

"I never doubted you."

"I think you doubted me a *little*."

"Okay. That's true. Learned my lesson."

We practiced a few more times. I went back to the front of the room, but the uptick in my pulse and the sweat on my brow didn't match how little I'd been moving. It had just gotten a lot hotter in here.

I clapped my hands. "Let's go on to body strikes. When you're in danger, you fight dirty. That means going after weak points. Eyes, throat, groin. Tim, would you join me? Mrs. Stuckey, you've got these moves down. Come up and demonstrate on Tim."

My assistant glared at me.

After strikes, we moved on to the bear-hug defense. "Let's say someone comes up behind you before you know he's there. He grabs you, pinning your arms. Immediately, he's limited your options. This is how to get them back."

Tim and I demonstrated how to get free, then I asked for a volunteer. Emma raised her hand. So did a couple of other women, but I picked Emma.

Because I had zero shame.

I placed her in front of me, facing the others. "I'm going to pin you. Try to use the defensive moves we showed to get out."

I came up behind her. We had no mirrors, aside from the window of one-way glass to the lobby, so I couldn't see her expression as my arms closed around her. But everyone else in the room was watching us.

Emma twisted her body, just like Tim had demonstrated. With a war cry, she mimed driving her elbow into my torso. Spun and aimed a hammer fist at my face, pulling the punch at the last second. Then, instead of retreating, she knocked me off my balance and had me flat on the mat in two seconds.

Damn.

"She's a ringer," Mrs. Stuckey complained. "Why haven't you taught us that move yet?"

"Sorry," Emma whispered as I got up. But her grin said she wasn't sorry at all.

It took every iota of my willpower to tear my gaze away from her. And to not pin her against the wall and see if she could get away from me then.

Everyone paired off to practice the bear-hug defense. I placed Emma in a threesome with two other ladies, while Timothy and I moved around to check form.

Then, since Emma had already taken me to the mat, I asked Tim to help me demonstrate a couple of jiu-jitsu-inspired defenses for the ladies to try on the ground.

By the end of the two hours, my students seemed happy and a lot more confident. They shuffled toward the lobby to grab their belongings. Tim was eyeing Emma again like he might ask for her number, so I clapped a hand on his shoulder and steered him toward the door. "Great job today, Timmy. See you next time. Say hi to your mom."

Emma lingered, grabbing a sip of water from her bottle. Every part of me was aware of her as I thanked the last of my students and made sure they were out the door.

Then I turned to face Emma, my blood zinging through my veins.

"I would offer to show you those advanced moves I promised. But now, I'm wondering how much you already know."

She shrugged, smiling. "Gotta admit, that was fun."

I put my fingertip beneath her chin and lifted it. Her eyes were blue as the cloudless sky outside the front window. "What else have you got?" I said, dropping my voice as deep as it would go.

I figured I was being obvious, but I didn't have it in me to be subtle right now.

Still smiling, she pivoted and went back to the mats. I followed. When she reached the center of the space, Emma held out her hand and beckoned. "Try me."

Yes, please. Whatever she had in mind, I was here for it.

I came toward her. Emma dodged out of my way, adopting an easy fighting stance. Nice. Her form lacked refinement, but she was confident and quick.

Mischief glinted in her eyes.

She feinted, but I didn't fall for it. Instead, I lunged. Took her to the mats to see what she would do.

Emma's pupils dilated. Her lips parted.

Then she wrapped her legs around my waist to put me in the guard position, the proper defensive move. Her body wriggled against mine. *Nngh.* She tried to get me in a chokehold, but she didn't quite close it.

"Like this," I said, changing her arm position slightly, which drew us even closer. Our bodies pressed together. We were sparring, but this was also a *very* intimate position.

Lavender and vanilla flooded my senses. My cock twitched with interest.

She released me, and I got up, holding my hand out to help her stand. Phew, I needed a cold shower right about now. This woman was dangerous.

Honestly, I didn't know how much of this was practice. How much was foreplay. I knew what I *wanted* it to be, but I couldn't tell yet if Emma was really on board.

"Go again?" I asked.

She nodded.

This time, I let Emma take me to the mat. She straddled my torso. I hugged her tight around the middle and flipped her. Not too rough. When she was on her back, she tried the same chokehold. My head was tucked close against her, enough that her pulse thrummed straight into my skin.

"That's it," I said. "You've got it."

We were both breathing hard. She loosened her grip enough that I could look down at her.

Two stormy blue eyes gazed up at me.

Fuck, I wanted her.

I'd been teaching defensive moves all afternoon, but really, I was at war with myself. If I kissed her, there was no going back. No matter how she reacted.

Emma glanced away.

We both got up and went to grab our water bottles. My mind was a buzz of conflicting thoughts. I was teetering right on the edge.

No. I had to play it safe.

"We should stop while we're ahead," I said. I studied her expression for disappointment, for any kind of hint she was feeling what I was, but she just shrugged.

"Good idea. Thanks for the lesson. My turn next time."

"You're going to teach me music? I'm warning you now, that's hopeless."

"Won't know until you try. I'm a good teacher."

"I'd rather sit and listen to you play."

"Play what?"

"How about the piano?" I nodded at the keyboard in the corner. It had a protective cover, and I'd had to be strict with the jiu-jitsu kids to stay away from it.

"Do you mean *now*?"

"Yeah," I decided suddenly. "Why not?"

We had a few until Callum would bring Maisie home from uncle time. Now that Emma had mentioned it, I couldn't imagine a better way to spend these minutes.

And I didn't actually want her to go yet.

"Play something for me?" I asked softly.

For some reason, I was holding my breath.

She went to the keyboard, removed the cover, and switched it on. I drifted closer as she sat at the bench and played a few notes. It sounded exactly like a real piano rather than an electronic instrument. Fancy.

I couldn't tell if she was warming up or searching for some melody. She stopped and started, shaking her head a few times, before her fingers began to move swiftly across the keys.

I was not ready for it.

My feet carried me toward her until I was standing at her shoulder, watching her fingers gracefully move. At the same time, her body swayed and her head nodded, like she was playing with her entire being.

I didn't know the words to describe what I was hearing, except things like *jaw-dropping*. *Heart-stopping*. The fact that it was Emma playing these notes in my training room just made it more surreal.

It was over too soon. When she stopped, I just stood there dumbstruck.

She turned and looked up. "What did you think?"

Emma's spine was straight, head high, but I saw vulnerability in her eyes. Like she didn't know what I was going to say and my uninformed opinion was somehow important.

"That was...wow." I straddled the bench, facing her. "What was that called? Who wrote it?"

"It doesn't have a name yet. And *I* wrote it. I've been trying to figure it out for a few weeks, but it suddenly came together. You liked it?"

I still didn't have words that would do justice to what I'd heard.

Or words that would do *Emma* justice.

She was so far out of my league.

This incredible woman who I had tried so damn hard not to care about. But then she went about her day, stealing my breath again and again just by existing. A man was only so strong.

I reached out to tuck a stray lock of hair behind her ear. She didn't pull away.

Fuck it, I thought.

I leaned forward and brushed my lips against hers.

She made a small, shocked sound. But her fist grabbed hold of my T-shirt, keeping me close instead of knocking me off the bench.

So far, so good.

I eased my mouth onto hers again. Slow, sensuous. Even though I wanted everything and I wanted it *now*. This was something I shouldn't rush.

If I was going to have her, then I planned to be thorough about it.

Her lips pressed back, sliding against mine in a gentle exploration. Emma's breath hitched. I felt the soft nudge of her tongue. I groaned, opening up to meet her tongue with mine. She tasted sweet. Like never-ending summer.

One of my hands went to her waist, the other to the back of her head where I lightly gripped the root of her ponytail.

Then came the unwelcome sound of a door opening, of voices. Emma wrenched away from me. I caught her wrist before she could get up. "Wait," I whispered. "Please."

Emma stared at me, uncertainty written on her face. I heard my brother out in the lobby, along with Maisie. But the door to the training room was closed.

Callum and Maisie headed upstairs to the apartment. The sound of their footsteps receded.

I scooted closer and cupped the side of Emma's neck. My thumb traced up and down her rapid-fire pulse. Her chest lifted and fell as she breathed.

I leaned in for another deep kiss, my mouth lingering against hers before we separated again.

"We have to go," I said, "but can we talk later? After Maisie goes to bed?" Without waiting for an answer, my lips went to her jawline, then her neck. I wasn't fighting fair. But I knew what I wanted, and I was pretty set on having it. If she wanted it too.

"Yes," she breathed.

That was all I needed to hear.

FIFTEEN
Emma

When Ashford and I got upstairs, Maisie was in the living room with Stella. She must've let Stella out of my room, where I'd left her during the couple hours of Ashford's self-defense course.

"We were looking for you two," Callum said, lounging on the couch. "How was the class?"

"It was...informative." Did my voice sound strange?

Crap. It did. If the amused expression on Callum's face was anything to go by.

Ashford's fingers brushed my side as he passed me. "Hey, monkey. Tell me about your day." While Ashford sat with his daughter and caught up, Callum followed me into the kitchen.

"You all right, Emma?" he asked. "You're a little pink. Must've been an intense class."

"Great exercise." I grabbed the kettle and filled it under the tap.

I had kissed Ashford. Kissed him *back*. After flirting with him all afternoon.

And it had been epic. Fireworks and the swelling sound of violins. The best kiss I'd ever had the pleasure of experiencing. The kind where all rational thought wiped away, and it was just our lips, our heartbeats, our tongues gently stroking.

Now I was overheating. I fanned my face.

Callum chuckled.

Geez, I needed to get out of this apartment for a while. I had *kissed Ashford*, and he wanted to "talk" later after Maisie went to bed, and I couldn't deal with that while also dealing with his brother's knowing laughter. I wasn't used to someone's entire family, and by extension everyone in town, knowing my business.

"I should take Stella on her walk," I said to Callum.

In my room, I pulled on my Nirvana hoodie and grabbed Stella's leash. My sneakers were by the front door, and I stopped there to slide my feet into them. "I'm taking Stella to get some exercise," I called out. "And I told Dixie I would drop by."

Maisie came running. "You have to go, Emma?"

"Promise I'll be back later. At the very least, I'll see you tomorrow morning. We can have frozen waffles for breakfast again. With honey butter, like I made last time."

She didn't look pleased. But she nodded. My compromise had been accepted.

Ashford held my wrist just before I opened the door. "You okay?" he whispered.

"Yeah."

"Is something wrong?" He glanced toward the kitchen. "Did Callum say something stupid?"

"No. Really. I'm going to stop by Dixie's. I told her I'd swing by with some dinner."

"Okay. Let me know if you need anything. I'll see you later." His hand moved down my arm and squeezed my fingers. He glanced at my mouth, and I had the feeling he was replaying the mental image of our kiss. Just like I was. I wanted to kiss him again right now.

All the more reason to excuse myself and take a walk so I could *think*.

Hooking Stella's leash to her collar, I tugged her toward the door. She dragged her feet, reluctant to leave without Maisie. "Stella, *come*."

Even my dog was getting attached to our life here. I just didn't know if that was the wisest thing.

In short, I was freaking out a little bit.

Outside, we aimed in the direction of Main Street while I texted Dixie. It wasn't *exactly* true that I'd already agreed to swing by her place. She'd suggested we have dinner one of these evenings. Why not this one?

She texted back that she was free, so I told her I would pick up some food. After placing an order at the Italian place, I had fifteen minutes to kill before our pasta would be ready. So I grabbed a bench around the corner in a quiet spot.

And I called one of my best friends. My stepmom, Madison.

"Emma! So you *do* have phone service out there in Colorado."

Just hearing her voice soothed some of my nerves. "Ha ha. I've sent a million texts."

"But that doesn't stop your dad from complaining that he never hears from you. He's out with Kelsea. They're having a daddy-daughter day. Thompson's with me, and he's, *erg*, really squirmy."

"That's fine. I just wanted to hear your voice. And maybe get some advice?"

"Hold on, I'm going to put your brother down in the playroom so he can smash some toy trucks together."

My sister Kelsea was five, and Thompson was two. I loved spending time with them whenever I got the chance. I'd started teaching Kelsea piano, and she'd caught the music bug like me. But she was Madison's little girl, so she was also sporty, blond, and loved wearing anything pink and covered in glitter.

Maisie would probably adore her.

"Emma?" my stepmom asked. "Are you still there?"

"Uh, yeah. Sorry. I zoned out."

"Something on your mind?"

"A lot, actually."

"Are you sure you don't want to wait until Nash is home? It should only be another half hour or so."

"It's not that kind of conversation."

There was a pause. But I knew Madison had her thinking face on.

"Babe, I would do just about anything for you. But if you're about to tell me something important is going on with you, you know I can't keep that from Nash. When it's pillow-talk time, things come out."

Curse their perfect marriage. My inner teenager was sticking her tongue out in disgust because, ew, my dad.

This was why I hadn't told Madison the real reason I was transferring.

"What if it's about a friend?"

"Okaaay. What's happening with this friend?"

Neither of us were buying my friend story. But at least she was going with it.

"She met a guy. A very sexy older guy who has a daughter."

"This is sounding familiar."

"Can you stop bringing up my dad?"

"I can't help it. You said *sexy older guy*." Madison laughed. "Sorry. How much older is your friend's guy?"

"He's thirty-four. A year older than *you*."

"That's not so bad. You do recall that your dad is thirteen years older than me."

But I doubted my father would see it that way. Because when it came to *me*, Nash Jennings tended to be unreasonable. "My friend really likes this guy. A lot. He's thoughtful, kind, an amazing father. And *really* sexy."

I sighed, remembering that kiss.

"You mentioned the sexy part. But what's the problem?"

I bent over to stroke Stella's soft fur. "It's complicated. Right? Seeing a man with a daughter. Especially when my friend likes this little girl and spends a lot of time with her. And my friend is leaving at the end of the summer. She can't stay."

"She could enjoy a good thing while she's got it. And just see what happens."

"But she's screwed up with relationships in the past, and she can't do that again. People get hurt." I pressed my face to Stella's neck.

Madison didn't say anything for a long moment.

"Em, did something happen last semester? You seemed really happy for a while, and then suddenly you were avoiding our calls and making plans to run off to Colorado for the summer. I didn't want to push you about it, but..."

A lump gathered in my throat, made of all the things I couldn't tell her. "I don't want to talk about it."

"All right. When you're ready, I'm here. So is your dad."

"I know." Except I would *never* be ready to share those details. No, thank you.

I got up from the bench, walking aimlessly with Stella down the street.

"But we were talking about your friend and this older man she likes. I do have some advice for her. If you want to pass it on."

I smiled and huffed a laugh. "Yes?"

"Tell your friend she's right. Relationships can hurt. But they can heal, too. When two people take a chance on each other, they might find it's everything they needed. Even if the relationship doesn't last. Does that help?"

I glanced up at the blue sky. "It does. Yeah."

We talked for a while longer. Madison told me all about what was going on with my family in California. Then shared recent stories from her job as a West Oaks PD hostage negotiator. But my mind started to wander to the blue brick building a few blocks away.

I wanted to see Maisie and Ashford.

I wanted to kiss him again.

Because no matter what other complications existed, he wasn't my ex. Ashford wasn't the type of man to keep some big, dark secret.

It was scary to take a chance on him. But my gut said it could be worth it.

✧

When I got back to the Big Blue Monster, there was a stack of mail on the floor in the lobby. Saturday mail delivery had arrived.

Holding Stella's leash with one hand, I scooped up the envelopes and flyers with the other and headed upstairs.

Dixie and I had enjoyed a relaxed dinner on her patio. As usual, she'd asked about Ashford and Maisie. I'd gotten tongue-tied, probably giving away that something was up from the way Dixie had grinned smugly.

I didn't even know what Ashford wanted. I couldn't imagine he was only interested in a one-night stand with me. Since we lived together, that would invite far too much drama, and Ashford seemed to prefer as little drama as possible.

Neither of us wanted to risk Maisie getting hurt. But we couldn't stay away from each other either. Touching him was electric. Kissing him? It was unforgettable.

I wanted that. Even if it was just for the summer.

Upstairs, I set the mail on the kitchen counter and sorted through the junk. The sounds of bedtime filtered down the hallway from Maisie's room. Ashford was reading stories, doing the voices of the characters just the way Maisie liked.

I smiled as I found a large pink envelope in the stack of mail. It was addressed to Maisie and had stickers of stars and rainbows all over it. So cute. I almost brought it to Maisie's room right then, but I didn't want to disturb bedtime.

I flipped it over absentmindedly, not meaning to be nosy. But my eyes went straight to the return address before I could stop myself.

A post office box in Los Angeles.

Who did Ashford know in LA?

Maisie's bedroom door shut, and Ashford's footsteps padded along the hallway rug. "You're home."

I turned around, leaving the envelope behind me on the counter. "Hi."

"How's Dixie?"

"She's good. She said hello. Did you have dinner with Callum?"

"Yeah, he stayed. Asked what was going on with you."

"What did you tell him?"

"Nothing. Wasn't sure what to say." He touched my hip, his fingers playing with the edge of my shirt. "I wasn't sure how to take the fact that you ran off after our kiss."

"It wasn't *right* after. But I needed to do some thinking."

"Come to any conclusions?"

"That I missed you."

"I missed you too." He came closer and rested his hands on either side of me on the counter. "I had a hard time thinking about anything *but* you all evening." He leaned in like he was going to kiss me. I lifted my chin.

Then his brows knitted, and he peered past me.

"What's that?"

"Oh, the mail? I brought it up."

He moved to one side of me and reached for the pink envelope. Flipped it and read the return address.

His skin went ashen. "This arrived today?"

"Yes. What's wrong?"

Ashford walked toward the other side of the kitchen. Facing away from me, he tore open the envelope and glanced briefly at whatever was inside.

My eyes widened as he tore the card and envelope into several pieces and shoved them deep inside the trashcan.

"What was that?" I asked.

"Something that shouldn't have come here. It was a mistake."

"But it was addressed to Maisie."

"And you shouldn't have seen it." His voice was tight. Angry. "Just pretend you didn't."

"How can I pretend I didn't see it?" I knew I wasn't entitled to Ashford's private business. But how could I just ignore that?

He was upset. More than that. Ashford was *afraid*. Something I had never seen.

"The return address was in Los Angeles," I said.

"So?"

"Someone called you from an LA area code the day I had a migraine. Was that really a wrong number?"

He didn't answer for a while, and when he did, it wasn't satisfying. "There are things I can't tell you."

"Is this about Maisie's safety?"

"Yes. I believe it is."

I exhaled. "Then you don't have to say anything else. I'm sorry I brought the envelope upstairs where she could see it."

"You didn't know." He wiped a hand over his face. "But it would be best if you don't mention this to Grace or Callum."

My stomach sank. All of this felt off. *Wrong.*

"You don't want me to tell your siblings? I...I don't know if..."

"It's hard to explain."

"I get that. But this seems really weird. And concerning. This is some kind of secret from your family?"

"Emma, you don't understand," he snapped.

"Clearly not."

He scrubbed his hands through his hair. "I'm an asshole."

"You did sound like one just then."

He leaned against the counter, hunching his shoulders. Neither of us spoke. I was so bewildered.

A few moments ago, he'd been smiling. Happy. Now he looked like he hadn't slept in a month.

"Ashford..."

"I shouldn't have kissed you earlier. That was a mistake. I'm sorry."

My mouth opened, then shut. His sudden shift had blindsided me. Especially the way he'd said it, so devoid of emotion.

"I'm sorry too."

If this affected his daughter's safety, then of course that should be his priority. But I had a hunch why he was pushing me away.

I was getting too close. Interfering with the careful boundaries he'd put up, just like when I first got to town.

Well, I called bullshit.

But I wasn't going to stick around to prove him wrong. I'd already gotten involved with a man who had secrets, and I couldn't put myself in that situation again.

It hurt, though. So, so much. Because every cell in my being kept telling me to trust him. But if Ashford refused to let me in, there was nothing I could do.

SIXTEEN
Ashford

I WAS SITTING ALONE at a dark corner table at Hearthstone, nursing my second beer, when Grace came up to me. "What are you doing over here all by yourself? You look like you're brooding."

"Probably because I *am* brooding."

The majority of my anger was directed at myself. But still. Brooding.

"You want to tell me why? Or do I have to guess?"

I took a long pull of my beer.

Maisie was staying at Piper's tonight. Teller had bought Ollie a telescope, and the kids were going to stay up to see stars. Maisie had begged and pleaded until I agreed. Which had left me to my own devices.

It had been two miserable days since that incident in the kitchen. The pink envelope covered in stickers and addressed to my daughter.

The fucking nerve, sending that to my home.

What if Maisie had gotten to it first, instead of me? But in a way, it wasn't surprising. Those phone calls from Los Angeles had been getting more frequent. I had known she would escalate eventually. Not that I had a clue what to do about it.

The real issue was me. How I had reacted in front of Emma. I hadn't known what to say to make her understand. How could I, when this was a secret that even Grace and Callum didn't know?

So instead of coming up with something that would make me look like a reasonable human being, I had impulsively told her that kissing her was a mistake. My actual mistake was hoping I could somehow wish my problems away. That if I ignored them hard enough, they would disappear.

But nothing about Emma could *ever* be a mistake.

Those words had been haunting me in the two days since. Yet I couldn't take them back, either. Because then I would have to explain.

Hence the reason I was brooding.

"I think Emma's going to move out," I said.

Grace got a strange look on her face. Then she pulled out the chair opposite me and sat down.

"That wasn't an invitation for you to make yourself comfortable."

"Since when do I need an invitation?" She reached across the table, snagged my glass, and took a sip. "Why do you think Emma's going to move out?"

"Because I overheard her saying something to Dixie."

"But she hasn't said anything to you?"

"Not really." Probably because Emma and I had gone back to not speaking much. She was amazing at being the ideal babysitter and all-around fairy godmother to my daughter, while having as few interactions with me as possible.

Grace rolled her eyes. "Why don't you just ask her about her plans? She's here tonight."

"Where?" I sat up straighter, glancing around at the other tables and at the bar.

There she was, sitting at a table by herself and writing in her journal. The one *I'd* bought her. I took some satisfaction in that. At least she didn't despise me so much that she'd gotten rid of it.

"All right, enough sad broody faces," my sister said. "Out with it. What happened, exactly?"

I couldn't tell her that. So I went with, "We had a fight."

"That's exactly why fucking your roommate is a bad idea."

I sat back so hard my chair bumped the wall behind me. "Geez, Grace."

"Did you think your little sister didn't know that word? You and Grayden taught me the f-word by the time I was ten."

"Still don't want to hear you saying it in that context. Especially about *me*."

She smirked. "What about when I'm discussing *my* conquests? Not that I have a lot of those."

I cringed. "Please stop. I'm not sleeping with Emma. Just so you know."

"But you want to."

I wasn't denying it. I swiped my beer from Grace instead.

"What about the fact that she'll be leaving in a couple months?"

"I'd say that's low on the list of my worries at this point. She's barely even speaking to me."

"You're really upset about this."

"*Yes*, I am."

Grace tapped her fingers on the table for a few seconds. For some reason, she looked guilty. "Did Emma tell you I stopped by to have a chat with her?"

"You did *what*?"

"Elias told me she'd moved in with you. I thought that was pretty sudden. So, I went over to meet her. I basically told her not to get involved with you unless she's serious about it."

"Who said I'm looking for something serious?" Though as I said that, it hit a wrong chord inside me. What I felt for Emma wasn't just casual. Otherwise, why would I be so torn up over it?

"I just don't want you getting hurt," Grace said. "I'm aware that Callum has been telling you to have a fling, but the woman sharing your business space *and* your apartment might not be a good choice. I should've told you I spoke to her, though. For that, I'm sorry."

Like me, my sister was cautious about taking risks. I never had to worry about Grace getting into dangerous situations or being careless with her wellbeing. That was probably why I'd felt comfortable being in the Army, stationed on the other side of the country, while she was in college.

But it wasn't a great feeling for my little sister to be stepping in to protect me. It was supposed to be the other way around.

"I messed up with Emma all on my own," I said. "That wasn't your fault."

"Yet you won't tell me exactly how you messed up."

"And I'm not going to."

She sighed and adjusted her glasses. "There's one more thing I need to say."

"I am not going to like this, am I?"

"Is it possible you've been lonely for so long that you're latching on to the first pretty, nice woman to fall in your lap?"

I looked over at Emma's table again. Longing throbbed in my chest. Was Grace right? Was I so closed off I couldn't even see my own motives?

"There's so much stuff we don't discuss in this family," Grace said. "Like about our childhood. We all pretend like none of it matters anymore, but it does."

"Do you remember me telling you about my best friend from the Army? Dane Knightly? He grew up with more privilege than you or I can imagine. Mansions and nannies and boarding schools."

"You told me about him. I seem to remember he offered to fly us all to New York one Christmas, and you didn't take him up on it." She poked my shoulder. I chuckled.

"That may have happened. But Dane's childhood wasn't happy either. We all have shit to deal with."

"I wasn't talking about how much money we had. I meant how Mom practically had to raise us herself, and when she died,

Dad couldn't be bothered to step up. And Grayden's issues. We could try to find our brother. Don't you ever wonder how he is?"

"*No*," I said sharply. "Absolutely not."

"But it might help if you and Cal and I face that stuff instead of hoping it'll disappear. This family is worth it. *You* are worth it. You've done so much to make Maisie the joyful, healthy little girl that she is, but you have to take care of yourself too." She got up to hug me. "I love you."

"I love you too."

But this conversation hadn't made me feel any better.

✧

After Grace left, I ordered some food. I saw Emma do the same over at her table. Every time I glanced at her, she was looking away. Maybe she hadn't noticed I was here at all.

My potato skins arrived. I stared at the basket of food and decided I was being stupid. I had to say something. Be a man about this and apologize. What was the point of us both sitting here in this crowded brewery by ourselves?

But as I picked up my beer and food to join her, I saw some guy walk over to Emma's table and start chatting her up. Beating me to the punch.

What the hell was this?

I'd never seen this guy before. Looked like a tourist, with his expensive athletic clothes. Probably came here after a day of mountain biking. He was leaning over Emma's table and grinning at her, the flirtation obvious even from across the room.

She wasn't going to fall for that. Was she?

But then she picked up her plate of nachos and her drink and joined the tourist guy at another table, where his friends were waiting. A mix of men and women, all in their twenties. I couldn't hear what they were saying, but it was obvious greetings were being exchanged.

I sat back down heavily in my seat, my mood even blacker than before.

"Excuse me. Is this seat taken?"

I turned to see a blond by my table with her hand on the empty chair across from me. I nodded, thinking she needed to take the chair. "Go for it." Not like I needed it, since I was very much a one-man show at the moment.

But then the blond sat down, smiling and biting her lower lip nervously. When Emma wore that expression, it usually made me want to pull her closer. But on this stranger, it made me wary.

"My friends dared me to come over here." She flipped her hair past her shoulder, gesturing at another table of women who were watching us and grinning. "My boyfriend and I broke up yesterday, and apparently I've been moping, so they're peer pressuring me to meet new people."

"That's not very nice of them. Moping can be very satisfying."

"I know, right? I was doing fine at home with my gallon of ice cream before they shoved me in the car and drove me out here." She smiled again, eyes crinkling. "I'm Callie."

"Ashford."

"I have to admit, I was curious why you're sitting here by yourself. Waiting for someone?"

I grunted noncommittally. "Not really."

She brightened, as if my response had encouraged her.

Shit.

Callie tried to make conversation with me, and I did my best not to be rude, though my best wasn't that great. She was probably in her thirties, like me. Seemed like a nice person. I was sorry she'd had a bad breakup. But it was hard to muster the energy to be friendly.

Not when I could barely look away from the horror movie unfolding across the room.

Mountain-biker guy had his arm draped on the back of Emma's chair. As if he hadn't met her all of ten minutes ago. Then he leaned closer, saying something into her ear.

The vein at my temple pulsed.

"So, who is she?" Callie asked.

"What?" I grunted.

"That pretty brunette at the other table. Someone special?" She smiled and took a sip of her martini. "It's okay, I already figured out I have zero chance with you. I'm just wondering why you're over *here*, since you so clearly would rather be over *there*."

I heaved a sigh. "She's my roommate. We had an argument the other day. Haven't made up."

"Why not?"

"It's complicated."

"But you miss her." It wasn't a question.

"I do. She's..." I sorted through the words that surfaced in my head. *Smart. Determined. Funny. Beautiful.* "She means a lot to me."

That realization hit me like a left hook. Should've seen it coming, but it stunned me all the same.

I wanted to make Emma laugh. Spend time with her, and feel the warmth of her smile on me. I wanted to hang out with her and Maisie. The three of us.

Grace had it wrong. I wasn't going for the first woman to come my way. I'd had opportunities before. Emma was the first woman who'd broken past every barrier I put up just by being *her*.

"Then what's stopping you? Is it the guy she's sitting with?"

"*Him*? No. He's nobody." Unless she decided to leave here with him, but I didn't care to consider that possibility. "It's me. My last relationship...ended badly."

Callie tapped her glass against mine. "I feel you there."

The other day, when that envelope from LA had arrived, it forced me to think about Lori's secrets. Things that still weren't resolved, even three years after losing her. I'd been holding on to the idea that I would understand her death someday. I was stuck picking up the pieces and trying to make some sort of picture with them.

They were never going to fit.

I was afraid of what might happen if the world knew the truth I was hiding. But the tighter I held that secret, the harder it was for anyone to get close.

I wanted to hold Emma close. So damn much.

I glanced at her table again. Then I cursed. My head swiveled as I looked for Emma, but she was gone.

"Oh, no." Callie gave me a sympathetic look. "The guy next to her is gone too. They must've left together. I'm sorry."

No way. I was not going to let this happen. Not after what I'd just realized. "I gotta go."

"Are you going after her? Please say you're going after her."

"Yeah. I am."

"Good luck!"

I ran for the door.

SEVENTEEN
Emma

From the corner of my eye, I watched Ashford chatting up some blond. Unbelievable.

The man had kissed me two days ago, but just like that, he'd moved on to the next.

"I'm going to head out," I said.

Josh, the out-of-towner I'd been sitting with, looked disappointed. "We were just going to play some pool. You don't want to stay for a round?"

"No, thanks. Have fun though. It was nice meeting you." I finished my soda and got the heck out of there.

The last thing in the world I wanted to see was Ashford hooking up. I now had confirmation that our kiss the other day had meant nothing to him.

Ugh, my chest was in a vise.

Just outside the brewery, Main Street was busy, but the crowd thinned as I walked. It was a cool summer night with a bright moon overhead. The air smelled of pine, and I tried to focus on all those pleasant sensations instead of the fist currently crushing my heart.

The only reason I'd gone out tonight was to get away from Ashford's apartment. Maisie had a sleepover at Piper's, so I would've been alone with him. Not something I could handle. But the brewery had been the wrong call.

I had been taking some space the last couple of days, just for my own wellbeing. Cuddling up with Stella, writing in my journal. I'd been spending just as much time with Maisie as before, since this had nothing to do with her. But after two days of rehashing what had happened and writing about my feelings, I still felt the same about Ashford.

I liked him. Wanted to be around him.

Which made me such a fool.

In the brewery tonight, it had been so hard not to stare across the room at the burly, bearded martial arts instructor. Even when Josh had invited me to join him and his friends. I'd tried to appreciate the distraction, but there was no hope of some new face taking the place of Ashford in my thoughts.

It wasn't even about him being sexy as hell. It was the man underneath the gruff exterior. The sides of him he let me see when he finally let down his guard.

The man who'd listened to me play my work in progress for the very first time—a nerve-wracking thing for any artist—and who'd kissed me right after.

And then pushed me away that same night.

I turned the corner. There were fewer streetlights over here, leaving the sidewalk mostly in shadow. At least I didn't have too far to go. But I couldn't stay at Ashford's anymore, not now.

I had to move out of his apartment. There was no other solution. It would be a stretch for my budget unless I moved in with Dixie's friend and her potentially creepy grandson. Or accepted Dixie's offer of her couch, but as much as I loved her, that wasn't my top choice. She had a tendency to mother, and I already had two of those.

I hoped I would be able to find a new place that was in walking distance of the Big Blue Monster.

But even if I moved, I would still have to see Ashford almost *every single day.* Especially if I continued babysitting Maisie, which I wanted to keep doing. There was no escaping him.

The sound of footsteps snapped my attention back to the present moment.

I didn't think much of it at first. Silver Ridge was no metropolis, but there were always people out and about, especially this close to the business district.

But when the footsteps didn't disappear, instead continuing to echo behind me, I glanced back.

Nobody was there. Nobody I could see.

"Hello?" I said. No answer.

My skin crawled with a sense of unease.

While I had grown up in a small beach town, I had spent the last year living in LA. I knew how important it was to have situational awareness. And don't even get me started on my dad's lectures about safety. I had experienced danger myself when I was younger.

Something felt off.

I thought of that creep in the blue rain slicker who had been watching me and Maisie weeks ago. There hadn't been any sign of him since. Or of anyone else following me or doing anything suspicious. Until tonight.

Maybe I shouldn't have left the brewery alone. In LA, I never would've walked home by myself in a million years. But I'd gotten so comfortable here. After a month of living in Hart County, it felt like a second home. A far safer one than where I'd come from.

But now, my mind went to Lori. To the person who might've been on the highway with her that night three years ago. Who'd pushed her. Silver Ridge wasn't always safe.

Call Ashford, I thought. But he was busy tonight with his new *friend*. The blond. Calling 911 wasn't an option either. Not unless I knew for sure I was being followed.

I stuck my hand into my messenger bag to close it around my pepper spray.

"If you're following me," I said loudly, "don't. I have a weapon and know how to use it."

I sped up, ducking around a corner at the next building, and hid in an alcove. The footsteps started again and kept coming.

Breathe, I told myself, remembering all the advice my dad and Madison had given me over the years. And what Ashford had said in the self-defense class the other day.

Move fast. Be aggressive.

When the footsteps had almost reached me, I lunged out, holding my pepper spray up with my finger on the trigger. "Are you following me?"

The man on the sidewalk reared back, his face a mask of shock. "Jesus, you scared me."

"Are you following me?" I demanded again.

"No!" He brushed off his polo and khakis, blowing out a breath. Then he laughed, and I recognized his perfect white smile.

He was the dentist, Dr. Carmichael. Piper's ex-husband.

"Didn't expect my night to get so exciting. You thought you were being followed?"

"Pretty sure I was."

"Well, not by me. I was just heading home. I'm Danny Carmichael."

I lowered the pepper spray, though I didn't put it back in my bag. "I know. I've seen your photo in your office window on Main Street."

He laughed again. "Of course. And you must be the new girl who's staying with Ashford O'Neal. I've seen you around. Sadly, I don't recall your name."

His eyes traced down my body, slowly moving back up again.

I gave him a brittle smile. *Eyes to yourself, buddy.*

"I'm Emma. I know your ex-wife, Piper. She's a good friend."

His smile dulled.

"I should get going," I added.

"Happy to walk you."

After the way he'd just ogled me, I didn't relish the idea of him escorting me home. But maybe it was better than nothing. Especially if I texted several friends that I'd be with him.

Then a gruff voice said, "I'll walk her," and a very different kind of shiver passed across my skin.

Ashford had just turned the corner. He frowned at Danny, whose smile turned into a smug smirk. "Ashford."

His nostrils flared. "Danny. You can go now."

"I see you haven't learned civility since the last time we spoke."

"Nope, I'm the same. I assume you are too."

Danny's gaze slid back over to me. "Pleasure to meet you, Emma. See you around."

"*Asshat*," Ashford muttered as Danny walked away and disappeared around the corner. "Never liked that guy."

I was about to ask why, but then I noticed how hard Ashford was breathing. "Are you okay? You're out of breath."

"I just ran up and down all the surrounding streets trying to find you." He pushed back his hair from his forehead. "Didn't know which direction you were heading after you left the brewery."

I tucked the pepper spray back into my bag. "You could've called my phone."

"Would you have answered? I thought you left with that tourist you were cozying up to and went back to his hotel room."

I'd had similar thoughts about Ashford and the blond. Which only stoked my anger. "Why on earth would I do that?"

"Because I assume he's not a jerk if you spent so much time with him tonight. And he's age appropriate. Probably has a carefree lifestyle and multiple zeros in his bank account."

My brow wrinkled. "Do you think I *should've* gone with him?"

"Fuck no," Ashford growled, and closed the distance between us.

His hands cupped my face. I inhaled, chin lifting as I looked up at him.

"I'm sorry," he whispered.

Warmth spread from every place he was touching me. "What about the blond?"

"What blond?"

"The woman you were with."

"Callie? I told her about you. She wanted me to go after you."

"*She's* the reason you came after me?" I started to push back from him, but he held on to me, not letting me move an inch.

"No. I came after you because I've been a complete dumbass."

"You mean a D-word?"

He huffed a laugh. "Exactly. I'm sorry. It wasn't a mistake, kissing you before. I should never have said that."

My hands traced a path up his T-shirt from his stomach to his chest. "I had no interest in that guy at the brewery. There's only one man I can't stop thinking about. Even if he is a D-word sometimes."

"So you don't hate me?" His nose brushed mine.

"How could I possibly hate you? But we still need to talk."

"We do. I have a lot to explain. If you'll give me another chance."

I whispered, "What do you think I'm doing right now?"

Ashford rested his forehead against mine, eyes closing. And it felt so *right*. The cold chill of the night air didn't matter anymore. The unease I'd felt earlier. It all disappeared.

I wanted this man so much. He had the power to hurt me. Yet my whole heart told me to trust him.

When he pressed a kiss to my temple, it felt even better. Then he took my hand. "Come on. Let's go home. I'll tell you everything."

EIGHTEEN
Emma

STELLA BOUNDED over when we opened the door to the apartment. I bent down to give her some love. "You would think I didn't even walk her and feed her dinner."

Ashford knelt beside me to rub Stella's belly. "She hates being alone."

"Yeah, she does. That's why I try not to leave her too long."

"If someone's alone for a long time, they get used to it. Until eventually, they're afraid of *not* being alone instead. Even if they're really fucking lonely."

I didn't think we were talking about Stella anymore.

I reached for Ashford's hand and laced our fingers.

We'd held hands the entire walk home, which had been the best feeling. Touching him was electric and exciting, every time, yet it made me feel grounded too. Like nothing bad could happen as long as he stayed beside me.

But we still had to talk, and I had no idea what to expect.

Ashford stood, pulling me up with him. "It's a nice night. Should we go up to the roof?"

"I didn't know there was anything up there."

"I would've shown you before, but I don't let Maisie up there. Too afraid she'll fall. But I bet you'll love it."

We went to the kitchen window. Ashford pushed the frame up, revealing an old-fashioned metal fire escape with a ladder leading up to the roof, and another ladder that could lower down to the ground.

We climbed outside onto the rickety metal landing. "You sure this is safe?" I asked.

"If it can hold me, it'll hold you. It's solid." He put a hand on my lower back, steadying me. I held on to the hand rails and climbed. At the top, I came out onto the flat roof of the building. Someone had laid out squares of fake grass, topping them with two faded lawn chairs. Planters with fake flowers completed the impression of a backyard garden. It was nowhere near fancy, but something about the colors and the cheerfulness, even at night, made it endearing.

He was right. I loved it. "This is adorable."

"Lori set this up." Ashford led me to the chairs. He pushed them as close together as possible, and we sat, our arms pressed together and hands clasped. "But the best part is when you look up."

I sat back, my gaze drifting upward. And my jaw dropped with a gasp.

Stars. Millions of them. They seemed infinitely far, yet also close and bright enough I could touch them. The Milky Way stretched directly overhead, a gauzy ribbon waving its way across the sky.

I had noticed there were a lot more stars visible in Silver Ridge than Southern California, but somehow I hadn't been in the perfect time or place to see them in such spectacular fashion. Until now.

Maybe I'd been waiting for just the right moment. The right person to share it with.

I gripped Ashford's hand. "This is amazing. Why aren't you up here every night?" He probably didn't want to leave Maisie alone, but surely he could spare a few minutes to sneak away. That girl was a deep sleeper. And this was too incredible to miss.

"Too focused on other stuff." He squeezed my hand back. "Lately, the sweet, beautiful music teacher who lives down the hall."

"I thought you didn't like that music teacher," I teased.

"I tried not to like her. But it turns out she's irresistible."

I leaned across the arm rests of our chairs to put my head on his shoulder.

For a while, we took in the view together. It was so quiet here. Dark, but the darkness felt comfortable and peaceful instead of threatening.

But I didn't forget for one second that Ashford and I needed to talk.

"So," I prompted. "That pink card someone sent to Maisie…"

His Adam's apple moved as he swallowed. "Lori's younger sister sent it. Maisie's aunt."

"Is she dangerous somehow?"

"In a way, yes. Very dangerous. If she wants to be."

"Okay." I tried to imagine what he could mean, but my mind drew a blank. "Ashford, you don't have to tell me if you don't want to. It's all right."

His brown and gold eyes pinned me. "No, I need to. But it's going to sound strange. You might not even believe it. So I'd better just spit it out."

I nodded, ready to listen with an open mind to whatever he was about to tell me.

I waited.

"Lori's sister is a famous singer. Ayla Maxwell."

I wished I could say I had a calm, mature reaction.

"*Shut. Up.* You're not serious."

"See? You don't believe me."

"No, I do." I shook my head, trying to catch my brain up to this new reality. Because *wow*. "You mean, cover of Vanity Fair Ayla Maxwell? Grammy for best album of the year? Face of a billion-dollar makeup brand? *That* Ayla Maxwell?"

"Yes. That's the one."

"You're sure."

His lips pressed flat together. Zero humor in his expression. Holy cow. He was serious.

I folded up my legs in the lawn chair and turned all the way to face him. "I'm guessing this is a long story. Start wherever you want. I will do my best not to have Ayla's latest song running through my head."

"Emma." His mouth twitched in a half-smile.

"I'm sorry, it's just—"

"I really want to kiss you."

My heart thumped. "I'm sitting right here. Not going to stop you."

Ashford leaned forward, tilting his head. His lips looked so inviting.

But then he grimaced. "It *is* a long story. It's not my favorite either. If I kiss you, I won't be able to stop, and I need to get this out."

"Okay. Kissing later, then."

He took a deep breath. Blew it out again.

"I told you about Lori's family. How her dad, the colonel, was so cruel to them. But Ayla got the worst of it. She was a sensitive kid. Different. After their mom left, Ayla ran away to New York City. She was sixteen. This was about a year after I'd met them. Lori tried to get in touch with her. To send her money. But Ayla wanted nothing to do with any of her family."

"I assume Maxwell is a stage name."

"You assume right. Lori googled her constantly over the years, trying to keep track of her sister the best she could. By the time Lori got pregnant with Maisie, Ayla was developing a fanbase online. Then her career blew up like wildfire. Ayla was all over TV, radio, socials. The damn magazines in the grocery checkout line. Lori was proud of her sister, but it hurt too. Since Ayla didn't want Lori in her life."

"I bet."

"It was wild. Suddenly, Ayla was a household name with

millions of people clamoring for any scrap of info about her. We decided it would be better if nobody knew Lori was her sister. We didn't want any of that attention on us. Much less to seem like we were capitalizing on her fame. I couldn't tell Callum because my little brother has trouble keeping his mouth shut. But if I didn't tell Callum, that meant I couldn't tell Grace."

"That must've been hard."

"A little, but really, Ayla's life didn't have anything to do with us. Her fame was like a galaxy out in space. We could see it, but it might as well have been another universe. A couple of years went by. Then Lori's father died, and we went for the funeral. Ayla didn't come. She sent some assistant. But I think that's how Lori managed to get Ayla's number."

Ashford pulled a phone from his pocket. His device had a black case, but this phone was glittery purple. His knuckles were white from how hard he was squeezing it.

"Was that Lori's?" I asked.

"She dropped it the night she died, and the police found it. I guessed her passcode after a couple tries. Checked her call log. Lori had called a Los Angeles number several times in the weeks before she died. Including the last night of her life."

"Ayla?"

He nodded. "Ayla didn't show up to Lori's funeral either, thankfully, because that would've been a circus. But I called that LA number. Ayla answered. She claimed Lori had left her a voicemail the night she died, but there was too much static to hear what she'd said."

"Do you believe that?"

"Not really. But what can I do? Before then, I'd realized Lori was keeping something from me. I thought it was about dating some new guy. But what if Lori was worried about something, and called her sister? Because for some reason, she couldn't trust me."

I knew he was thinking of what the driver had seen just before Lori was hit. Someone else on the highway who'd pushed her.

"After Lori's death, why would Ayla keep that from you? Or from the police?"

He shook his head. "Wish I knew."

"What's going on now? Why has Ayla been contacting you?"

"To see Maisie. Be a part of her life. Ayla finally realized that Maisie is the only family she has left, and she won't stop calling. I block one number, and she just gets another. Always an LA area code, even though I assume she's calling from all over the world."

"But you don't trust her."

"Not even close. I still think she knows more about Lori's death, but for her own reasons, she'll never tell me." He rubbed his face. "Ayla has the kind of money and power to destroy our lives if she wants to. Even if she means well, can you imagine paparazzi swarming all over Silver Ridge? Knocking on our door? Following us around?"

I shuddered. "Definitely not."

"I don't want Ayla giving Maisie expensive gifts or taking her to movie premieres or who knows what. That's not the life I want for my kid. But it's more than that. What if she demands visitation? Or worse? She could hire a team of lawyers to challenge me for custody of my own daughter."

"But she has no legal rights compared to you. She's not Maisie's parent."

"Would that matter if she gets in front of the right judge? How do I fight back against somebody with the resources she has? Someone like her could turn the whole world against me. She hasn't told the media about us yet, but what'll happen if she does?"

I couldn't imagine the stress he'd been under all these years. Fearing that a celebrity could upend his life, and he'd have no way to fight back against it. For a man with multiple black belts, who'd made a career out of teaching people to defend themselves, that had to be terrifying.

"I have to protect Maisie from that," he said. "The only way is keeping Ayla out of our lives. There's only one other person I've told any of this, my Army buddy Dane, but I never told him Ayla's specific identity. He said he'd front me the money to hire lawyers if it comes to that. I hope it doesn't."

"Wish I could do more to help. I want to smuggle you guys into protective custody. My uncle Jake works for the government. He could pull some strings." I was only half kidding.

He smiled and pulled me closer, burying his face in my hair. "You've helped a lot just by being here."

I was honored that he'd trusted me. "I won't say anything to anyone."

"I know you wouldn't." Ashford sat back to look at me, cupping my face with his palm. His thumb traced my cheekbone. "But it feels so good to tell you. I've been holding that in for a long damn time."

We went back down to the apartment. Ashford descended the ladder first, then waited on the landing, grasping my hand to help me down as soon as I was in reach. We climbed through the window.

In the kitchen, he folded me into his arms. "I like you, Emma. I *want* you. I can't remember the last time I wanted anyone like this."

"I want you too." Shivers of anticipation ran across my skin. I wanted to feel his bare skin on mine, to feel him inside me. But this was perfect too. Just holding each other. Sharing comfort.

"Would you spend the night with me?" He rubbed his soft bearded cheek against my temple. "We don't have to do anything you're not ready for. But I'm dying to have you close. I want to hold you tonight."

"Definitely." I wanted that too, and I figured we should take advantage of Maisie being gone for the night. "My bed or yours?"

"Mine. I've been imagining you in my bed for a while. Already feels like you belong there."

✧

We separated to get ready. I went to my room, shutting the door and leaning back against it.

I had not expected that I'd spend tonight in Ashford's bed. Thank goodness I had shaved my legs.

Stella jumped up from her bed where she'd been lounging and blinked at me. Almost like she was asking, *Are you sure about this?* I sat on the floor, nearly getting knocked over when she climbed into my lap. "I'm good, Stella. I promise."

I still had some doubts. But not about Ashford. I never would've guessed his secret, but he was exactly the man he seemed to be. A really good one.

After some debate, I changed into a loose top without a bra and cotton shorts. Ashford wasn't in the bathroom, so I quickly took care of business, brushing my teeth and washing my face. When I emerged, I found Ashford there in the hallway. He wore the same T-shirt as before but had traded his jeans for comfy pajama pants. His smile looked just as soft.

"Ready?" He held out his hand.

I slid mine into his grip, and he led me into his bedroom. The lights were low, and he'd already turned down the covers. He kissed my cheek as we stood beside the bed. "Get comfortable. I'm going to double check everything's locked up."

"Have you heard from Piper?"

He grinned. "Yeah, just texted with her. The kids finally went to bed after using Ollie's new telescope in the backyard."

"Perfect night for stargazing."

He touched my chin affectionately. "Yep. It was. But the prettiest thing I saw wasn't in the sky."

"That's very sweet, Mr. O'Neal."

"Too much?"

"Just enough."

He brushed his lips over mine, the gentlest hint of a kiss, and then went to check the apartment. I climbed into his bed, snuggling under the covers and inhaling the scent of him that clung to the sheets.

After a few minutes, his warm, heavy body slid in behind me. I turned and rolled right into his arms.

"Thank you for tonight," he said.

"Thank you for sharing so much with me."

He was just looking at me, fingertips tracing lines back and forth along my side. So I added, "If you don't kiss me soon, I'll take matters into my own hands."

He laughed, his tongue darting out over his lower lip.

Our kisses were gentle at first. But when I moaned against his lips, Ashford's grip on my upper arm tightened. He shifted me onto my back. His tongue nudged at the seam of my mouth for entrance. I opened up, loving when his tongue pushed inside and glided against mine.

I draped my leg around his hip, inching closer, and the hard line of his cock suddenly pressed into my other thigh. "*Oh*," I breathed.

I felt him smiling against my mouth. "Don't mind him. You're getting me excited. But don't worry, we'll take this slow."

"I'm not as innocent as you seem to think."

His gaze was dark and intense as it moved over me, assessing. "Is that so?"

Ashford took my hands and pinned them onto the mattress above my head. His thumbs pressed firmly into my palms. His hips moved, erection rubbing between my legs through our layers of clothes.

I whimpered.

"Have you thought about this before?" he asked. "You and me, here, in my bed?"

"Mmhmm."

"Did you make yourself come?" he murmured into my ear.

"Yes. But I wanted it to be you." I gasped and sighed at the way his hard length massaged my core at the perfect spot. "Your cock. Your tongue. On my clit, inside me. All over me."

"Show me how you touched yourself."

He shifted to unpin me. I traced my hand down my stomach

and into my shorts. Using two fingertips, I rubbed circles over my clit while not breaking eye contact with him.

"Spread your legs wider."

The bossy tone of his voice made me wet. I bent my knees, letting them splay open. Ashford made a growly sound and nudged his own fingers along my inner thigh until they reached the juncture between my thighs. He pushed aside the thin cotton of my sleep shorts. "*Fuck*, Emma. No panties."

While I rubbed my clit, he played with my opening. Pushed one thick finger inside, then two. I moaned at the sensation of fullness.

And then I cried out, an orgasm suddenly taking me over with a rush of pleasure.

Sliding his hand away, he grinned deviously. "You're right. You're not innocent at all."

A sudden jolt of insecurity hit me. I felt myself flinch, and I glanced away from him.

"Hey, you okay?"

"Yeah." But a tiny thread of guilt had just wiggled its way into my mind, even though I'd tried to keep it away. Ashford had been honest with me tonight. Didn't I owe him the same? "There's something I should tell you. About why I left my grad program."

"You said it was a bad breakup."

"It was. Very bad. But I didn't tell you exactly what happened, and I don't know if..." My voice got thick. I cleared my throat. "If you'll see me the same way after you find out."

Ashford lay on his side next to me. He propped up onto his elbow. "Emma, look at me."

I did, blinking fast to keep my eyes from filling with tears.

"I see everything I need to. You listened to me earlier, and I'll do the same for you if you want to tell me. But it's not going to change anything."

I nodded. Breathed through my uncertainty. "My ex was a theater director. I was a musician for a show. He insisted we keep our relationship secret, and I thought it was because he was my boss. But it turned out, his real concern was that he's married. I found out when his wife returned from teaching in England. She's a professor in the music department at my school. Everyone knows now, and there's no way I can show my face there again."

"Why should you be ashamed? Why should you be the one to leave? You did nothing wrong."

I disagreed, but it meant everything to hear him say it.

His mouth twisted, eyes narrowing dangerously. "Good thing we're in a different state. Otherwise, I'd be tempted to sneak up on this ex of yours and put him in a chokehold, and there's already one O'Neal brother with a prison record."

Laughter snuck up from my chest. I pressed my lips together, but soon I was shaking with it. In an imaginary showdown between Ashford and my ex, there was zero doubt about who'd win. "I shouldn't be laughing at that violent mental image, but I can't help it."

"You can tell me all your bad thoughts."

"If you tell me yours."

"Deal. But for the rest of tonight, I don't intend to do anything more than hold you and kiss you. Because no matter what we do together, you're safe with me."

"What about..." I glanced down at the obvious erection tenting his pants. "I'd love to help you with that."

"Another time. I can wait." Ashford switched off his bedside lamp and put his arm out. I snuggled into him, and he tucked me against his side like I was his matching puzzle piece. He dropped a kiss to my head. I was all cozy and relaxed when he sat up again.

"What is it?" I asked.

"Is Stella in your room?"

"Yes."

"Just thought she might want to come in with us. No point in her being alone."

"She'll get on the bed," I warned.

"I don't mind." He got up and went into the hall. I heard another door open, and a moment later, Stella bounded in. Just as

I'd expected, she jumped up onto the mattress and lay down next to me. She knew the rules for my room, but in a different space, all bets were off. Ashford returned right after.

"Hold on, that's my spot."

"Told you. She thinks it's a slumber party."

He nudged Stella toward our feet. She scooted, still happy as can be. If she thought it was strange that Ashford and I were in bed together, she didn't show it.

He pulled me against him, and we got settled. Stella inched back between us as much as she dared. I heard him laugh softly. And then he moved his legs to give her a bit more space.

If I hadn't already been swooning for this man, it would've happened right then. For Ashford, I was a goner.

NINETEEN
Ashford

WAKING up next to Emma was better than I could've imagined. It had been way too long since I'd woken up next to a woman. But this wasn't just any woman.

Emma's mouth was a pink rosebud in sleep, and I was dying to kiss it. Her dark eyelashes splayed over her olive-toned skin. My sheets smelled like lavender-vanilla, and I hoped it would be a long time before that scent faded.

I didn't want to be thinking already about her leaving. But it was there. Never leaving my mind. Even though I'd decided, *to hell with it*. I was tired of letting fears drive me. In my classes, I taught my students to overcome fear. What the hell was wrong with me if I couldn't do the same?

I couldn't believe I'd told her about Ayla though. Part of me still thought I was a fool for risking that. People did unconscionable things to get access to fame or money. But Emma would never do anything that could jeopardize Maisie's wellbeing.

Now that Emma was here in my bed, in my arms, it seemed like the risk had paid off. Hard to focus on negative what-ifs when I felt so damn comfortable right now.

Stella's head popped up like she'd realized I was awake, and she jumped down to wait by my bedroom door.

"Alright, I'm coming," I whispered.

I took Stella downstairs and out the side door. She did her thing in the stretch of grass by the sidewalk. Then it was back upstairs, but I held open the guest room door. "In you go. Sorry, girl. I need private time with your momma now."

Slipping back into bed with Emma felt like an indulgence. Mmm, that was nice. She rolled to her side, ass pushing against me in her sleep. I bit back a groan so I wouldn't wake her. But my cock was definitely awake. My morning wood had softened earlier, but now it swelled to full mast.

I couldn't wait to finally get Emma naked and make her forget about her piece-of-shit ex. Or any other guy for that matter. Well, I *could* wait, but my cock wished it didn't have to.

Emma yawned, butt wiggling against me again. *Nngh.*

She looked over her shoulder. "Somebody's up."

"Pun intended?"

"Yep. I couldn't resist."

I nudged her onto her back and lifted up to hover over her. "There's something else in this bed I can't resist."

"I thought you'd be grumpy first thing in the morning."

"Usually. But there's this gorgeous woman in my bed. What's there to be grumpy about?"

"Bet I could make you even happier." She cupped her hand around the tip of my cock in my pajama pants. "Can I suck you?"

My phone rang, and I saw Piper's name on the screen on my nightstand. At almost the same moment, the bell on the door downstairs rang. Damn it. No.

"Maisie's back?" Emma asked.

"Yep. Missed her, but not the best timing." I dropped my forehead to the pillow next to Emma. If I were a lesser man, I might've whined about impending blue balls.

Instead, we both jumped up. I grabbed for my jeans. Before Emma could scurry away, I held on to her wrist and stole another kiss. My lips refused to rush, lingering over hers.

Downstairs, Piper rapped on the door again.

"We'll finish this later," I murmured.

"Promise?"

"Cross my heart."

Emma's fingertip drew an X on my chest, and the muscle beneath gave an answering thump.

✧

I increased the speed on my treadmill, as if that would make my morning go by faster.

"Geez, bro," Callum complained next to me. "Somebody's got energy."

"You're makin' the rest of us look bad," Judson said with a smile from my other side. He was jogging at a steady, methodical pace, the way he did everything.

I'd finished with my sole client appointment this morning, and now I was working out with Callum and Judson. Something I usually enjoyed. Today, though, my mind was elsewhere.

"Something happened last night." Callum reached over to smack my arm. "Didn't it?"

"Hey, hands to yourself. People are injured on treadmills every day."

"This isn't your classroom. Even if I *might* be acting like a child." He grinned.

I snorted. You'd think my brother was sixteen instead of thirty-two.

"Heard about you and some blond hanging out at Hearthstone last night," Callum said. "Even though I was pretty sure you and Emma were getting close just the other day."

Judson lifted his thick brows, glancing over curiously.

"What happened?" my brother asked. "Because Elias and I might have twenty bucks riding on it."

I hit the stop button. The treadmill belt slowed. "I have no comment. Except that you need to grow up." Grabbing my towel to wipe my face, I went to the locker room to get my gym bag.

I had no idea what to tell my brother and my friends about me and Emma. And suddenly, that seemed like the most pressing matter. I needed to talk to her. This was Silver Ridge, and any moment, people would be gossiping about the two of us even more than they had already.

Keeping something quiet around here was not easy. A fact I knew all too well.

I made it to the Big Blue Monster just as toddler music class was letting out. I hovered in the doorway, nodding politely at the moms and babies streaming past. But my eyes were on Emma as she put her guitar in its case. Also on her long legs in her cutoff jean shorts.

She smiled when she saw me. "Hey. Maisie still at her camp?"

"Few more minutes." I schooled my face into a stern frown, aware all those nosy moms were watching us. "Can we go to my office? We need to talk."

Emma sighed. "If this is about the trash cart again..." She followed me down the hall. The moment I had her in my office, I pushed her up against the closed door.

"Hi."

Her eyes glinted with mischief. "Only about half of that audience bought our act."

"I might not actually care."

I crashed my mouth onto hers.

Grabbing onto the seat of her jean shorts and hiking her up, I braced her against the door and explored her mouth with my tongue. The kiss was hot and dirty and fast. When she broke away, she was panting. "Wow. That was quite a hello."

I set her down and grabbed her hand. Pulling her over to my desk chair, I sat and tugged her into my lap. "I did want to talk. We didn't discuss how we want to handle this. Us."

Her brows knit. "What do you mean?"

"People are going to be gossiping. We should be on the same page about what to say."

Emma looked down at where our hands were entwined. "You want to keep this a secret." Slowly, she pulled her hand away from mine. Her shoulders sagged.

Oh, crap. Understanding hit me. She was thinking of her douchebag ex-boyfriend. The way he'd kept their affair on the down low, which was the exact opposite of the way Emma deserved to be treated.

I wasn't so sure I *could* keep this a secret, much less wanted to. And that was mind-blowing in itself.

I hooked her chin with my finger and turned her to face me. "You can let me know what you'd prefer. But I'm up for letting people see and think what they will. I won't be able to keep a straight face around you anyway. My brother already guessed this morning that something was up with me."

"You're okay if people know about us?"

"More than okay."

A pleased smile grew on her pretty lips. Which meant I had to kiss them. What else was a guy to do?

"The only issue is Maisie," I said when we broke apart again. "I don't want to confuse her."

"Of course. We can be discreet around her. I think that's wise."

"As far as what we tell other people..." I began.

"Like you said, let them think what they want."

I squeezed her hip. "What *I* want is for every other guy in town to know you're taken."

"That won't be an issue."

I hummed. "Good." My hand wandered down to massage her bare thigh. "How much time do we have?"

"Not enough for whatever you're thinking."

"Not fair," I grumbled. If I didn't get this woman naked soon, I might explode. But I didn't want a quickie with her. Emma meant a lot more to me than that.

She deserved to be wooed first.

"Will you go out with me tonight? I'm thinking you, me, Maisie, and Stella."

"The four of us? I'm in. Where are we going?"

"It's a surprise." Which I hadn't planned yet, since I'd just come up with this.

"I can't wait."

"Me too."

I was not usually a spontaneous guy. At least, I hadn't been for a long, long time. Being responsible, holding up every aspect of my life so it didn't cave in around me, didn't lead to spontaneity. But she made me want to try something new. Made me want to grab onto the parts of life I'd been missing and just hold on for as long as I could.

✦

"Daddy, Emma, can Stella splash in the creek? She really wants to."

"Not here, monkey. The current is too strong. Just wait."

My daughter pouted. I had no idea where she'd gotten that impatience, because I had the patience of a saint. Felt like it today, anyway.

I'd packed some snacks and water, dressed Maisie in her hiking gear, and knocked on Emma's door at four sharp this afternoon. My mouth had watered as soon as she'd appeared. Long, dark hair back in a braid, snug cropped shirt, and high-waisted hiking pants. Even a touch of gloss on those sexy full lips.

I'd figured a hike was a good bet for a first official date. Especially on a trail that showed off Silver Ridge to the highest degree. We'd walked up a series of shallow switchbacks to a panoramic vista, then descended into a valley full of wildflowers with an oxbow creek. Now that we were on flatter ground, Maisie took

Stella's leash, and the two of them ran ahead. Stella's tongue lolled to the side, shaggy fur flying.

Most trails around Silver Ridge were busy with hikers every summer, but we'd gotten lucky, probably because there was an art festival in the square today. One of the endless number of festivals going on during July and August.

But out here, we had the trail and this secluded valley to ourselves. This was exactly what I wanted right now. The three of us—make that four of us—just being together without anyone else interfering or commenting.

Since Maisie wasn't watching, I reached for Emma's hand. "Those two are having a great time."

"So am I." She glanced at me coyly, eyelids heavy. "I want you to know. After the drama with my ex, I got tested. All negative. I haven't been with anyone else since. And birth control is taken care of."

Just like that, a fire lit in my belly like a furnace roaring to life. "I'm negative too." I tugged her closer, putting my arm around her waist and enjoying the contact with her bare skin. I would rather be licking it, but for the moment, this was good enough. "I'm kind of dying here," I murmured.

Emma's hand sneaked back to grab my ass through my hiking pants. "Same here. I want to know what you feel like and taste like. How you sound when I've got my mouth on certain parts of you."

The sound I made was far from dignified. I took my metal water bottle from my pack for a drink of water, just to cool off a little. "I'm not just dying. You're killing me."

She laughed, teeth digging into her lower lip.

We reached a calmer stretch of the creek with a shallow portion where Maisie could safely get her feet wet. Stella charged right in, splashing in the icy-cold water. It was snowmelt down from the mountains, so it was always frigid, even in summer.

After I helped Maisie get her boots and socks off, she tip-toed in and bent to examine the river rocks beneath her feet.

"Don't go past that boulder there," I said, pointing.

"Okay!"

Emma and I sat on a large flat rock by the bank. I'd worn a baseball cap. I took it off and put it on backward, then leaned in and whispered, "I want to know what you taste like, too. Every part of you. I want to bury my face between your legs and feel your thighs squeezing me while I drive you wild with my tongue."

Emma made a small, choked sound. "*Urgh.*" She squeezed her thighs together, like I'd described.

One corner of my mouth twitched in a satisfied smirk. My hand inched nearer to her, my pinky crossing over hers.

We watched Maisie and Stella splash in the water. Stella shook herself off, and Maisie squealed at the sudden shower of cold droplets.

"Emma?" she asked. "When you're back in California, will you take a picture of the ocean beach for me?"

"Sure, Maisie-doodle," she replied evenly. Like it was no big deal to talk about her returning to the West Coast.

I grabbed my pack and dug through it, needing a distraction from that topic. I didn't want to think about Emma leaving yet. So I wouldn't.

Very mature of me, I know. But I just wanted to enjoy this instead of focusing on the negative. For once in my life.

Yet Emma's expression had turned cloudy, and I wondered if I'd been wrong. If she dreaded the thought of her leaving too. "I forgot to mention something that happened last night after I left the brewery," she said.

"Oh. What's that?"

"I thought someone was following me."

That got my attention. "*What?*"

Keeping her voice down, Emma told me she'd heard footsteps behind her on the dark, isolated street. She'd actually gotten her pepper spray and prepared to use it. "Then Danny Carmichael showed up."

"Was *he* the one following you?"

"I don't think so. Unless he's a really great actor, because he seemed shocked when I jumped out at him with my pepper spray."

"Should've sprayed him," I grumbled. "He's earned it."

"Why is that? Apart from being Piper's ex."

Where did I begin with that guy? "He was shitty to Piper during the divorce. He's a crappy father to Ollie. Plus he was Lori's boss, and he was a dick to her too. Didn't even show up for her funeral."

Yet Lori had always defended him.

Whenever possible, I drove Maisie and myself out to another dental office for cleanings. If I never had to deal with Danny and his fake smile again, it would be too soon.

But Emma's feeling that she'd been followed... It reminded me of the incident a couple of weeks ago. The man in the blue rain slicker outside her apartment building. Was there some connection?

I squinted at the mountains in the distance.

"Maisie!" Emma screamed.

She launched off the rock, running for the water. I turned to see my daughter slip beneath the rushing surface of the creek and disappear.

TWENTY
Emma

ONE MOMENT, Maisie was laughing at Stella dog-paddling in the creek. And the next, the little girl had fallen beneath the surface.

"Maisie!"

I rushed into the creek, ignoring the icy pull of the water on my pants and boots. Stella started barking at a rapid, fearful pitch. Reaching for the dark shape under the surface, I grabbed hold of Maisie and yanked her upward. She came up coughing and sputtering.

Ashford was suddenly there next to me. He wrapped his arms around me and Maisie both. "Daddy!" she screamed, terrified.

"I'm here." He took her and put her against his shoulder like she was a much smaller child. His worried gaze connected with mine, and then he reached for my hand as he carried her to the bank.

Once there, he lay her on her side on the soft grass. She kept coughing. Thank goodness she'd only been under the water for a second or two, and the current had been weak in that spot.

Ashford's hands were steady as he checked his daughter over. But from the concern in his eyes, I could tell that he was shaken. "How you feeling, monkey?" He rubbed her arms to warm her up.

"My nose hurts. Water went in there. And in my mouth. I was scared."

"I know you were. I would be too. But Emma grabbed you, didn't she?" Ashford looked gratefully at me.

"I just got there half a second before your dad."

"Thank you, Emma." Maisie reached out to hug me. I returned the embrace. Poor thing was soaked and shivering. Stella edged in and gave Maisie kisses to help warm her up too. In no time, the little girl was giggling again.

But Ashford didn't seem the same. Like a dark cloud had descended over his mood.

I took his backpack, and he carried Maisie all the way back to the car.

When we got home, I toed off my damp shoes. Maisie bounded off to her room to change, though our clothes had mostly dried. Stella followed. Ashford stopped in the kitchen and braced his hands against the counter, taking a breath.

"You okay?" I rubbed my hand over the thick muscles of his back.

"I know she's fine. But close calls like that get to me. Hard not to think about what-ifs."

"You're allowed to worry."

"Am I? Callum loves to tell me how useless it is, and he's probably right. But if I lost that little girl..."

I didn't tell him that he'd never lose her. Because we both knew that loss was always a possibility. So instead I dug my thumbs into the knots between his shoulder blades. Ashford groaned.

"Is this okay?" I asked.

"Amazing."

I worked on loosening his tight muscles for a while. Until he stepped to the side and pulled me in front of him, trapping me against the counter. "That felt great. I want to return the favor." His fingers searched out the points of tension in my upper back.

But he added soft kisses to my neck. His tongue swiped the juncture where my neck met my shoulder.

"I'm sweaty from the hike."

"I know. You taste good." Those strong fingers kneaded down my back to my butt cheeks, digging into my soft curves. "Can't wait to have you spread out and at my mercy," he whispered. "I am going to make you come so hard. Harder than last night."

I bit into my lip so I wouldn't moan. I'd never been with any guy who could turn me on this quickly. Not just interested but raring to go. If he had unzipped my hiking pants and let those fingers wander inside my panties, he'd find me dripping.

"Stop," I said, keeping my voice low.

His hands instantly lifted away from me, going to the counter instead. Though his body still caged me in. "Too far?"

"No, not far enough, but we can't right now. Anybody ever told you you're a shameless tease?"

He chuckled and leaned to kiss my neck again. "I enjoy teasing you. It's fun for me."

"Mean." I kissed him firmly on the mouth, just once, before pushing him away. "No more of that. We need to make dinner."

He boiled water for the pasta and chopped vegetables. To a big pan, I added olive oil and garlic to start a quick, lemony tomato sauce. Shrimp and fresh greens would go in last. We'd had this dish last week, and it had been a hit.

"I can't believe you can get Maisie to eat shrimp," Ashford said. "And spinach."

"Anything covered in lemon-garlic sauce is a crowd pleaser." Though I'd subbed in penne instead of linguine. Much easier for a six-year-old to eat without making a huge mess.

Ashford poured us glasses of white wine and a cup of milk for Maisie. The three of us ate at the dining table, Stella sitting dutifully beside her new best friend. Ashford smirked as his socked foot nudged mine. But I got him back by teasing my foot along his thigh. Until he grabbed hold of it and wouldn't let go.

"Why are you laughing, Emma?" Maisie asked, delicately spearing a cherry tomato on her fork.

"Just thinking about how much fun I've had today."

"Me too. Daddy is smiling a lot, and that makes me happy."

I locked eyes with Ashford, my heart doing a dance in my chest. "I like when he's smiling too."

We sneaked more kisses while doing the dishes. Then Maisie brought in her favorite board game, a Disney-themed version of Monopoly that I'd played with her only two dozen times before. Give or take a few.

"Can we play this? Please?"

"If Emma wants to."

"I'd love to. You set it up, Maisie-doodle, while your dad and I finish loading the dishwasher."

Ashford leaned over to murmur in my ear. "Sorry. This is probably not the most exciting date you've ever been on."

"I disagree. I wouldn't change a single thing about it."

I took a quick shower while he was getting Maisie ready for bed. Ashford hadn't minded earlier that I was sweaty, but I did. I had hopes for tonight, and I wanted to be ready.

In my room, I changed into a pair of leggings and my favorite oversized sleep shirt, a vintage Pixies concert tee. Through the wall, I heard Ashford and Maisie talking, and it made me grin. I loved that bedtime was a special ritual for them. He never missed it if he could help it.

His voice changed to a steady, soothing tone. It was time for her bedtime story. The past few days, Ashford had been reading her *The Mouse and the Motorcycle*.

I sat on my futon and grabbed my journal, jotting down what had happened today. Aside from the brief mishap in the creek, I couldn't imagine a more perfect summer date.

I'd been relieved that Ashford didn't want to keep us a secret. I'd had enough of that in my past. We hadn't defined our relationship, but I didn't need labels either. We were exclusive. That was enough. I just needed to feel like he was proud to be with me, even if we kept things quiet around Maisie.

I hadn't known them very long, yet our connection felt natural. It was so tempting to think of us as a unit. But my pen stopped, hovering above my journal page.

I had to rein myself in. I couldn't latch on to ideas that were simply impossible.

Ashford appeared at my open door. "Hey, Maisie asked if you would tuck her in."

Happy flutters cascaded in my belly. I closed my journal and set it aside. "Of course. I would love that." It was the first time she had ever asked me to participate in bedtime.

I went into Maisie's room with Ashford right behind me. The lights were turned low. Her bedside lampshade featured cut-out shapes to splash bright shooting stars and fairies on her walls and ceiling.

Maisie held her arms out. "Can you hug me good night?"

"Absolutely." I bent down to hug her, then pulled up her blankets and tucked them around her. My heart felt too big for my rib cage.

"Can Stella sleep in here with me?"

"No," Ashford said, gentle yet firm. "I already told you that."

"What about one more story?"

"Maisie, I already read you five chapters."

She blinked those big green eyes innocently. "But Emma didn't read anything."

I looked at him, blinking my eyes the same way.

"Fine. One."

Maisie picked a different book, this one about a mermaid. From the way Ashford laughed and crossed his arms, I guessed he had read this one many times before as well.

As I turned the pages and read her the story, Maisie's eyes started to droop. Then she yawned, and her eyes stayed closed.

She didn't budge as we left the room, closing the door behind us.

We went into the living room and sat on the couch. Ashford put his arm around me and pulled me into his lap, burying his nose behind my ear and inhaling. "You showered."

"I didn't smell my best."

"I disagree. But this is good too. I love that smell. Your shampoo." He kissed me, nibbling at my lower lip. It was gentle, no urgency behind it. But now it didn't feel like a tease. This was pure anticipation.

"I would've been fine with Stella sleeping in Maisie's room," I said.

His frown reappeared for the first time in hours. "I know. But I don't want her getting used to that."

Right. Now that he said it, it was obvious. My place here was temporary.

Why did I keep conveniently ignoring that fact?

But before I could apologize, Ashford kissed me again with more purpose this time. He repositioned me so I was straddling his lap. I felt his cock thickening against my behind.

"I want you tonight," he said.

A shiver wound its way through my belly and settled as a throb of desire between my legs. "I want you too."

"How far we take this is up to you. I need you to tell me if there's anything you *don't* want."

I put my hands on his chest, dragging them down his flat stomach. When I reached the edge of his shirt I dipped beneath, finding his hot, smooth skin, ridged with muscle beneath. "I just want to feel like I'm yours."

For as long as I can.

With a swift movement, he grasped me around the hips and tossed me up as he stood, palming my ass in his big hands. I yelped and grabbed him around the neck. In just a few seconds, he'd carried me into his bedroom and dropped me on the edge of the mattress, my legs hanging off the side. Then he went back to his door and shut it quietly, flipping the lock and dimming the light switch.

Ashford stalked toward me, eyes devouring me like a predator. "I know exactly what I want to do first." He dropped to his knees at the edge of the bed. "Make you come on my tongue."

He reached for the waistband of my leggings and tugged them down. But he paused, nostrils flaring, when he saw my panties.

"Damn. You really are trying to kill me."

I smirked. "That wasn't what I had in mind."

"Did you put those on for me?" His gaze roved over my body.

I nodded. After my shower, I'd chosen a pair of lacy pink panties and a matching bra. A set I didn't wear often and had packed on a whim. I'd forgotten that stupid raincoat and remembered these instead, but right now, I had zero regrets.

"Feels like I'm unwrapping a present."

But he didn't take the panties off me yet. Ashford stripped my leggings off and tossed them aside. His hands made a slow journey back up my shins, over my knees, then my thighs. His gaze didn't waver from that triangle of pink lace, his breathing unsteady. I had never felt sexier.

"Lay back. Let me make you feel good."

I relaxed onto the mattress. Ashford stroked my inner thighs with his calloused fingertips. Again and again. One of his big hands traveled back to my knee, bending it and widening my legs. His mouth went to that same joint, kissing the inner side of my knee. His beard gently abraded my skin.

Then the thumb of his opposite hand grazed the crotch of my panties, sending tingles of need through my clit and out into the rest of my body. I whimpered.

"You're wet. I feel it through the fabric." His thumb stroked again.

"I've been wet for you all day."

Groaning, he went back to kissing a line up the inside of my thigh as his thumb rubbed circles over the lace, so close to what I needed but not quite there. I had no doubt it was on purpose. The man had no shame about teasing me.

But when it came to sex, I didn't have much shame either. I

was younger than him, possibly less experienced, but I knew what I wanted.

I reached for the stretchy band of lace at my hips and started pushing them down. But Ashford stopped me. "Did I say you could do that?"

I pouted. "Bossy."

"Your point?"

"I want your mouth on me."

"Soon. I promise."

I made a sound of frustration. He had the nerve to laugh. But okay, I liked it. This dark and wicked side of him. Making me wait, while also leaving me with no doubt it would be worth it.

His mouth edged closer and closer until his thumb finally pushed the damp scrap of lace aside.

The flat of his tongue dragged over my bare pussy. I cried out and shoved my fist to my mouth, biting my knuckle to muffle the sound.

As far as I knew, Maisie was a deep sleeper, but I had to stay quiet. Which was *not* easy as Ashford made a meal out of me. His tongue worked up and down, slowly at first, then switching to fast before he sucked my clit between his lips. Every time the pleasure started to coil up inside me, tense and hot and so close to releasing, he switched back to slow again.

He'd promised to drive me wild, and the man was delivering and then some.

Every part of me seemed to be quivering. Heat prickled all over my skin. I arched my back and moaned around the knuckle in my mouth.

"Do you need to come, baby?" he asked.

"*Please.*"

He redoubled his efforts, his tongue massaging me in exactly the right spot. But instead of backing off this time when I got close, he buried his face between my legs and held my thighs in his hands. A hard jolt of pleasure shuddered through me, unleashing wave after wave of sweet release. I couldn't have stopped it if I'd tried. My teeth sank into my knuckle as I tried to keep my moans quiet.

I was still shaking when he lifted his head, licking his lips, and smiled up at me. "Did you like that?"

All I could do was nod. It felt like my entire body had just rebooted. Speech functions were still loading.

He dropped a few more kisses to my inner thighs. "I hope you're ready for more, because I'm just getting started."

TWENTY-ONE
Ashford

I stripped off my shirt, then my pants and boxer briefs in one go. My cock bobbed in front of me, achingly stiff. I had loved making Emma feel good. There was no bigger turn on than feeling her come apart because of me.

But a close second was having her appreciative gaze on my body. My fist stroked my erection as the muscles in my chest, abs, and arms flexed. Emma had accused me of being shameless, and it was true. But only for her.

"Come here?" she asked, voice lifting at the end to make it a question.

"I'm getting there."

"Get here faster."

Watching me undress seemed to give her a renewed burst of energy, because she sat up and tugged her own shirt over her head. *Ungh.* "Matching bra, huh? You are so sexy it should be illegal."

"I was going to say the same about you." She scooted back until she rested against the pillows. I knelt on the bed and crawled toward her. When I was close enough, I tugged her by the ankles, forcing her to lay flat so I could stretch out on top of her. Emma laughed. "Manhandle me, why don't you?"

"Thanks. I will."

The tip of my cock brushed against the lace of her panties, which I still hadn't taken off of her yet. I kept myself propped up on my elbows to get a long look at the beautiful woman beneath me. The lace of her bra was translucent, so I could see her pink nipples beneath. I lowered my head to lick one through the fabric, then the other, and she moaned.

"Sexy as you look in this, I have to think you'll be even better without it." I reached beneath her with one hand to unlatch the hooks on her bra. Emma did the rest, pulling the straps down her arms and tossing the undergarment aside.

"Somebody's getting impatient," I said.

"Just making things easier for you. Hint, hint." She draped her arms on the pillow above her head and arched her back invitingly.

Grinning, I licked each pert nipple again, then sucked, this time with no barrier between my tongue and her skin. Mmmm. Definitely better without it. I laved and sucked at each one until she was panting.

The last thing was her tiny pair of lace panties. Time for those to come off too. I sat back against my heels, hooked my fingers in the lacy band, and dragged them over her hips, not stopping until they were somewhere on the floor.

We were both naked, and I wanted to do so many naughty things to her.

"You're incredible." I pressed my palm to her chest, where her heart was fluttering like a bird, then caressed down between her breasts and along her stomach to the V where her thighs met. So pretty, every inch of her.

Her fingertips grazed over my cock head. "What do you want now?" she asked. Like she'd say yes to whatever it was.

I had some ideas. My dick was harder than it had ever been and craved some relief. But now that we were both bare, I didn't see any need to hurry. Why not make this last? My kid was safe and asleep. I had nowhere else to be all night. That was a damn good feeling.

Sometimes it was nearly impossible to banish all the worries from my head. Right now, they were quiet.

"There's no rush."

"I thought you were dying."

"It's true, but the waiting also makes it better." I lay down beside her and got comfortable, keeping my hand on her softly curving stomach. Emma turned her head on the pillow to face me. I kissed her. Savoring her plump lips, the sweet way her tongue nudged mine.

I could've kissed her all night and all day without getting tired of it. Especially with that heavy-lidded, dizzy look her blue eyes got when I'd been kissing her a while, and she was breathless.

She tucked her head against my shoulder. "Tell me about your tattoos? I've seen them so many times, but I've never asked."

"Sure." I didn't always think about them either. They were just a part of me. I lifted my left hand, glancing at the design of a mountain range and a sun on that forearm. "This one was inspired by the mountains here in Hart County. I got it just before my last deployment." I hadn't needed a reminder of what I was fighting for. Not exactly. But on the hard days, I'd needed that small piece of home to keep me going.

"And this one?" She traced the evergreen branches on my inner right forearm.

"Got that after Maisie was born. Her birthday is here." I pointed at the stylized numbers inked between the branches, beside the words, so small you could barely read them: *My love for you is forever.* "I'm sure it'll embarrass her when she's a teenager."

"That's one of the sweetest things I've ever seen." Emma grinned. "You're blushing."

"No." I ran a hand over my beard. "My skin is chafed from rubbing it on your thighs."

"Oh, sure."

Growling, I crawled on top of her. Having her naked body up against me made my cock take interest again. My erection had flagged a bit, but now it swelled and pushed eagerly against her thigh as I kissed her. And for the record, the skin of her thighs was buttery soft. Pure heaven. I'd totally been blushing a moment ago.

I rolled us so she was above me and I could let my hands roam as much as they wanted. Cupping her round breasts, traveling down to squeeze her butt cheeks. Emma moaned into my mouth, and I ate up the sound.

I wanted more of that. Her sexy whimpers. The little sounds she made when she was getting close and desperate. I had to discover them all.

"Crawl up here," I said, tapping my upper chest.

"What?"

"So I can get my mouth on you again."

Now Emma was the one blushing. "Straddle your face?"

"Exactly." I knew she wasn't a virgin, and she hadn't come on my tongue like a virgin either. But the thought that she hadn't done this exact thing with anyone else before? A caveman part of me liked that thought. A lot.

Making her come made me feel invincible. Like it was my superpower.

I spun her around and maneuvered her so her knees were on either side of my head, her upper body draped over my stomach. My cock jerked as I admired the view.

Hold on. What was this?

"You have a tattoo?" My thumb traced the outline of a black-ink music note on her right butt cheek. Pushing a pillow under my head, I lifted up to nibble playfully at the tattoo, then licked it.

She laughed. "Got it when I turned eighteen. My friends dared me."

I would have to memorize this and keep it in my naughty mental slideshow forever.

I tugged her hips to move her a bit lower. Then my tongue darted out to lick her clit, and she gasped, hips shaking.

"Like the new angle?" I asked.

Her response was unintelligible, but she sounded happy.

I'd already made her come twice, so I knew a lot better what Emma liked. Exactly how to get her where I wanted her. When her hips started to rock, rubbing her clit gently against my tongue, I knew she was enjoying it.

Then she started to pump my cock with her fist, and her lips closed around the tip and sucked. I faltered a moment, because that felt unbelievable, but now I was even more determined.

I needed her to come again before I did. My tongue pushed inside her, sliding as far as it would go.

Emma's thighs quivered. She dropped her forehead to my stomach and moaned breathlessly. I held on to her hips and flicked my tongue until she finally crested over the edge.

When she'd finished, she crawled off of me and turned, falling back against her elbows. Her hair was wild and tangled. "I am *definitely* going to need you to do that again."

I laughed as I sat up, moving toward her. "Next time." Gently nudging her so she was flat on her back, I positioned myself over her.

"Kiss me?" she asked.

"I can't get enough of kissing you. But right now, I need my cock inside you." The swollen head teased her slick opening. "Yes?" I asked.

"*Yes.*" Emma wrapped her legs around my waist, and I finally sank all the way into her.

Mmm. Oh, hell yeah. The way her body hugged my cock was perfect. Even better than I could've imagined, and I'd imagined this plenty.

But even more perfect was the way she smiled up at me, those pretty blue eyes blinking languidly.

I rocked my hips into hers, my cock pushing deep. I wanted to stay just like this all night. But after so much buildup, I didn't know how long I could last. She felt too good. Her soft breasts and beaded nipples brushing my skin. The sighs she made with every thrust.

"*Emma*," I groaned.

I lifted up on my arms so I could watch my body strain against hers. My hips snapped, driving my cock into her again and again. Her fingers dug into my biceps.

I ached for release. Yet I still held myself back by some last thread of willpower, not wanting this to end.

She clenched around me and cried out my name. My vision swam. The climax hit me hard. A hot, all-consuming surge of bliss roared through me.

As the pleasure faded into contentment, I hovered over her, sharing kisses. Emma's hands moved over my arms, my shoulders, into my hair, like she couldn't stop touching me.

After a while, I shifted my weight to one side of her and pulled her as close as possible. I struggled to keep my eyes open.

"I should go back to my room," she whispered.

I made a grumbly sound of protest. "Not yet." What I really wanted was Emma in my bed the rest of the night. Waking up beside her and finding her asleep on my pillow. Kissing and sinking inside of her a second time before we'd even had coffee. Then maybe a third time against the counter in the kitchen.

But I also had a six-year-old whose favorite morning activity was barging into my room and shaking me awake. Even if Emma and I got dressed in PJs, Maisie would have questions I couldn't answer.

Like, *Can Emma stay with us forever?*

No, I supposed I did know the answer to that one.

Eventually, after several more kisses, we got out of bed. Emma put on her clothes, while I tugged on my boxer briefs. I walked her down the hall to her room. Once there, she turned around and leaned against the closed door. Stella was sleeping inside.

I rested a hand on the door above her head. Emma tipped her chin to look up at me. The lights in the hall were off, but starlight streamed through the living room windows and tipped the strands of her dark hair with silver.

"I had a good time," she whispered. "Best date ever."

"For me too." I cupped her cheek and bent to kiss her. One more time. "Maybe we can do it again tomorrow."

Her smile lit me up inside. "Goodnight, Ashford."

"Night." I stood there until she'd gone inside her room and quietly closed the door.

TWENTY-TWO
Ashford

I SAT at the desk in my office, staring at my computer screen. But really, I was listening for the end of Emma's piano lesson with Mrs. Stuckey's grandson. Mrs. Stuckey had taught piano herself for the last several decades, but apparently, her own grandkid was the one student she couldn't handle. Yet for Emma, the kid was sitting still and making progress.

Objective evidence proved it. Emma was amazing.

Within minutes of Mrs. Stuckey and her grandson leaving the building, Emma opened the door to my office. She closed and locked it behind her, resting against it. "How long do we have?"

I was already out of my chair and rounding the desk to meet her, tugging off my T-shirt along the way. "Twenty minutes. Grace is taking Maisie to lunch."

"Perfect." Emma took off her top, revealing a skimpy, translucent bra underneath. Simple, yet so sexy.

I pushed her up against the door and claimed her mouth.

The past two weeks had been like this. On the surface, my life was pretty much the same as always. My summer schedule of classes. A few new training clients. Plenty of father-daughter time with Maisie, with the welcome addition of Emma in all our daily activities.

But in between, at every opportunity we got to be alone, Emma and I fucked like wild bunnies.

My tongue drove between her lips. She moaned and sucked on it with abandon, just like she'd sucked my brain out through my cock last night. Just thinking about that, combined with the sight and scent and feel of her right in front of me, made me so hard I was lightheaded.

Tugging down the straps of her bra, I pulled the cups below her breasts and flicked her nipples with my thumbs. Emma pushed her hands past the waistband of my athletic pants and palmed my ass.

She pulled her mouth away from mine. "Commando?"

"Figured that would save a couple of seconds."

Emma grinned wickedly. "I had the same thought."

With a growl of lust, I spun her and bent her over my desk. A couple of papers fluttered down to the floor. A moment later I had her shorts down around her ankles so she could step out of them. Her bare bottom was right there beneath, that naughty little music-note tattoo greeting me. No panties.

While I teased her between the legs to make sure she was wet, I tugged at my own pants with my other hand. My erection popped out, thick and eager.

Within minutes of her appearing in my office, I was pumping inside of her, both of us taking advantage of the empty building by being as loud as we wanted.

"Ashford," she begged, "touch me. I'm so close."

"I've got you, baby." I reached around to find the sensitive nub of her clit and massaged it, the rhythm matching the thrusts of my hips. "That's it. You take me so well. Come for me. I need to feel you squeezing my cock."

She cried out, grabbing hold of the edge of the desk. More papers went flying. I sank myself into her as deep as I could go and groaned through my release.

"Holy shit," I said hoarsely.

She hummed with her eyes half closed and smiled.

Clean up was a necessary evil. But by the time we were dressed and eating the sandwiches we had made together in the kitchen that morning, we still had another few minutes. I sat in my desk chair with Emma in my lap. The best spot for her, in my opinion.

"Mrs. Stuckey kept winking at me after her grandson's lesson. Asking if I've been up to anything interesting. She definitely knows."

"I think all of Silver Ridge knows by now. I stopped at the market this morning, and Dixie put a case of sports drinks in my cart. She said I needed to, and I quote, 'replenish all the electrolytes I've been losing'."

Emma snorted.

Last week, Callum, Elias, and Judson had asked me point-blank at the gym if Emma and I were seeing each other. I had confirmed it. My brother had gotten all smug, acting like the whole thing had been his idea and he deserved the credit.

"Dibs on being best man at the wedding," he'd said.

"It's a summer fling, dumbass," I had responded. "Don't be an idiot."

Then Judson had asked, in that serious voice of his, "Are you sure that's all it is?"

As if it could be anything else.

But they had respected my request to not say anything around Maisie. I couldn't let her get the wrong idea. We had blurred enough lines already. Like having almost every meal together and making Emma a part of bedtime.

Plus inviting Emma and Stella on the camping trip I had planned for the beginning of August. A couple weeks or so from now.

The only member of the Lonely Harts club who hadn't brought up my "fling" was Grace. I had no idea what my little sister thought of it, and if she wasn't speaking up, then why should I go looking for trouble? Same with the sudden lack of phone calls from Los Angeles area codes.

Maybe Ayla had finally given up.

I didn't want to question it.

Usually, my baseline was making sure that my kid was happy. But these days, I actually felt good too. Thinking about all the shit that could happen, that *would* happen at the end of the summer, would just ruin it.

Emma made me so happy, and why shouldn't I get to enjoy that while I could?

By the time we said goodbye in my office, Emma's lips were swollen from kissing me. "Send Maisie up when she's home?" she asked. "I'll feed her a snack and then take her and Stella to the park for the afternoon."

"Sounds good."

I watched her jog upstairs, then waited in the lobby with the front door open for Grace and Maisie to arrive. They charged up the sidewalk a couple of minutes later, laughing about something.

"Head upstairs for a snack, Mais."

"I get to play with Emma and Stella?"

"Yep. You're going to the park."

"Yay! Bye, Aunt Grace!" Maisie ran upstairs.

I thanked my sister for watching her. Grace also needed some upgrades done in her kitchen, which I'd volunteered to do for her, so I double-checked her paint color choices and let her know I'd stop by in a couple days.

But after all that was settled, Grace lingered in the lobby. "Seems like Maisie is getting really close to Emma."

"She is."

"What about you? From what I hear, you've been getting very close to Emma too."

Uh oh. This was the conversation I'd been hoping to avoid. "You already said you don't approve of Emma and me being together."

"That's not what I said."

"That's how I remember it."

"I said I didn't want you getting hurt, but I also acknowledge you're a grown man who can make his own decisions."

"Who's also older than you."

"Do you really want to have a discussion about age differences?" She smirked, knowing she had me there. "I don't disapprove. I'm glad you're happy."

"Yet you don't sound happy yourself."

She made a face. "I told you I wanted to work through some things." Grace glanced at the open doorway and sighed. "Elias asked me out."

"He did *what*? When?"

"Yesterday. But you can't get mad. Not after you basically just told me to stay out of your business."

"It's different. I'm your older brother." I had a big brother's instinctual skepticism of any man who asked out his younger sister. Elias was a great guy though. One of my best friends.

"I'm not going to acknowledge the inherent sexism in that statement. Or the fact that it's not surprising." Grace pushed her glasses up her nose and crossed her arms over her middle. "I just wanted to let you know. I haven't even decided whether I'll say yes."

"Why not? You've known him long enough. If you like him, I can deal with it."

"I know. But when Elias asked, it dawned on me that I hadn't dated anyone since college." Grace shifted uncomfortably. "And it's not like I don't want to. Something's been holding me back, and I don't know what it is."

I pulled my sister into a hug. "You'll find the right person, whether that's Elias or someone else. And I'll be there for you. The O'Neals stick together."

"So we're good? You and me? Even with my unwelcome opinions on you and Emma."

"Of course we're good. Always." No matter what happened, I had my family's back when it mattered. And I knew they had mine.

I could trust that Grace would never say *I told you so*.

Grace took off, and I had my afternoon martial arts classes.

The little kids were only here a couple times a week, but nearly every day I offered classes for teenagers and adults working toward their higher-level belts. Those classes were fun and satisfying, and I felt the good sort of worn out afterward.

Not as good as the kind of worn out I got after alone time with Emma. But still. Satisfying.

While I was in class, Emma had sent me a text of Maisie and Stella rolling in the grass at the park. I smiled and sent back a reply, saying I was about to head out to join them. I was feeling left out. Maybe we'd grab burgers after. Or mix it up and go to the taco truck.

I just had a few chores to deal with on my way out the door.

After showering and changing into jeans and a fresh shirt, I emptied the lobby trash, grabbed my keys, and headed out the back door.

Then I froze when I saw some asshole in a hoodie digging in my trash cart.

"Hey," I bellowed. "What the hell are you doing?"

Not like I would've minded if somebody was hungry and looking for scraps of food. If he was that desperate, I would've bought the guy a meal myself. But this person didn't look homeless. He wasn't holding food, either. The guy had ripped open one of the plastic bags and held some crumpled papers in his fist.

He shoved the papers into the pocket of his hoodie and took off at a sprint.

"Hey!" I dropped the trash bag I was holding and ran after him.

The guy was rangy and fast. He broke left, cutting through a gap between two buildings. But I was gaining on him. I swiped at the back of his sweatshirt, my fingertips brushing the fabric. The guy darted right, treading over Mrs. Dominguez's prized vegetable garden. Which delayed me slightly because no *way* was I trampling her tomato plants. I'd never hear the end of it if she caught me on her doorbell camera.

As he crossed the next street, I tackled him on a burst of

speed. He landed in the dirt. I still hadn't seen his face, and I wanted to know who I was dealing with.

Pinning him in place so he couldn't run again, I yanked the guy's hoodie back.

"*Sheldon?*"

It was the property manager from the Ponderosa Apartments. The jerk who'd been so rude to Emma about her leaky ceiling.

He held up his hands in a warding-off gesture. "Don't hit me, bro. Don't hit me!"

I let go of his collar in disgust and stood. "I'm not going to *hit* you."

"Or karate chop me. Whatever. I didn't mean anything by it, okay?"

"You were stealing from my trash!"

Sheldon pulled the papers out of his pocket. I swiped them from his hand and looked them over. A few packing slips from deliveries I'd received. Stuff nobody could care about.

I didn't get it.

"The hell were you doing going through my trash? Have you been following Emma around? Are you stalking her?"

"No way. Just peeked in the cart a few times. You threw the stuff away, so you didn't want it anyway, right? The guy said it was easy money. If I found anything interesting, I could send him a picture of it, and I'd get a deposit to my Venmo."

I grabbed his collar again, yanking him up to standing. "What guy? *Who?*"

"I don't know. I swear. He sent an email to me. I never met him in person."

"Which of us were you spying on? Emma or me?"

"Both of you, I guess. Plus, you know…your little girl."

I saw red. Fury surged through my system. It took all my self control to keep from throttling him. "*Why,*" I said, low and dangerous.

"I didn't ask. I just wanted the money. All I've found so far is some store receipts and a ripped-up greeting card and stuff, and he paid me like a hundred bucks."

A greeting card. Oh, no. My stomach sank.

Please let me be wrong, I thought.

"I want this person's email address, or I'm calling the cops right now." I hoped it wouldn't come to that, though. If I called our local police department, there'd be no hiding my secret. Not anymore.

At least it seemed like Sheldon had no clue about Maisie's famous aunt.

He took out his phone and opened his email app. "I didn't do anything illegal. He told me if you throw the stuff in the trash, it's abandoned property. But fine, whatever. He hasn't wanted any of the stuff I've found lately anyway."

Sheldon showed me the email chain. It was pretty much what he had said. Some creep had offered him money to paw through our building's trash.

Besides, now that I thought about it, Sheldon was too tall to be the guy I had seen in the blue rain slicker.

I studied the email address of the man Sheldon had been communicating with. I didn't recognize the name. But the website sounded familiar. A quick search on Google on my own phone confirmed it.

Sheldon had been emailing with someone from the *Hollywood Star Post*. A sleazy gossip tabloid. But what did they want with info on me?

Unless they knew about Ayla.

TWENTY-THREE
Emma

PIPER AND OLLIE met us at the park. The two kids played a chaotic game of fetch with Stella, who was loving every minute, while Piper and I grabbed a sunny spot on the grass to stretch our legs.

"How are things with Ashford?" Piper asked.

I smiled. "Wonderful."

"You two are way too adorable." She stuck out her tongue.

"Hey, you were in favor of this from the start."

"I know, but now I'm jealous. Reminds me how cold my bed is at night." She playfully bopped me on the arm, and I bopped her back.

"Says the woman who views love as a terminal diagnosis."

"Hold on, *love*?"

I scrunched up my face. "I didn't mean it like that."

Piper was the first person I'd told about me and Ashford getting together. Make that the *only* person, because it seemed like everyone else somehow just knew, even though Ashford had barely told anyone and Piper had sworn she hadn't repeated the news to another soul.

But I had not meant to use the *L* word. In fact, I'd been trying to avoid any and all thought of it.

"Forever is a heck of a long time when you turn out to be wrong about your partner," Piper said. "But if any guy has a heart of gold hiding on the inside, it's probably Ashford."

I agreed with her. But this conversation had made a dangerous turn, and I needed to steer it back toward less treacherous waters. "We're having a great time together. That's all."

She hummed thoughtfully. "Have you heard back from any of the other schools you applied to?"

"Still waitlisted at one. I have an advisor who knows the dean there, and it helped, but doesn't guarantee me a spot. A couple rejections from others."

"What if you can't transfer?"

I watched the kids and Stella explore near the play structure. "I don't know. I haven't really planned that far."

I'd thought about it though. If I had to wait another year to resume my master's, would I stay in Silver Ridge during that time? Would Ashford even want me to?

He hadn't asked about my exact plans for after the summer. Like he simply assumed I would be gone. He had never suggested once that he wanted me to stay longer.

But if I did, wouldn't that make it so much harder to leave? Because I did have to leave eventually. To do otherwise would mean giving up my master's. Everything I'd imagined for my future.

Yet as my gaze followed Maisie and Stella, that idea didn't seem like such a sacrifice.

After a couple of hours, Piper started packing up. "Want to head back with us?" she asked. "We can swing by Silver Linings and raid the day-old pastries that haven't sold."

That did sound tempting. But my phone chimed with a text. "Ashford's about to head over. I'll stick around here."

"So you can have adorable family time in the park?"

I knew she was kidding, but an ache settled between my ribs.

Her face turned serious. "Hey, I shouldn't have said that. Please ignore me."

"Will you save me an iced mocha donut?"

"I always do."

I pasted on a bright smile. "Then I will forgive anything you say. I will sell out for sweets."

"Thank you for being easy." She winked, grabbing her bag and calling out to Ollie that it was time to go.

Maisie came over after they'd gone and sat in my lap. "Will you tell me a story?"

"What kind of story?"

"One about a dog with yellow fur named Stella."

"Who could ever imagine such a thing?" I tickled Maisie until she giggled. Then I made up an elaborate adventure, complete with pirates and princesses, about the dog stretched out in the grass beside us.

When I finished, Ashford still hadn't shown. Most everyone else in the park had cleared out to head home for dinner. "I wonder where your dad is?" I mused aloud.

"Maybe he's on a pirate adventure."

I tickled Maisie some more, but a sense of unease was growing in my stomach. Prickles spread over the back of my neck.

That feeling of being watched. Like I'd had on our first visit to the park, when I'd seen the man in the rain slicker.

I glanced around, not seeing anything suspicious. But the feeling only increased.

Still scanning the park, I dialed Ashford's number on my phone. He didn't answer. Which really wasn't like him. Had a client reached out, last minute? Was he working?

But then why wouldn't he let me know?

My instincts said something wasn't right. And when it came to Maisie, I trusted my instincts. Especially after what Ashford had told me about Ayla Maxwell.

"Let's head home, Maisie-doodle. We can meet your dad there."

"Okay." She'd gotten quiet in the last few minutes. Like she could feel it too.

I tried Ashford's number again. It went to voicemail.

I stretched out my hand to Maisie. "Should we skip? Or walk backwards?"

She laughed. "Skip!"

We left the park, crossing to the opposite side of the street to walk on the sidewalk. The skipping only lasted a block. Then we walked, keeping a fast pace. We passed a stretch of businesses, including Dr. Carmichael's dentist office.

Suddenly, a man stepped into our path. He was slightly taller than me, wearing dark trousers and a button-down shirt.

I stopped short, holding Maisie against my side. Stella backed up, growling low.

"Excuse me. Emma Jennings? Could we chat a moment about Ashford? I promise you, it'll be worth your while."

"You know my dad?" Maisie asked.

The man's focus sharpened on her. "Hi, sweetheart. Are you Maisie? Have you seen your aunt Ayla?"

Protectiveness flooded my body. "*Hey*," I barked at the man. "You need to *step back*. Get away from us or I'm calling the police." I tried to go around him, shielding Maisie on my other side, but the guy grabbed my elbow.

"A hundred thousand for an exclusive if you know where Ayla Maxwell is."

I tried to pull my arm free of his grasp. "Let go of me."

"Go away!" Maisie shouted and kicked at his shin.

"Emma," another voice said behind me. "Come on. In here."

I barely had time to register the fact that this was Danny Carmichael before he'd shoved the other man away. The reporter's fingers dug painfully into my arm for another moment before he was forced to let go.

Danny steered me, Maisie, and Stella into the open door of his office. He closed and locked it. My ears rang with the sudden silence, and my heart felt like it would beat out of my chest. I wondered if that man was still hanging around nearby. I assumed he was a reporter. He'd offered money for info on Ayla.

Which meant the media had found out about her connection to Ashford.

I had to tell him. This could be the exact situation he'd feared.

I knelt beside Maisie. "Are you all right, Maisie-doodle?"

"I didn't like that man."

"I know, me neither. But you were really brave." I hugged her. "We're okay now."

Then Stella barked and growled. I glanced up to see Danny with his hands up, backing away. "I was just going to check on Maisie," he said. "Can you call off your guard dog?"

"She's hardly a guard dog." But it was clear that Stella did not care for the dentist. Still, he'd helped us out, and I appreciated that. I stood, holding Maisie against me. "Thank you. I'll just call Ashford, and he'll come get us."

I felt around in my pocket for my phone. But it wasn't there.

Maisie looked up at me. "Emma, why was that man asking about Ayla? Did he mean the singer on your phone?"

My skin flushed. I couldn't help glancing at Danny again. He was frowning at us, and his expression was far too knowing.

I dug into my bag, but I still couldn't find my device. Had I dropped it somewhere? "My phone's not here. I need to call Ashford."

"I don't have his number," Danny said.

Seriously? My pulse sped up with impending panic. Should I go back and look for my phone? But I couldn't take Maisie out there, and I didn't want to leave her here with Danny.

He'd stepped in to help us, yet I didn't feel safe right now. The dental office was quiet and dark. Nobody else was here.

And even though I couldn't explain it, I had that same creeping feeling I'd had in the park.

Stella growled again.

"I think we should go," I said. "That man is probably gone. We'll walk home."

"Don't be ridiculous. I can drive you myself."

"Not necessary."

"You're being a little rude to the guy who saved you." He smiled like that was a joke. But it didn't feel like one. "For the second time, I might add."

"Second time? When was the first?"

"Outside the brewery a couple weeks ago. When someone was following you. I scared him off."

"That is not what happened," I snapped. And why was I even arguing about this?

Maisie had hidden her face against my leg. She was scared. I reached down and picked her up, resting her weight against my hip. She was a slip of a thing, but still heavy. My arms strained to keep hold of her.

"You seem to find yourself in trouble a lot," Danny commented. "Now you've lost your phone?"

"I must have dropped it. Please call Ashford and let him know where we are. I'm sure you have his number somewhere. Ask Piper for it."

That same smug smile played across Danny's lips. "Ashford and I are hardly friends."

"Is that because of Lori?"

The smile dropped away, leaving cold assessment in its wake.

The sharp sound of knuckles banging on glass made us turn our heads. Ashford was right outside the door. The sight of him was like a drug in my veins, instantly filling me with relief.

"Unlock the door," he shouted.

At an unhurried pace, Danny walked to the door and flipped the lock. Ashford yanked it open.

"What is going on? Are you both okay?" He strode over and pulled us into his arms, holding us tight.

Grace and Elias were behind him, both of them hovering anxiously outside on the sidewalk. I wasn't sure yet how much they knew, or how they'd known to come for us, but I was grateful.

"We're fine. A little freaked out."

"Some guy was harassing them," Danny cut in. "I got rid of him and brought them inside. Where exactly were *you*, O'Neal?"

"Trying to find them. And I'm here now." Ashford aimed a fierce scowl at him. Danny glanced away and shrugged.

"Ashford, my phone—"

"I found it on the street by the park. When I couldn't find either of you, I got nervous. Called Grace and Elias. They were a block away at Flamethrower. Came to help me look for you." He dug into his pocket and handed my device to me.

"Daddy, I want to go home."

"Sure, monkey. That's exactly where we're gonna go." Ashford lifted her from my arms and into his. Unlike me, he could balance her easily one-handed against his hip. He wrapped his other arm around me.

"Everything's okay now," he said. "I promise."

But the worry in his eyes suggested the opposite. Something more had happened. I just didn't know what.

✧

We piled into Ashford's truck. Grace and Elias went back to Flamethrower to grab some food and meet up with us in a bit. We headed back to the Big Blue Monster.

As soon as we got upstairs, Ashford carried Maisie to her room and laid her down. I stopped in the doorway, but he beckoned for me to come in with them.

"There was a scary man," Maisie said. "I kicked him to make him let go of Emma."

Ashford petted her head. "You did a good job. But he's gone now."

Maisie talked about the scary man on the sidewalk for a few minutes longer. She didn't mention Ayla. Ashford cast questioning glances at me, though. Like he knew there was a lot more to what had happened, but he didn't want to ask about it in front of his daughter.

We read her a couple of chapters of her latest book, *The Tale of Despereaux*, until she was settled, and Ashford agreed to let Stella come in and lay down with her.

"Just until dinner time," he said. "Emma and I are going out to the living room. We'll be right there if you need us."

"Okay, Daddy."

"Love you."

"I love you too."

He closed Maisie's door most of the way. Then took my hand and walked with me to the couch, where he tucked me tightly against him.

"You have no idea how freaked out I was when I couldn't find you."

"You said you were coming to the park, but you hadn't arrived. And I got this uncomfortable feeling, like somebody was watching us. I decided to take Maisie home. I tried to call you and you didn't answer. I must've been rushing, and that's why I dropped my phone. I'm sorry."

He moved my hair back. "No, don't you dare be sorry. I'm sorry for not being there."

"Forget about what Danny said—"

"I don't give a fuck what Carmichael said. He just enjoys being a dick to me. I got held up with something here, and that's why I was running late and didn't answer my phone. That's on me. Would you tell me what happened?"

I recounted every detail that I could remember about the man on the sidewalk. How he'd asked about Ayla. And how he knew my name. And Maisie's name.

"He touched you?" Ashford growled. "That's assault. You should press charges, if you're comfortable with it."

"Absolutely. You know I'm a cop's daughter. I have no problem filing a report. But the police will ask questions. They'll find out it was about Ayla."

"Your and Maisie's safety is more important." He kissed my forehead. "I'll text Teller. See if he or one of his officers can take your statement." Ashford got out his phone and sent off a message.

"What about the rest of what the reporter said? He asked if I knew where Ayla is. Is something going on with her?"

Ashford checked the news. And cursed. "It says Ayla Maxwell canceled the rest of her world tour last night, and has refused to make a statement. What the hell."

"She hasn't tried to call you?"

"No. Not in weeks. And I was the idiot who was relieved." He gripped the skin between his eyes, a pained look on his face.

"Maybe that reporter had some random tip and was hoping to exploit it, but if he doesn't find a story here, he'll go looking for one somewhere else."

"I think it's worse than that." He told me about how Sheldon, my former property manager, had been rifling through our trash.

"Sheldon? You're kidding." Thankfully I hadn't thrown away my old journal. I'd dried it out and kept it as a keepsake. A lot of the ink was smeared, but the thought of Sheldon reading it disgusted me.

"A reporter put him up to it. Someone from the *Hollywood Star Post*, a tabloid. But they've been in touch with him for a while. Months. Remember how the trash cart was tipped over not long after you got here?"

My hand went to my mouth. "Do you think it was the same reporter who came up to me today? Is that who Sheldon was working with?"

"I don't know. It's possible. But there could be more than one sniffing around. If Ayla suddenly took off and people are looking for her, a lot more could follow."

If Danny Carmichael had heard that reporter asking about Ayla, would he be able to connect the dots? Who else in Silver Ridge might be willing to spill details about Ashford and his daughter in exchange for a payoff?

Maybe they already had. That reporter had known my name.

"I always knew it was possible that people would find out," he said, "and I'm still not ready. I'm just glad you're here."

"Me too. I'm not going anywhere." In that moment, I meant it with my entire heart. There was nothing in the world that would make me want to leave his side. "We're going to figure this out. But you have to decide what to tell Grace and Elias when they get here."

Because if more reporters showed up in Silver Ridge looking for a story about Ayla Maxwell, Ashford's secret was not going to stay that way for long.

✦

Grace and Elias arrived with an obscene amount of food, plus Judson. "Look who we found," Elias said.

Judson took off his cowboy hat. "I heard someone accosted you, Emma. Are you okay?"

"Yeah, I'm all right."

Elias had brought burgers and grilled chicken sandwiches, to-go boxes of tots, and chocolate milkshakes. Between the food and the visitors for dinner, Maisie was all smiles. I was so glad that she'd already shaken off the upset of what had happened.

Callum showed up halfway through the meal, instantly doubling the energy around the table. I was surprised that Ashford had texted him. But if he planned to tell his siblings the truth, that made sense.

Everybody kept conversation light for Maisie's benefit. But there was definitely an unspoken tension.

Chief Landry showed up next. Unfortunately, the crowd riled Stella up again. She was barking and misbehaving, so I had to put her in my room until Maisie's bedtime. She kept whimpering until Ashford agreed to let her sleep on the floor right beside Maisie's bed.

After that, we all gathered in the living room. The police chief introduced himself to me.

"I'm Teller. Sorry to hear about the trouble you had today, Emma."

"It wasn't fun. But I'm glad to meet you. Piper's told me about you."

"Same. Would've introduced myself earlier, but I don't get out much for socializing. A visit from me isn't something people look forward to." He sounded apologetic about that.

Teller was a handsome guy in his department uniform, his blond hair cropped close to his head. I could see the family resemblance to Piper, both in his height and his striking pale-green eyes. But he didn't have Piper's easygoing smile. Instead, he had the penetrating gaze of an interrogator. Burn scars stretched over the right side of his neck and cheek.

Callum brought out a bottle of whiskey, passing around glasses. "Did you bring that bottle with you?" Ashford asked his brother.

"Hell yeah, I did. I could tell from your text that something big was up, and you never have anything decent to drink."

Teller shook his head when Callum offered him one. Callum kept going around the circle, handing whiskey to Elias, Judson, and Grace. I sucked down half my glass in one gulp. I wasn't usually a big whiskey drinker, but tonight, I wasn't turning down a shot of liquid courage.

"Do we need to call in Piper too?" Callum asked. "Make this a full club meeting?"

"We'll catch her up later," Grace said. "Ashford, just tell us what's going on."

We sat on the couch, and Ashford's hand rested on my knee as he told them about Lori's famous sister. They were all as shocked as I had been when I'd first heard it. Except for Teller, who said he had no clue who Ayla Maxwell was.

"Well, trust me," Grace said, "everybody else in the world definitely knows who she is."

"Unfortunately," Ashford muttered.

Teller crossed his arms. "So you think that was someone from the media bothering Emma and Maisie earlier?"

"We're getting to that part." Ashford explained about Sheldon digging in our trash for dirt to sell to the tabloids, and then I recounted what had happened after Maisie and I left the park.

"He hurt you?" Teller asked.

I pushed up the arm of my sweatshirt. Bruises were forming around my elbow where the man had grabbed me.

Ashford bared his teeth, a growly sound rumbling from his throat. Not unlike Stella earlier, but a whole lot more threatening. He put his arm around my shoulders. "There has to be something you can do, chief."

Teller rubbed his chin. "You said Dr. Carmichael was a witness. I'll bet the reporter is staying in a hotel somewhere in the vicinity. I'll have an officer call around and find out which one. I can get the sheriff's department involved if need be."

Elias sat forward, resting his forearms on his knees. "Then again, if you arrest this guy, it'll just provoke the media further."

Ashford nodded. "Fair point. It might be better if we encourage the guy to leave town and not come back. I'm happy to make that clear."

"No, I'll convey the message," Teller said sternly. "If that's what you would prefer over pressing charges, Emma."

"You make the call," Ashford said softly to me.

It might've been satisfying to see the guy in jail after he had frightened Maisie. But that was pointless. It would only draw attention, making the media think we had something to hide. "I would rather he leave us alone."

"I'll take care of it." Teller took out his cell phone and started typing something. A message to one of his officers, I assumed. "I'll also have a word with Sheldon. He may not have done anything illegal. I'll look into that. But I'm not going to put up with my citizens being harassed. If the tabloid media thinks they're going to cause a circus in Silver Ridge over some celebrity, they will find themselves sorely mistaken."

I believed him. He couldn't be a day over forty, and from what I'd heard, he'd been a Green Beret instead of a SEAL, but Teller reminded me of my dad. A no-nonsense special forces guy. Decorated hero, reliable through-and-through, but in the right scenario, extremely scary.

"And what if Ayla Maxwell actually shows up here?" Grace asked.

Which was what we all had to be thinking.

The police chief frowned. "Then hopefully she'll move on as soon as possible, and take her problems elsewhere. Because we certainly don't want them."

TWENTY-FOUR

Ashford

TELLER STUCK AROUND for a few more minutes, then left to head back to the station. He assured us he'd be in touch soon with whatever he found.

Hopefully, the reporter who'd harassed Emma and Maisie would be getting his ass out of town before morning. I doubted Teller would do anything out of line. He was the straight-and-narrow type. But he'd taken what happened seriously, and I was grateful for that.

After Teller took off, the rest of us sat around the table. Elias, Judson, Callum and Grace had stayed. "Thanks for being here," I said. "It means a hell of a lot. I should've told you all a long time ago."

I'd been sweating as I told them all about Lori's sister. But I should've known they would be great about it. Though Elias and Callum would definitely give me shit for keeping my superstar sister-in-law a secret.

Callum shrugged. "Yeah, but we all know you're the least likely to ask for help when you're in trouble. So thanks for trusting us. I gotta say though, I'd be even more thankful if I can meet Ayla Maxwell in person. Think she's single?"

The rest of us frowned at him.

"Oh come on, did you guys even *see* the outfit she wore to the Oscars last year?"

"It was a showstopper," Emma agreed.

"Didn't know you were so into fashion, Cal." Grace gestured at his jeans and tee. "You think Ayla will be impressed by volunteer firefighter chic?"

"My style hasn't failed me yet." He pushed the sleeve of his shirt back and flexed his bicep.

I wadded up a napkin and threw it at him. But we were all laughing.

Callum brought out the whiskey bottle again. I nodded, and he tipped another half-inch of brown liquor into my glass.

Callum went around topping up everyone else's glasses. "Here's what I want to know. How did the media find out that Ayla was Lori's sister in the first place? Obviously, Ashford has been keeping that under wraps for a long time. It's hard to imagine Ayla telling anyone, either. Don't celebrities hate the tabloids?"

"What about Danny Carmichael?" Grace asked. "Lori could've told him her sister's identity."

Emma's gaze sharpened. "Why him? Because Lori worked in his office?"

Grace tilted her head thoughtfully. "That. But I used to think...well, I wondered if maybe Lori was seeing Danny. Since we're all being honest tonight."

Judson took a sip of whiskey. "Lori was around the dentist every day. Proximity counts for a lot."

I shoved my glass away, bile rearing in my throat. "Why would you think that? Lori couldn't stand him."

"*You* can't stand him," Callum corrected. "Are you sure Lori felt the same way?"

"I..." Shit. I didn't actually know.

There was so much I still didn't know.

Emma crossed her arms on the tabletop. "Danny got Maisie

and me away from that reporter, and I appreciated that. But he was pretty rude to me afterward."

My eyes narrowed. "Rude to you?"

She waved her hand, like that part wasn't important. "I had the feeling he'd heard the name Ayla before. Like he knew something, and he was smug about it."

"Danny and I get along okay," Elias said. "I could try talking to him about what happened today. See if he lets anything slip about Lori or her sister. Or anything else Lori might've told him."

I scrubbed a hand over my face. "I guess. Thanks, man." Honestly, too much had happened today. It was hard to wrap my head around all of it.

I was wiped.

Grace and Callum hugged me on their way out. Judson tipped his hat to Emma.

Elias clapped me on the back. "I hear you asked out my baby sister," I said under my breath.

Elias smiled sheepishly. "I thought it would be easier to get forgiveness than permission. Plus, I didn't know if she'd say yes. She still hasn't."

"I could be okay with it. I know you'd be good to her."

"If she gives me a shot, I will."

I was grateful for all of my friends and family, but when Emma and I were finally alone again, I pulled her against me and just held on.

Damn, I was relieved. That Emma and Maisie were okay, but also, that I wasn't carrying around this secret anymore. Funny that I'd always dreaded this very scenario, yet now that it was here, I almost felt better.

A big part of that was Emma. Knowing she'd protected Maisie. Though it frustrated me to no end that I hadn't been there.

"You sure you're okay?" I smoothed my hand over the bruises on her elbow.

"Fine. What about you?"

"Pretty good. Considering. But there's something else I need to do." I took out my phone, went to my settings, and unblocked the last of those Los Angeles numbers. I held my phone to my ear. The number rang.

Voicemail answered, and I said, "Ayla, this is Ashford. I'm willing to talk. Call me back, but *don't* come to Silver Ridge. We had a reporter show up here and scare Maisie, and if that happens again..."

Emma reached over and squeezed my bicep reassuringly.

"Just call me back," I finished. That was all I could do for now.

No—there was something else I could do. Take care of Emma the way she deserved.

"Can I get you anything? Some tea?"

"Just you." Emma tipped her head back, and I knew exactly what she wanted. I kissed her, slow and deep. Bending down, I put my arms around her hips and lifted her up.

"Want me to make you feel good?"

She shuddered against me. "Yes. Make me forget everything else."

That, I could handle.

Emma's bedroom was closer, so I carried her inside and quietly pushed the door closed with my foot. When I set her down, she reached for the hem of her shirt, but I stopped her hand. "Let me do it. Let me take care of you."

With a shaky breath, she nodded.

I undressed her piece by piece. Pressed kisses to her exposed skin, and stroked her warm, smooth curves. Once she was down to her bra and panties, I pulled off my own shirt and opened the fly of my jeans to give my cock some more room. I was so hard that I was uncomfortable.

Sitting on her bed and scooting all the way back against the pillows, I patted my thigh. "Come here, baby."

She crawled toward me, and when she was close enough I nudged her to turn and sit between my legs. Grabbing some lotion from the nightstand, I slicked my hands and started massaging her shoulders.

After kneading the muscles up and down her spine, I unhooked her bra and reached around to cup her breasts. Emma turned to kiss me.

We'd only been together a couple of weeks, yet intimacy with her was as easy as breathing.

She got onto her knees and faced me. Kissed her way down my stomach, and then her tongue darted out to lick the tip of my cock where it poked out of my fly. I clenched my teeth on a groan.

Suddenly, all I needed in the world was to be inside her. With our bodies connected, eyes locked. I couldn't wait another second. I shoved my jeans and boxers down.

"Ride me."

Emma pushed her panties over her hips, then worked them off and straddled my lap. She opened her mouth on the sweetest sigh as she sank onto my cock, enveloping me in her tight heat.

"That's so good, baby," I murmured in her ear, and she whimpered.

I held her by the waist and pumped myself inside of her. We kissed and kissed. Trying to draw this out, make it last.

But nothing, especially not the very best things, could last forever.

✧

The next morning, Teller called with an update. Maisie was watching a show on my iPad in her bedroom, so Emma and I sat at the kitchen table and put him on speaker.

Teller got straight to the point. "We found the reporter who accosted Emma and Maisie yesterday. Guy was in an extended-stay motel outside town. I went myself along with one of Sheriff Douglas's deputies. Had a word with the suspect."

I put my hand over Emma's on the table. "How long has he been there?"

"Off and on for a couple of months. Wouldn't reveal any sources, but he admitted he's fishing for info on Ayla Maxwell. Seemed *very* concerned about anyone scooping his story."

"Who does he work for? The *Hollywood Star Post*?"

"No, claimed to be freelance."

I cursed under my breath. "That means there's more than one of them sniffing around. The person who was paying Sheldon to go through our trash was someone else."

"Yep. I sent an officer to the Ponderosa Apartments to chat with Sheldon as well. We let him know that if he goes near you again, you might press charges for harassment. Sadly it's difficult to convict someone of harassment or stalking, but I think in this case the warning will be enough."

"And the freelance reporter?" I asked. "Did he agree to leave town?"

"You bet he did. Was already packing up when we arrived. He knew he'd gone too far. He's driving out of the county as we speak."

Emma exhaled. "Chief Landry, did you by any chance see a dark blue rain slicker in the reporter's motel room?"

I lifted my eyebrows, locking eyes with her. I hadn't thought to ask about that.

"Huh." The chief thought a moment. "You know, I believe I did see one. A raincoat hanging on a hook by the door. What's the significance?"

"Someone was watching me and Maisie about a month ago wearing that coat. Then followed me to my apartment. Ashford saw him."

"I chased him off," I said. "Didn't report it because we couldn't be sure he'd done anything wrong."

But now, I was kicking myself for not realizing what it meant.

"There probably wasn't anything I could've done at that point," Teller said. "But now we know the situation. So does

Sheriff Douglas. Next time someone shows up in Silver Ridge digging for info on your sister-in-law, we'll at least know what's up. But Ashford, I've gotta be honest with you. If these reporters follow the rules, there's very little I can do. They have First Amendment rights. I can't banish them from town or forbid Silver Ridge residents from talking to them. Much as I might like to."

"I know. Thanks for all your help, though."

"Keep me posted, and we'll keep doing what we can."

I ended the call. "Now we know who was following you the day of the rainstorm. The whole time, it was that reporter. He could've followed you other times, too. Like the night you left the brewery."

"It's possible. Kind of anticlimactic, in a way. The guy's a nuisance, but he wasn't actually that dangerous."

"He *hurt* you yesterday. Bruised your arm."

"I know. But he wanted information. Not to actually hurt us." Emma glanced in the direction of Maisie's bedroom. We could still hear her Netflix show playing. "If more reporters show up, there has to be something more we can do to fight back."

I smoothed a lock of hair from her cheek and tucked it behind her ear. "Aside from leaving messages for Ayla on every possible phone number, I don't see what else I can do."

Exactly why I'd always dreaded the media's discovery of this secret. I was all for reporters exposing corrupt politicians and important news events. But my child's blood connection to a celebrity wasn't news. And yet they could upend our lives because of it.

Emma seemed like she wanted to say more, but she was hesitating.

"What is it?" I asked.

"Do you think, if you speak to Ayla, you'll ask her again about what Lori was keeping secret around the time she died?"

For a moment, I struggled to respond. "I don't know. That's a tough question to answer. Part of me still wants to know the truth. But the other part of me..." I shook my head. "Just wants to never see or speak to Ayla Maxwell again."

Emma nodded. "Then maybe you should get legal advice about this. My dad and stepmom are friends with a bunch of lawyers. Including one of the top private attorneys in West Oaks, Jane Holt. I'm sure she knows lawyers who practice in Colorado."

"I don't want you worrying about this. It's my problem to fix, not yours."

"But—"

I stopped whatever she was about to say with a kiss. If I really got desperate for legal representation, I could call my Army buddy Dane for a loan. But that wasn't anything I wanted Emma stressing about. "I just want to enjoy spending time with you and Maisie," I said. "Couple more weeks until we can get out in the wilderness for our camping trip, and it can't come soon enough."

"You still feel okay about going?"

"Absolutely. I want to get away more than ever."

I had little control over this situation with Ayla, and I hated that feeling. All I could do was keep Maisie and the other people I cared about close.

I had to enjoy whatever time with Emma I had left. After this summer, I would go back to focusing solely on my kid. That had been enough for me before Emma. It could be enough for me again.

Even if I knew deep down that I was lying to myself.

TWENTY-FIVE
Emma

"Don't put your feet on the dash," Ashford grumped at me. "It's dangerous if we get in an accident."

"You're such a dad." Smiling, I took my socked feet down.

"Daddy? Can I put my head out the window like Stella?"

I turned to look in the backseat of Ashford's truck. Stella had her paws on the door, tongue and ears blowing in the wind from the half-open window.

"Not a good idea on the highway, monkey. But maybe in the parking lot of the campsite. When we get there."

"But she's having so much fun," Maisie said, kicking her legs in her booster seat.

Ashford heaved a sigh. "All right. You can stick your hand out. But that's it."

"Softie," I whispered.

Shaking his head, Ashford buzzed Maisie's window down, filling the cabin with a rush of air that had my dark locks swirling around my head. I laughed, pulling my hair into a knot, then turned up the radio.

"Oh! Our road-trip playlist." Bending to search through my bag at my feet, I found my phone and cued it up.

"You made a playlist?" he asked.

"Of *course* we did. Maisie and I."

I was *so* ready for this trip. It was the first Friday of August, the sun shone down from a crystal-clear blue sky, and we had about five days of camping, breathtaking scenery, and open road to look forward to. We planned to camp for three nights and then meet up with Grace for a final night at a hot spring.

"I love this song!" Maisie shouted when a new one came on. "Daddy, we all have to sing. You too."

"Not happening."

"*Please?*"

"I don't know any of these songs."

"What music *do* you like?" I asked.

He shrugged, being all mysterious.

After that reporter had left town, we'd been on pins and needles for days wondering when the next might arrive. But no one had. Then the news broke that Ayla had resurfaced. She'd checked herself into a rehabilitation facility in New England for exhaustion. A media frenzy followed her there.

Ayla hadn't returned Ashford's call. I knew almost nothing about her, and I wished her well. I couldn't imagine the pressure that her level of fame would put her under. But I was glad that the focus was off of Ashford and Maisie. At least for now.

As far as what would happen after we returned to Silver Ridge, what the last few weeks of the summer would bring, my plans for the fall...

Nope. Not thinking about any of that. Thinking about the future was off limits this week.

But I *had* made it my mission to discover what kind of music Ashford liked. Whenever I asked him about different genres, whether it was alternative or country or classic rock, he claimed to have no opinion. But I refused to believe that somebody had no opinion on music.

I turned and winked at Maisie. "We put a lot of different songs on this playlist. I bet we'll have your dad singing along by the end of this trip."

A few hours later, we pulled into the campsite. It was a perfect spot, surrounded by tall pine trees with craggy mountains looking down on us. The nearest other campsite was barely within view. Maisie and Stella had already run off to explore.

"How long ago did you book this?" I asked.

Ashford laughed as he unloaded gear from his truck bed. "After Maisie and I took our camping trip last year. Best bang for your vacation bucks, and spots book up fast."

"It's gorgeous."

He hefted the bag with the tent on his shoulder, stopping to kiss me. "Even more gorgeous with you here. I'll have to book it again for next year."

His smile faltered, like he'd just realized what he'd said. *Next year.*

"You should," I said quickly. "Maisie clearly loves it." But I wouldn't be there.

We set up the campsite, then hiked a nearby trail that took us up to a waterfall. Ashford didn't let Maisie get too close, but she was able to splash a little with Stella right beside the bank. Then it was back to the camp, where we started a fire.

"Everything okay?" I asked. I'd noticed Ashford checking his phone.

"Just seeing if there's reception. No service."

I pulled out my phone and found it was the same. "That's good though, right? No news is good news."

He huffed a laugh. "That's my motto lately."

Around sunset, and after a dinner of campfire-grilled steak tacos, Maisie begged for s'mores. I grabbed my guitar. Because how could we have a proper campout with no music?

I started with the opening strains of "Dust in the Wind."

Ashford chuckled. "I know what you're doing."

"What, Daddy?" Maisie was sitting in his lap. She looked up at him while she licked her sticky, marshmallow-covered fingers.

"Emma's trying to get me to sing along to something."

"I'm not giving up. I *will* find out what you like."

I strummed and sang the words of "Dust in the Wind," quickly losing myself in the lyrics and the melody and wishing I could play the solo on my violin, but I'd only brought my acoustic Yamaha. That song became another. And another. Until the campsite was dark around us, and embers from the campfire rose up toward the starry sky.

Then I started "Let it Be," and Maisie said, "Daddy loves this one!"

I gasped. Ashford laughed softly. "Got me. See, I'm not that interesting."

"I disagree. The Beatles are timeless." I played my heart out, singing along, but nearly lost my place when Ashford started singing along. He shrugged at me and kept going. As if this wasn't a minor miracle.

He had an amazing voice, too. Smooth and deep.

I played every Beatles song I could think of. When I stopped, Maisie was sound asleep in Ashford's lap, and the fire had burned down.

"You have a great voice," I said quietly. "Why don't you ever sing?"

In the couple of months I'd known him, tonight was the first time I'd ever heard him. He was better than me. I had a serviceable voice, enough to get a song across. But Ashford had that extra special quality to his tone. Something rare and beautiful.

"I used to. Sang to Maisie when she was a baby. Lori could *not* carry a tune." His teeth flashed in the dark as he smiled. "I guess I forgot how good it could feel. Letting go like that."

I set my guitar carefully aside and moved closer to them. Ashford wrapped an arm around me while cradling his sleeping daughter. And suddenly, it felt like my chest was ready to break open with all I was feeling. Tears stung my eyes.

I told myself it was the smoke from the campfire.

"I'm glad you could do this with us," he whispered.

"Me too."

"Do you... Is everything settled for your new school? Does it start this month?"

What are you really asking me? I wanted to say.

"The semester starts at the beginning of September. I'll have to be there by the end of the month. Unless..."

"Unless?"

Unless you ask me to stay.

I was shocked when that thought surfaced in my head. It was one thing to consider sticking around Silver Ridge if I hadn't gotten into a new program. But turning down an offer to transfer? Giving up my master's? To do what?

I loved teaching music to the kids of Silver Ridge. And I loved a lot of other things about my life in Colorado. But my lease with Dixie ended soon. I didn't have my own place here. Ashford didn't want to share his space with me forever.

"Unless I don't get off the waitlist," I finally said.

"You will. They'd be idiots not to want you."

I stared into the remains of the fire, no longer sure what *I* wanted.

✧

"Aunt Grace is here!"

Before Ashford could stop her, Maisie dashed across the parking lot. Thankfully there were no cars moving anywhere near us. Grace had just gotten out of her sedan, and she knelt down, opening her arms for Maisie to run into them. The girl knocked Grace's glasses askew and nearly sent the both of them sprawling on the concrete.

"I swear, I've taught her better than that," Ashford said through clenched teeth.

"You've been blessed with a courageous kid."

"Or maybe cursed."

Grabbing our bags from the truck, we walked over to meet

them. Grace hugged her brother, then opened her arms to me.

"Warning you, I smell bad," I said. "Haven't showered in days."

"I'm sure I've smelled worse. Oh. Wow, that *is* intense."

We both laughed.

For the last three days, Maisie, Ashford, and I hiked, sang, and stargazed to our hearts' content. Now we'd arrived at a hotel next to a public hot spring. All three of us could use a shower. Make that four, because Stella needed a more thorough bath than she'd gotten in the creek.

It had been idyllic, though. Spending every waking moment with them. Laughing at Maisie's jokes and Ashford's dry humor. Nestling in our sleeping bags in the tent with Maisie's in between us. And no internet access.

Of course, I saw Ashford scanning his phone the first chance he got during check-in.

I leaned in. "All good?"

He nodded, tucking his phone away. "No news."

"I've been keeping an eye on the tabloids and gossip sites," Grace chimed in. Maisie and Stella were over by the hotel lobby's aquarium, watching fish swim around. "Everything on Ayla has gone quiet since she checked into the rehab facility."

"I hope she's okay," I said.

Ashford scowled. "I hope she stays on the other side of the country. And forgets my number."

The clerk at the reception desk finished with our check-in and handed us key cards for two rooms.

I nudged Grace. "Guess it's you and me, roomie." I assumed Ashford and his daughter would take the other.

"Oh, I'll stay with Maisie."

"You don't mind?" Ashford asked.

"Please, like that wasn't your plan all along, big brother. A romantic hotel stay. Just keep it down, okay?"

"I would say something obnoxious, Gracie, but I don't want you to change your mind."

"I accept payment in Swiss chocolate. And French cheese."

Ashford grinned. "If they have any of those things at the pool, I'll buy it for you."

Sadly, we didn't have time for any hanky-panky right away, even though it had been days since Ashford and I had been truly alone together. We took lightning-fast showers, then got our swimsuits on to head over to the hot spring.

While Ashford took Maisie into the pool, Grace and I went for the hot tub. "That is gooood," I said as I sank into the water. After chasing around a six-year-old in the woods for three days, plus a man in insanely fit shape, it felt amazing to unwind.

"So good," Grace agreed. "Maybe better than an orgasm. Not that I have many prospects there. Unlike some people."

I didn't know whether to laugh or apologize. But at least she was loosening up around me. She'd left her glasses off and tied her auburn hair into a twist. Grace could've been a model if she'd wanted to. Her bone structure was incredible, yet she'd chosen a style of glasses that hid her face as much as possible.

Made me wonder what other parts of herself she was hiding. Maybe she had more in common with her brother than just her sharp cheekbones.

"It's sweet of you to room with Maisie," I said. "I'm sure that's not why Ashford invited you."

"Then my brother is more devious than you realize. But it's fine. I love that girl. I've been missing her while you guys were gone." She ruffled her hands through the water. "I had to turn down Elias for a date, though. Second time he's asked me out. He's persistent."

"Yeah? You haven't said yes?"

She side-eyed me. "Ashford hasn't mentioned it to you?"

"No."

"Well." Grace turned on the bench so she was facing me. "Elias and I have been friends forever. We work together too. I do freelance accounting, and I handle his books for Flamethrower. Don't you think it would complicate things? If I cross that line with him?"

I couldn't believe it. Grace was asking me for advice. "It *could* complicate things. But it could also be amazing. Since you've been friends with him so long, you know what kind of man he is. You know what you're getting into."

"You sound like Piper, with her lectures about marrying the wrong guy and getting a nasty surprise."

I barked a laugh. "Piper came by that opinion honestly. I don't blame her for it."

"You haven't known my brother that long."

Her words could've been harsh, but she'd said them gently.

"I feel like I know Ashford." I glanced at the pool, where Maisie was screaming with joy as Ashford tossed her around. All his sexy muscles were on display, wet and golden in the sun, but it was his smile that really drew me. The adoration he showed to his daughter. The kindness and attention he showed to me.

"I really like him," I whispered.

"What are you going to do about that?"

When I looked back at Grace, her dark eyes were sympathetic.

"I wish I knew."

TWENTY-SIX
Emma

AFTER HOURS of swimming and eating junk food for dinner, Maisie was about ready to drop. "I'm going to take her back to the room," Grace said.

She'd offered to take Stella for the night too. I hugged Maisie goodnight, and Ashford gave her a bunch of kisses before she and Grace went to their room to get ready for bed.

"We owe your sister a bottle of wine or something," I said. We were sharing a lounge chair by the pool, squeezed in together. Ashford was still shirtless, his tan skin hot against mine in my bikini.

"I promised her a new vanity in her bathroom. I would've done it anyway. But this way, she doesn't feel guilty about asking me. Grace is always giving to other people, but she sucks at accepting anything for herself."

I kissed his whiskery cheek. "You're a good brother."

"I am." He smirked. "I'm installing it in a few weeks as soon as it arrives."

A pang of longing hit me. Because in a few weeks, I'd probably be gone.

But I was here with Ashford now. We had most of the rest of this month.

We had tonight.

"Want to head back to the room?" Ashford asked, his tone low and husky.

"There is nothing else I'd rather do."

First stop was the shower. Ashford switched on the water to get it heating, while I teasingly undid the ties of my bikini.

He stepped toward me, hands going to my hips and his mouth dropping to lick along my collarbone. "You are so sexy. I'm starving for you. It's been days since I could last have you."

I closed my eyes as his mouth went lower, capturing my nipple between his lips. "I've missed this too. But I really had fun. The past few days..."

Ashford's tongue smoothed over my sensitive nipple before he released me and stood. "I had fun too. Never been camping with a dog before. I have a feeling Maisie will refuse to do any other kind of camping from now on."

I knew he was kidding, but that longing in my chest only increased.

We'd spent twenty-four-seven together at the campsite. I hadn't felt bored for a single second. I loved my friends, but as an introvert, I was the type to need some time to myself to recharge. But not with Ashford and Maisie. With them, I could've stayed a lot longer.

Maybe forever.

We pulled off the rest of our swimsuits and stepped beneath the hot water. Ashford pumped shampoo from the dispenser and washed my hair, then lathered my body with shower gel. I relaxed against him, and his erection slid against my lower back.

Spinning in his arms, I held on to his shoulders and kissed him. Our tongues glided, stroking. He moaned, his hands squeezing my curves as he rubbed his stiff, swollen cock against me.

"I could take you up against this wall," he said.

"You could." When his eyes flashed with lust, I added, "But I haven't had my turn to wash you yet."

We had nowhere else we had to be, which was a rare luxury. Usually one of us had a class to teach, or an appointment to run off to, or Maisie would be back soon. But tonight, it was just us. All the way until morning.

I stepped back and pumped shampoo into my palm. My fingers dug into his scalp as I reached up to wash his hair. Then I washed and rinsed the rest of him thoroughly, enjoying the way his body responded to my touch. I liked seeing *exactly* how turned on he was.

Finally he growled and pushed me against the tile. "You're driving me wild."

"What are you going to do about that?"

"I'm trying to decide how I want you first." His gaze dragged down my body, following the trail of the water that dripped along my curves.

He switched off the water, got out, and wrapped me in a towel. The cooler air outside the shower prickled against my skin.

"Here. Right here. Can't wait another second." He turned me around, leaning me over the bathroom vanity and stroking my bare behind beneath the towel. My gasp echoed against the bathroom tile as his cock filled me in a single thrust, making me lift up onto my tiptoes.

Our bodies met, wet skin sliding, as the heat built between us. Our towels fell to the floor. The sight of us together in the mirror was scandalous.

"I needed this too badly," he said. "I'm not going to last." Ashford brought his hand between my legs and ruthlessly stroked me where I was most sensitive. Within minutes, we were both tumbling together over the edge.

After another rinse in the shower, we stumbled into the bedroom and fell naked into bed, towels strewn across the floor as we kicked the covers down. Kissing. Touching.

We'd been together enough times now that we knew each other's bodies. What the other liked. Yet tonight felt completely new as well. Like something had changed between us in the last few days. Every kiss was more intense.

"I finally get to have you all night." He lowered his head to whisper in my ear. "I hope you're not tired, because I plan to give you such a workout you'll be feeling me the rest of the week."

"Big promises."

He rubbed his thickening cock against my thigh. "My promises aren't the only thing that's big."

I tipped my head back and laughed. Even though he was *not* wrong.

I'd learned that Ashford's sense of humor came out whenever he was at ease. I loved that he felt that way around me. I could be myself with him too. I'd never had this intense a connection with a lover before.

When I was in Ashford's arms, everything seemed easy.

We kissed until we were both aching again. Desperate. Ashford slid his cock inside me, our bodies meeting like we were made for each other. But he took a more gradual pace this time. Driving us both slowly and deliberately to the edge.

"*Please*," I begged, angling my hips to meet him on every thrust, but still needing more. What only he could give me.

His brown and amber eyes held more passion than ever as he gazed down at me. "Tell me what you need."

"Don't stop. Don't let me go."

"Never, baby. You're mine."

But I had meant more than just the heat of this moment. More than something physical. Because, as I stared into his eyes, what I felt was suddenly so clear. Even if I didn't have the courage to say it.

I need you to love me, I thought. *Because I'm in love with you.*

✦

Morning light glowed in the windows, slowly nudging me awake. I felt Ashford beside me. His breathing was smooth and regular. But when I opened my eyes, I found him already awake and watching me.

"Morning," he said, voice scratchy. A yawn stretched the end of the word. We hadn't gotten much sleep.

I snuggled against his bare skin. "Hi."

"First time I've ever woken up next to you naked." Ashford shifted, and his half-hard cock bumped my hip. "You had enough yet?" The amber in his eyes sparked, and he smiled.

"Not yet."

He rolled me onto my back and kissed me. A short while later, he was moving inside me again. Insatiable. But I felt the same.

More, more, more.

Afterward, we showered. We were both sated for the moment, so our kisses and wandering hands were purely affectionate. But I still couldn't get enough. We stood under the spray, arms around each other. I rested my cheek on the swell of his pec beneath his collarbone. He touched the back of my head, smoothing my wet hair.

"Hard to believe you'll be gone in a few weeks."

I looked up at him. "It is. The summer's going too fast."

"Maisie's going to miss you."

I smiled, even though I was shrinking inside. I adored Maisie, but how did *he* feel about me going? "I'll miss her too. And you. I..." The words got lost on their way out.

"I am going to miss you so damn much." Ashford's voice was just as thick as mine. Which gave me a sliver of encouragement.

"I could visit sometime. If you'd want."

"*Yeah.* Of course I want that." He cupped my face. Searched my eyes with his. "Emma..."

I held my breath. Aching to hear the words I couldn't manage to say myself.

"Do you hear that?" he asked.

"What?"

Ashford twisted the shower valve. The sound of a phone ringing filled the quiet. "My phone." He got out, wrapping a towel around his waist and tossing another to me on his way out of the bathroom. I followed, water streaming from my hair and down my shoulders as I held the towel to the front of my body.

He grabbed his phone from the dresser. "It's my sister." Putting the device to his ear, he said, "Grace? Everything okay?"

I couldn't hear what she was saying. But the color drained from his face. Without another word to his sister, Ashford lowered his phone and thumbed at the screen.

"What's going on?"

"Grace just saw this. Callum sent it to her, and she forwarded it to me." He turned the phone so I could see it. There was an article from a tabloid website on his screen.

Exclusive: Ayla Maxwell's Secret Grief.

"Oh no. What does it say? Does it mention Maisie?"

"I don't know yet."

I tangled our fingers together. "Maybe it's not so bad."

Ashford's expression was made of stone. We sat on the bed and looked at his screen.

Singer Ayla Maxwell has long been secretive about her background, though many of her song lyrics hint at a dark history of personal grief. Now, we know why.

Three years ago, Ayla's sister Lori O'Neal died tragically on a deserted highway outside the small Colorado town of Silver Ridge. Questions still swirl around her death. Local police shut down the investigation and ruled it an accident.

But even more problematic questions surround Ayla's brother-in-law, Ashford O'Neal, a martial-arts enthusiast with a violent family history.

While they were both members of the US Army, Ashford's older brother Grayden was courtmartialed and convicted of manslaughter.

Ashford's chest lifted and fell as he breathed. His fury radiated off of him in waves. "That's a low blow, bringing up my brother."

I wanted to stop reading this train wreck of an article, but of course, I couldn't.

Sources report that O'Neal has kept Lori's young daughter away from Ayla for years, even though the singer has begged to see her niece to confirm the girl's wellbeing. Yet just recently, he invited a much younger woman, Emma Jennings, into his daughter's life.

But Jennings has a checkered history of her own.

"Some of this is about *me*." My body went tight and cold. Like numbness was spreading through me. I read the words, but they wouldn't sink in.

Just months ago, Jennings left her graduate-level music program in disgrace after an affair with the husband of her professor. While Jennings avoided official discipline, the professor has had to take a leave of absence from her own position.

"I was humiliated," the professor said when asked for comment on the scandal, though she's asked not to have her name revealed in this article.

Those words seemed to echo. *Disgrace. Humiliated.*

Oh, God. All my friends from college and high school might see this. My family.

My *dad*.

"Hell." Ashford switched the phone screen off, blotting out the rest of the article. "I figured Ayla might go after me one day, but now they've brought you into it, and that is so far beyond the pale."

He got up, doing something on his phone, then held it to his ear. "Ayla, you need to call me back. *Now.*"

Numbly, I got up and grabbed my phone. I'd had it on Do Not Disturb overnight, but now I checked my notifications. There was a dozen. Calls, texts, emails. Including from my stepmom, Madison.

My knees went weak. My stomach roiled.

Ashford appeared at my side, strong arms closing around me. "Baby, I am so sorry about this."

"It's not your fault. At least they didn't reveal Maisie's name. I'll call that lawyer I mentioned. You need someone representing you."

"Probably, but what they said about you... We're not going to take this. I'm going to do everything I can to get that article taken down. This bullshit reporter needs to apologize to you." He held my face, studying me.

"I don't see any of that happening. Don't worry about me. I'm fine. Let's focus on Maisie."

"Are you sure you're all right?"

"Not really. But we have Maisie to think about."

He couldn't argue with that.

Somehow, we got dressed and packed, then went to the lobby to meet Grace and Maisie. I felt like I was sleepwalking. But I pasted on a smile and gave Maisie a hug. I couldn't let her see how upset I was.

"How are you?" Grace whispered to me while Ashford took Maisie through the free breakfast line. I wasn't hungry.

"Been better," I said.

"Can you call a lawyer or something?"

"I will. For Ashford." The article hadn't gone so far as accusing him of a crime, but the implication was there. We had to do damage control.

"But what about—"

"What the article said about me is true."

Grace clenched her jaw in a grimace. Shame rocked through me.

I hadn't realized my ex's wife had taken a leave of absence. Of course she was humiliated by what had happened. So was I. We'd both been lied to. But between the two of us, I was *the other woman*. The villain. The article made it sound like I'd gone after my professor's husband on purpose.

It was absurd that my ex had suffered so little for what he'd done, not even losing his job. From what I'd heard, he'd received no more than a slap on the wrist from his superiors. Fair? No. But that was reality. It wasn't like the school administration had kicked me out. I'd left voluntarily. But everyone's reactions to the scandal made it clear that I wasn't wanted there.

He was a beloved director. I was no one.

And right now, I really felt like it.

"Could I ride with you on the way back?" I asked Grace. "Would you mind making a detour?"

A line appeared between her eyebrows. "Why?"

"A favor. Please."

"Sure, if you want."

When I told Ashford I was leaving with his sister, he pulled me to a quiet part of the lobby. "What do you mean you aren't coming home with us?"

"I'm worried reporters will show up to your place. If they see me with you, that could make things worse."

"So what? I *want* you with us." He held my hand in both of his, pressing it tightly. "That's where you belong."

I blinked fast so my tears wouldn't fall. I didn't want to make this about me. Ashford had enough problems without adding mine.

"I've been texting with Callum," Ashford said. "He hasn't seen any reporter-type people around. They'll probably come eventually. But it's only a couple of hours back to Silver Ridge. Once we're home, then—"

"I need some space to think. And to call my family and figure out what I'm going to say. I can't do that in front of Maisie. Please."

"Then where are you going, exactly?"

"I'm going to Hartley. I'll stay with Uncle Aiden and Jessi and make my calls and figure out what we're going to do."

"I am not okay with this. But if it's what you need, then I'll be patient. When will I see you?"

"In a few days or so."

"I need a specific number."

"Maybe three."

"Fine. Three. Then I'm coming to get you."

Maisie ran up, crashing into Ashford's legs. "Daddy, can I have another waffle?" She looked over at me. "Emma, what's wrong?"

I knelt. "Nothing, Maisie-doodle. But I have a bunch of work I need to do, and I'll be gone a few days."

"You have to?"

"I do. I'm sorry." I gave her a hug, closing my eyes as a tear slipped free. "You are so special," I whispered. "So precious."

"When are you coming home?" she asked.

"I'm sure I'll see you soon. But remember, I'm only here for the summer. That's just a few more weeks."

She frowned. "I know. I remember." After another squeeze, I let her go.

Ashford kissed me on the cheek. "Call me later."

"I'll text."

He was going to keep arguing, but Maisie called out for him to help her.

"Go," I said. "I'll be okay."

Grace asked me a few questions on our way to Hartley, but I struggled to form any coherent answers. My phone kept buzzing with more calls and messages, and I couldn't avoid them forever.

What was I going to tell them?

In a way, the truth about last semester was easier to face now. I was deeply ashamed of what had happened and the way I'd left my master's program. But now, it was out there. Dad knew. I couldn't do anything about that.

The far worse part of it was that I'd hurt Ashford by association. That tabloid was trying to use me to make him look like an unfit father. It was ridiculous, but plenty of people would think worse of him because he'd welcomed me into his daughter's life. Hard to believe some people still thought that way, but they did. As that tabloid reporter had expected. People loved salacious gossip, and they loved to pass judgment.

I'd thought I was wiping my slate clean by coming to Silver Ridge for the summer. That had been a fantasy. My past had followed me.

Silver Ridge wasn't really home. I'd known it all along. I didn't belong with the O'Neals. It was time for me to face that fact.

I never should've let myself fall in love with Ashford and his sweet little girl. Because I was *never* supposed to stay.

TWENTY-SEVEN

Ashford

I'D AGREED to give Emma a few days. Three at the most. It had been two.

I was *miserable*.

"You should go to bed. Get some sleep." Grace walked into the kitchen in her pajamas. "Or at least turn a light on. Sitting here in the dark is creepy, and it can't be making your mood any better."

"You think a light is going to help my mood? It'll just signal to the vultures outside that we're up."

It was the middle of the night, and I was sitting at my kitchen table doom-scrolling through social media. My phone had dozens of emails and voicemails from reporters seeking comments. I'd given up on deleting them.

The reporters had descended within hours of us returning home after our trip. We'd had to cancel classes. Chief Landry had increased his officers' patrols down our block, but if the reporters and news vans stayed on the public sidewalks and street, there were limits to what he could do to keep them away.

Grace and Callum had been braving the paparazzi to bring us supplies, but Maisie and I were pretty much trapped here, and my little girl had no idea why these strangers were suddenly bothering us.

All she knew was that Emma wasn't here, and she didn't understand why.

As promised, Emma had texted once she arrived in Hartley. *I'm with my family, and I'm safe. I'm sorry about that article. But I will try to make it right. I miss you so much, Ashford. You and Maisie both.*

Which sounded very reasonable, if completely unsatisfying.

I wanted to put my fist through a wall, but I couldn't act like an impulsive teenager. I was a father. Had to set an example. But it would've felt good. Better yet, I might put my fist through some reporter's face. That article had lumped me in with my older brother. I had a *violent family history*.

Well, I could show them violence. *Just give me an opportunity*.

Grace opened the fridge and came back to the table with a takeout container and two forks. "Eat something."

"Not hungry."

"That wasn't a suggestion, O'Neal." She handed me a utensil and opened the lid. We both dug into cold leftover noodles.

"Have you spoken to Emma?" Grace asked.

"A little. On the phone. She won't tell me where she is."

"Because she knows you'd show up there."

"Hell yes, I would."

I'd tried to find out where exactly Emma was. Grace had dropped her off at a diner on Hartley's Main Street, so that wasn't much help. I didn't know her Uncle Aiden's last name. It wasn't Jennings, because I'd looked for an Aiden Jennings, and there wasn't one in Hartley.

If I'd known where Emma was, I would've followed her out there already. Screw being patient. Screw all these reporters. Screw three days.

I shoveled noodles into my mouth, barely tasting them.

Yesterday, I'd received a call from Emma's lawyer friend in California. Jane Holt. I assumed that was what Emma meant by "making it right." She was still trying to help me and Maisie, after everything.

Jane had offered to find me a lawyer in Colorado who had expertise in media relations and privacy laws. Not something I'd ever wanted to know about. But from what Jane had told me, we probably couldn't get that article taken down. All the facts it had stated were technically true, even though it had drawn ridiculous implications.

Not like it mattered at this point, anyway. That article was out there. People were talking about us. Posting about us. Coming up with wild theories about Ayla's lyrics and how they were about me and the awful things I'd supposedly done to Lori.

It was pure madness. I didn't want my kid to have to deal with this. But the constant ache in my chest wasn't really concern for Maisie. She was safe here surrounded by me, Grace, and Callum. Jane Holt had assured me there was very little Ayla could do in a court of law to take Maisie away from me.

I couldn't sleep because Emma was out there, and she was hurting. I got the feeling she blamed herself for somehow making the situation worse, and it couldn't be further from the truth.

I wanted to make it better. I wanted her with me.

"I think I'm in love with her." My voice sounded like it was made of a thousand broken pieces. Missing her had me in a chokehold. I couldn't breathe.

"Oh, Ashford." Grace set her fork down and rested her hand on mine. "I already figured."

I'd realized it that last night we were together. In the hotel. I'd almost told her. And again the next morning, when she woke up in my arms and I couldn't take my eyes off of her. I wanted to tell her now, but I refused to do it over the phone.

"It snuck up on me," I said to my sister. "Falling in love with her. I'd never felt anything like that."

Being Maisie's father was fulfilling, but loving Emma was a different kind of happiness. She'd stitched together the broody, rough-hewn parts of me into a whole person. A whole man.

All those evenings we'd had dinner together, laughing. Afternoons in the park with Stella. Reading Maisie stories at bedtime. Sharing things I'd never confessed to anyone.

Lingering kisses and hours spent in my bed, skin to skin. Burning up the sheets. Burning away all my resistance. I'd made her mine in every way. How had I ever thought I could let her go?

Emma had suggested she could come back and visit. It had been an opening, right? Maybe she wanted us to keep seeing each other after the summer ended. There had to be a way to make this work.

But why would Emma want to keep seeing me now that her private business had been splashed in front of the entire world, and it was because of me?

Grace rubbed my hand. "What can I get you? Some of that whiskey Callum brought?"

My brother was in my room right now, snoring. Grace had taken the couch. It probably would've made more sense for her to take Emma's room, but Grace hadn't suggested that, and neither had I. All Emma's stuff was in there. Stella's doggy bed and toys.

I'd been in there earlier, and that had not been a good idea. I'd been drowning in the scent of lavender-vanilla, and only Maisie calling for me had brought me back to the surface.

"I'm going to go downstairs and work out," I said. "Maybe I can exhaust myself so I can sleep."

"Let me know if you need anything else."

"Just stay close if Maisie wakes up in the night."

"Yeah, I've got it."

"Thanks."

I went down to the training room. Did pushups, sit-ups, and banged out pull-ups on the bar over the doorframe. The exercise helped some. Yet I still wasn't tired.

Then someone knocked, and I realized it was the external door at the back of the building. Probably another vulture reporter.

Fury rushed back, setting my pulse racing. *Seriously?* It was the middle of the night. My kid was sleeping. Did these people have no decency?

Don't do anything stupid, I told myself. But I was already storming to the door. I felt just reckless enough to welcome a fight, no matter how idiotic that would be.

I yanked the door open.

But there was no reporter outside.

Ayla Maxwell stood on the concrete outside my back door. She had a baseball cap pulled over her platinum-blond hair, no trace of her signature dramatic makeup, but her heart-shaped face and green eyes were unmistakable. Same face and eyes that Lori and my daughter shared.

"Are you *insane*?" I growled.

"It's quite possible," she muttered.

I grabbed her arm and pulled her inside, glancing around. But there wasn't a single reporter or photographer in sight.

I closed the door quietly, thinking of my daughter asleep upstairs, and locked the bolt. "Haven't you done enough to fuck up my life?"

"I'm so sorry about the article. That wasn't me, I swear."

"It was your fault, though."

She couldn't argue with that.

Under the harsh light of the hallway, dark circles ringed her eyes. Not unlike the ones I'd seen in my own mirror. Her lips were chapped, and her skin was sickly pale. A baggy T-shirt and a backpack swallowed her petite frame.

I refused to believe that Ayla felt worse than I did. But she wasn't in good shape. That was for sure.

"How'd you even get here?"

"I snuck out of the rehab facility, bought a car with cash, and drove here. Parked a couple blocks away and walked to your building. I made sure nobody was around to see."

"You drove here from New England? By yourself?"

"Didn't have much choice."

"Then why isn't the news reporting that you disappeared again?"

"My people are probably keeping it quiet as long as they can. But I left my phone behind and I've avoided using credit cards so they don't know where I am. I swear I would never wish to cause you or Maisie any harm. I just really, really need a friend. And I have nowhere else to go."

I scrubbed my hands over my face. I didn't need this.

My veins pulsed with all the anger and frustration I could unleash on this woman. But what good would that do? It wouldn't bring Emma back home.

Except for magazine covers and screens, I hadn't seen Ayla since she was a teenager. Yet right now, she seemed far more like Lori's younger sister than a superstar.

If Lori were here, would she want me to turn her sister away?

"Do you like tea?" I asked.

"What? *Tea*?"

"Yeah. Hot tea. The froo-froo, flowery kind. Do you like it?"

"Um, yes." She eyed me warily. "Tea would pretty much be the best thing ever."

I heaved a sigh. "Come on, then."

Turning, I headed for the kitchenette, not waiting to see if she'd follow. Part of me hoped she'd think better of this and leave.

But she didn't. Ayla followed me and stood in the doorway while I poured water into the kettle to heat. I grabbed the box of tea from the shelf.

"You don't seem like the flowery tea type," Ayla said.

"It's Emma's."

"Oh. Is she here with Maisie?" Ayla's voice lifted when she said my daughter's name.

I gritted my teeth. "No, Emma left. Because of that article."

"I really am sorry about that. I had no idea anyone knew Maisie was my niece until the story broke. Is Maisie okay?"

"She's fine."

"And Emma?"

"I wish she was here. But yeah, she's safe." I loosened up, just a little, at the concern I'd heard in Ayla's voice.

When the water boiled, I poured some into a mug and pushed it across the counter.

"Do you have any cookies?"

"*Really?*"

"Come on, Ford! I've been driving for hours. I only stopped for gas and to pee. I'm hungry."

Snorting a laugh, I found a sleeve of cookies in a drawer and handed them to her. Lori had used to call me *Ford* sometimes. Especially when she was annoyed with me.

We sat down at the tiny table against the wall. She dropped her backpack to the floor. Ayla shoved a cookie in her mouth, then dipped a second one into the tea.

"So what kind of rehab facility did you escape from? One of those cushy celebrity ones?"

"You think I could go anywhere else? Even there, paps were still hiding in bushes to take my picture. Pretty sure my own staff sold me out. I can't trust anyone." She ate her second cookie. Took a long sip of tea. Then Ayla sighed, eyes closing, and sank back against her chair. "I really was there for exhaustion. It wasn't code for a drug addiction or anything like that."

That was good, because I didn't want anything drug-related near Maisie. I had no idea what kind of rock 'n' roll lifestyle Ayla had been living.

"What happened?" I asked. "I heard you canceled your world tour."

"You know how they say, be careful what you wish for?" She took another cookie from the sleeve. "I just got to the point that I couldn't take the pressure anymore. The nonstop traveling. Not having anybody I could trust. It's really hard doing this without family who will be there for you, no matter what. Who see you as a real person and not a commodity."

"But I thought that's what you wanted. You didn't want anything to do with Lori back when she tried to get in touch."

"I messed up with my big sister. But I apologized. We started talking again before she died."

"I know. I saw her call log. You refused to tell me why she called you the night she died."

"*No*, I told you the truth. Her voicemail was garbled. Like the connection was bad. But we did talk other times. We had reconnected. We were friends."

"Then why didn't she tell me?"

"Ashford," she said softly, "there's a lot Lori didn't tell you."

I knew that. But still, it stung. That same old hurt.

"So you're admitting you knew something was going on with Lori. Yet you didn't tell the police about it after she died. If you didn't want to talk to me, fine. But there was an investigation. There are still questions about what happened. And you're the only one who might have any answers."

"I never told you because I suspected you."

"Are you kidding me? Why would you think I'd do anything to hurt Lori? She was my best friend."

Ayla burst into tears.

Dammit.

I handed some napkins to her. She accepted them and wiped her face. Then I noticed the goosebumps on her skin. She was shaking, hugging one arm across her middle. I didn't even know how long it had been since she'd slept. Maybe longer than it had been for me.

Leaving the kitchenette, I grabbed a plaid flannel I'd left in my office.

"Wear this." I draped the flannel around her shoulders. "It gets cold down here at night."

Ayla stuck her arms into the shirt and took a big gulp of tea. I went to get the kettle to fill up her mug.

Eventually, her sobs quieted. "Thanks. Sorry. I just miss my sister."

"Yeah. Me too." I sat across from her, wondering if we shouldn't have this conversation tonight. But if we didn't do it now, when would we? How did I know that Ayla wouldn't disappear again?

"At Dad's funeral, Lori got my number from my assistant."

"That's what I thought."

"I called her back. We talked about Maisie a lot. About old times. About how it was when we lived in that house growing up. Our father was so cruel."

"I remember." I spoke without emotion, but it had seemed like she needed an acknowledgment. She nodded and took a breath.

"When I left home, I just wanted to put all of that behind me. I know it was wrong of me to cut off Lori along with our dad, but I was sixteen. I wanted my own life. After we reconnected, Lori and I worked through it. She forgave me. And then she started to open up. She always said you were a wonderful father. There was never any doubt about that. But she admitted she was really unhappy in your marriage."

I looked down at my hands on the tabletop.

"Then Lori told me she'd met someone. A man. Someone who lived here in town."

"Who?"

"She never told me his name. She only ever called him by his first initial. L. Same as hers. It started out great. She used to joke around, saying *L and L* like she thought it was the funniest thing. Lori told me she was falling in love, but her biggest concern was *you*. What you would think."

"I was okay with her seeing other people. We made that clear to each other from the beginning."

"But she was still anxious about how you would react. That's why she wanted to keep it secret until she knew for sure if it was going to last. She didn't want to change the life you guys had with Maisie unless this new guy was the one."

"But something happened. A friend of mine said she walked in on Lori crying at the dentist's office."

"Yeah. Lori told L about *me*." Ayla pushed the last of her tea away, like she couldn't stomach any more of it.

"She told him your identity?"

"Yep. Once he knew, he told Lori to ask me for money. Supposedly so they could start a new life together."

"Did she?"

Ayla shook her head. "No, but Lori told me about it. She was so upset. She said L got angry when she refused. I even said I'd give her the money, or a loan if she preferred, but she thought she'd made a mistake by trusting him. She actually said she was scared." Ayla leaned forward, her green eyes going hard. "That was just a few days before she died."

"Scared of what? Of L? Did she think he'd hurt her?"

"She didn't say exactly. Believe me, I tried to get it out of her, but she said she'd figure it out on her own. When I heard about her death, I freaked out. Hired a private investigator to come to Silver Ridge. I refused to believe it was an accident. I had two suspects. This L person, and you."

"Me? Why?"

"Because you were her husband. Everyone says it's the boyfriend or husband who usually does the woman in. So it was L or you. I thought you could have found out about her secret affair, and you'd gotten angry that she wanted to leave you, and maybe that was why she was scared."

"She never told me. Never."

"I believe you. My investigator figured out you had an alibi. And he searched all over Hart County for someone who could be L, but couldn't say for certain who the guy was."

"The driver who hit Lori saw someone else on the highway that night. Said this other person could've pushed her."

"I've read the police report. But my investigator came to the same conclusion the police did. Not enough evidence to suggest it was anything other than an accident. I had to accept that I would never know exactly how or why Lori died."

"I still haven't accepted it." My mind worked, trying to

untangle the mystery. "When did you plan on telling me all of this?"

"Would it have mattered if I did? It took a long time before I was convinced you had nothing to do with it. And by then, when I tried to get in touch with you, you wouldn't answer. You had no interest in anything I had to say. Every number I called you from, you blocked it."

Yeah, that was true.

What a damn mess.

I got up and went to lean against the counter. "How did those reporters find out about your connection to me and Maisie? They've been poking around here in Silver Ridge since the beginning of the summer."

"I don't know that either. But I had an assistant early this year who was stealing money from me. I told you I have trouble finding people I can trust. She sold at least one story about me to the tabloids. It was about me crying in my dressing room before a show."

"Geez."

Ayla gestured at her tear-streaked face, the corner of her mouth quirking in a rueful smile. "Not so hard to believe, is it?"

"What about this L guy, whoever he is? Could he have told the reporters, since he knows you're Lori's sister?"

"Maybe. But that would be dangerous. Because if he really had something to do with Lori's death, why would he invite more attention? It's far more likely that someone on my team gave some reporters a tip about my secret family members, and they did the rest. I wish you and your girlfriend never got dragged into this."

My heart twinged painfully at the mention of Emma. "She's not really my girlfriend yet. I'd like her to be, but that article publicized some really personal things about her, and I have no idea if she'll want to keep seeing me."

"I truly am sorry. I left messages with my publicist and my lawyers, asking them to do whatever they can to shut this story down. Especially if it could put Maisie in danger. I don't care how much it costs. Whatever I have to do to protect her, I will. And I'll help Emma too. However I can. But my team doesn't know where I am at the moment, and I'd like it to stay that way. At least until I've had some time to rest. So I can think about what I want for my future, because how things are now isn't working."

My head ached. Two days' worth of exhaustion had just crashed into me. After the revelations about Lori, this entirely new perspective on Ayla, and her offer to help... I'd had just about all my brain could process.

And I still missed Emma so badly.

"You can stay here a few days," I said. "My brother and sister are already upstairs, so I guess you should take Emma's room."

"You sure?"

"Not really, but there's no other beds. So unless you want to sleep down here on a training mat, it's Emma's room or nothing."

"And Maisie? Can I finally meet her in the morning?"

"It'll be hard not to. My apartment isn't that big."

She clasped her hands together, eyes shining. "Thank you. *Thank you*. I promise, Ashford. You won't regret this."

I really hoped not. Because I already had too many regrets at the moment.

TWENTY-EIGHT

Emma

THE LAST REFUGE Inn and Tavern was perched on a mountainside, with a view of Hartley's commercial district in the valley below and panoramic vistas in the distance.

Yet it did nothing for my inspiration. The only melody running through my head was a lonesome one. Sad enough to break your heart. Even my journal hadn't been helping.

I left the deck and went inside, where the staff was preparing for breakfast. My aunt Jessi bustled around giving directions, looking more beautiful than ever with a healthy blush in her cheeks and a small baby bump under her dress.

"Jessi, can I do anything?" I asked. Just like I had for the past couple of mornings. And just like the past two days, she gave me the same answer.

"Nope. Park yourself at one of the tables. I hope you're hungry."

I wasn't hungry, exactly. But was I going to turn down any of Jessi or Aiden's incredible cooking? No, I was not.

Grace had dropped me off at Jessi's Diner on Main Street. From there, I had called my aunt and uncle to give me a ride here to Last Refuge. Jessi and Aiden owned the diner, but this place on Refuge Mountain was their pride and joy.

The main building that housed the restaurant had once been part of a ranch. It was a log-cabin style, with wide plank floors and open rafters. The hotel side was a more modern addition, but they'd kept the mountain cabin aesthetic, with warm colors, fireplaces, and lots of wood.

I'd been here last year for their wedding outside on the deck, overlooking that breathtaking view. But I didn't know Jessi well, and the last couple of days with her had been nice. Just getting to hang out and get to know her. Uncle Aiden rarely came out of the kitchen, where he was head chef, but they had both made me feel welcome. I wasn't technically a blood relation to either of them, since Aiden was my stepmom's brother, but I didn't feel any difference.

I was beyond thankful for them. They'd made special food for Stella. I'd taken her out first thing this morning to run in the woods, and now she was lounging back in my room. So spoiled.

I had no doubt that Jessi and Aiden had seen that article along with everyone else in my family, so there couldn't be too much of a mystery about why I had suddenly turned up on their doorstep. But they hadn't pushed me for explanations.

I still didn't know what to say for myself. Just like I hadn't known what to tell Ashford. I didn't want him worrying about me.

Of course, being away from him had only emphasized the fact that I was head-over-heels in love with the man. And how selfish would it be to tell him that now? When he had so much else to deal with?

Anything I could do to help Ashford and Maisie, I would. Even if that meant staying away from them.

Jessi brought over a couple plates of biscuits and gravy. "Mind if I sit down and eat with you? I need to get off my feet, or Aiden will come out here and boss me around. I like to maintain the aura that I'm the one in charge around here."

"I certainly wouldn't mind the company."

She slid into the seat across from me. "I bet. Seems like you have a lot on your mind. If you need a friendly ear to share the burden, you just let me know."

"Thank you. I should've come here to visit sooner, not just when I needed to escape."

"Don't even mention it. When I came up with the idea for Last Refuge, that's exactly what I wanted it to be. An escape, a very literal one. You know we take people in, right? Anyone who needs help. Especially women and children. We protect them."

"I know. This place is amazing." They also had a lot of security. Both a state-of-the-art system and several beefy guys patrolling the premises at all times. Even if a reporter figured out I was here, they wouldn't get very far.

Jessi and Aiden were the best.

Plus, the food here was so dang good.

We both dug into breakfast. Someone had already poured me a cup of coffee, and I sipped it between bites. Maisie would've loved these fluffy biscuits. They had a hint of sage. She wasn't always an adventurous eater, but when I could coax her into taking a taste...

Ugh, I had been doing that a lot. Letting my mind wander like it was still summer, and Maisie and Ashford were still a daily part of my life.

I wanted them to be. I just didn't see how to make it happen.

"It's true," I blurted out.

Jessi looked up, her fork poised in front of her. "What's true?"

I already wished I hadn't said anything, but now that I had started, it would be better just to get it out. Even though my breakfast rebelled in my stomach.

"I did what that article said. Slept with a married man. I had no idea he was married, but there were probably signs I missed. I should have figured it out. I should've known better."

I wrapped my hands around my coffee mug and stared into it. A distorted reflection of myself looked back from the surface.

Jessi put down her fork. Reached across the table and put her hand on my arm. "Emma, I am so sorry that happened to you.

That man should be ashamed. I'm sure it's hard for you to talk about, so I appreciate you telling me."

I nodded, still feeling sick.

"Believe me when I say this, honey, because I found myself in bad situations too before Aiden came along. No matter what signs there may or may not have been, it wasn't your fault."

"Thanks." I knew all of those things in theory, but that wasn't the same as believing them. Hearing it from Jessi helped me get one step closer.

"What about the father and daughter mentioned in that article?" She bit her lip guiltily. "I tried to resist reading it, but that's all people seem to be talking about around here. How Ayla Maxwell's family lives over in Silver Ridge. All the family she has, from how that article made it sound."

Another rush of longing hit me at the mention of the O'Neals.

"I was shocked about that too. When I first got to know Ashford and Maisie, I had no idea they were related to her. They're both..." There I went, getting choked up again. "The article makes Ashford sound like the bad guy. But he's not. Not even close."

"Tell me about him."

I started with meeting him at the beginning of my summer. How Ashford and I had to share a space. How I wound up living with them.

Falling for them.

Once I got to talking about Ashford and Maisie, I couldn't stop. Even with all the heartache I felt, I was smiling. But that smile faded as I got to the end.

"I was only supposed to be in Silver Ridge for the summer. Until I could get things sorted out with transferring to a new music program. But then I fell in love with him. Fell in love with them both. And I feel like I'm torn in two different directions. Which is aside from the fact that I don't even know how Ashford feels."

"Was it his idea for you to come here after the story broke? Or yours?"

"Oh, definitely mine. He didn't want me to leave. And he's called and texted every day. He's trying to be patient, but I know he wants me to come home."

Home. Just saying that word twanged a chord in my heart.

She hummed. "That seems to be an indication of how he's feeling about you."

"Maybe."

Jessi took another bite of biscuit. "There's someone else who's been calling. Madison and your dad."

"They've been calling you too?"

"Only about five thousand times. They said you haven't responded."

"Just didn't know yet what to say."

"What you just told me explained it all. But if you could do me a favor and call them back, it would clear up my phone line. They know you're safe, of course, but they just want to hear it from you."

"I know. I will. I have several calls to make."

"Want to make them in my office? I can sit with you."

"No, I'm a big girl. I've got this." But her offer somehow solidified my courage. Just knowing I had that support. She was going to be an incredible mom.

The moment I got back to my room, I called Ashford. And...

He didn't answer.

"Dang it." I plopped onto my mattress. Stella came over to check on me, so I scratched her behind the ears. "I guess that means I have to call Dad." I made a whiny sound. Stella looked sympathetic.

Get it together, I told myself. *You've got this.*

I chickened out and called Madison's phone instead of my dad's. She answered on the first ring. "Emma! Hey, sweetheart." Then she yelled, "Nash! Emma's on the phone!"

I paced. A few seconds later, my dad's deep voice spoke. "Em. Are you okay?"

"I'm at Last Refuge with Aiden and Jessi." *Deep breaths*, I reminded myself.

"I know that, but that's not what I meant. You say the word, and that so-called director who messed with you will find out what it's like to have a SEAL sniper on his ass."

I sputtered a laugh. "*Dad*."

"I'll use a paintball gun. Not a real one. It'll still hurt like a bitch, though."

"The paint would be wasted on him." I knew Dad wasn't being serious. He'd been a sniper on the West Oaks SWAT team for many years now, and he rarely stepped a toe out of line. Unlike my uncles Aiden or Jake. But they were Madison's siblings, not my dad's. Those Shelbornes could be trouble.

"Em, I wish you'd told us," Dad said, all joking gone. "We're on your side. One-hundred percent. In case there was any doubt."

I looked up at the ceiling, tears filling my eyes.

But before I could respond, Madison chimed in. "We're definitely on your side, and we'll support you if you really want to transfer schools. It's your choice. But babe, you should consider going back. You were so excited when you got in. It's not right for *you* to suffer because of what that man did. It's not like you to run away."

For a moment, I was speechless. Because she was right.

We talked a while longer. I told them about Ashford and Maisie and how I'd gotten closer to them this summer, though I left out the part about being in love. Too awkward.

"Jane Holt is going to help Ashford find a lawyer. I gave her his contact info."

"That's smart of you," Madison said. "Tell my brother hi and ask him to call me sometime. Aiden's the worst about keeping in touch. Even worse than you."

"I love you both."

"Love you too, Em," Dad said. "No matter what."

After we ended the call, I lay down on the bed. My nerves were still ragged. Yet it couldn't have gone better. They'd said everything I needed to hear. I still needed to call my mom, but I needed a few minutes.

Stella stretched out right over my stomach. "Oof. You're heavy." I didn't make her move, though. I ran my fingers through her soft fur. "Madison had a point. I *did* run away from grad school. I ran instead of staying and fighting for my place there." A place I was no longer sure I wanted anyway.

But I'd done the same thing with Ashford. I ran because I thought it would be easier.

Could I go back and fix it? Fight for what was mine? Or had I already messed it up?

✦

Less than an hour later, my room's phone rang. "Emma," Jessi said. "You need to come down to the lobby. Like, *now*."

"Okay. But—" She hung up before I could finish asking what this was about. I looked over at Stella. "I don't know what's going on, but I guess I'd better hurry. Can't upset the pregnant lady."

I heard voices as I made my way down the stairs to the lobby. One of them made my breath catch. I rushed the rest of the way.

Ashford was here.

He was facing off against my uncle Aiden. Two bearded mountain men in jeans and dark T-shirts, thick arms crossed and wearing similar grumpy expressions. Jessi stood behind the reception desk, rolling her eyes and keeping out of the way.

"I know she's staying here."

"But we don't give out information on our guests. No exceptions. I don't care who you are."

"I'm the guy who's about to start shouting her name and disturbing all your guests unless—"

"Ashford." I hurried across the lobby. "I'm right here."

But Uncle Aiden put out an arm to bar my way. "Are you sure about this guy, Emma? If he's harassing you, I will remove him from the premises."

"Aiden, stop," Jessi muttered.

Ashford pushed Aiden's arm out of the way. And then his arms were around me, lifting me up until my toes left the ground. I held on to him just as tightly.

"How did you find me?"

"A friend. Would've been easier if you'd told me where you were."

He set me down and I brought my hands to either side of his face. We had a lot to talk about. But I was just so glad to see him and feel him. So relieved that he was here.

Then I realized we had a growing audience. Two of my uncle's scary ex-military buddies, Trace and River, had turned up and were standing over by the reception desk. Trace looked just as grumpy as Uncle Aiden, but River was smirking like he enjoyed the show.

"Nothing to see here," I said loudly. Then I grabbed Ashford's hand. "We can go to my room."

I headed toward the stairwell, but Ashford pulled me into a short hallway as we were about to pass it. The elevator. He pushed the button.

"What floor are you on?"

"Three."

The moment the door opened, he pulled me inside the elevator car and crowded me against one wall. "I know I agreed to give you three days, but I couldn't wait any longer. I asked Sheriff Douglas for help finding you. Took some convincing, but he agreed. Even called ahead here to vouch for me. But your uncle was being a stubborn asshole. He still wouldn't let me see you."

"They're serious about security here. Aiden thought he was protecting me."

"And I respect that. But protecting you should be *my* job. If you'll let me."

I stroked my hand down his bearded cheek. "I left because I didn't want you worrying about me."

"If you had any idea how I feel about you, then you would realize that statement makes absolutely no sense. Since you left, it was hard to think about anything *but* you."

The scent of him surrounded me. In the soft light of the elevator, the amber flecks in his eyes glowed gold. The shadows beneath suggested he hadn't slept, and his hair was messier than I'd ever seen it, but he was so beautiful to me.

"I couldn't think of anything except you either. You and Maisie both."

"Doesn't that tell you where it is you belong?" Ashford's lips brushed over mine, his tongue stroking at the seam. The kiss was sweet. Aching with longing. I held on to his strong shoulders, feeling like I would slide right to the ground otherwise.

I had missed this. Just two days away from him, yet it felt like ages. Like his kiss was breathing life back into me. Ashford's lips moved to my jaw, then my neck. His teeth dragged lightly over the skin there. It felt like he was staking a claim.

He pulled back to look into my eyes again. "Emma, I love you. I've been in love with you for a while. But I was the idiot who didn't see it, and once I realized it, I didn't tell you. I'm not saying this isn't complicated. I'm just asking for a chance to win you over."

"That won't be necessary." My breath pushed out of my lungs. "I love you too. I was already packing my things to go back to Silver Ridge."

He exhaled a curse. "That was easier than I'd expected."

When we kissed again, we were both smiling.

The elevator doors opened. We looked over to find a white-haired couple standing just outside. We hadn't pushed any buttons, so we were still there on the ground floor.

The woman grabbed the man's arm and said, "See? I told you there's something in the water here."

I snickered. We stepped back to make room for them, and

Ashford hit the button for three. But he didn't step away from me, positioning me right in front of him with my back to his chest and his arms tight around me, like he couldn't bear to have any more separation than that between us. The elderly woman kept sneaking smiles at me until they got off on the second floor.

The man stepped out with his cane. His wife winked and said, "Enjoy your stay. I certainly intend to."

Then she pinched her husband's butt on their way down the hall.

When the elevator doors closed, I spun around in Ashford's arms and we collapsed against each other in helpless laughter.

He kissed me on the forehead. "Take me to your room."

"Will you kiss me some more?"

"I certainly intend to."

TWENTY-NINE
Ashford

I KEPT my hands on Emma as we made our way down the hall. I pressed in close to her back as she waved the key card in front of the lock. And then, finally, we were inside. Kissing again. My fingers in her hair, Emma's hands pushing up my T-shirt to touch the overheated skin beneath.

But a big, furry weight crashed into both of us. I caught myself, hands landing on the door so I didn't crush Emma against it.

"Oops," she said. "I should've expected that. Stella's excited to see you too."

"Down, girl." I bent to rub her flanks and scratch behind her ears while her tail whipped from side to side.

"She missed you."

"I missed her too." Which kinda surprised me. But who was I kidding? I'd come to love Stella, dog hair and all. Why else had I let her shed all over my truck seats during our road trip? "Missed both of you. Like crazy."

"Where's Maisie?"

"At my place with Grace and Callum. And Ayla."

"*Ayla?*"

"Yeah. Long story." I let Stella lick my face, then turned so she could lick the other side. "All right, that's enough." I stood, wiping at my beard. "Yeah. Ayla's in Silver Ridge."

"And you left Maisie there with her? I'm not saying you shouldn't have. You said Grace and Callum are there too. But... that's big."

"It is." A few months ago, I got anxious just leaving my daughter with my siblings. Ayla Maxwell had been enemy number one.

She'd explained herself, and that had made a huge difference. But really, I credited Emma with helping me realize that I couldn't be the best father to Maisie unless I welcomed other people into our lives. That meant taking chances, even scary ones.

"I should catch you up on everything that's happened."

Once Stella had calmed down a bit, we sat on the bed up against the headboard, and I gathered Emma against me, fitting her into my side where she was supposed to be.

I put my nose in her hair and inhaled. She didn't smell exactly right. She'd been away from her lavender shampoo for too long. But the hints of it were still there.

And more importantly, the sweet smell that just belonged to her. Some magical mixture of pheromones that I was addicted to. "I was miserable without you."

"Same here."

"You said you needed some space to think. Did you get what you needed?"

"I guess so." She snuggled closer to me. "I spoke to my dad and Madison. My mom too. They told me they support me completely. All this time, I was terrified of them knowing what happened. I was so ashamed of it. But my ex is the villain in that story, not his wife and not me. I know the truth, and it doesn't matter what anyone else thinks."

"Didn't I tell you basically the same thing?"

"I know. Logically, I knew that was true. I shouldn't have doubted how my parents would react. I shouldn't have run away from you either."

"Baby." I kissed her on the nose. "Sounds like you're still trying to blame yourself, and I won't have that. Maybe it's a good thing that you ran from me." I couldn't believe I was saying that, but I was pretty sure it was true. "Because it made me realize that I can't live without you. I don't mind chasing you. It's worth it if I get to have you. You're worth it."

I didn't mention the fact that she was still supposed to leave for her music program in a few weeks, assuming she got off that waitlist. After what had happened, I was more determined than ever that she get everything she wanted. Those music schools would be beyond stupid if they didn't see her worth.

I could've sat there for hours, just basking in her glow, but Emma asked, "Will you tell me what happened with Ayla?"

"She showed up last night on my doorstep."

"Does the media know? I've been trying to stay offline."

If only I had been doing the same. But I was glad she hadn't been subjected to all the rampant speculation that was going around. "Nobody knows yet except for you and my siblings. And Maisie, obviously. She and Ayla met this morning. She was excited to meet a celebrity. Especially when Ayla sang her latest hit. A personal concert for Maisie's dolls and stuffed animals."

"Oh, bringing out the big guns."

I chuckled. "There's no way the rest of us could compete with that. Except maybe you, when you play for us. You're every bit as good a musician as her. Probably better."

Emma poked me in the ribs, her face turning crimson. "That is so not true. Not even close."

"I'm not entitled to my opinion? It's you and the Beatles. With music, I only go for the very best."

She laughed, tucking her face against my chest. "Go on. How did Ayla convince you to let her stay?"

I recounted what Ayla had told me. How she and Lori had reconnected. The secrets Lori had shared with her sister. "She suspected me of doing something to hurt Lori. Apparently that's why Ayla wouldn't tell me anything. And when she finally decided to reach out..."

"You didn't want anything to do with her."

"Exactly."

"You trust the private investigator she hired? Maybe you or the local police could find this *L* person Lori was seeing."

"It's hard to say." I had been racking my brain ever since Ayla had told me those details. I had also passed on the new info to Teller and Sheriff Douglas. But the file on Lori's death had been closed for years now, and it wasn't easy to reopen it.

Besides, the investigation into Lori's death wasn't even our most pressing concern. Not by a long shot.

"I need to get rid of the paparazzi that's hanging around in Silver Ridge. If they get wind of the fact that Ayla is there, it's going to get a hundred times worse."

She nodded, sighing. "Do you need to head back?"

"Soon. But you're coming with me. I'll sneak you back into the Big Blue Monster."

"I was thinking I'd stay on Dixie's couch. If I go home with you, won't it draw more attention?"

"Does that really matter at this point? I want you to be comfortable with this, but I also need you with me, and that's not negotiable. Any reporter who messes with you had better watch out. But if they help spread the word that you're mine? I don't have a problem with that."

She tilted her head to kiss me. I pressed her into the pillows, letting my weight rest partly on top of her. Just enough so that I could feel her beneath me.

"This bed was very cold and lonely the past two nights," she said.

If I had actually slept in mine, it would've felt the same.

I kissed her more deeply, getting lost in the sweetness of her mouth as my tongue stroked inside.

She loved me. I hadn't even had the time to relish that fact. I wanted to make love to her right now, knowing that we both felt the same. My cock firmed up as I imagined it. And she certainly seemed willing. She whimpered, her legs lifting to cinch around my hips.

Reluctantly, I turned down the heat on our kisses. "I would love to spend the rest of the afternoon in this bed with you. But I need to go back downstairs and properly introduce myself to your family."

"You don't have to. Uncle Aiden will be fine."

"No, this is important." Aiden had been trying to take care of her. He'd also served, and given the fact that we were around the same age, our time in the Army had probably overlapped. I needed a do-over on that first impression. Because I intended to be a part of Emma's life and I wanted her family to know it.

Her Navy SEAL father and her stepmom in West Oaks were on the list too, but one thing at a time.

"Also, I haven't eaten since cold takeout last night, and something smelled amazing downstairs. I'm starving."

She laughed. "Then we can knock out both things at once, because we'll most likely find Aiden in the kitchen."

✧

I didn't want to interrupt Aiden while he was working, because I would've found that annoying if it were me. I'd already done enough to get Emma's uncle on my bad side.

So we swung by the tavern to grab a bite to eat, just like any other customers. The food really was delicious. Then went to the inn's front office. When we knocked, Jessi opened the door, and Aiden was there right behind her.

He frowned as soon as he saw me. "You again."

"I'm Ashford O'Neal," I said, offering my hand. "I apologize for barging in the way I did earlier."

Aiden grunted an acknowledgment, glaring at my extended hand. But Jessi pushed past him and pulled me into a hug.

"Jessi Shelborne. And trust me, I understand. If Aiden hadn't been able to find *me*, he would've been equally loud and insistent." She gave her husband a pointed look.

We stepped into the office, and Jessi closed the door. It was a small but welcoming space, with a wood desk and a couch up against one wall. Jessi took a seat, a hand on her small belly.

"I'm Aiden." He clasped my hand in his grip. And squeezed. I squeezed back. "You don't think you're too old for Emma?"

Emma and Jessi both made frustrated sounds. But I appreciated Aiden being straightforward. The sooner we could get this part over, the better.

"I wasn't sure at first. But now, after getting to know her, I think we're perfect together."

Aiden held eye contact with me another moment, then shrugged. "That's a decent answer. Nash might still have a problem with it, but he married my little sister Madison. Questionable decision in many ways. I've satisfied my uncle duties."

Emma punched Aiden lightly on the arm.

"Ow! What was that for?"

"I figured Madison would want me to. Also, for interrogating my boyfriend."

Boyfriend. I really liked that. When I'd shown up at Last Refuge earlier, I'd had every intention of claiming Emma as mine. Now, she'd just claimed me in front of her family. My chest puffed up with pride.

Jessi reached out to take Aiden's hand and pull him down on the couch beside her. He managed to land softly, arm going protectively around his wife. "Ashford, Emma told me how much she's enjoyed spending time with you and your daughter," Jessi said. "Clearly you mean a lot to her."

I palmed the back of Emma's neck as our eyes met. "She means a lot to me. I love her very much."

"Love you," Emma whispered back.

"Awww." Jessi waved a hand in front of her face. "Don't mind me. Since getting pregnant, I cry about absolutely anything.

Do not show me a diaper commercial unless you want waterworks."

Aiden smiled fondly at Jessi. "She's not exaggerating." He pressed a quick kiss to her lips.

"How old is your daughter?" she asked me.

"Maisie is six."

"You two should bring Maisie to have dinner with us sometime. After things have settled down, I mean."

"I'd like that. Thanks. The food here is amazing. I'd make the trip any time."

"I hope you will," Jessi said.

Aiden didn't add anything, but he looked pleased. I doubted he and I would be best friends. But we did have a lot in common.

My phone buzzed in my pocket. "Excuse me, I should check this. It could be about Maisie."

When I pulled my phone out, I found messages from Grace and Callum. Photos, to be exact. News about a sighting of Ayla Maxwell in Silver Ridge had hit social media about an hour ago, and even more reporters than before were swarming outside my building, like they were multiplying. Maybe they'd already been on their way, but still.

Dammit.

"What's wrong?" Emma asked.

I turned my phone around to show the others. "The media somehow found out about the guest who's staying at my place. Local police are trying to rein them in, but this is bad. There's no way the media will leave us alone now."

Jessi cringed. "From the other stuff we've been seeing online, I'm assuming your guest is your famous sister-in-law?"

"She turned up last night, begging for a place to stay. But my apartment is hardly equipped to handle the attention a superstar celebrity gets. I don't think Silver Ridge is ready for this, either." My stomach swirled with unease. "My little girl is there, probably scared by all the noise and chaos."

I had zero regrets about coming to find Emma, but I needed

to get back to Maisie. And I also needed a solution to this mess. Kicking Ayla out on the street wasn't an option, because she was family. Even if I'd denied that fact for a long time, it was undeniable now.

"We might be able to help," Aiden said.

"I need a discreet, secure place for Ayla. And probably a twenty-four-hour professional bodyguard detail." I waved a hand. "Do you have that tucked away somewhere around here? If not..."

Aiden grinned. First time I'd seen that expression on the man. "Come with me next door, and we can talk."

✦

"Emma! Did you pursue your professor's husband?"

"Emma, did you start dating Ashford because you knew his connection to Ayla? Were you hoping to make your own shot at fame?"

I kept Emma in front of me as we pushed through the gauntlet of reporters to our door. "Get off my property," I growled. Plus a few other choice words. Videos of me would end up online, but I couldn't help myself. They were messing with my girl.

Luckily, Stella's barking drowned out most of what I had said. I was carrying her big furry body in my arms. Callum held the front door open for us, taking Emma's bag as she rushed inside. I followed.

Callum gave her a one-armed hug. "Glad you're back, Emma."

"Me too."

I set Stella on the ground and made sure the door was locked and all the curtains were drawn. Then I enclosed Emma in the circle of my arms, dipping to kiss her temple. "You all right?"

"Fine. But that was bonkers. I don't see how Ayla lives that way."

"When we get upstairs, you can ask her."

Emma shivered. "So weird. I can't believe I'm about to meet Ayla Maxwell. I'd better get my fan-girling out of my system."

"She's very much human. Just like the rest of us." Mistakes and all.

"Do you think she'll sing my favorite song of hers for me? I've never heard her do it a cappella."

I lifted my eyebrow.

"Okay, maybe I shouldn't ask the first day we meet."

I had to kiss her again because she was adorable. I didn't know how I could love her more.

Callum carried Emma's bag. Upstairs, Grace was in the kitchen, stirring something in a heavy pot and something else in a skillet. Food sizzled. The air smelled like cooking meat and garlic.

The moment we walked in, Maisie came running, and Stella let out a happy bark.

"Emma! You're here!" Maisie jumped into Emma's arms, nearly knocking both of them over. "I can't wait for you to meet my aunt Ayla. She sings just like that lady on your phone."

Emma set down Maisie, who fell to her knees and hugged Stella.

"Little busy around here," Callum said, moving around them. My small entryway had never been this full.

Ayla peeked out shyly from Maisie's room. She nodded at me, and I nodded back.

Maisie took Emma's hand. "Come on. This is Aunt Ayla."

The two women met in the hallway. "I'm *such* a fan," Emma gushed. "Is that awkward? It's probably awkward."

Smiling, I left them to it and went into the kitchen. Callum had joined our sister, and they were already bickering over the pots and pans on the stove.

"I didn't touch your sauce, jerk."

"Looks to me like you messed with it."

My apartment was way too small for all these people. But I

actually didn't mind it. I put one arm around each of my siblings, pulling them in for a rough hug.

"What's happening?" Grace asked.

"I love you both. I really appreciate everything you've been doing."

Callum smirked. "You say that like you're surprised at the feeling."

"We love you too." Grace waved a wooden spoon at me. "And we're glad Emma is back, since she's clearly the real reason you're in a good mood. Now set the table for dinner."

"I will. Cal, you haven't been hitting on Ayla, have you? Is that why she was hiding in Maisie's room?"

My brother looked offended. "I haven't done a thing. I'm a gentleman."

"She doesn't meet his usual standards," Grace said. "Because they'll definitely be seeing each other again."

Callum flipped her the bird.

"What was that about you being a gentleman?" Grace deadpanned.

"I learned it from Ashford."

I moved to the next topic, ignoring their bickering. "Emma and I have a plan for getting Ayla to a secure location where she can stay as long as she needs. If everything goes well, the media will have no idea where she is. But they'll know she's not here."

"Sounds good." Grace bent over the stove again. "Tell us all about it after dinner. I never cook like this, so you people are going to eat it and enjoy it, so help me."

Dinner was delicious. Grace had made chicken parmigiana and a spinach salad, with Callum's penne alla vodka on the side. My table wasn't made to hold so many, but somehow we managed it, with extra chairs pulled from various other spots and Callum standing and eating by the counter.

Ayla insisted on handling the dishes. Afterward, we gathered in the living room. Emma squished against me on the couch with Maisie on her lap. Stella tried to climb up too, but when there wasn't room, she settled for lying on top of Callum's feet. Ayla and Grace took the two upholstered chairs.

"I don't want you feeling like I'm kicking you out," I said to Ayla. "But this..." I pointed at the windows, where paparazzi vans were camped up and down the street. "This isn't good for any of us."

Ayla pulled her feet up into the chair and tucked them beneath her. "I really am sorry. I wouldn't have come here if I thought the media would find out."

Maisie got up and crawled into the chair with her aunt. "But I'm glad you're here." Ayla shifted to make room for her, closing her eyes as she kissed Maisie's head.

"Thank you, sweet girl." Ayla looked so much like Lori in that moment. I got a little choked up.

"I'm glad you came too," I said. "This was long overdue. But Emma's uncle in Hartley made us an offer that might solve the issues we're having."

I told them the rough outline of the plan. We had two objectives. Leading the reporters away from here, and getting Ayla to Last Refuge without the media knowing.

"My uncle and his friends have a lot of experience protecting people in danger," Emma explained. "People who don't want to be found."

"He can keep me hidden at this Last Refuge place?" Ayla asked her. "I thought you said it was a hotel."

Emma nodded. "They have secure areas with a heavy security presence, and they're on an isolated mountainside. Plus, before you go, we'll have a couple of decoys leave here separately disguised as you. Myself and Grace."

I nodded at my sister. "Would you be up for that, G?"

Grace grabbed a blanket and draped it over her head. "Just give me some sunglasses and I'll be ready for my close-up. Or maybe not, but it'll be dark."

Callum scratched his stubbled chin. "Think I've seen this same plan in a bunch of movies and TV shows."

"That's because it works," I said. "Callum, you'll leave with Grace. We're hoping you two will lead away most of the reporters. Then I'll escort Emma outside as the second decoy. We'll head to a different location. Ayla, you'll leave last with my buddy Judson Lawrence."

Ayla pressed her lips into a straight line. "But where will Maisie be?"

"Our chief of police, Teller Landry, and his sister Piper will come get Maisie and Stella before any of us leave. I texted them both earlier, and once I give them the final word, they'll head over." Judson was already on his way here. I'd spoken to Elias as well, and he had his own important role to play.

"But I want to stay with Ayla and Emma." Maisie hugged her aunt around the neck. So much for Dad being her number one. But I was smiling.

"I know, Maisie-doodle," Emma said, "but you'll have Stella with you. And then you and your dad and I will meet up afterward."

"Really?" Now, Maisie looked to me for confirmation. I nodded. Dad was still good for something, at least.

"Ayla, Judson will drive you out near Hartley," I continued, "where you'll meet with one of Aiden's contacts, who will take you to Last Refuge. The rest of the world will have no idea you're there."

"And if anyone somehow finds out," Emma said, "the security team at Last Refuge will protect you for as long as you need. You can stay there until you're ready to go wherever you want to go. What do you think?"

Ayla stroked Maisie's hair with a shaky hand. "I'm grateful for this. I really am. You've gone to a lot of trouble. But I don't know any of these men you're talking about." She glanced at the window with a pained expression. "Maybe it would be better if I just leave right now. Drive away and let the reporters follow me and…I don't know. I guess I'll figure out that part later. I came here without a plan. None of you should have to deal with this."

Emma exchanged a glance with me. "What if Ashford drives you to the meeting location instead? I can make sure my uncle Aiden is there at the pickup. You can trust him. I swear. You'll be completely safe the whole time."

My immediate reaction was to protest. If I drove Ayla personally, I would be separated from Maisie and Emma for several hours.

But they'd be with my friends. There was no way I'd let Ayla drive away by herself, knowing the lengths these tabloid reporters would go to get their story.

"I can do it," I said. "I'll drive you, and Judson will go with Emma." I would reunite with Maisie and Emma afterward as soon as I could. "Agreed?"

Ayla hesitated. But finally, she nodded. "Okay. I'll do it."

"Good." I started sending off texts to Teller, Piper, Judson, and Elias. "We'll make our move tonight."

THIRTY

Emma

I WATCHED from the window as Judson arrived in his cowboy hat and snug T-shirt, followed a minute later by Teller and Piper. All three pushed past the throng of reporters on the sidewalk. A couple of Silver Ridge PD officers waved their arms, trying to keep the path clear.

When Ashford let them into the apartment, I grasped Piper in a hug. "Thanks for being here."

"Hey, the media can take as many pics of me as they want. I did my makeup." Piper fluttered her lashes.

Judson smiled and touched my arm in greeting, then reached to clap Ashford on the shoulder. "Happy to help." He was so big that he took up most of the entryway by himself.

Ashford waved Ayla forward. "This is my sister-in-law. Ayla, this is Piper Carmichael. Judson Lawrence. And Chief Teller Landry."

Teller was in his police uniform, his expression grim. His intense gaze swept over Ayla, taking in her simple tank top and shorts, her long platinum hair in a ponytail. "So *you're* who all that fuss is about?"

Her pink lips opened slightly. Then she let out a shocked laugh. "Sorry to disappoint."

"Would've been wiser if you told someone before you showed up here," Teller said. "We could've prepared."

"I didn't ask for anyone to make a fuss over me. But isn't it your job to keep these reporters from harassing your citizens?"

Teller turned to Ashford. "If you weren't right on the public sidewalk, we would have more leeway to get them away from your building. But this is a touchy situation as it is."

"I get it," Ashford said.

Teller eyed Ayla again, and she returned his glare with equal force before sweeping her ponytail over her shoulder in a dramatic gesture. She spun and walked away.

Well, then.

Until now, Ayla had been extremely low key given her superstar reputation. But within seconds of appearing, the chief had brought out her inner diva.

Judson crossed his arms, eyes impossible to see beneath the brim of his hat. Piper looked like she was stifling a laugh. "Does Maisie have her bag packed?" she asked.

"Yep," I said, welcoming the subject change. "Right, Ashford? I can grab it."

Ayla was in Maisie's room. When I walked in, Maisie ran over and hugged my legs. "I really have to go?"

"Yes, but we'll be back together later tonight."

"Can I stay up late and watch shows? And have extra dessert?"

Ayla snickered, meeting my eyes. "Girl knows what she wants. I love that."

There were more hugs and kisses as we got Maisie ready to go. Ayla promised to FaceTime Maisie as soon as she could. "I'll have to send you the new songs I'm working on."

"Will you sing for me some more?"

"Of course. I would love to."

Maisie glanced over at me. "Emma can play the music for you. She's super good at violin and piano and guitar too. And Daddy's also an *excellent* singer." She shrugged. "For a boy."

Ayla winked at her niece. "You've got a promising future as a talent agent, Maisie."

"What's that?"

"I will tell you *all* about it next time I see you."

Ashford came in and picked up his daughter, holding her tightly and whispering to her. It was time for her to go, and I felt how anxious he was. But Maisie would be in good hands.

He carried her to the entryway. Ashford handed Maisie over to Teller. "You're going with Ollie's uncle. You remember the chief, right?"

"I've heard from your dad how brave you are," Teller said.

"I'm taking jiu-jitsu," her tiny voice replied.

"Of course. Just like my nephew, right?"

"Is Ollie coming with us?"

"Ollie is at Dixie's." Piper leaned in to tickle her. "Maisie, you can protect us with your fancy fighting moves."

Teller frowned at his sister. "No need for fighting moves. Everything's going to be fine."

Ashford draped a blanket over Maisie. "This is just until you're in Teller's police car, okay monkey?"

He reached for my hand as Teller carried Maisie out the door and Piper followed with Maisie's bag. Then we both watched from a window as they made their way toward the waiting police SUV. Once the reporters realized it was the chief of police and a child, they stepped back. Only the most zealous kept shouting questions.

Everyone in the apartment seemed to breathe a collective exhale when Teller drove away.

Callum and Grace were up next. They didn't wait long. Less than ten minutes after Maisie's departure, they hurried out the door. Grace had a thick shawl draped around her face and a big pair of sunglasses, which Ayla had loaned her. It helped that they were a similar height. She'd also added Ayla's signature bright pink lipstick, never mind the fact that Ayla herself hadn't worn a swipe of makeup her whole time in Silver Ridge.

I held my breath, peering down from the window. Another police SUV had just pulled up, driven by another officer.

I couldn't see Grace yet from this angle. But I knew the exact moment she stepped outside. The waiting crowd gasped.

And then *lunged*.

Shoving each other, waving cameras and phones set to record. Their shouts rose in a cacophony. Callum barred his arm in front of the frenzy of reporters, yelling for them to get back.

An officer opened the back door of the SUV, and Callum pushed Grace inside, leaping in after her. The SUV's tires peeled as it accelerated, reporters chasing it down the street with their cameras held high. Then a dozen media vans took off after the SUV's taillights.

Afterward, less than half a dozen people were left milling on the sidewalk, talking excitedly into phones.

I smiled at Ashford. "They bought it."

"Callum did get the lead in the third-grade spring pageant. Kid wouldn't shut up about it for months."

"He and Grace both deserve Oscars for that performance."

They were headed to Judson's ranch. Out of anyone in the Lonely Harts club, he lived the farthest out of town, so that goose chase would lead the reporters nearly a half hour away from Silver Ridge. His property was also surrounded by acres and acres of land with a gate and fencing, so they wouldn't be able to get too close.

Ayla was sitting on the couch in the living room, hands clasped around her knees. "Well?" she asked. I assumed she'd been too nerve-wracked to watch.

"It's working," Ashford said. "Next it'll be Emma and Judson's turn."

I planned to wear a similar disguise to Grace's. The remaining reporters would definitely get suspicious when I appeared, and they might call back some of the vans that had followed Grace and Callum. So we were going to wait until it was fully dark and use a different exit, so it seemed like the real Ayla was trying to sneak away.

By the time Ayla and Ashford would leave, another hour after that, they'd hopefully be able to slip away without a single eye on them.

"Talk to me a minute?" Ashford murmured.

We left Judson and Ayla making polite conversation in the living room and went to Ashford's bedroom, closing his door partway.

"You sure you're okay going with Judson instead of me?" he asked.

"It was my idea."

"I know. Still not happy about it, though. I'll get to Elias's as soon as I can."

Judson was going to drop me off there before heading to his ranch to meet Grace and Callum. I'd never been to Elias's place, but apparently Ashford would be able to head there without passing through Silver Ridge on his way back from the rendezvous with Aiden.

I had no doubt that a bunch of scary *what-ifs* were going through Ashford's mind. Now that I knew him so well, I understood that he focused on the negative because he was determined to protect those he loved. As if he could outrun anything bad if he saw it coming in time.

But everything was going to be fine.

I rubbed my nose against his. "I love you."

"Love you more." He dropped his mouth to mine. I put my hand on Ashford's chest over his beating heart.

There was a noise in the hallway. "Oh, gosh. Sorry." Ayla started to turn away.

"It's all right," I said, putting a few inches between Ashford and me, though he didn't move his hands from my hips. "What's up?"

She turned back, smiling sheepishly. "Wanted to thank you

both again for your help. And apologize that you got mixed up in this mess, Emma."

"Oh. It's really okay." I shrugged. "I should've told my family about the drama at my school last semester. That tabloid article saved me the trouble. Or rather, forced me to deal with it."

"And your family? Are they supportive?"

"They've been great about it."

I was lucky. Plenty of people, like Ayla and Lori, didn't have that support system. Which was so unfair.

I'd been fan-girling about Ayla earlier, but she was a genuine person. Sweet and kind. She deserved to have people around her who loved her, and who she could trust. *Everyone* deserved that. Money and fame couldn't buy it.

Ayla shuffled her feet in the doorway. "I hope you don't mind me bringing this up. But it's not right what happened with your ex. How you were treated by the school. They should've done more to defend you. Maybe there's some way I could help."

I didn't see how she could, but I appreciated her offer. "Thanks. If *you* need anything else, please let me know." Ayla's life was so much more uncertain than mine at the moment. Her world tour was on hold. She probably had a manager, agent, and countless others demanding to know when she'd be back at work. What she needed was some peace and rest.

"You've done so much already. I'm glad we got the chance to meet. And I'm sure it won't be the last time."

"I hope not."

Ashford rested his hand on my lower back, his expression carefully neutral.

When it was time for me to go, I gave Ashford another kiss goodbye. One turned into three.

"Tick, tock," Judson reminded us.

I grabbed my scarf and sunglasses. No pink lipstick, though. Which was a good thing, because Ashford would've been wearing it too.

We'd already switched off all the lights. Judson and I went to the kitchen and climbed out the window onto the fire escape. He extended the ladder leading down. Once we'd climbed to the ground, he pushed the ladder back up, and Ashford secured it into place.

The creaking of the metal ladder had created just enough noise to draw the few remaining reporters' attention. Behind the building, Judson rushed me into his truck while the reporters dashed around from the front, snapping pictures and shouting questions.

Judson slammed the door shut on the passenger side. Seconds later, he jumped in, and we took off. The reporters dashed toward their vehicles to follow.

In the rearview, I watched the Big Blue Monster disappear into the darkness.

THIRTY-ONE
Ashford

THE LAST OF the reporters followed Emma and Judson, just as we had hoped. Which left me and Ayla in a dark apartment. After all the life and excitement here just a few hours ago, it was depressing as hell.

Or maybe that was just me.

I hated that Maisie and Emma weren't with me. Even if that was irrational, I still felt it. And that wouldn't go away until I'd met up with them again.

A text came in from Teller, letting me know they'd arrived with Maisie at Elias's place. About half an hour later, Emma texted that Judson had dropped her off. I tried calling her just to hear her voice, but the call didn't go through. Reception outside town could be spotty though. I figured she was busy with Maisie.

Grace and Callum had arrived at Judson's a while ago. Judson himself had gotten held up for some reason and hadn't gotten to the ranch, but aside from him, everyone was in place.

Something irked me. A feeling that not everything was right. Yet I couldn't put my finger on it, and I didn't have time to spend pondering it.

I went to the living room, where Ayla was resting, and said, "We should go."

We left the building as quietly as possible, not daring to turn on any lights. My truck was parked about a block away. Ayla kept her head down and her arms wrapped around herself. She was wearing some of Emma's clothes, as well as a baseball cap. No big sunglasses or scarves to make it look like she was hiding.

We didn't see a single person on our way. Once we were in the truck, I pulled away from the curb. Her car was still here in town, but she'd said she would deal with it later.

A few minutes later, we passed the boundary of Silver Ridge and drove along the deserted highway.

The moon was bright tonight. Just like the night Lori had died, which was a morbid thought. Especially when we drove past the white cross marking the scene of the accident.

Emma had driven this way over an hour ago with Judson.

"That's it?" Ayla asked softly. She'd noticed the cross too.

"Yep."

"I really miss her."

"I do too. I'm..." I pushed out an exhale. "I'm so sorry I wasn't there for her the way she needed." If only Lori had trusted me. If she'd come home and talked to me instead of going out that night. Same thoughts I'd had so many times.

"I wasn't here either. But when I showed up in Silver Ridge the other night, you let me in. You let me meet Maisie. It means so much to me. I'm not going to forget that."

"You're Lori's sister. It's what she would've wanted. I'm glad you came."

Ayla glanced over at me. It was dark in my truck cab, but I caught the curve of her smile.

This isn't like the night Lori died, I reminded myself.

Everyone I loved was safe right now. Surrounded by friends. And soon, Ayla would be in a safe place as well. Hopefully getting the space and time she needed to deal with what she'd been going through. If it had been feasible, I would've invited her to stay with us in Silver Ridge for longer. Because that was what family did.

Maybe we'd get that chance at some point, when her fame wasn't such an obstacle.

"I wondered about something," I said. "You mentioned there might be some way you could help Emma."

Ayla looked over again. "Sure. Got any ideas?"

"I do, actually. She's trying to get into a new music school. Any chance you could pull strings? You are *the* Ayla Maxwell, after all."

"I do know people. And those people know people. But the best schools aren't anywhere near here. Are you sure you want that?"

I wasn't sure at all. I didn't want Emma to go. I selfishly wanted her to stay in Silver Ridge with me and Maisie. I wanted to change that sign downstairs to *O'Neal Music and Martial Arts*, and how ridiculous was that?

But even more, I wanted Emma to reach her goals. Get her fancy graduate degree.

"I want all of Emma's dreams to come true. Even if that takes her away from me."

Ayla huffed a small laugh. "You're a good guy, Ashford."

"I guess I am." Even if that sucked sometimes.

Good guys didn't always get their happy endings.

We drove through the night, following my GPS to the coordinates Aiden had given me. A quiet stretch of road where no other drivers might spot us. An SUV with dark windows was already there.

When I pulled toward it, the SUV's door opened, and Aiden stepped out. My headlights washed over him. Then another man emerged, Trace Novo.

Aiden had introduced his buddies to me at Last Refuge. When I hadn't been creating a ruckus in their lobby, they'd been extremely nice guys.

I put my truck in park. Ayla grabbed my wrist. "Which one is Emma's uncle?"

"That's Aiden. Beard, short hair. The one with the longer hair is Trace, Aiden's brother-in-law." Then, to my surprise, a tall woman got out of their vehicle. "I don't know her," I said, "but if she's here, that means Aiden trusts her."

"But you didn't tell me they'd have guns." Ayla's hand tightened on my arm.

"It's just a precaution. They have military training." And from the stories they'd shared with me earlier, they'd been through some dicey situations. Even in a sleepy place like Hart County.

"And my dad was a colonel," Ayla reminded me. "I know most soldiers were nothing like him, but it still makes me nervous."

Shit. I hadn't anticipated this. Ayla's father was the whole reason she had run away as a teenager and broken ties with Lori. "You remember how you and Lori met me, right? I was one of those soldiers on the base too."

"I know. It doesn't bother me when it's you. But..." She exhaled. "I'm okay. I can do this."

"You don't have to. We can figure something else out."

Instead of answering me, she opened the passenger door and jumped down. Keeping her chin high, Ayla marched over to the SUV.

I got out, grabbed Ayla's bag where I'd stowed it in the backseat, and followed.

"This is Brynn Somerton," Aiden said, nodding at the woman who'd come with them. "She's part of our team. When she's in town."

Brynn smiled and reached for Ayla's hand. "I happened to be in Denver when Trace called. He said they had an op that might need a feminine touch. The rest of the team can be a *lot* of masculine energy."

Ayla laughed. "You're not wrong."

"We'll take good care of you," Brynn said. "Doesn't matter how many people out there in the world are searching for you. We'll keep you hidden for as long as you need."

That seemed to soothe the last of Ayla's nerves.

She gave me a quick hug. "Pass on that hug to Maisie for me when you see her tonight?"

"Will do."

I watched as she got into the SUV with the others, and they drove away. Thank goodness that was done. Now, I could get back to Emma and my daughter.

Jumping into my truck, I sped off, still buckling my seat belt. I used my Bluetooth connection to my phone to call Emma.

Her phone rang. But she didn't answer.

It was after ten o'clock. Way past Maisie's usual bedtime, but I expected they'd end up staying awake until I arrived.

I tried calling Elias next, and he didn't answer either. Maybe they were doing something that had distracted them. Watching a movie, or...hell, I didn't know.

But it bothered me.

I almost relaxed when a call came in. But it was Grace. "Hey," I said.

"Did the drop-off go okay? You sound tense."

"The rendezvous with Aiden went fine. Ayla's with them, and I'm heading back. Just anxious to see Maisie and Emma."

"There are still a few media vans waiting outside Judson's gate. That was kinda fun, actually. But Piper says the rest of the reporters have descended on Main Street. They're going up and down questioning every citizen they can find, hoping someone will reveal where Ayla went tonight. And some people are losing patience, yelling at them to go. Teller's officers are responding to half a dozen different disturbances."

Maybe our plan had worked a little *too* well. I tapped my fingertips on the steering wheel. "But Judson's there at the ranch? He's arrived?"

"Of course. Been here a while after leaving Emma at Elias's. But there's something else I wanted to tell you. Ayla let me and Callum know about what Lori was hiding before she died. The guy she was seeing."

"Yeah." I accelerated down the dark highway, my high beams on. "Ayla asked if I was okay with her telling you. I didn't mind."

"Well, I decided to follow up on a hunch. And I came across something weird. Remember how I thought before that Lori could've been seeing Danny Carmichael?"

"But his initial isn't L."

"That's just it. It took some digging, but I figured out his middle name. It's Lachlan. What if Lori called him by his middle initial?"

Was that possible? For a long time, Danny Carmichael had tripped my instincts. Yet Lori had refused to speak poorly of him. Was it really because they were having an affair?

"Maybe I'm wrong," Grace said. "But it's worth looking into. Ayla's investigator might not have made the connection with his middle name. Lori would've had a lot of reason to keep their relationship secret. He was her boss, and he was married to Piper."

"And Lori knew I hated him."

"It's a theory. I'm working on a list of other *L* names. First, middle, and last initials. Not Teller Landry, since he was still in Army Special Forces and didn't live in Silver Ridge three years ago. But I put Judson on there, since his last name is Lawrence. Ridiculous as that is."

"Totally ridiculous." I'd had a passing recognition of the fact that his last name started with *L*, but had dismissed it immediately. Still, the thought gave me an odd feeling now, since Judson had driven Emma tonight.

But he was back at the ranch. He'd left Emma hours ago. Hadn't he?

"Just being thorough," my sister said. "How far are you from Elias's?"

"About forty minutes." Though from the way I was speeding, it would be less. My lungs were tight. I wouldn't be able to relax until I'd made it there and seen that Emma and Maisie were safe and sound. Even though I had no reason to think they were otherwise.

"I still haven't decided about that date with Elias," Grace said.

"He's being patient, then. Good."

"He is. Say hi to him for me. And if El says anything about the date, which I doubt, but if he does—"

"Spit it out, Gracie."

"Geez, give me a minute. Just tell him I'm leaning toward yes. Maybe. Definitely maybe yes."

A quick response was right there on my tongue. But then my brain worked through the last few things Grace had said.

"Wait. You just called Elias 'L'."

"E-l. The first part of his name. I wasn't really thinking. I didn't mean—"

"Does anyone call him that? Did *Lori* ever call him that?"

Grace went quiet. "Ashford, you don't think..."

A sick, cold feeling washed over me.

I had no clue what to think. I had known Elias since high school. He was one of my closest friends.

But he was with Emma right now. And neither of them were answering their phones.

I pressed hard on the accelerator.

THIRTY-TWO
Emma

THREE HOURS EARLIER

As Judson drove us out of Silver Ridge proper, I looked up at the full moon overhead. A couple of news vans were still following us. But they didn't worry me. So far, our plan was working perfectly.

We headed down the highway that led out of town. Moonlight washed the valley in pale gray and blue, most of the landscape impossible to see compared to the glare of the headlights. But I caught a glimpse of a white cross up ahead.

I pointed to it. "Is that the marker for Lori?"

Judson nodded. "I say a little prayer every time I pass it."

The very first day I'd arrived in Silver Ridge, the day I had met Ashford, I'd walked past that cross. I hadn't realized its significance then.

But now, I said a few words for Lori too. *I'll take care of Ashford and Maisie*, I promised. *The very best I can.*

Judson turned onto a small side-spur of road just after we passed the cross. A moment later, his headlights lit up a sign for a campground and trailhead.

"I didn't realize Elias lived down this way," I said.

"His place is about a mile on."

"Not that far from the scene of the accident that killed Lori." Too far for him to have seen anything. But still, for some reason it surprised me.

"He and his wife Holly were some of the first neighbors the police interviewed about the accident," Judson said. "His ex-wife, I mean."

We drove past a dark, low-slung shape, and I realized it was an old abandoned cabin. Probably the one that Lori had visited that same night.

"That's one sad story. Lori's accident." Judson shook his head, which was bare. He'd left his cowboy hat in the backseat. "And then Elias's wife leaving him, when was it, a year or so later? That's the Lonely Harts club. If you're looking for sad stories, we've got plenty of 'em. As many as an old cowboy song."

"What's yours? If you don't mind me asking."

"I don't mind necessarily. But this conversation is enough of a downer. I'll tell you mine another time." His lips twitched in a half-smile. "Ah, here we go."

A couple of motorcycles were waiting by the side of the road up ahead. As we passed, they roared to life, both their headlights and their red and blue police lights flaring.

Chief Landry had arranged for a couple of Colorado State Patrol motorcycle units to help us out. They pulled onto the road, closing in on the media vans still on our tail.

Judson's smile grew. "I was speeding, and those vans were keeping pace. By the time CSP is done issuing warnings and running their plates, I'll have dropped you off and I'll be heading back the other way."

I relaxed more into my seat, glad we'd gotten rid of the reporters. But I wasn't going to feel secure until all of this was finished and Ashford had arrived to join us.

Judson pulled into a driveway leading to a two-story farmhouse with all its windows lit. The house had wooden siding, a wraparound porch, and intricate Victorian trim. "This is beautiful," I said.

"Used to be a ranch. Almost as big as my family's. I think Elias's grandparents bought it originally, but they sold off parts of it over the years."

A huge barn sat across from the house, along with a couple of other smaller wooden buildings.

Judson parked beside the other trucks already here. I grabbed my pack from the backseat. Slinging the strap over my shoulder, I walked toward the house.

A bark came from the porch. Stella was tied to the railing. I jogged up the steps, bending to pet her. "Hey girl, what are you doing out here? Were you being naughty in Elias's nice house?"

The front door opened, and Piper stepped out. "Poor baby has been upset since the moment we arrived. I wasn't sure what to do. Giving her treats didn't help."

"That's okay." I stood and squeezed Piper's arm affectionately. "How's Maisie?"

"She's watching a movie."

Elias appeared behind Piper in the open doorway. "Emma! Good, you're here. I set up Maisie in my office."

Stella lowered her head and growled. Elias took a step back.

"But I don't think Stella likes me." He gave her a lopsided smile, and Stella barked, making him flinch.

"It's probably not you," I said. "There's been a lot of excitement and stressful energy going around."

I knew Stella didn't like Danny Carmichael. But had she ever gotten upset around Elias before? I couldn't remember. Stella had been to Flamethrower Burgers plenty of times when Elias was there. Except she'd always been outside.

Elias took my bag and carried it in, while I calmed Stella down. It helped when Elias went upstairs. Teller was in the living room on the phone, and Stella didn't seem to mind him. She'd been fine when Teller and Piper had been at the apartment earlier.

"Maisie's in this room," Piper said, showing me the way.

After greeting Maisie and asking her to keep Stella with her, I went back out to the living room, where the others were all waiting.

"Need anything else?" Piper asked. "If not, we're going to take off. Ollie is at Dixie's, and I want to hurry and pick him up before he breaks something."

"We're good." I hugged Piper and Judson goodbye. Then figured, what the heck, and hugged Teller too. He smiled stiffly.

I checked the time. Ashford and Ayla were still at the Big Blue Monster, waiting a while before they set out toward Hartley.

A floorboard squeaked, and I realized Elias was standing there. Now that our friends had left, it was just the two of us in the entryway.

"I put you in the guest room. Upstairs to the left. I assumed Ashford would be sharing a bed with you." Elias laughed. "You're blushing. Sorry, didn't mean to make you uncomfortable."

"You didn't."

"Ashford could bunk with me if that's better."

Maisie still didn't know about Ashford and me. If I was leaving town soon, that was all the more reason to keep her unaware. But the thought of spending the night in Ashford's arms sounded wonderful. Especially after the last few days. "I'll see what he thinks when he gets here."

"Sure thing."

"I should text him. My phone is in my bag."

Elias pointed up the stairs. "It's on the bed. You'll need the wi-fi password. Cell reception here is terrible."

He told me the password. It was easy to remember. I went up the staircase, my palm trailing over the smooth banister.

In the guest room, I found a simple but cheerful space with a heavy, antique-looking dresser and a brass-frame bed. My bag waited on top of the quilt, just as Elias had said. Sitting on the mattress, I grabbed my phone and sent off a quick text to Ashford.

> **ME**
> I've arrived. Maisie is comfy watching a movie. The others left. Stella was stressed, but she's calmed down.

> **ASHFORD**
> Good to hear. We're still lying low. Will leave soon.

> **ME**
> Drive safe.

> **ASHFORD**
> You remembered your journal, right?

> **ME**
> Yep. 😊 I love you.

> **ASHFORD**
> Love you too. See you soon. 🩶

Ugh, I was so hopeless for this man. We hadn't talked about whether my plans for after the summer had changed. But *I* had changed.

We both had. Right?

Tossing my phone onto the mattress, I got up to head downstairs and check on Maisie.

I gasped when I nearly ran into Elias. He was right there at the top of the stairs. His hands grasped my arms. "Careful."

I stepped back, and he let go.

"I was about to check on Maisie. She wants to stay up and wait for Ashford to arrive, but I should start winding her down. Today has been a lot."

Elias nodded. Yet he didn't move, still blocking my way down the stairs. "The bathroom downstairs has a clawfoot tub. I've probably got some bubble bath somewhere that belonged to my wife." He flashed his charming, lopsided smile. "She didn't take everything when she left, and I'm the sentimental guy who can't get rid of it."

Elias edged past me, walking over to the bathroom down the hall, and emerged with the bottle of bubble bath.

I set my phone down again. "Thanks. Your home is beautiful. Judson said it's been in your family for a long time."

"Since my grandparents. My dad brought my mom here after they got married, and when they were gone, they left it to me. I don't keep animals any more, but I use the barn for my brewing equipment for the restaurant. Sadly my own marriage didn't last as long as my parents' marriage did. But hey. Maybe I'll end up bringing home someone else eventually."

"I'm sure you will." My thoughts immediately went to Grace, but this conversation was already awkward.

I started down the stairs, and he followed behind me.

"You know," Elias said, "I didn't get the chance to meet Ayla. What's she like? You would expect a celebrity to be difficult and stuck up, but her sister Lori was a sweet girl. Totally down-to-earth."

We reached the first floor, and I paused there to answer his question. "Ayla's down-to-earth too. She seems like she's struggling. But hopefully, now that she and Ashford have sorted out their differences, things will get better for her. And for Ashford too. That secret was weighing on him."

"Yeah, secrets tend to do that." Elias glanced away. "Did Ayla mention anything else about Lori?"

My brows drew together, confused why he'd even asked. I didn't feel comfortable telling him about Lori's affair with the mysterious *L*. "No," I finally said.

He shrugged and smiled. "I'm going to check my fermentation tanks and take care of some things in the barn. That'll give you and Maisie some privacy to get her ready for bed. Just holler if you need me."

"Thanks. It's really kind of you to let us all stay here."

"I'd do anything for Ashford. He's one of my best friends."

As Elias left and walked to the barn, I felt guilty that I'd been uncomfortable with him. Every time I'd been around Elias before tonight, I'd found him friendly and easygoing. He was going to a lot of trouble just to help us out. If he'd been acting strangely, it was probably the stress we were all under.

When I got to Elias's office, where Maisie was staying, she hadn't finished her movie yet. So she, Stella, and I cuddled up to finish the rest of it.

"Bath time," I said when the movie was done.

"I don't want a bath. I want Daddy to get here."

"I know. He'll get here as soon as he can. But I've got bubble bath, *and* Elias has a fancy bathtub with little feet on it."

She perked up. "Really?"

The clawfoot tub was a hit. Same with the pineapple-scented bubbles. Maisie pretended to be a mermaid and we told stories until her little fingers were wrinkled. I rinsed her with fresh water, then wrapped her in a fluffy towel.

But when we got to Maisie's room, Stella wasn't there. Dang it. I must've left the door partly open and she slipped out. What if she was chewing up an antique chair leg?

I went to the hallway and listened just as a crash came from upstairs.

Crap.

I pointed at Maisie. "You get your jammies on and brush your teeth. I'm going to find Stella."

"Can I come?"

"Absolutely not. You stay down here." Hopefully Elias was still outside. Since I didn't hear barking, I assumed he was. If Stella had broken something, I would have to fix it. Or pay for it. I groaned, imagining how expensive an item it might be. Probably something irreplaceable that had belonged to Elias's grandmother.

As I hurried up the stairs, I heard Stella's collar jingling. A glance in the guest room didn't reveal a naughty dog. Same with the upstairs bathroom. Which left Elias's bedroom, the only other door on the second story.

"Stella, get your tush out here."

I looked into Elias's bedroom, and there she was. Slipper

clenched in her teeth, growling and shaking it in a death-grip. "You are in so much trouble. What has gotten into you?" I got the slipper away from her. It was mangled beyond repair. Replaceable though. Not a priceless antique, thank goodness.

But what had caused that crash?

I couldn't see very well, so I switched the light on. Elias's bedroom was similar to the guest room, but with an unmade bed and more knickknacks and photos. Thick drapes hung over two windows facing the front of the house.

A tall chest of drawers stood just to the side of the doorway. Several framed photos decorated the top. But one frame was lying facedown on the wood floor. That explained the noise. Stella must've knocked it onto the floor when she was getting up to mischief.

When I picked it up, the frame came apart in my hands. I glared at Stella. "Big trouble. No treats tomorrow." She'd be lucky if Elias didn't make her sleep on the porch. We'd been guests in the man's house for an hour or two, and we'd already made a mess.

Flipping the broken frame over, I glanced at the photo inside. Then held it up for a closer look when I noticed Ashford.

The picture showed Elias, Ashford, Judson, and Callum, arm in arm and wearing Silver Ridge High School gear. The older boys looked around eighteen. I'd never seen Ashford clean-shaven before. Or with such a boyish smile. Adorable. If I'd been his classmate, I would've noticed him in the hall and developed a massive crush.

There was so much more I wanted to know about him. All his stories from high school, from the Army. From when Maisie was a baby. My chest ached with all the love I felt for him already. Once I got to know him even better, it would probably be worse.

He won't be able to get rid of me.

As I tried to gently set the frame back on the chest of drawers, a slip of paper fell out from inside it. Another photo, this one much smaller and printed on thin paper. It fluttered to the floor. I twisted, looking down at it.

And froze.

This photo showed Elias again, but he was grown. He had the same haircut as now. But the woman beside him was Lori O'Neal. The shape of her face, her green eyes... It was unmistakable. Even if I hadn't seen pictures of Lori at Ashford's apartment, I would recognize the resemblance to both Maisie and Ayla.

They had their arms around one another, cheeks pressed together. Not in a friendly way, either. It was an intimate pose. One of Elias's arms was extended like he was taking the photo.

I picked up the photo from the floor and turned it over. Someone had written *L + El* in a feminine scrawl with a hand-drawn heart beneath.

"There's no way," I whispered. But what other explanation could there be?

L wasn't an initial. It was E-l, short for Elias. He and Lori had been seeing one another before she died. This photo was the proof.

The front door closed downstairs. Footsteps thudded across the entryway. I jumped, the photo nearly slipping from my fingers.

Elias was back.

THIRTY-THREE
Emma

Elias was Lori's mystery man. He could've been there that night when Lori died. Could've pushed her.

And he was heading up the stairs right now.

Stella went to the open bedroom door, growling low. "Quiet," I whispered. I shoved the snapshot of Elias and Lori in my back pocket, then stuck the broken picture frame beneath the chest of drawers. If he found it there later, he would probably just assume it had fallen. Or maybe it wouldn't matter.

I had to tell Ashford. But first, I had to get Maisie and myself out of this house. *Now.*

Grabbing Stella by the collar, I switched off the light and hurried out into the hallway. Elias was just reaching the landing when I made it to the top of the stairs. Stella growled and barked, while I struggled to hold her back by her collar.

"Sorry!" I said. "She snuck up here while I was getting Maisie ready for bed."

"Is something wrong?"

"Aside from the fact that I have a very naughty dog?" I tried to laugh, and it sounded forced. "I'll take her back down to Maisie's room. They both need to settle down for bedtime."

Elias said nothing. And he didn't move, either. I even thought about letting go of Stella, but she was no attack dog. Elias might hurt her.

He might do a lot worse.

With this photo, plus Ayla's testimony, there would be enough evidence for the police to reopen the investigation into Lori's death. Even if Elias hadn't actually pushed her, he'd kept the secret of their affair from Ashford and the rest of the town for three years.

How far would he go to keep anyone from knowing? If he'd kept this kind of secret from Ashford, what else was he hiding?

"No worries." Elias slowly stepped aside, watching me. Stella and I went down the stairs. My heart pounded. I felt his eyes on me the whole way.

My pulse was racing, my vision feathering at the edges as I took Stella into Maisie's room and closed the door. It didn't have a lock.

"Emma, I brushed my teeth! I've been doing just like you told me." Maisie was lying in bed with the covers pulled up, reading one of her chapter books.

My chest filled with deep affection for her. This sweet, innocent little girl.

I knelt beside the mattress, feeling the photo of Lori crinkle in my back pocket. Stella stayed by the door to the hallway, growls still rumbling in her throat.

"Guess what, Maisie-doodle?" I whispered. "We're going to have an adventure."

"An adventure? Another one?" She didn't look excited, and I couldn't blame her.

"I know, there's been too many already today. But this is important."

"Is it more of those paporters?"

I smiled at her mispronunciation. "Yes. More of those mean reporters."

"Like that man from before? Who grabbed you and wouldn't let you go?"

I nodded. There was no way I could tell her the truth. Not right now.

Her lower lip trembled. "He was the meanest one. Even more than all the others that were shouting."

"I'm afraid someone like that is coming here. But I won't let him hurt you."

"Will Elias be okay?"

"He'll be fine. He's staying here." I grabbed Maisie's cardigan and shoes. Thank goodness we hadn't left them by the front door. Pulling back the covers, I lifted her to standing, helping her get dressed.

"What about Daddy?"

"I'll tell him where to meet us, and—"

With a jolt of panic, I realized I didn't have my phone. It was still upstairs.

Floorboards creaked overhead. Elias was up there. Shit, shit.

I had to get my phone. I had to warn Ashford. If he showed up here and we were missing, and Elias figured out the reason...

"Actually, you and Stella will go ahead of me. I'll come a few minutes behind you, and your dad will meet us. I want you to go to the neighbor's house." I took Maisie to the window. "See those lights?"

"That looks far. Can't you come with me?"

"It's only a little bit far. Stella will be with you, and I know how brave you are. I remember how you kicked that reporter's leg. You helped me."

"Can't I stay with you? I can help you again."

"No, honey. Not this time. It's very important that you do as I say. When you get there, tell the neighbors that there is a scary man here. He could be dangerous. They need to call 911. Send the police here to help. I'm going to warn your dad."

She whimpered. "Emma, I don't want to."

My eyes burned with tears. I hugged Maisie tight. "You can do it. I know you can."

I wanted to keep her with me. But I couldn't risk Maisie's

safety, and I couldn't risk Ashford's either. Even if I got my phone and called 911 right now, this could turn into a hostage situation if Elias was desperate enough. With a father on the SWAT team and a stepmom who was a hostage negotiator, I knew that far too well. Every minute was crucial.

I was out of options. Maisie had to go right now, before Elias left his bedroom. His windows faced the opposite side of the house, so he wouldn't see Maisie or Stella leaving.

Nudging the window frame open, I helped Maisie climb onto the sill and jump down.

Stella barked, and I reached over to hold her mouth. "*Shhh.*" When I lifted her, *not* an easy task, she jumped the rest of the way.

"I'll see you at the neighbor's house," I whispered through the open window. "You're so brave, Maisie. I believe in you. Now *go.*"

They took off toward the lights of the neighbor's house. The moonlight was a blessing and a curse. It would help Maisie avoid tripping and getting hurt along the way, but if Elias looked out a window on this side of the house, he might see the two of them.

I had to hurry.

Closing the window as quietly as possible, I turned and went to the door. Opened it. Looked out into the hallway.

Nothing.

With careful footsteps, I went into the hall and then climbed the stairs. The house looked the same as before, bright and inviting, yet everything now seemed slightly off. Like the wood floors and plaster walls were rotting just below the surface.

My heart hammered my ribcage as I stepped onto the landing. Elias's bedroom door was closed. Had he gone to bed? He'd left all the lights on, but maybe he'd assumed I would turn them off after Ashford arrived.

What if I was overreacting, and all of this was some kind of mistake?

But if it *wasn't*?

I reached into my back pocket, touching the edge of the photo. That picture didn't lie. Nor did the inscription on the back. Elias was hiding a major secret, and I couldn't afford to find out what he'd do to keep it.

In the guest room, I ran my hands over the bedspread looking for my phone. I could've sworn I had tossed it here earlier after texting with Ashford. But there was no sign of it.

I bent to look under the bed. Then searched my backpack. What the hell? Where was it?

Dread choked me, my stomach roiling with fear.

"Hey, Emma. Looking for something?"

The panic surged, almost whiting out my vision for a split second. "Just my phone," I said, not turning around. I was afraid he'd see it on my face. The accusations and distrust. "Have you seen it? Maybe you...picked it up or something."

"Why would I do that? It would be rude to take things that don't belong to me. Don't you agree?"

I spun around. Elias loomed in the open doorway. His usually friendly expression had morphed into something cold and menacing. His eyes were flat. Lifeless.

"Give it to me," he said in a low monotone.

"What?"

"Don't play dumb. I just saw it in your pocket."

Instinctively, my hand flew to my back pocket. The top of the photograph stuck out.

Elias lunged, his hands rough as he spun me and pushed me down onto the bed. I screamed. "Get off me!" He shoved my face into the mattress, while his other hand pulled the photo from my pocket.

"This is private," he growled. "Did you tell Ashford? Does he know?" His elbow dug into my back.

"You took my phone!"

"Does he fucking know?"

"Let me go. You're hurting me!"

Elias flipped me over. He had my phone now, like he'd just taken it from his own pocket, and held it in front of my face to unlock it. "Let's see what else you've been doing." Still pinning me to the mattress, his thumb scrolled and tapped at my screen.

Finally, he exhaled. "You have a missed call from Ashford from a couple minutes ago. Good thing you didn't answer." He let go of me, taking a small step back. "Look Emma, this is a misunderstanding. You need to give me a chance to explain. It's not what you think."

"You just showed me everything I need to know about you."

Bending my leg, I kicked him as hard as I could in the crotch.

Elias shouted, folding in half. My phone clattered to the floor. Leaping up, I grabbed my device and ran for the stairwell. My socked feet slipped, and I nearly fell on my way down.

When I reached the front door, I flipped the deadbolt, threw the door open, and ran down the porch steps and into the cool night air.

The barn. I'd be able to hide and call the police. Plus, I would be leading Elias away from the direction of his neighbors. Maisie probably hadn't made it there yet.

Heavy footsteps thundered down the wooden stairs inside the house. "Emma!" he yelled.

Rounding the side of the barn, I searched for a side entrance. When I reached the door, panic hit me again. What if it was locked? But the knob turned beneath my fingers.

I went inside, closing the door softly behind me. Elias wasn't far. He was running, yelling my name.

I had to hide.

The barn was a large, open space. It was dark. A play of moonlight and shadows. Once, there had probably been stalls for animals and hay, but now it was full of large, upright tanks. The brewing equipment Elias had mentioned. Metal shone in the darkness.

I found a small nook and ducked inside, unlocking my phone.

A door opened. "Emma, I know you're in here."

My phone had no service. I was too far from the house, so I must've lost my connection to wi-fi. I could still call 911, but could the dispatcher find my location? I couldn't risk speaking to anyone.

But any minute, Maisie would get to the neighbor's house. She'd be safe and warm, and they would call for help. They'd send the police. *Please*, I thought.

"Just come out, and we can talk about it," Elias said. "I was seeing Lori. That's true. Which you must've guessed from finding that photograph. Stupid of me to be so sentimental. I told you I can't throw things away. Though it's not exactly my fault that you decided to be nosy."

It sounded like he'd gone to the other side of the barn. A beam of light played off a high rafter in the loft. Instead of switching on the overheads, he was using a flashlight to search for me. Why?

The answer appeared in my mind. *He's keeping the lights off in case Ashford drives up. Doesn't want anyone to know we're out here.*

Carefully, I crawled deeper into the alcove, feeling around in the darkness. My hand closed around a heavy piece of wood. Something I could use as a weapon.

"I meant to tell Ashford a long time ago. I swear. But when Lori and I got together, it was complicated. Which is something I have to think you'd understand, of all people."

My grip tightened on the plank of wood. How dare he compare himself to me. But he was trying to draw me out. Get me to respond.

"Lori wasn't happy in a loveless marriage. Things weren't going well for me either, and that's what I confessed to her. It started out casual. Then we developed feelings for each other. She resisted it because I was married, but I won her over."

With lies, I thought. I had no doubt he'd said whatever was necessary to convince Lori to accept him. To make her believe he was in the process of leaving his wife.

The flashlight beam swept a far wall. His boots shuffled over the dirt. "Ashford was one of my best friends, but in case you haven't noticed, he can be a self-righteous asshole. As if he can do no wrong. He was the same back in high school. He acted like his family's problems were the end of the world. But Ashford never acknowledged how good he had it. He had siblings who loved him. A mom who took care of them, even if she later passed away. I fought for every friendship, for that spot on our wrestling team, for my girlfriend. Yet Ashford could go around being a jerk half the time and people still loved him."

Elias kept walking, coming closer to my side of the barn. I worked to keep my breaths even and quiet.

"When he and Callum left for the Army, they barely kept in touch with me. Just expected that their old friend Elias would be here when they got back. And you know what? I was. My restaurant was going okay. I got married to Holly because everyone expected it. I had managed to put together some kind of life for myself here. And then Ashford sweeps back into town with his beautiful new wife and their adorable baby daughter, and everybody acts like it's the fucking return of the king."

So you were jealous, I wanted to say. *And that's why you went after Lori.*

The leather of his boots creaked. He was getting closer.

"Lori was so lonely. I realized that right away. Ashford likes to pretend he's the hero, but he's the one who trapped her in that marriage. I felt trapped in my marriage too, and I wanted to find a way for us to be together. I looked out for Lori. Tried to do the same for you too, Emma. I kept an eye on you, like that night after you left the brewery. Making sure you were safe."

My skin crawled. Elias had been watching me? Following me?

"Ashford was Lori's jailer. I was trying to set her free."

He'd almost reached me. The flashlight beam darted behind a nearby fermentation tank. I held my breath, gripping the wooden plank.

Then he turned. Went the other way. Now was my chance. I had to get out of this alcove and try to reach the door.

Slowly, I got up and tiptoed across the space, stopping to hide behind another fermentation tank.

"That's why I told her she should ask her sister for money. So I could get my divorce, and we could start our new life together. But even though he didn't know what we were planning, it was like Ashford was inside Lori's head. Telling her that what we were doing was wrong, and that she shouldn't trust me. Poisoning her against me. Lori tried to end things with me. So what happened was his fault, not mine."

Crouching to stay low, I dashed out from behind the fermentation tank.

The flashlight beam hit me.

I screamed and ran. Elias was right behind me, closing the distance. The wooden plank whistled through the air as I tried to hit him, but it smacked into his arm and he knocked it to the ground.

He grabbed me, shoving me to the dirt and pinning my arms behind my back.

"I believe you!" I shouted, struggling. "You didn't mean to hurt her. Don't make the same mistake. Let me go!"

"For you to go running to Ashford, so he can turn the whole town against me? No way. I'll make it look like one of those reporters or a crazed Ayla Maxwell fan tracked us down. Broke into the house and kidnapped you." He leaned down, his voice a harsh snarl in my ear. "And I'll make sure that nobody ever finds you."

His hands closed around my throat.

THIRTY-FOUR
Ashford

I SPED down Elias's driveway. Nearly every light in the house seemed to be on.

It had taken me twenty minutes to get here. I'd been speeding so fast my tires had nearly spun out on some of the curves. On the way, I'd called Teller and reported everything we'd learned. I'd begged him to send an officer here to check on Emma and Maisie. Unfortunately, he and his officers were still on Main Street dealing with the reporters and irate citizens.

Teller had told me to be patient. That we had no specific reason to think Elias would hurt them, even if he was L. He'd promised to notify the sheriff's department, and someone would head this way as soon as possible.

No police cars were here yet. But I wasn't waiting. Not when the two people I loved most could be in danger.

I jumped out of the truck and ran toward the porch, dialing Emma's phone again at the same time. It went straight to voicemail.

Then I saw the front door. It was wide open.

I took a step over the threshold. "Emma!" I shouted. "Maisie!"

Silence.

A scream ripped through the quiet. But it hadn't come from the house.

Sprinting out the door, I crossed the yard toward the barn. The side door was open. I rushed inside. It was dark except for the faint glow of a flashlight on the dirt floor.

I saw the outline of heavy male shoulders crouched over something on the ground. Elias.

He was on top of Emma with his hands around her throat.

I yelled, not even recognizing my own voice, it was so feral. My body crashed into Elias, knocking him to the side. We both rolled in the dirt. He leaped onto me, trying to get me into a submission hold. I kneed him hard in the side. Slammed my fist into his chin. Faintly, I heard Emma coughing and retching.

Elias careened to one side, and I scrambled over him, wrapping my arms around him to put him in a chokehold as he tried defensive maneuvers.

Fury had nearly blinded me. My arms squeezed as he kept fighting against me. "I thought you were my friend," I gritted out. I clenched my teeth so hard that I bit my own tongue, tasting the metallic tang of blood.

His face was turning bright red. He struggled, but I held him too tightly for him to move. I was choking off his air supply.

My eyes stung with bitter tears as I thought of the depth of his betrayal. Everything he had taken from me and my daughter. And what he had almost taken just now.

"I should kill you for what you've done," I said. I was close. So fucking close. "But I won't. This is your one chance. Yield."

I eased up enough that Elias could nod.

Panting, I pushed off of him roughly, knocking him back against the dirt as I stood and put a couple of feet of distance between us.

"Ashford—" he started to say, coughing.

"Shut your mouth." I searched for Emma from the corner of my eye. "Baby, you okay?"

"I'm all right." Emma's voice was hoarse. She came up behind me, and I reached back to touch her, reassuring myself that she was there.

She was trembling. That, plus the ragged sound of her voice, made me want to lash out at Elias again. Make him suffer for hurting her.

He rubbed at his neck. "You've got this all wrong. Emma attacked me, and I was defending myself."

"You're pathetic. Blaming Emma for this. You killed Lori, didn't you? Was that her fault too? Only a weak, pathetic man blames women for his failings."

Pure hatred flashed through Elias's eyes.

He charged at me.

Keeping Emma behind me, I blocked his punch. Then slammed my fist in a vicious uppercut to his jaw. His arms pinwheeled as he fell backward. On his way down, Elias's head cracked against a jutting piece of metal on his brewery equipment. His body went limp.

Emma gasped as dark blood spread out beneath his head.

I turned and gathered her up, carrying her toward the door. It was dark in the barn, but she didn't need to see that.

Once we were outside, Emma grabbed hold of my shirt, her entire body quaking. Faintly, I heard the shrill whine of sirens approaching. Good. Saved me from finding where I had dropped my phone and calling emergency services myself.

"Ashford, I found a photo of Elias and Lori together."

I set her down, still holding her close. I was anxious to find Maisie, but first, I had to make sure Emma was okay. "You don't have to talk if it hurts too much."

"No, I do. When I realized Elias was L, I sent Maisie to the neighbor's house. I made sure she was safe. We have to get her."

"Thank you for taking care of her. Wish I'd gotten here sooner." She could barely stand without my help. I led her over to the porch, where we sat on the steps. The light bleeding from inside illuminated Emma's tear-streaked face.

I examined her neck. The sight of those marks, put there by a man I had called a friend, ripped me open in the worst kind of torment. Turned me raw and unforgiving. "I'm so sorry, baby."

If Elias hadn't already been bleeding on the floor of the barn, I couldn't account for what I would've done to the man.

"We'll get you checked out at the hospital."

"I'll be okay. I tried to get to my phone. I tried to tell you. But he caught me. Ashford, he was going to…"

"I know."

"You stopped him."

"I love you so much." I kissed her hair, holding her as gently as I could.

✦

Two days later, I went to look for Emma and found her in Judson's living room, her head bent with Piper and Grace as they whispered. We were at the ranch, the same place we'd been staying since the night everything had blown up.

Emma looked up, eyes instantly brightening when she saw me.

"I just got off the phone with Teller," I said. "Where's Maisie?"

"Outside with Stella and Ollie." Emma gestured at the expanse of windows, which overlooked the pastures behind Judson's home. I could just make out the edge of the corral.

Good, I thought, relaxing internally. I'd known Maisie was close. But it still felt better to be able to see her. And to have Emma here with me.

I'd almost lost her.

The police and paramedics had shown up just as I carried Emma out of Elias's barn. Maisie had asked the neighbors to call 911. My little girl had done amazingly, and she'd been so brave.

Maisie knew little of what had really happened. She knew a scary man had been at the house that night, and I'd said that Elias had to go away and probably wouldn't be back. But thankfully, she was young enough to accept what I told her without many questions. Though she had asked about the marks on Emma's neck.

"Did you have to fight with the scary man?" Maisie had asked her that night after we arrived here at Judson's.

I had picked up my daughter, holding her so close that she protested. Wishing that I could always keep her safe. Protect her. Not just from physical danger, but from all the ugly truths of the world.

Then Emma answered, *"I fought him, yes. Your dad did too. The scary man is gone now. We all did a really good job, especially you."*

Maisie smiled proudly. *"And Stella."*

"Yes. And Stella too."

The paramedics had pronounced Elias dead at the scene. Since Elias technically lived outside the boundaries of Silver Ridge, the sheriff had jurisdiction over the investigation. His deputies had reunited us with Maisie. The paramedics had checked Emma's injuries, but she'd refused to go to the hospital, insisting instead that she stay with us. With lots of TLC, she was recovering.

Judson offered his house, since he had plenty of bedrooms. Callum and Grace had already been here, and Piper and Ollie had arrived the next morning to join us. Judson's acres of land put a nice barrier between us and the media.

His ranch hands lived in a bunkhouse nearby, but they'd all had background checks when he hired them. Of course, it wasn't possible to know a person's soul on the inside, was it?

Elias had fooled me completely. Fooled us all.

"Ashford?" Emma prompted, bringing me back to the present.

"Sorry." I shook off those thoughts and sat on the couch beside her. "What did you say?"

"That Judson and Callum are helping the kids feed carrots to the horses. It's pretty cute."

I squinted again at the view. "Maisie hasn't talked Judson into letting her ride one by herself, has she?"

Piper laughed. "No. Much to the kids' disappointment. Ollie would be standing in the saddle right now at a full gallop if he had his way."

Judson kept goats, pigs, and chickens in addition to the horses. Maisie and Ollie had been keeping busy. Under close supervision, the kids had taken some rides on the horses, but of course they wanted to gallop off on an adventure without meddlesome parents getting in the way.

My daughter loved it here. She now wanted to be a cowgirl. Plus a superstar singer, of course. But I wasn't ready to let her ride on such a huge animal on her own. I would probably get there, but not until she'd had a lot more practice. And especially not if Ollie was being a bad influence.

Grace got up from the couch and took the chair opposite, tucking her legs beneath her. "So, what did Teller say?"

"Sheriff's deputies interviewed Elias's ex-wife this morning. Holly."

"Yeah?"

"She's filled in a few more of the pieces."

"Is it as bad as the rest of it?" Emma asked, voice still quieter than usual. She touched her neck just below the bruises.

"I don't even know what scale we're on anymore. But yeah, it's bad. Holly said she suspected he was having an affair three years ago. She didn't know it was with Lori. But Elias had also been getting more volatile at home. Threatening her, grabbing her arms and leaving bruises. Things like that."

This stuff was confidential, part of the investigation. Teller should *not* have been sharing it with me, since I was the guy who'd ended Elias's life. But we all knew it was self-defense. The final ruling from the sheriff's department was a pure formality.

"Then, on the night Lori died, Elias showed up back at their house completely freaked. He insisted that Holly say he'd been with her the whole evening."

After Lori died, Elias and Holly had been interviewed. Except for his wife, no one suspected he hadn't been at home that night. Certainly not me.

"So his wife lied about Elias's alibi," Emma said. "Does Holly know what really happened? If Elias intentionally pushed Lori into the highway?"

I shook my head. "No, Elias never explained any of that to her. But he told her he'd kill her if she contradicted his story."

Grace put her hand over her mouth. "That's horrifying. Maybe I can go out to Denver and see her. Holly was going through all that alone. Thank goodness she finally left him."

"Apparently she got fed up a couple of years ago, packed, and drove away to stay with her cousins," I said. "Elias never risked showing his anger in front of anyone else, so he just let her go."

Piper rubbed her eyes. "I feel like I should've seen it. All these years he was our friend. I never would've thought he could be capable of something like that."

"Me neither." I never would've guessed that Elias had been seeing Lori, much less that he could be so monstrous as to hurt her. Or hurt Emma. I reached for her hand, tugging her closer. "But I think he did it. He killed Lori. Even though we'll never know for sure."

Without Elias confessing what had really happened that night, all we could do was speculate.

But my hunch was this:

Lori had asked Elias to meet with her that night, planning to break up with him. She drove to the trailhead about a mile away from Elias's house. Maybe he walked there to meet her. Or drove himself.

We knew that Lori had walked the trail, dropping her phone near the old abandoned cabin not far from the highway. Elias had probably been with her. Maybe they'd been talking. He might've tried to convince her to give him another chance.

But when she wouldn't, when she told him it was over, he snapped. Lashed out.

Lori ran. Elias chased her. Maybe she went toward the glow of those headlights on the highway, hoping to find someone, *anyone*, who'd help her. But at the last moment, Elias shoved her into the car's path. An act of pure, reckless desperation.

He had done the same two days ago with Emma. Chased her down and tried to silence her. Thankfully he hadn't succeeded a second time.

After the car had hit Lori, Elias must've gotten out of there as fast as possible. It was simply luck of the draw that the driver had been elderly with poor eyesight, which made it all too easy for the police to dismiss what she'd seen.

And we still wouldn't know the truth if Ayla hadn't appeared in town. If Emma hadn't found that photo.

Elias could have gotten rid of it, but he had kept it, hidden away. I wondered about that. But now that I knew everything he'd told Emma, the grudge he had apparently borne against me since high school, it made sense. Elias wasn't the kind to let go of the past.

He'd had that darkness inside of him. Festering.

Elias had to have been nervous already. With Ayla's appearance, he would have expected she could say something to point the finger in his direction. There was no way he could've known how much Lori shared with her sister.

I knew what it was like to have a secret. That sense of a noose tightening when you knew it was bound to be discovered. Only, Elias's secrets were so much darker than any of mine.

He'd followed Emma at least once, supposedly to look out for her, but probably out of that same twisted jealousy of me.

He'd pursued my *sister*.

I hadn't killed Elias intentionally, and I was glad not to have that stain on my conscience, if only so that it didn't affect Maisie or Emma by association.

But was I sorry that Elias was dead? Fuck, no. I was not.

I wrapped my arm around Emma, brushing my nose over her hair. Taking that small comfort that I'd nearly lost forever.

THIRTY-FIVE
Emma

ASHFORD WENT OUTSIDE TO "SUPERVISE" the feeding of the carrots to the horses, while Piper went to take a shower. She, Grace, and I had spent all morning outside with the kids and Stella.

The exercise had been great to clear my head. Every minute that I got to spend with Maisie and my friends helped put what had happened with Elias behind me.

But having Ashford nearby was the best of all. Just knowing that he wasn't far.

He had been incredible. My personal superhero. He had saved my life. And whenever my mind dipped back into those terrifying moments, when I had thought I wouldn't survive, my love for Ashford brought me back out of it.

I finally understood exactly how my dad and Madison felt about each other. They'd been through life-threatening situations too. The kind of bond Ashford and I had now went soul-deep.

I wandered into Judson's kitchen and found Grace there already, staring into a glass of water. She startled and looked up.

"Don't mind me," I said. "I'm on a quest for sugar. I heard a rumor about chocolate in the pantry, and I figured I'd better get to the bottom of that before the kids beat me to it."

Grace smiled, setting aside her glass. "I'll be your wingwoman. Chocolate is exactly what I need. Or a can of whipped cream. But if I find one of those in the fridge, it's every woman for herself."

I barked a laugh. "Duly noted." Then I winced, because my throat was still a bit sore.

From the empathetic look on Grace's pretty face, she could tell. "How are you doing?"

"Getting better every day."

We went into the pantry to search the shelves. "Are your parents still threatening to come out to Silver Ridge?" Grace asked.

"After he heard, my dad got halfway to the airport before I talked him out of it. The media has already tracked Dad and Madison down in West Oaks, which did not go well for the reporters."

"Yikes. I bet not."

"How are *you* doing, Grace? I don't think I've asked you that yet. I should have."

The truth about Elias had clearly affected her. Like Ashford and Piper and the others, she'd known him since her childhood. But she'd been especially close to him.

"Me? I'm fine. I have nothing to complain about. I was incredibly lucky."

I turned to face her. We were standing a foot away from each other in the narrow pantry. "But Elias still hurt you."

Her eyes shone.

I touched her shoulder, and Grace closed her eyes, a tear slipping down her cheek. I grabbed a napkin and used it to dab her face.

"I cared about him. Trusted him. I feel so guilty about that. There was one night that I was doing the books at Flamethrower, and we almost kissed. It disgusts me."

"But you *didn't*. You kept saying no. Maybe, down deep, you felt that something was off about him."

"Maybe. If that was my inner voice talking, I wish it had spoken louder."

"Stella didn't like him either. She kept barking at him. But I didn't put it together. You know what I realized? The first time Elias was around Stella at Ashford's apartment, she was barking and growling. I just didn't get it. But if it wasn't for her, I never would've found that photo."

"There's one thing I do know for sure. Piper is right. Falling for someone is a huge risk. Even if it's someone you've known most of your life, they might turn around and betray you. Or you might lose them and end up alone." She blew her nose in the napkin.

It twisted me up inside to hear Ashford's sister say that. I wanted Grace to find happiness. But was she wrong?

Love was a risk. It could slip away so easily.

Unless you fought for it.

We hugged, not letting go for a long while. "I'm so glad you're all right, Emma."

"Thanks. You'll be all right too."

She sighed and nodded.

✧

That evening, Maisie, Ashford, and I camped out on a huge air mattress, like we had been doing the past couple of nights. We were downstairs in Judson's basement game room. Pool table on one side, a huge entertainment center on the other. I was just relieved Stella hadn't chewed up any wires.

Of course, since arriving at Judson's, she'd been an angel. She'd reserved her aggressive behavior for Elias. Next time, I was going to pay closer attention to her. Like the way she'd barked at Dr. Carmichael. He hadn't killed Lori, but he was definitely still a sleaze ball.

What a good girl Stella was. Treats for life.

And everyone else seemed to feel the same way. She'd been getting more adoration and attention the last couple days than I could usually provide in two weeks. Ashford especially had been generous with belly scratches and fetch sessions. Stella seemed to love being near the other animals, too. Though some of them, especially the chickens and Judson's old farm dog, were not so sure about her.

"I don't want to get ready for bed," Maisie said. "Ollie doesn't have to go to bed yet."

"I'm sick of hearing about what Ollie does," Ashford grumbled.

"Get used to it, Dad," I muttered.

Ashford ran Maisie a bath, while I took a few minutes to myself and pulled out my journal.

I bit on my pen cap, words evading me.

I hadn't written anything since Elias had attacked me. I'd retold what happened to a bunch of police, to Ashford, and to my parents. But I hadn't written it down.

I wasn't sure yet that I would. It probably would help. I *knew* it would help. Then again, when I wrote down exactly what I'd gone through that night, I didn't want to put it in the journal Ashford had bought me. I wanted to write that somewhere else. And then be able to set it aside, or even burn it if I wanted.

The rest of my entries in this journal, detailing my time with Ashford and Maisie, were too precious.

Maisie wandered out in her jammies with Stella on her heels. Ashford was still in the bathroom draining the tub.

"Emma, you and Daddy are sleeping on the mattress with me again, right?"

"Yep. We sure are."

I'd been worried that I might wake Maisie if I had a nightmare. And I *had* woken each night so far, sweating and breathing hard. But having Maisie and Ashford there had soothed me. Each time, Ashford woke with me and put his hand over my racing heart. Breathed with me until the panic had passed.

She crawled into the middle, the air mattress bouncing beneath her. "I like having sleepovers. Can we do this always?"

"Nope, eventually you'll have to go back to your own room at your apartment. The reporters will all be gone, and everything will go back to normal."

Her face scrunched up. "But will you still be there? Or will you have to go back to California and the beach, like you said before?"

I was pretty sure I knew the answer. Though I couldn't tell her yet. Ashford and I hadn't had the chance to discuss it.

But I did know what I wanted. And I took it on faith that he wanted the same. After what we'd been through, we both knew we couldn't stand to be apart. Right?

"I'm still figuring that out," I said. "But no matter where I am, I'll be thinking of you. Because you're one of my favorite people."

"You're one of my favoritest people."

I laughed and kissed Maisie on the forehead.

THIRTY-SIX
Ashford

WHILE MAISIE WAS BRUSHING her teeth, I got a text. The moment I saw who it was from, I snuck down the hall for some privacy to read it.

> **AYLA**
> About that favor you asked for. I have good news. Not final yet, and it's a different opportunity from the one you wanted. But it could be life-changing for Emma's career. Let me know when you want me to tell her.

I squeezed my phone in my fist, knowing what I wanted to say. *Sorry Ayla, I was wrong. I changed my mind. Pretend I never asked.*

I was such a selfish bastard.

> **ME**
> Thanks. Let's wait until it's final. I don't want to get her hopes up unless this is for real.

My text was a cop-out. A way of avoiding the inevitable. But I just couldn't upset the peace we'd found here in the past couple of days.

Ayla had never met Elias herself, but she'd been shocked to hear about what happened. The truth about Lori's death had reopened her grief. And she was essentially dealing with it all by herself, which I hated. I'd offered to arrange for her to come to Judson's, but she'd declined, saying that she didn't want to risk the media finding her again.

She was comfortable at Last Refuge. In fact, she'd been raving about the food and the beautiful surroundings. That, along with several FaceTime sessions with Maisie, and it did sound like Ayla was getting the escape she needed.

And now, she was coming through on that favor I'd asked for. I was going to owe her for this one. Even though it would take Emma away from me.

You're a good guy, Ashford, Ayla had said a few days ago.

Yeah, I was. It kinda sucked.

"There you are." Emma walked down the hall. "Maisie's ready for bed."

Tucking my phone into my back pocket, I leaned down to kiss her. "Then I'd better help tuck her in."

We went together into the game room. I read Maisie some more of her current book, then made sure she was comfy with a glass of water on a small nearby table. Emma and I would join her later, all three of us squeezing onto the king-size air mattress.

If anyone had asked, I would've claimed it was for Maisie and Emma's benefit. But it was for me too. I needed my girls. Even Stella, who had been sleeping curled up at our feet.

"Go to sleep now," I said. "Emma and I will come and join you soon."

Maisie yawned. "Okay, Daddy."

The first night, we'd all gone to bed at the same time. But last night and tonight, Maisie didn't seem to mind going first. I was relieved she hadn't been too scared for that. She knew Emma and I, along with her aunt and uncle and our friends, would be close.

Someday, I would sit her down and explain what really

happened to her mom. Who Elias really was. But not for a very long time.

Emma and I retreated to the hallway, where we were out of sight. "Should we go upstairs and hang out with everyone?" she whispered.

"I'd rather stay right here and kiss you. I haven't had enough of that."

My fingers slid into her hair to cradle the back of her head, and my tongue licked teasingly into her mouth. Unfortunately, it couldn't be more than a tease with so many people staying here and Emma still recovering. Not that I really needed more.

I just needed to touch her. Savor every moment that we had.

We stood in the hallway and kissed and touched until our lips were swollen. Then we both went to change and get ready for bed.

When we carefully lay down on either side of the mattress, Maisie was deep asleep, her lips parted as she dreamed. I kissed my daughter's head, then reached over her to smooth Emma's hair, my thumb tracing along Emma's cheek.

I was so in love with her. Now more than ever.

But love wasn't always enough.

So I had to memorize each moment and live off of those memories later on. Because there would never be anyone else like Emma Jennings for me.

✧

Another week passed. When news broke about Elias Camden being Lori's killer, there was another flurry of media interest. But the crush of attention finally stopped, eclipsed by some other celebrity controversy somewhere else.

I got back to work, and Emma started up her toddler music classes again to finish out her lease. We spent every single day together. I tried to somehow keep the sun from setting through sheer will.

Spoiler alert: it didn't happen.

I spied on her through the one-way window as she sang and strummed her guitar. The babies made me smile as I thought of Maisie at that age. How cute she'd been, even with the mess and the late nights.

Yet time always moved forward.

Today was the day. Ayla had texted me earlier, letting me know she'd gotten the final word on that opportunity for Emma. After Emma's class, I planned to pull her into my office and call Ayla so my sister-in-law could deliver the news.

Was she still my sister-in-law? I didn't know how that all worked. I just knew she'd quickly started to feel like a real sister to me. Lori would've approved.

Ayla didn't know she was engineering my heartbreak. But I'd asked her to do it. And if it made Emma happy, how could I regret that?

"Must feel good to be back."

I glanced over to find Dixie beside me. Her frame was so slight that I hadn't heard her come inside, even with those big gold sneakers she loved.

"It does. Thank goodness things have calmed down."

"I saw the latest video Ayla Maxwell posted," Dixie said.

"You've been following those?"

"Oh hon, who hasn't?"

Ayla had been doing a series of video interviews with the editor of the Hartley Gazette, Genevieve Blake. Genevieve also happened to be the girlfriend of Sheriff Douglas and a friend of Emma's aunt and uncle. Ayla had spoken openly about her struggles with the pressures of fame. A little about Lori's death, keeping the details vague. She'd asked the public to give her family and friends privacy. For now, it seemed to be working.

There had also been a social media campaign to support Emma. I had no idea who had started it, but Ayla had reposted the videos to help them gain traction. There'd been a public outcry against

Emma's cheating ex in LA and an online petition urging his bosses to fire him for his behavior. Just yesterday, he'd resigned from his director position. His wife, the music professor, had announced she would file for divorce, and she'd even reached out to Emma via socials to ask Emma to return to school in Southern California.

Emma didn't want to go back to that school. Not because she was ashamed, but because it would feel like going backward. But she'd told me she felt vindicated. I was glad too, because it meant I didn't have to fly to California, track down the cheating asshole, and deal out a punishment of my own.

But it could've been a bonding experience for me and Nash, Emma's dad.

"Did you hear about the boycott against Dr. Carmichael?" Dixie asked.

I grunted, scowling at the one-way glass. "I don't even want to hear his name."

We'd learned that Danny was the one who'd tipped off reporters about Lori being Ayla Maxwell's sister. Years ago, Lori had let something slip at work. Danny had kept that secret in his pocket, and earlier this summer, he'd finally decided to sell the info because his dental office wasn't making as much money as it used to.

Dixie sniffed. "The boycott wasn't my idea. I'm staying out of it. Don't want to penalize any of his staff, since it's not their fault. But I *have* been organizing a donation fund for Elias's ex-wife to cover any legal expenses she might have."

"That's good to hear."

Elias had died without any heirs, and his ex Holly was working with lawyers to claim his assets, including his house and Flamethrower Burgers. It sounded like he'd intimidated her into accepting less than her share during their divorce, even though she'd worked hard to build the business with him.

Holly didn't plan to move back to Silver Ridge. But I thought she deserved any proceeds from the sale of Elias's assets. Lawyers were expensive though, and they would probably take a hefty chunk of the money.

Dixie reached up to pat my shoulder, making me feel like a kid though I towered over her. "I just want you to know that Silver Ridge is on your side. This town loves you and your family, Ashford. Nobody blames you for keeping the truth about Lori's sister private."

"Thank you. That means a lot."

Dixie aimed a meaningful glance at the one-way window, where Emma was singing the goodbye song that ended every class. "The town loves Miss Jennings, too. We'd sure love to see her stay."

So would I, I thought. But who said we always got what we wanted?

"Emma's lease is almost up," Dixie reminded me. As if I needed a reminder. "I stopped by today to offer some new terms. I just emailed them to you and Emma. I know this month hasn't been easy for you with all the class cancelations, so I'll throw in a discount on the first month of the new term. *And* an updated sign for the building. That piece of paper in the window for Emma's music classes just isn't cutting it."

"Thanks, Dixie," I said, jaw so tight it barely moved. "We'll let you know."

"Please do. Don't let these lease terms pass you by, Ashford. Who knows when you'll get a chance like this again?"

"Yep. Okay. I'll talk to you later."

"Think about it." She gave me a stern glare on her way out.

The door to the classroom opened, and parents streamed into the lobby. Emma saw me and smiled as she grabbed the cleaning spray.

"Don't worry about cleaning," I said. "I can wipe down the mats later. Come to my office? I have something for you."

Her smile turned mischievous. "*Oh*. Do you?"

We made our way down the hall. Once my door was closed, Emma pulled me down to kiss her. "What do you have for me? Is it this?" She palmed my crotch, where my cock was quickly getting interested. But for once, I hadn't pulled her into my office for *that*.

I kissed her again, reluctantly stepping back and leading her toward the desk. "Actually, it's something else. Something Ayla and I have been working on."

"Really? You and Ayla?"

I sat in the chair, guiding Emma to sit in my lap. "She's expecting our call."

I set up the video call on my computer. My stomach burned, and my pulse increased. My grip tightened on Emma's hip where I was holding her.

Ayla's face appeared. She looked far better rested than she'd been the night she showed up here unannounced.

After some greetings and small talk, Ayla got to the point.

"Emma, I know you really want to get your masters, and you could absolutely still do that. But I have another opportunity for you to consider. I work with a private music coach here in LA. She's amazing. She's helped me take my music to the next level, and she works with a lot of other big artists as well. Names you would definitely know. I've been in touch with her about you, and she's willing to take you on for a paid internship. You can learn to do what she does. Teach the best in the business."

"*Me?*" Emma shifted in my lap, glancing at me, then to the screen again. "Are you serious?"

"Ashford hoped I could get you into a new master's program. But trust me, this could be even better. I don't think I can stress enough what a unique opportunity this is. All the contacts you'll make. You'd be near your family in West Oaks, too. Back home in SoCal."

Emma's mouth opened and closed, clearly speechless. "Yeah, I...I have to think about it. But thank you, Ayla. That is so kind of you."

"I did pull some strings, but I hope you don't see this as a favor. Those sing-a-longs we've been having with Maisie over video? You are incredibly talented. You have a real knack for teaching too. You've earned this."

"Thank you," Emma whispered.

"My coach needs a decision in the next week. Let me know, okay?"

Ayla signed off. For a long moment, there was silence. I squeezed Emma's hip. "What do you think?"

"You did this for me?"

"I want you to have the best," I said softly. "Ayla really delivered."

"I do appreciate it. It's an unbelievable opportunity. But do you think I should take it? Do you *want* me to take it?"

I touched her face, turning her to look at me. Even though her pretty blue eyes cut straight through my heart. "You deserve the world. And the moon and the stars too. LA seems to be full of those."

"That doesn't answer my question."

My eyes stung. I pulled her closer and cradled her against me. If only I could hold her and never let go. "This summer has meant everything to me, and sometimes good things end. But you'd be going on to something even better."

Her hands went to my shoulders and pushed, forcing my grip on her to loosen. "Wait a minute. Are you breaking up with me?"

"No. I mean, I don't want to. But you're twenty-three. You'll be moving back to LA and hanging out with a bunch of celebrities. Do you really want to be saddled with some small-town guy in his mid-thirties with a kid?"

"I happen to *love* that guy and his kid. And this small town." Her cheeks flushed red. "I can't believe you're saying this to me."

"I love you too. But I'm being realistic. I don't want to hold you back."

"So you'll happily wave goodbye to me, knowing it's for the best."

"Pretty much."

"*Bullshit.*"

"Which part?"

"I want to know what you really want. Can you honestly say you want me to go back to LA and live a life without you? You want me to meet some other guy."

I tried to swallow down the bile in my throat. She went on.

"If you turn on the TV one day, and you see me at some award show on the arm of the hot lead singer of some band, you'll just smile and be happy because—"

"You really want to know what I want?"

"Please, Ashford," she whispered. "Please tell me."

I cupped the back of her neck and tugged her close again. Her arms folded against my chest. Our noses were inches apart, close enough I could fall into the endless blue of her eyes.

"I want you to have everything. And I would love the chance to give that to you. I want you to stay here with me and Maisie and wake up every morning next to me. I want to share my training room with your music classes. Stay up late stargazing on the roof at night. Kiss you and make love to you until we're both exhausted, and then do it all again the next day. But only if you're sure that's enough for you. Because it would kill me if you settle for anything less than the happy ending you deserve."

She blinked at me. "I want everything too. Everything with *you*. You're my happy ending."

The tip of my nose nudged hers. "Then stay."

"All you had to do was ask me."

Epilogue

Ashford, Six Months Later

"Ollie, honey, the cake server is not a sword." Piper dashed past me, chasing after her son.

Grinning, I left her to it. We weren't serving cake for another half hour. I had no doubt Ollie would return the server by then. Thankfully it was plastic, so it wouldn't do any permanent damage.

I only felt a *tiny* bit smug that my little angel would never do such a thing.

"Hey, birthday girl and Aunt Ayla," I said, lifting my phone for a picture. "Smile."

Maisie looked up from her art project. Ayla leaned in with her arm around her niece. "*Cheese*," they both said.

I lowered my phone. "Anyone seen my girlfriend?"

"No, I haven't seen Emma." Maisie went back to gluing music notes onto the edges of a picture frame. "You shouldn't call her a girl though, Daddy. She's a *woman*."

I arched my eyebrow. "Are you sure you're turning seven, monkey? Or twenty-seven?"

Maisie stuck out her tongue and blew a raspberry at me. Much better.

It was March, and a fresh layer of snow blanketed the ground outside the Big Blue Monster. Maisie's birthday party had taken over our entire building. Maisie had been thrilled that her aunt Ayla could make it in between studio recording sessions. And because our connection to the superstar was old news at this point, no reporters bothered to show. She could even walk down Main Street without drawing a crowd. Any tourists who tried to film her were gently, but firmly, scolded by Silver Ridge locals.

Ayla was one of ours now, and we took care of our own.

Grace stopped me, her party hat askew on her head. "I think I saw Emma go into the kitchenette."

"Thanks."

I left the training room and headed down the hall, though partygoers kept stopping me to chat. Then my phone rang, and I took a detour into the office to answer it.

It was Dane. My best friend from the Army.

"You calling to wish Maisie a happy birthday?" I asked.

"Of course I am! It's her birthday again? Didn't that just happen?"

I snorted. "Exactly how I feel."

"Sorry for bugging you on her birthday."

"No worries. I would've invited you to the party, but you'd probably parachute here off a private jet or something equally obnoxious. Emma might decide she likes you better than me. And then I'd have to kill you."

Dane barked a laugh. "How's Emma doing, man? How's everything?"

"Good," I said sincerely. "She's pretty damn amazing."

The past six months had been the happiest of my life. Our business was booming. Emma had a slew of music students, including Maisie, who was now learning violin. I'd hired a couple of new teachers. We'd accepted Dixie's new rent terms, and we had extra every month to go into a piggy bank toward...something. We hadn't decided yet.

I had ideas, though. Maybe a special trip. Nervous energy had me shifting from foot to foot as I thought about it.

"I didn't just call to catch up," Dane said. "I have an ulterior motive. You know we're always looking for new investments. I've been looking into opportunities around Silver Ridge."

"*Here?*"

After insisting on his independence for years, Dane had finally agreed to go to work for his dad's company. They invested in properties all over the world. I couldn't imagine why they'd be interested in my hometown.

"Yep. Rumor has it the ski resort is looking for a new owner. They've got an expansion underway and a hotel most of the way finished, but it's run into financial trouble. They can't complete the project."

I'd heard about that. "So you're going to swoop in? I guess that would be good for the local economy and the people who work at the resort. As long as it doesn't cause too much extra traffic."

"I see a tremendous upside. Not just the investment. I've never met Emma or your brother or sister, and I haven't seen Maisie since she was a baby. Just wanted to see how you felt about it. If you'd mind me showing up in your backyard."

"Not at all. You're always welcome. Don't take this the wrong way, but I thought you were too much of a jet setter to bother with Silver Ridge, and I didn't take that personally."

Dane exhaled into the phone, pausing, and I sensed that he hadn't liked what I'd said. "Maybe Silver Ridge is exactly what I need."

"Then don't let me stop you."

"I wasn't, actually. But I figured I'd try being polite."

I tipped my head back and laughed.

Someone knocked at my office door, and it opened. "What's so funny in here?" Emma asked.

I tilted my head, beckoning her closer. "My buddy Dane is on the phone." I put him on speaker and introduced them. My chest lifted in pride, the way it always did whenever I had the chance to claim her as mine.

"Hey, Emma. Hoping to meet you in person soon."

"Anytime. Ashford's told me all about you." She smiled at me.

I didn't know what exactly was going on with Dane. But I hoped he would find his happy ending. Maybe even here in Silver Ridge.

I was sure I'd found mine.

✦

Emma

I climbed onto the roof of the Big Blue Monster and shivered. "Springtime in the Colorado mountains sounds far more idyllic than it actually is."

Maisie giggled. "Stella loves it!" Our dog bounded around the tiny square of space on the flat roof. Stella and Maisie were both riled up from the party. It was too cute.

Maisie's party was over, and our guests had all finally gone home. Callum, Grace, and Ayla had stayed until the very end and helped us clean up. Then Ayla had to take off. Her driver had whisked her away to the nearest private airport. She had an event in London tomorrow.

Now, we were up on the roof for birthday stargazing. Ashford and I had bought Maisie a telescope. She loved the one at Ollie's house and had been begging for her own. Ashford had carried the box up earlier to assemble it.

"All of you be careful," Ashford said, his head appearing as he mounted the ladder. "It could be icy." Even though he'd cleared every inch of snow from the roof this morning.

"We're being really careful, Daddy." Maisie had a puffy coat and a beanie with a pom-pom on top. She clutched a thermos of cocoa in her mittens. "Come on, hurry. I want my hot chocolate."

"Because you're in desperate need of sugar? You ate every bite of that slice of birthday cake. Aunt Grace cut it way too big." Ashford stepped up beside me, his arm going around my waist.

His daughter held out the thermos for him to unscrew the lid. "Ollie said I should get blue icing on my cake next time. It will turn my poop green!"

Ashford made a horrified face.

I couldn't have held back my smile, even if I'd wanted to. They were so much stinking fun.

This was my first Colorado winter, and I'd loved every moment of it. Not so much the snow. I was tired of that. But Ashford and Maisie brought me more joy than I'd ever known I could feel. I didn't regret turning down the internship Ayla had offered. Here in Silver Ridge, I taught music every day. My students challenged and delighted me. I had time to compose my own music and even perform on occasion.

And in between classes, Ashford and I snuck into the office downstairs for hot quickies. *Our* office.

We had Maisie and Stella. There was nothing that could make our lives any better. Except maybe finding the same happiness for the rest of our friends in the Lonely Harts club.

Ashford fiddled with the telescope. "Okay, monkey. Let's try it out." He stepped back. The telescope stood on a stand, pointing upward at the sky. It was a clear night. Even though it wasn't that late, a rich tapestry of stars already painted the sky.

"I want Emma to go first!"

Ashford and Maisie stood on either side of me as I peered into the eyepiece. But it didn't look right. "It's blurry."

"Huh, pretty sure I followed the instructions," Ashford said.

Maisie stood on her tiptoes, trying to get a glimpse of the lens. "Emma, I think something is in the way. What is it?" She wiggled like she could barely contain her excitement. And I suspected it wasn't just the cocoa and birthday cake. But I decided to play along.

I stepped closer to examine the business end of the telescope.

There, balanced on the ledge of plastic that bordered the glass, was a ring.

I gasped.

Ashford reached over and carefully plucked the ring from the end of the telescope. He held it between his fingers, and the tiny diamonds glinted in the starlight.

A lump gathered in my throat.

"What if you'd scratched the glass of the lens?" I asked helplessly.

"I didn't." He went to one knee. Stella crowded him, wanting in on whatever he was up to. "Emma, you and Maisie are both the brightest stars in my sky. You've brought so much beauty into our lives. Last summer, you agreed to stay. I'd like to make that permanent, because I can't live without you. *We can't.*"

"Can we keep you forever?" Maisie asked.

Hot tears gathered in my eyes, a contrast to the cold. "Yes."

Ashford stood up and slid the ring on my finger. Then kissed me. "I love you."

"I love you too. I love you both."

He picked up Maisie, his other arm pulling me close. Stella whapped our legs with her tail.

For the moment, the telescope was forgotten. All the other countless stars overhead. Those could wait.

Everything we needed was right here.

✦

Grace

I was so thrilled for my brother and Emma. As spring turned to summer, the strength of their love amazed me every day. If anyone could beat the odds, it was those two.

But *me*? No way. After what had happened with Elias, I was done with men.

As I walked into the ballroom of the new ski resort hotel, feeling the gazes of at least a dozen men rake over my body, I reminded myself of that resolution.

The surroundings were opulent. The chandeliers overhead glowed with a warm, flattering light. My dress was equally fancy. A floor-length, body-hugging gown in a silky red fabric. Mesh cut-outs teased the lines of my figure along the sides.

It was the hotel's grand opening party. Not only a black-tie affair, but a masquerade ball. Like something out of a movie. Piper had talked me into coming, and it was *so* not my usual scene. The dress belonged to Piper too. Why did a small-town coffee shop owner have an extra evening gown waiting in her closet? My best friend was quirky like that.

Yet the dress, combined with the new glittery red mask hiding my eyes, made me feel confident. Like I could pretend, for one exciting night, that I wasn't some mousy accountant with an abysmal dating history and zero trust in the male species.

Tonight was about *me*. Feeling good in my skin and nothing else.

I didn't see Piper or her date anywhere. The bar seemed like a safe bet. That was what I needed to soothe my nerves. A drink.

"Glass of merlot, please," I said, elbows on the bar top with my purse clutched in my hands.

Then a heavy grip landed on my shoulder and squeezed. "You were supposed to wait for me in the lobby."

"*Excuse* me?" I looked over to find a gray-haired man scowling at me, his face ruddy beneath his blue jeweled mask. I tried to shake the man off, but he wouldn't let go. "You must have me confused with someone else."

"I don't know what kind of game you're playing, but this isn't what we agreed."

"I have no idea what you're talking about."

A new presence loomed at my side, towering over the guy in the blue mask. The newcomer was close enough I could feel the heat from his body, though he didn't touch me.

"There you are, gorgeous. I've been looking for you everywhere."

He had thick dark hair, broad shoulders. His full lips slid into a charming smirk. But when I met his steely gray eyes, which were framed by a satiny black mask, they were full of concern.

I almost told him he had the wrong woman too. But something about the newcomer's soft smirk told me to wait.

Then he angled his body, which was clad in an impeccably tailored black tuxedo, and winked at me. Like this was a joke, and we were both in on it. *Go with it*, he mouthed silently.

Who was this guy?

The creep in the blue mask hesitated, no longer so sure of himself. "This is *your* date?"

"Exactly." My would-be hero's gaze turned cold and menacing as he glared at the other man. "So unless you want me to break every one of those fingers, you'd better take your hand off of her."

Find out what happens next for Grace in MOONLIT COLORADO, a billionaire, brother's best friend romance.

A Note from Hannah

Emma's story began a while ago, back when I was writing another book called **The Five Minute Mistake** (also about a single dad, with an age gap, suspense... I'm sensing a theme). That book was about Emma's dad Nash and her stepmom Madison. Emma was just a teenager, but something about her struck a chord with me, and I knew I wanted to give her a happily ever after of her own someday!

I just didn't know when, or how, or *who*.

Then Ashford started talking to me, and he was *so* grumpy, y'all. He had a lot of hurt underneath his tough exterior. And I just knew that Emma would not only understand him; she'd be able to give him exactly what he needed, and vice versa. I'm so glad these two found their story. Thank you for reading it!

And many thanks as always to my ARC readers, and to my fans who keep reading and enjoying my stories. It means so much to me to be able to share them with you.

Until next time—
Hannah

More from Hannah Shield

Hannah Shield writes steamy, suspenseful romance with pulse-pounding action, fun & flirty banter, and tons of heart. She lives in the Colorado mountains with her family. Visit her website at www.hannahshield.com, where you can join her newsletter for access to bonus content, info on new releases, and more!

✦

Hart County

Starcrossed Colorado (Ashford & Emma)
Moonlit Colorado (Dane & Grace)
Stormswept Colorado (coming soon)
Sunkissed Colorado (coming soon)
Homeward Colorado (coming soon)

✦

Last Refuge Protectors

Hard Knock Hero (Aiden & Jessi)
Bent Winged Angel (Trace & Scarlett)
Home Town Knight (Owen & Genevieve)
Second Chance Savior (River & Charlotte)
Iron Willed Warrior (Cole & Brynn)

✦